MICHAEL J. BOWLER

ONCE UPON A TIME IN AMERICA

CHILDREN OF THE KNIGHT V

Published by Michael J. Bowler, USA
stuntshark2.0@gmail.com

Cover Art and Interior Formatting by Reese Dante
www.reesedante.com

Edited by Heather Sowalla, Windy Hills Editing
h.sowalla@gmail.com

Print: ISBN: 978-0-9908711-0-1
Mobi: ISBN: 978-0-9908711-1-8
epub: ISBN: 978-0-9908711-2-5

Printed in the United States of America
First Edition
November 2014

Praise for *Children of the Knight* (Book I of The Knight Cycle)

"In a novel that realistically and sometimes uncomfortably displays societal failures like run-away drug abuse, child molestation, indifferent adults, bigoted contempt for gays and lesbians, economic injustice, dispirited teachers and cops, and corrupt politicians, the novel threatens to overwhelm the reader with a sense of pessimism and fatalism at times. But Bowler manages to do just the opposite. Optimism and hope are its ultimate tone, as a bunch of rejects come to accept the challenge laid down by King Arthur and join his quest." –author Jay Jordan Hawke

"Learn to be brave by saying what's in your heart. You may not have the chance to say it before its too late. As a resident in LA during Mayor Villaragosa's term in office it was a unique fantasy. The fantasy set up of the novel is extraordinary and the delivery is triumphant. I cannot wait to read the continuation!" –Jerry on Goodreads

"Part Arthurian legend and part urban fantasy, this very ambitious novel by Michael Bowler addresses a very real and shameful problem. Why are so many children, and some very young ones at that, left neglected, abused, and abandoned? And even more importantly, whose responsibility is it to save these children? All too often it's seen as "not our problem" but Mr. Bowler and I seem to be in agreement on this issue. It truly is society's responsibility, for the children are the future." –Shawna

Praise for *Running Through A Dark Place* (Book II of The Knight Cycle)

"On another note, this book is more "real" than I would like it to be. I've met these optional, disenfranchised, violent, and "difficult" children everywhere. On the whole, adults don't tend to give them much of a chance. This is a crime to our children. I've witnessed first-hand how much these "optional" children are capable of when taken seriously and given a chance, and it is incredible. Read this book. May it ignite a fire in you to pursue justice for the youngest "least of these" in our society." –Nora

"Taking a historical figure made mythological and imagining what his crusade would be in today's age is really ingenious, and is a testament to Michael J. Bowler's skill, but hat I like best about his writing is that he does not pull any punches. He lays the tough issues out there as they are and shows his characters' struggles in tackling these issues. While many of his characters are what would be considered at-risk youth, Running Through a Dark Place, and the rest of Michael J. Bowler's Knight Cycle, will appeal to all youth and those adults who work with youth." –Rikki

"Michael manages to draw you in like you're under one of Merlin's spells and traps you in this world that he has created and not turn you loose. But I, personally, would not WANT to be turned loose. His characters have great depth and complexity, something a lot of writers seem to have trouble achieving, and he does it without boring you with a whole lot of un-needed details like some very famous authors I could name tend to do." –Dallas

"Just like the first volume in the cycle, this book is not only beautifully written, but also touches the reader on a deeper level. It's not just entertainment, but a story that changes your outlook on life. It is a story that explores the depth of human madness and hate, but also the depth and beauty of the various types of love. Such a fantastic book!" –Kim Anisi for Reader's Favorite

Praise for *There Is No Fear* (Book III of The Knight Cycle)

"'I'm not ready to be a grownup yet.' With that simple admission, author Michael J. Bowler sums up the essence of young adult literature. So often, writers try to make their teenage characters seem more put together than they really are. It could be a ploy, telling young readers what they want to hear, that authority figures suck. It could be a marketing strategy that love equals sex because sex sells. It could be the belief that teenagers are looking to escape their problems, not solve them, so let's keep them disconnected because they want to be. But that kind of mentality is shortchanging a smart and capable teenage audience. Yet again and again, publishers choose to spit out the same old story that teenagers don't need adults, feeding them the line that they can overcome any obstacle on their own. All they need is a hot love interest and they're all set, able to conquer anything that gets in their way. The adult characters in THERE IS NO FEAR are just as important as their younger counterparts. King Arthur is a father figure, the stabilizing influence for a group of troubled teens who aren't sure where they fit in or where they belong." –Nicole Langan

"Lance is conflicted, yet that's what makes him such a deep and influential character. He's growing up on the page before readers' eyes. He's figuring things out as he goes along. He's not fully formed because he's not supposed to be. He's a teenager in the flux of transition from boy to man. His heart is pure, it's only when he allows outside forces to penetrate his inner peace that he's thrown off course. Whenever he remains true to himself, he flourishes. Whenever he doesn't, trouble is usually right around the corner." –The Character Connection

"Search no further for a book that will ignite your passion to work for the good of those whom society has deemed "the least of these", a passion for justice served as well as rights protected and accountability realized. This amazingly well written book drew me into its action, into the very lives of these characters, in a way that made me want to assign this series as mandatory reading for every high school graduate. It made me feel." –Elnora Romness

Praise for *And The Children Shall Lead* (Book IV of The Knight Cycle)

"I am primarily a romance writer. In fact, the tag line on my author's blog is "Love is what I see." And of all that I see in Michael Bowler's Children of the Knight series, the depth of love between the characters is my personal favorite aspect. Profound love—that of friends and brothers and sons and romantic partners—infiltrates this contemporary and mystical adventure series, that I once likened to an action-filled motion picture. And this constant presence of the characters' selfless devotion to others is why the fourth novel of the series, And the Children Shall Lead, touches me so deeply and will stay with me for years to come." –Mia Kerick

"And The Children Shall Lead is as wild a ride as its series predecessors. Included are plenty of action, mystery, adventure, and even some US History. I highly recommend And the Children Shall Lead to all readers, to those who enjoy witnessing the thrill of the chase, human rights activism at work, and skillfully devised, witty slang-packed repartee amid courtly formality."
–Kristen

"The myth of King Arthur was always fascinating, but experiencing how he saw modern society and his determination to help todays youth definitely altered my perspective on how our laws effect their lives. Arthur's acceptance and understanding helped all the knights overcome their pasts to create a brighter future for everyone. Watching Lance's growth from a homeless child to the strong, confident young man he became who brought hope to so many was inspiring."
–Teresa at Fallen Angel Reviews

First off, I want to thank everyone who helped me bring this series to life, most notably my amazing beta readers who provided valuable insights and comments that kept me on track with all the characters, locations, and situations. Couldn't have done it without Mia, Dallas, J.g., and Betsy. You guys rock.

Since this is my last book, the one that brings The Knight Cycle to a close, I'd be remiss if I didn't share some feelings about this epic journey. This is a true coming-of-age story that illustrates what all kids can achieve if given half a chance. Overall, however, the series is about heroism, though not the kind where someone puts on a cape and has super powers. This is about real, everyday heroism such as I've seen in kids my whole life, kids that no one wants or cares about. My characters are, in spirit, and in terms of life experience, based on these kids I've met as a teacher and a volunteer. Life grabbed them by the throat from the moment they were born and slammed them time and again into the ground, trying mightily to break them. But hope endures. The human spirit is indomitable. A hero is someone who rises above those who try to break him, and proves to the world that he is better than the worst thing he ever did, or the worst thing ever done to him. The characters in my series, teen and adult, are true heroes in the most real sense of the word. No, they don't wear a cape. No, they can't fly or cling to walls like a spider or a bat. They are heroes because they keep hope firmly lodged in their hearts, hope that the world which so abused them can be made better if only enough people like them stepped up to make it so. They are heroes because they can look past the superficial differences within each other and see the humanity we all share. And they are heroes because they make a clear choice about how to move forward in life – to do what's right, rather than what's easy. If more of us make that simple choice the world will be filled with heroes, and life for children everywhere will vastly improve. And then we can all fly.

The
End
Is At
Hand

Chapter One

Because I Had a Choice

Once upon a time in the City of Angels, a boy led the way, and the people followed.

Passing through Los Angeles in the large school bus, painted myriad colors and scrawled with hundreds of signatures, Lance and the young people, except Kai and Dakota, felt on secure, familiar ground. Once the bus passed San Bernardino, however, there was not a tall building or paved street in sight. That both fascinated and freaked them out in equal measure.

Helen had her own *ABC News* van driven by her cameraman, Charlie, and there were also two black unmarked Secret Service sedans accompanying the bus, one leading and the other bringing up the rear. Agents Brooks and Andrews remained aboard the bus in case of attacks along the way. Andrews also doubled as bus driver if evasive maneuvers were required.

New Camelot was operating on a skeleton crew. Sir Enrique and Sir Luis were in nominal command. They'd given Lance boxes of stickers to pass out to kids along the way, as well as t-shirts and New Camelot bobbleheads for special giveaways.

Seventeen-year-old Sir Khom had been given the key to the armory and had taken charge of the Training Centre; sixteen-year-old Sir Charley had been placed in charge of security for gatherings; and fifteen-year-old Sir Phillip took command of the Computer Lab.

Mayor Soto was living at the venue while the main body traveled the country, so there would be an adult presence amongst the youth, an arrangement that eased Arthur's mind.

By the time the bus passed through Palm Springs and Indio, there was nothing much to see but pure flat scruffy desert, all dirt and stubby little plants and rocks and low hills. At first, the kids sat and gazed out at the sheer emptiness of it all. For Lance, the peaceful beauty lulled him into a calm he normally didn't feel. Holding

Ricky's hand and pointing to this cactus or that faraway hill, he felt freer than he ever had in the city.

After about three hours of travel, most of it through empty desert, the caravan rattled into Blythe, the last bit of civilization before entering Arizona. They decided to stop for lunch and chose an easily spotted Denny's on Donlon Street. Everyone piled happily from the old bus to stretch and walk and shake off the long ride, and then gasped at the one hundred ten degree heat slapping them in the face and practically sucking the air from their lungs. The bus was air-conditioned, so the sudden change in temperature hit hard.

Blythe was a tiny little desert town whose biggest claim to fame seemed to be the two state prisons located nearby in the desert. As they entered the crowded restaurant and mercifully left the staggering heat behind, Lance wistfully wondered how many youngsters were in those prisons, convicted under Prop 21 before his own Prop 51 had done away with that law.

Being such an instantly recognizable group, Arthur's entourage drew the eye of everyone in the place. Most people looked curious, and some kids excitedly grabbed their parents and pointed, but no one spoke to them or approached. Lance surmised the towering and scary-looking Brooks, as well as the other three dark-suited agents, instantly put off any autograph hounds.

When everyone had eaten and Arthur paid the bill with his debit card, they all circulated amongst the patrons shaking hands—especially the children—and handing out stickers. The Denny's diners expressed excited joy at the gesture, and many wished them well on their journey.

Then it was back into the bus for the final two-hour ride into Phoenix. The interior had been remodeled, with the addition of softer upholstery, and even seat belts. Lance had often wondered as a kid why every vehicle in America was required to have seat belts *except* the ones carrying what should be considered America's greatest treasure—her children.

Ah well, he decided as they pulled out of Blythe and into the steaming hot desert, *more evidence of America's "children are property" philosophy.*

†††

Lance knew they were nearing civilization when he spotted an obvious cell phone tower masquerading as a giant palm tree. He pointed it out to Ricky and they both got a laugh. However, they quickly logged onto their iPads and sent updates to Sir Phillip and tweeted their progress before pulling into Phoenix itself.

The odd-looking caravan passed through the outskirts into downtown and pulled into the parking lot of their hotel. The manager greeted the group as they spilled from the bus and trudged into the lobby carrying their bags. Since they would likely stay in each city only a few days, they'd attempted to travel light. Everyone but Reyna, who just had to have everything she owned. The boys pulled the "You're such a girl" routine on her again as she made Esteban carry her three bags along with his one, and she flashed that nasty smile she'd perfected. Even Sylvia, the only other girl, had packed a single bag and laughed along with the boys.

Sleeping arrangements for the entire journey had already been decided before departure. Reyna had arranged rooms with multiple beds for all but Arthur and Jenny. She and Sylvia would share a room, Kai, Dakota, and Techie would be together, Lance, Ricky, and Chris, Esteban, Darnell, and Justin, and lastly Ryan, Gibson, and Merlin. The Secret Service made its own arrangements, as did *ABC News* for Helen and Charlie.

After everyone showered and cleaned up, they headed out for dinner. As in Blythe, the group elected to eat at a regular restaurant so they could interact with ordinary people and their families. This time they chose Sizzler, and the sight of twenty-two people entering the line to order food turned many a head in the establishment, especially when it became evident who was in that group.

Since the temperature in Phoenix hit the hundreds by day and was still ninety-one at six p.m. when they entered the Sizzler, Arthur allowed the group to forgo the usual New Camelot attire for more casual clothes.

The boys all wore tank tops of varying styles, while Reyna and Sylvia sported sleeveless shirts, and everyone wore shorts, even Arthur and Merlin. Lance and Ricky couldn't help but laugh at the sight of these two men wearing shorts and t-shirts. Jenny wore shorts and a light shirt and looked as relaxed and happy as Lance had ever seen her.

The Secret Service agents always wore their standard dark suits, and Lance figured they must be dying from the heat. Brooks kept joking with the Native Knights, as he'd taken to calling his four long-haired charges, that they were trying to get as buff as him. "You just want to show me up with those tank tops." The boys laughed.

Helen was dressed casual, but still looked well-coiffed and professional. Charlie carried a small HD camera that could go live on ABC at a moment's notice.

Dinner was loud and fun and lively, and many of the patrons dropped by their table to say hello or get an autograph. Most of the children in the restaurant begged their parents to let them say "hi," and all of the knights greeted each of them with a smile, passing out stickers, inviting them to their public Town Hall meetings. Lance and Ricky found it amusing when teen girls flirted shamelessly as they asked for autographs.

Later that night, the Native Knights sat in their hotel room discussing strategy for the legislative appearance the following day. Lance wanted both Kai and Dakota up front with him. They'd been given information from Native sources within the state to pass on to the legislature, and Kai's personal expertise, being a Navajo Nation resident, would be invaluable. Once the Indians left, Lance asked Ricky if he still wanted to attend mass with him on Sundays whenever they had the chance.

"Of course," Ricky replied at once, taking Lance's hand in his. "I like sharing you with Jesus."

Lance smiled. "Fool."

In the room next door, Techie sat on his bed texting Ariel, while simultaneously updating Sir Phillip on their progress. He glanced up when Kai and Dakota entered the room after their meeting with Lance and Ricky. The two young men held hands as they stepped inside and closed the door, and Techie's eyes immediately dropped to those clasped hands.

Both Indians noted his look and quickly let go. They approached the Vietnamese boy and Kai asked uncertainly, "Does it make you uncomfortable, Techie, to room with us?"

Techie looked mortified and quickly slid his falling glasses back up onto his nose. "Uh, no, not really." Then he turned red and looked back down at his computer. "Well, um, I mean, well, we're going to be rooming together for a lot of months and, well, if you guys want time alone just let me know." He looked more embarrassed than either Kai or Dakota had ever seen. "But I'm not real comfortable if you guys, like, start making out in front of me." Then his face turned even redder, if such a thing was possible. "It's just my background, you know. I don't even make out with Ariel in front of anyone else and—"

The laugher from Kai, and even Dakota, cut Techie off and he gazed uncertainly at them. "What?"

Kai grinned. "It's okay, Techie, we're *much* more hung up about stuff like that than you are, man. Cultural and all. No worries."

He raised a fist as he'd so often seen Lance do, and Techie raised his. They bumped, and Techie grinned. "Cool."

In the next room over, Esteban chatted with Justin and Darnell, the three of them sharing war stories from their former lives as gangsters on the streets. They laughed and joked and tried to one-up each other with outrageous or crazy things each had done, and Esteban couldn't help once again marveling at how life had changed in just a few years. Here they were, three former enemies who would've killed each other had there been a turf war, sitting around yucking it up as a team. Amazing!

Reyna and Sylvia readied for bed, and Reyna noted the independent streak in the younger girl that seemed so much like her at fourteen. *Independent, smart, and incredibly capable*, she thought. She felt proud of her protégé and Sylvia seemed grateful for the older girl's attentions.

Merlin had brought along his iPod and a small Bluetooth speaker so he could listen to music while shaving or getting dressed. As the wizard brushed his teeth and the strains of a country song wafted out of the bathroom, Gibson, already changed and lounging in his bed texting Sandra, glanced over at Ryan, who likewise sat up in bed with a book, rather than a phone, in his lap.

"What?" Ryan asked, apparently oblivious to the problem he saw in his partner's hard brown eyes.

At that moment, the door to the bathroom opened and the music got louder. Merlin stepped out wearing his Sons of Anarchy robe and carrying the speaker and iPod.

Gibson turned his glare from Ryan to Merlin, causing the wizard to eye him with amusement.

"You did bring your ear buds, I trust, Merlin?" Gibson asked, his voice authoritative.

Merlin's eyes seemed to twinkle with amusement. "Naturally, Sergeant."

"Then please use them, at *all* times," Gibson insisted. "*Please.*"

Merlin looked even more amused, but Ryan looked over at his partner. "Hey, Gib, I like that music."

Now Gibson gave his partner such a "look" that Ryan laughed.

"Then you can do what the kids do, partner," Gibson shot back. "Use one ear bud while he uses the other. I'm with Lance and Ricky on this one."

Ryan and Merlin exchanged a look, and then grinned.

Catching their expressions and realizing he'd been played, Gibson snatched up a pillow and tossed it across at Ryan. The older man easily ducked and then all three of them laughed.

Jenny adjusted the room air conditioner before slipping into the queen-sized bed beside her husband. Arthur was looking over their itinerary on her iPad and gave her a warm smile as she snuggled up close to rest her head on his shoulder. He set the iPad onto the night table and wrapped his arms around her, pulling her in.

Jenny sighed. "I think this is what they call a working vacation, Arthur."

He chuckled. "A lengthy working vacation, to be sure."

She fell silent and he instantly noted her shift in mood. "What?"

She tilted her head up and fixed her light blue eyes onto his. "Lance is growing up."

His face clouded. "I know."

She rested her head against his chest, uncertain and filled with dread. Nothing more was said.

†††

The Arizona State Capitol Building, located on Washington Street, was originally constructed in 1901 and had been enhanced over the years. Designed in classical revival style, the four-story building was built out of materials unique to Arizona and designed to withstand the brutal desert climate with its thick masonry walls that insulated the interior. There were also numerous skylights and round clerestory windows to allow heat easier escape from the legislative chambers. Atop the center rotunda stood a highly visible wind vane.

As had been the case in Washington, and would continue throughout the next five months, Lance, Ricky, and occasionally some of the others would address a joint session of both houses and answer questions about the CBOR. Despite having already spoken before the most important body in the country, Lance felt jittery. Flanked by the two detectives and four Secret Service agents, he gingerly stepped out of the bus into a throng of people held back by barriers and local police. He and all the others were attired in their formal tunics, pants and boots to clearly represent New Camelot to all observers.

The size of the crowd stunned Lance, and he looked aghast at Ricky, almost afraid to pass through the jubilant members of the public. As he had when he'd first "come back," he felt on display, like an animal in a zoo.

He stopped a moment to observe the cheering children, many of whom sported plastic New Camelot swords that Esteban and Luis had sent out to those whom Arthur "virtually knighted." There had to be three or four hundred people, Lance noted, and even a fair number of the adults were calling out his name. But more of them simply gawked, pinning him with their eyes, and it suddenly hit him why: since he became The Boy Who Came Back, none but people in L.A., San Diego, or Washington had beheld him in the flesh. These people now looked at him as though seeing a miracle, and it awed them.

So rather than feel pinned down, Lance flashed his smile and waved to the crowd as he began following Brooks. He elbowed Ricky, who grinned and started waving too. So did Arthur and the others. They shook hands as they strode past the barricades and thanked the people for coming out.

Then he and the others were through the throng and crossing the front courtyard leading into the imposing state capitol. The three arched entrances were surrounded by grey stonework, while above the doors the stonework was beige and the façade split by six columns. Hanging between the middle four were three enormous banners commemorating Arizona's centennial. Lance barely noted these as he followed Brooks through the center doorway, his mind on his mission.

The lobby was huge, with a view straight up beyond the four stories at the glass rotunda adorning the roof. Hanging from the center of that rotunda was a gigantic chandelier. Lance was stunned when, among the reception committee awaiting them, he found a grinning Edwin wearing a casual light-beige suit and his trademark designer glasses with the bluish tint to the frames.

"Edwin!" he nearly shouted around the huge grin breaching his face. He sprinted over to the young man and clasped the hand awaiting him.

"Surprise," the intern said, still grinning as the others joined him. He released Lance's hand.

"What are you doing here?" Lance asked, happy to see a familiar face in this sea of potential detractors.

Edwin shrugged. "The senator assigned me to travel with you and help you guys navigate the 'shark-infested waters' of state politics. Ha! He figured I could advise you, ya know, about what to say, and mostly what *not* to say."

"That is so cool!" Lance gushed as Ricky stuck out a hand to shake that of the newcomer.

Arthur stepped forward and shook Edwin's hand. "A most welcome surprise, Edwin," the king said graciously. "Please send the senator our gratitude."

Edwin nodded, his glasses slipping slightly. He pushed them back up and grinned sheepishly. "Not sure if a lowly intern can be much help, but I'm here to serve."

He introduced Lance and the others to the Speaker of the Arizona State House of Representatives. The Speaker, a balding, round-faced man with a double chin and wire-rimmed glasses, welcomed the group and invited them to follow him into the chamber so the session could begin. Lance noted the cordiality of the man, but there was no indication in his voice or face as to his own opinion of the CBOR, or they themselves, for that matter.

These politicians are so slick, he thought wryly.

The house chamber was much smaller than the one in Washington, but similar in its circular layout with two raised three-sided seating areas up front, a center aisle flanked by desks for each of the representatives, and side seating areas where, at the moment, members of the public sat awaiting the start of the session.

The Speaker led them down the center aisle toward the front. Every desk to either side was occupied and the place resembled a gigantic college lecture hall with the senators crowding in alongside the representatives. Everyone burst into applause when the group entered, and the clapping sounded enthusiastic to Lance, rather than just perfunctory.

Maybe we got some supporters here, after all, he thought as they arrived at the front.

He, Ricky, Kai and Dakota were led to the higher of the two raised bench-like desks, while the others filed behind the one below.

The Speaker stood in front of Lance and banged his gavel several times for silence. Everyone sat and leaned forward attentively. Lance could tell that whatever their opinions were on the CBOR, they were obviously excited to have The Boy Who Came Back in their midst and most gazed up at him in wonder.

The middle-aged Speaker called the meeting to order and introduced Lance, adding with a chuckle, "Though this is one boy who needs *no* introduction." Applause filled the chamber as the Speaker sat behind the four boys and Lance stepped to the microphone, Ricky to one side, his Indian brothers to the other.

He graciously thanked everyone for allowing him to address them. "I don't plan to be like adults are with kids and ask if you all did your homework." There were a few chuckles. "I did that in Washington and you saw the result." More laughter. "I figure if you all haven't read our Children's Bill of Rights by now, you never will, so whatever. I don't plan to talk a lot because I want to listen to you and your concerns and answer your questions."

He glanced a moment at Ricky and the other boy smiled with encouragement.

"I do wanna talk about one issue because our supporters in this state keep bringing it up and it's one that I know real well - children's services taking kids away from their parents and putting them into homes they don't wanna be in. Mainly, I'm talking about Native American children being put into homes with white people."

He turned to Kai and Dakota and waved them forward. The Indians stepped to Lance's side, though Dakota looked ready to faint. Kai appeared nervous, but far more in control.

"This is Sir Kai of the Navajo Nation," Lance went on, placing a hand atop Kai's shoulder briefly before moving it on to Dakota's, "and Sir Dakota of the Lakota Nation." He removed his hand and looked back at the assembled lawmakers. "Since Arizona is the primary home to the Navajo nation, Sir Kai will talk about our concerns in this area and why we included the taking of Native children in our CBOR."

Lance stepped back and indicated the microphone. Kai warily stepped forward as though the mic might leap off the podium and bite him. He reached into the pocket of his pants and slipped out a paper onto which he'd written some notes. Unfolding the wrinkled sheet, he smiled sheepishly at the attentive crowd. "Sorry, I'm not used to talking all slick and fancy like my brother here."

He nudged Lance with his shoulder and the other boy grinned, while the assembled lawmakers chuckled. Then Kai spread open his paper on the podium and began. "We know that historically native children were taken from their people and put with white people to, I guess, make them white cuz that was supposed to be better," Kai began, his voice a bit shaky, but still easily understood. "The Indian Child Welfare Act was supposed to stop that, but it hasn't. Ninety-nine percent of the Native children taken away from their homes are because of neglect, and only one percent for abuse, but this state and every other one have weak definitions of neglect, like every kid doesn't have his own bedroom. I did on my rez, but I'm an only child."

Some in the assemblage laughed at that, and Kai frowned. It struck Lance as almost disturbing not to see the young man smiling or laughing.

"This isn't something to laugh about," he went on, his voice trembling with contained anger. Dakota's hand on his arm seemed to steady him. "How many poor white families don't have a bedroom for every kid? I don't see the social workers rushing in and snatching those kids away and placing them with *native* parents, do you?" He looked around the room as though expecting a response. When none came, he said, "Our children need protection from people who want to keep stealing them away from us. Thank you for listening." He stepped back and Dakota patted him on the back in praise.

Then Lance took his place and waved a hand out to the murmuring and agitated lawmakers. "This is as good a time as any for some questions since Sir Kai seems to have pressed somebody's buttons out there."

Many hands rose into the air and Lance pointed to a woman legislator wearing a staid-looking dress and severe hairstyle. "Sir Lance, what if there is genuine abuse going on? Isn't it our job as adults to protect those children?"

Lance nodded. "Course. I know about abuse better'n anybody in this room. Our amendment doesn't stop kids from being taken away when there's real abuse, only if the main problem is cuz the parents are poor."

Ricky stepped forward now and Lance stepped back. "My parents were poor when I's growing up, but that wasn't what made them bad parents. 'Poor' can be fixed. My parents were lousy people who treated me bad cuz I was different from them, and there was nothing I could do to help myself. If the CBOR passes, kids will have standing under the Constitution to help *themselves*."

He stepped back again. Lance resumed his place at the microphone and pointed to another waving hand. "Sir Lance, have you seen some of these Indian reservations?" the lady asked pointedly. "The level of poverty is staggering."

Lance eyed her soberly. "If there's so much poverty, how come *you* don't help them?"

The woman looked indignant. "Sir Lance, tribes are sovereign nations unto themselves and the law is murky as to how much a part of this state they are."

Lance sighed heavily. "America gives billions of dollars every year to countries that hate our guts, and we can't even help our own native peoples right here? That sounds pretty lame to me."

He pointed to another man, this one older and smug-looking. "Why do you think Native children *aren't* better off with white families?"

The question caught Lance off-guard. "How do you mean?"

The man chuckled. "Well, it worked out pretty well for you, didn't it?"

Lance froze, and more agitated murmurs wafted throughout the chamber. Ricky's breath caught in his throat, and he was sure he heard Reyna's voice cursing from the row beneath him. He reached out a hand and gently placed it on Lance's arm. He felt the arm trembling with contained anger. But Lance kept his cool, as he'd promised his parents he would.

"You're right, sir, it did," he responded, his voice cool and calm. "But for one reason only."

The man raised his eyebrows. "Because your adoptive father is the most famous man in the world?"

Lance shook his head, locking his eyes on the man. "Because I had a choice."

The murmuring intensified a moment, and then many in the room burst into applause. The smug senator or representative—Lance didn't know which he was– –lost the smirk and saw he'd been trumped, so he lowered his eyes to the desk before him and fell silent.

Lance looked over the edge of the desk and met his father's eyes. Arthur looked both proud and happy at the same time. Lance grinned and flashed a thumbs up. Arthur returned it. Then Lance said, "Hey, Chris, c'mon up."

Having already known he would be called, Chris leapt from his chair and sprinted around the table and up to the next level to joyfully lean against Lance.

"The CBOR is about rights," Lance went on, "and one of those rights is choice. You all think you know what's best for us and your social services people are even worse. I went through it my whole life, so don't bother telling me it's great." He stopped to cast his fierce gaze over each and every one of them before resuming. "This is my brother, Chris, and he's my brother because he chose to be. Chris."

Lance stepped back and let Chris step onto a small platform and lean in to the mic.

"I didn't pick the mother I got," Chris said, his young-boy voice sailing out over the chamber like ringing church bells, "and the one I got stuck with dumped me in an alley so she wouldn't hafta feed me anymore." He pointed dramatically down at Arthur and Jenny. "*Those* are my real parents," he announced like a newsboy shouting out a headline, "because they chose me and I chose them. Social workers tried to take me away from them cuz I was just a kid and didn't know what I wanted. Don't tell me you all didn't know by the time you were three or four if your mom and dad loved you or not, cuz I know you did. Us kids aren't stupid. You all just wanna control us cuz it's good for you. Well, it isn't good for us and that's why we need this bill of rights, why we the *very* young people of the United States of America need to be human instead of just toys."

He turned his head to Lance and grinned. Lance grinned right back and leaned in to kiss the boy on one cheek. Chris grabbed Lance in a tight hug before turning his head back to the mic. "Oh, and this is my big brother cuz *I* chose him."

Laughter and applause soared upward from the seated representatives to the high, cavernous ceiling, and Chris grinned even more. Lance scooted him off the podium and the boy ran back to Arthur and Jenny, enfolding both in his arms.

The remainder of the session went smoothly, with senators and representatives asking serious, well-thought-out questions about various amendments while Reyna took copious notes. When everything concluded, Lance and the family waded out onto the floor shaking hands and chatting with various lawmakers one-to-one. Several invited Lance to their offices the next day to discuss the CBOR in more depth. He graciously agreed, and suddenly the joint session was over and everyone made to leave.

Edwin slapped Lance, Ricky, and Chris on the back and praised their "Masterful performance," adding that they were better at presenting their arguments than most politicians in Washington who tended to ramble on trying to "Be all PC." The boys laughed and thanked him.

✝✝✝

The following day was hectic due to meetings much of the day with senators and representatives in their offices, and then a town hall-style Q&A meet-and-greet with the public in the late afternoon. Despite Edwin keeping everyone in stitches with his snarky and hilarious mocking of certain Arizona lawmakers and the faces they were making during the boys' appearance the day before, he was the consummate professional when greeting some of these same lawmakers in their offices that morning.

Lance marveled at his easy schmoozing style that enabled him to disarm even those he personally disliked, realizing that this was the reality of politics, and an area in which he needed to hone his own skills as the tour spread out across the country.

The outcomes of these meetings looked positive. Lance could tell these lawmakers were reluctant to like him when he'd first entered, but by the time they exited each office, the ice had melted and he knew he'd earned at least a reluctant ally in their fight. His young Mr. Lincoln skills were still intact, with Edwin showing him a few new tricks to add to his arsenal.

The town hall Q&A was wildly successful. The people seemed almost in awe of The Boy Who Came Back and many questions revolved around his death and return. He graciously answered these, but always steered the reason for his return back to the CBOR so every child could have "A kind of rebirth under the law."

Most of those present seemed supportive of the CBOR, partly because they'd seen more than a few injustices perpetrated against children, often by their local school system. But mainly, the parents had listened to their own kids talk about the CBOR and how it was necessary, and that it wouldn't in any way harm them as parents, but rather make the country as a whole stronger.

The following day was spent in a similar manner, with Lance disarming the barriers put up by this senator or that representative and then wowing the public with his humor and charm at another town hall meeting. He and Ricky yucked it up and goofed around with Chris, and the people were smitten.

What happened at the conclusion of that town hall meeting, however, shocked everyone, Esteban most of all. As the Secret Service agents, led by the always formidable-looking Brooks, guided the group from the venue and out to the parking lot, a crowd had gathered. These were obviously locals who couldn't get into the meeting because of overcrowding. Many waved signs of support, and almost all cheered and waved. Lance and the others cordially greeted the people, and passed out stickers.

A man stood at the fringe of the crowd, close to where the bus was parked. Lance noticed him first. The man was short and stocky, maybe mid-thirties, though Lance wasn't too good at guessing ages, with an almost bald head, wearing jeans and a short-sleeved work shirt. Even as he moved along the crowd shaking hands, Lance felt the man's eyes on him. No, not on him. On someone behind him. He turned and found Esteban glad-handing eagerly, not nearly so shy with the public as he once was.

Lance glanced back at the man and saw the gaze fixed on Esteban. He studied the man's face a moment, and then gasped. Grabbing Ricky, he nodded his head in the direction of the man, who loomed ever closer as the group moved toward the bus. Ricky turned and looked. He must've seen what Lance saw because he gave him a quizzical look.

Lance turned to Esteban and nudged his arm. The older boy looked over and Lance indicated the man with a nod of his head. "He's watching you."

Esteban lost his smile and frowned as he looked over and met the man's eyes. The man did not turn away, and a chill ran up Esteban's spine.

You don't take no shit from no one! You learn that now, boy, or else!

Esteban had been five, maybe six, when he last heard that voice, and those words. Uncharacteristically trembling, Esteban bunched his hands into fists at his side, causing Reyna to eye him with concern.

"What's wrong, Este?"

When he didn't turn, she followed his gaze and saw the other man, now barely ten feet ahead.

Watching them both, Lance noted that she must've seen the same thing he and Ricky had, because she gasped.

"Este, he looks like—"

Esteban didn't let her finish. He strode purposely forward to the edge of the crowd and stopped before the man. Most of the crowd was unaware of anything occurring because they were engaged with Arthur and Jenny and the others. But Lance, Ricky, and Reyna hurried after Esteban to prevent an incident that might otherwise spiral out of control.

Esteban looked into the man's face with a fierce intensity. They were nearly the same height, with Esteban sporting a couple of more inches in height and more muscularity in the arms and chest. But their builds were remarkably similar, Lance noted, as he hurried to his big brother's side. And their faces, especially the eyes... it was almost as if... and then he got it.

"Este, chill, man," he whispered desperately, his voice as calm as he could make it.

"What're you doing here?" Esteban growled, his fists tightly bunched, his look pure hate.

The man did not return hate. His expression reflected guilt and shame. Lance saw that at once, but would Este?

The man made no threatening moves. To Lance he didn't look big and powerful like he must've when Este had been young, but small and broken and sad.

"Just wanted to see you one more time," the man answered.

Reyna was at Esteban's other side and slipped her arm in his, pulling him in close to calm him. "Well, I don' wanna see you! You ditched me and mama."

The man nodded sorrowfully. Lance eyed him uncertainly. *This was the big, bad gangster who'd made Este so badass by age six and then split?*

"I killed an enemy. The homies sent me to Mexico."

Esteban continued to mad dog the man, clenching and unclenching his fists. "That's yer excuse for not talking to me in fourteen years?"

The man shrugged. "No, that was cuz I was young and full 'a shit. Go ahead, *mijo*. Hit me. That's how I taught you."

Esteban's eyes narrowed. "Don't call me that. Arthur's my *jefe* now."

Esteban's father didn't look hurt or even surprised by his son's words. "And he's done a better job than I did. You're a good man, Esteban, *un hombré importanté*. I got no right to say this, but I'm proud of you."

That caught Esteban off guard, and a slight gasp passed his lips. The young man looked into the eyes of the older one who'd abandoned him, and saw sincerity within them. "So what now? You just drop in and play papa? I'm a man now."

His father offered a look of admiration. "Yeah, ya are. And I can't stay. Got business with the homies."

Esteban made a disgusted snort and shook his head in dismay. "Still the homies over yer own flesh and blood. Some guys don't change for shit! C'mon, Reyna."

He grabbed her by the arm and started past his father toward the bus.

"*Mijo*," his father said quietly.

Esteban whirled around, looking enraged again. "Don't call me that!" But something in the man's eyes must've been genuine because Estenan suddenly calmed. "What?"

"You won't see me again, not becuz I don't want to. Just becuz."

Esteban sneered. "Just because?"

The man nodded. "The business with the homies gots to do with you, but I got yer back. Remember me that way, if ya can."

Then, before Esteban could respond, the man ducked away into the crowd as Brooks pressed his way through the people toward them.

"Everything cool here, guys?" the big man asked, eying the faces expectantly.

Esteban's gaze never left his father's back until the man vanished down the street. Lance watched Esteban, saw Reyna sliding her hand up and down his arm to calm him, and turned to Brooks. "We're cool, Brooks."

The enormous agent gestured for them to enter the bus. As Reyna led Esteban up into the vehicle, Lance turned and eyed his father as Arthur approached.

"You saw?" he asked.

"Yes," Arthur said pensively, as Chris and Jenny joined him.

"He told his *jefe* you were his real dad," Lance said with a smile.

Arthur returned it with a nod, placed an arm around his son's shoulders, waved one last time to the cheering crowd, and then boarded the bus.

Their next stop, per Reyna, would be the Grand Canyon, not to campaign, but because "I've always heard it's, like, the most amazing thing to see in the country."

Then, from the Grand Canyon, the tour would move on to Kai's reservation, Many Farms, located in northeastern Arizona.

✝✝✝

The entire group bid farewell to the hotel staff and a gathered crowd of supporters who turned up early the next morning to see them off. Lance, Ricky and Chris, the "poster kids" for the campaign, waved and grinned and smiled at the well-wishers before boarding the bus. They would travel north on I-17 for the three and a half hour journey, most of it through vast expanses of hot, dry desert. Despite Reyna's enthusiasm for seeing the Grand Canyon, Esteban expressed the sentiments of the other young people – what's so great about a big crack in the ground? Reyna, who'd seen lots of pictures of the landmark, simply smiled and ignored them.

Lance and Ricky found it amusing that Edwin, rather than spend the trip working on business for Senator Cairns or even the tour, spent nearly the entire ride playing games on his iPad, or watching movies. He told Lance and Ricky he especially liked old adventure films, movies he'd watched growing up, and he didn't even care that most were in black and white. His favorite old film was something called *The Most Dangerous Game*, which he promised to show them at some point along the way.

As for games, Edwin favored the first-person shooter variety, which the boys found doubly amusing given his terror in Washington when they'd been attacked the previous summer. The calm and non-threatening intern's two favorite games seemed to be any of the *Modern Combat* and *Call of Duty* ones, but he also enjoyed the bloody *Resident Evil* stuff. Sometimes Lance or Ricky would take him on in these games, but his most frequent competitor was Sylvia, who seemed to enjoy them as much as Edwin.

Lance was grateful Chris stuck to *Madden Football* and kept challenging everyone on the bus to go against him. Sadly for them, they all lost, which made Chris ecstatic with joy.

"The boy knows his football," Lance told Ricky with a laugh as they settled down beside each other to sleep. The previous few days had been hectic and snuggling next to each other for a nap seemed like a great idea.

✝✝✝

Lance woke to find Kai shaking him gently. As he stirred, Ricky's head moved against his shoulder and the two boys pulled themselves into uncertain wakefulness. Kai stood grinning before them.

"We're here."

That got both boys awake quickly. They sat up and rubbed sleep from their eyes as they looked out the window at a large stonework sign proclaiming: "Grand Canyon National Park." The sign slid on past as the bus entered into the green lushness of the park.

Everyone had a face pressed against a window hoping for a glimpse of the canyon itself, but as the bus pulled into Grand Canyon Village and stopped before a rustic-looking, unpainted building that looked like some kind of lodge, they all quickly realized the canyon would not be visible from the bus.

Everyone piled out carrying their overnight bags to check into their hotel as quickly as possible, drawing a large crowd of gawking tourists as they did. They waved and smiled as the people, especially the children and teens, waved back excitedly. Since they had only today and part of tomorrow, despite feigning indifference to Reyna, now that they'd arrived all of the boys were anxious to see the canyon itself, if for no other reason than to rag on Reyna for wasting their time.

Edwin booked a room for himself, and once everyone had checked in and gotten settled, they gathered down in the lobby for the trek out to the rim. Jenny insisted on sunscreen and hats for herself, Arthur and Chris, who had the lightest complexions. She offered the sunscreen to the others, but only Reyna and Sylvia used any. The guys all laughed in that macho ways boys do when a female suggests something, and turned down the offer, especially Darnell and Justin. "We could use a little red to go with the black," Darnell joked, and Justin high-fived him.

Lance and Ricky thought Arthur looked hilarious in the large floppy hat Jenny had placed on his head, and ribbed their dad mercilessly as they made their way along the path they'd been told would take them to the rim. The three started shoving each other and laughing, and then Chris jumped into the fray, the four jostling and joking, the boys bagging on Arthur's hat, and Arthur acting unusually boyish for a brief, endearing moment.

Jenny captured video of their antics with a wistful sadness that caught up in her throat and almost stopped her breathing. *If only this moment could last forever*, she thought, lowering her camera and just enjoying the light, carefree moment her family was sharing. But, of course, she knew it couldn't.

Kai and Dakota walked side-by-side, trailing Arthur and the rest of the team. Neither had ever been here before, even Kai who'd grown up in the state, but obviously wide-open spaces and mesas and canyons were nothing new to them. They watched the group approach a low stone wall set back from the South Rim to keep tourists from getting too close to the edge, noting with amusement how everyone suddenly fell silent. Lance and his brothers stopped messing around with Arthur as gradually more and more of the canyon rose into their field of vision. Everyone lined up at the stone wall and gazed outward in stupefied silence. Kai and Dakota grinned at one another and joined them.

Lance nearly lost his breath as the immense, timeless beauty of the canyon filled his vision and stopped his heart. He gasped lightly, and heard Ricky beside him suck in a breath. Far below, the blue snake that was the Colorado River wound its way through intricate rock formations and towering cliffs carved out over eighty million years. The rock patterns shimmered beneath the hot summer sun, gleaming red and brown and green, with so much detail they looked like they'd been carved by the hand of God himself. Lance had never seen anything so incredible in his entire life.

Ricky, eyes riveted to the splendor spread out below and before him, whispered in an awe-filled voice, "I finally found something more beautiful than you, Lance."

That momentarily broke the spell and Lance glanced over at him with a shake of his head. "Dumbass."

Ricky grinned and returned his eyes to the magnificence below.

Lance heard Kai chuckle to his left and looked over. The Indian was grinning. "I guess you city boys never been to the country, huh."

Lance and Ricky shook their heads simultaneously, their expressions still reverential. That made both Indians laugh.

"Welcome to my world, Lance," Kai announced proudly. But then his face clouded and for a moment looked eerily like Dakota's. "Well, the world of nature, anyways. My rez is a shithole."

The boys nodded and turned to observe everyone else. Reyna had her head on Esteban's shoulder as they gazed outward, Jenny rested up against Arthur, and the others merely stood with their mouths agape, even Justin and Darnell, who thought they'd seen it all on the streets of L.A. Even Edwin looked awed by the view. It was a moment, Lance knew, that none of them would ever forget.

After spending several hours wandering around, snapping pictures of the canyon itself or themselves with the canyon behind them, the hot, sweaty group headed back to their hotel to get cleaned up for dinner.

†††

The following morning, during a raucous breakfast in the hotel dining room, the group chatted up tourists and their children, handing out stickers and encouraging everyone to email their representatives to support the CBOR. Lance and Ricky hated the constant politicking and vowed once more that, after this campaign concluded, to never venture into politics again.

Then it was back onto the bus heading east through the Arizona desert on AZ-64E toward Many Farms. Lance noticed that Kai seemed more subdued as they drew closer to his home, rather than displaying elation at seeing his mother again.

Dakota tried to draw him out, joking that Many Farms was not as ghetto as Pine Ridge, and Dakota's use of the L.A. slang drew a smile to Kai's face.

Hair tied in his traditional twin braid style, Kai looked over at Dakota resting comfortably against him on the bus seat, their bare forearms touching, their shoulders pressed in against the other's, and sighed. "I guess I'm just stressing over what everyone'll say about… us."

Dakota brushed his waterfall of hair away from his face as he sat forward in surprise. "They know you're Two Spirit, right?"

Kai shrugged. "I mean, I never told nobody 'cept my mom, so I don't know."

Dakota's face clouded over. "Are you… embarrassed to be with me, cuz of what I did?"

Now Kai leaned in close and spoke with an urgency that touched Dakota. "Hell, no! I love you, Cloudy Boy, and I'll tell that to the whole world."

That broke the mood and Dakota grinned shyly. He felt self-conscious around *any* Indians after what he'd done to his brother, and he dreaded the reception he'd receive when they finally pulled into Pine Ridge. But Kai's love and support filled him with warmth and courage. Kai rested his head against Dakota's shoulder and they settled in to nap.

†††

Many Farms, located in Apache County, was only around eight square miles, Lance knew from checking Wikipedia before leaving L.A., and only had thirteen hundred forty eight people living there according to the last census. Just the smallness and dearth of people amazed him. Kai had told him that a quarter of the households were run by the mother only, his being one of them. His father had died as a result of alcoholism when Kai was very young, and he had no siblings.

By now, most of the city kids had become bored looking at empty expanses of desert, and slept during much of the drive. Ricky had dosed off against Lance's shoulder, but Lance wasn't able to follow suit. His eyes kept returning to Esteban, sitting two rows ahead across the aisle, gazing solemnly out the window while Reyna slept beside him. Lance knew his big brother was deeply troubled by the unexpected encounter with his long-absent father, and felt he understood the other's ambiguous feelings. How would he feel if out of the blue a man approached him and claimed to be *his* father?

Of course, Este had known his father at least until age six, whereas Lance never had. Still, the emotion would be one of turmoil, he knew, anger mixed with curiosity, and he wished for something to say that might calm Este's troubled heart the way the older boy had helped calm him on more than one occasion. Alas, he could think of nothing to say, and so merely sat eyeing his big brother and silently praying the young man's heart would be healed.

The road into the reservation was two lanes and sparsely trafficked, with a lone green sign with white letters announcing: "Many Farms." Way in the distance was a huge mesa rising up out of the desert like some kind of monolith monster. Some of the buildings looked new, while others were run down and shabby. From the road, he could see a large white cross standing beside a small wooden building adorned with the words "Red Ridge Friends Church" in peeling brown wood, but there was little around it – just empty dirt. No landscaping and no paving for cars to drive or park.

With nowhere to stay on the reservation for so many people, Reyna had booked a hotel for them at nearby Chinle, fifteen miles south. For now, their destination was Kai's house, and Lance spotted it from a distance, even though he'd ever been there before. It was small and rectangular shaped, single story, made of faded, weathered wood with few windows and only one door visible from this distance. But what made it instantly recognizable as Kai's was the massive wolf mural painted across the entire front of the small home, spilling onto and covering the front door. It was unmistakably Kai's style, same attention to uber-realistic detail. As the bus drew nearer Lance felt as though the eyes of the wolf were following him. Sadly, the house sat in an empty lot with nothing but dirt around it. Dirt, it seemed, was the preferred building site, with paving and concrete conspicuously absent.

By this time, the other young knights had stirred, and Arthur awakened Chris, who'd been slumbering peacefully with his head in his father's lap. All turned their eyes to the windows and gazed out at the emptiness of the reservation, the dirt roads, the small, unadorned homes interspersed with newer buildings off in the distance.

"Man, this is worse than South Central by a mile," Darnell said to Justin, shaking his head in amazement. Justin nodded in agreement, but didn't reply. He just glanced over at his dad in the next row and smiled gratefully, as though suddenly realizing just how good a life the man had tried to make for him.

Reyna and Esteban eyed Kai's house as the bus turned off the road to park. "This makes my mom's house look like a palace," he muttered to Reyna, who said nothing. He glanced over at her openmouthed expression of horror as she stared at the shabby home, and knew she was feeling guilt over her parents' lavish lifestyle and her own griping about not having this or that growing up. Real poverty had a way of putting everything into perspective, and for these city kids, even those who'd grown up with little to nothing, the sight of such extreme neediness was sobering.

Kai had already stood, Dakota beside him, as the bus rolled and rattled to a stop. Lance noted the taut posture of his Navajo brother and again wondered why the other was so tense. He glanced at Ricky beside him, soaked up the wonder of the boy's smile, and then stood into the aisle to approach the two Indians. He placed one hand on Kai's shoulder. The young man flinched in surprise, but then relaxed when he turned and found Lance grinning at him with support and confidence.

Kai smiled, enlightening his face. As everyone began filing off the bus, Lance noted a stout, short, swarthy-looking woman with weathered skin and long, braided black hair step from the house onto what Lance surmised constituted a porch. It was just a platform of wood raised above the ground and extending out from the doorway. The woman had dancing, laughing eyes exactly like Kai's and there were gray strands running through the black of her hair. Dressed in simple black pants and a plain purple t-shirt, she still looked somehow stately and regal with that magnificent wolf as her backdrop.

As Lance followed Kai and Dakota out of the bus, he noted they weren't holding hands and considered that might be the cause of his trepidation, especially with all the locals gathering around, spilling in across the vastness of dirt like curious ants. Everyone stood and waited while Kai approached his mother, Dakota trailing shyly behind.

Kai's mother threw her hands to her hips and frowned as her son stepped onto the wooden porch to face her. "It's about time you came home," she said in a chastising tone, but then broke into a huge grin and grabbed her son in a tight hug. Relieved, Kai joyfully hugged her back while Dakota stood looking down at his feet and shuffling nervously.

Kai's mother released her son and stepped back to assess him. "You're taller and even handsomer."

Kai grinned at the compliment. Then he quickly turned and grabbed Dakota's arm, dragging the reluctant young man forward. "Uh, *má*, you remember Dakota, right?"

Her eyebrows shot up in surprise. "What, no more *Cloudy Boy*? Of course I remember him." Then she stepped forward to envelope Dakota in a tight hug, catching him off guard. Then she stepped back, her hands on his shoulders. "And what a handsome man you've grown into." Dakota turned red around the ears, and Kai tossed off a laugh. "I've missed you and your family at the powwows."

Dakota's face clouded over instantly, and he lowered his shame-filled eyes to the wood beneath his sneakered feet. Kai instantly stepped to his side, fully aware of the locals standing around in silent observance. "Uh, -*má*, you know Cloudy and me have known each other since forever, right?"

She nodded knowingly. Even from a distance, Lance could see in her eyes that she already knew what her son was going to say.

Kai glanced nervously at Dakota, his insides churning with dread, and then looked his mother in the eye. "Well, now he's my boyfriend," he blurted quietly, hoping his fellow Navajos, especially those he'd grown up with, couldn't hear.

His mother merely smiled and nodded. "Honey, he's been your boyfriend since you were six. It just took you this long to figure that out."

Kai and Dakota had such openmouthed looks of shock that Lance and Ricky nearly laughed.

"You knew?" Kai whispered to his mother. "All this time?"

"Of course," his mother replied, her eyes dancing with amusement. "Everyone on the rez knew."

Now Kai's heart pounded with terror and his mouth dropped open in shock. He turned and gazed out over the heads of his New Camelot family to focus on his fellow Navajos. None seemed surprised or distressed, but merely looked at him with the traditional Navajo impassivity that kids were taught from a young age so as to hide their true feelings from others. Then he turned back to his mom. "How did you know?"

She looked at him like he was crazy and shook her head. "Don't you think you should introduce me to your new family?"

That made Kai burn with embarrassment. "Oh, sorry." He turned to the gathered Indians and announced, "My *diné* brothers and sisters, I'd like you to meet my brothers and sisters of the Round Table, and the man who leads us, King Arthur."

There was reserved applause, but nothing enthusiastic, Lance noted. He knew out here in the middle of nowhere with no Internet and little television, most of these people probably didn't know much about their crusade. Kai led his mother down off the wooden platform to the dirt and walked her over to Arthur, Dakota trailing mutely behind. Kai introduced his mother to the entire team, and everyone thanked her for allowing their son to join them, and praised his heroics when it came to protecting Lance.

She gave Lance, in particular, a stronger appraisal than the others, studying his face and almond-shaped eyes with her own. "You're Native, likely Mayan." Then she looked Ricky over in the same way. "Your boyfriend too."

That made both boys redden, though Lance knew it shouldn't have.

Kai's mother smiled at their reaction. "You blush like my son."

That drew a laugh from everyone, Reyna most of all. She still loved ribbing Lance for his tendency to turn red with embarrassment at the slightest compliment.

The Navajo woman invited the entire group into her tiny home. Arthur and Jenny thanked her graciously, followed her up onto the porch and entered through the wolf mural. She proudly pointed out the wolf as "My son's gift," and everyone praised Kai profusely. To Lance, the wolf seemed more lifelike up close and he marveled at Kai's ability to capture real expression, even in an animal, and bring it to such vibrant life.

Kai's mother insisted everyone call her Dezba and assured Arthur that their tribal council representative, as well as the president and vice-president of the council, would meet with the king and his team that night during a communal supper with the people.

The house felt cramped with such a large group crowding in, and there wasn't even a place for everyone to sit, so the younger people planted themselves cross-legged on the floor. Dezba ducked into the tiny kitchen and quickly returned with fry bread and a red berry beverage she called *Chilchen*. Kai and Dakota, of course, already knew these traditional foods, but the others had never tasted them before and proclaimed them "delicious," "fantastic," "amazing," and a host of other adjectives, which caused Dezba to laugh with delight. Lance and Ricky almost choked on their fry bread because her laugh was exactly the same as her son's. They grinned at Kai, and he shrugged.

"-*Má*, how did you know I liked Cloudy so much?" Kai suddenly asked around a mouthful of Frybread. "I only saw him, like, once a year. And I *never* talked about him."

Dezba chuckled in that tired, exasperated fashion only mothers seemed able to pull off. "You didn't have to." She rose from her chair and pointed to a pencil or charcoal drawing—Lance couldn't tell which—of Dakota as a young boy tacked to the wall above a ratty-looking end table. Dakota rose to check it out while Kai looked on red-faced.

"Okay, one drawing," Kai mumbled, suddenly wishing he hadn't asked his mother in front of everyone else. "And I drew that when I was, like, ten."

"This was a hint," his mother said, chuckling again as she picked up a sketchpad from the end table, handing it over to Dakota, who took it gingerly like it might bite him. "I found it under his bed."

Kai blanched slightly, having forgotten about that particular sketchpad. He'd had so many growing up, but he recognized the cover of this one, and knew what it contained.

Dakota flipped it open and gasped. Lance and Ricky jumped up and hurried to his side to look at the open pad in his hands. As he flipped the pages, they saw sketch after detailed sketch of Dakota at different ages in his life, starting when he was six. Kai had written in the year for each. At first, his drawing skills were good, but not great. Dakota was clearly recognizable and in every shot he wore fancy powwow regalia.

But as Dakota, and Kai the artist, aged, the drawings became more and more detailed until they were almost photographically lifelike. Dakota's mouth hung open the entire time as he saw himself age from small boy to teenager before his very eyes.

"Do you like them, Cloudy?" he suddenly heard as merely a whisper of breath, and he turned to find Kai gazing at him with uncertain trepidation.

Dakota was speechless, not an unusual occurrence for him as he was never good with words. "They're amazing," he whispered, his voice filled with awe.

By now, Arthur, Jenny, Reyna, Chris, and even Edwin had crowded around to see the images, and everyone expressed once more, as they had so often at New Camelot, great admiration for Kai's artistic abilities.

"That's not all," Dezba finally said after everyone had admired the various sketches. "There's still your last one."

Kai looked at her quizzically as she turned and walked down the single hallway past several doors to one at the end, a door clearly leading outside. As he and the others followed and he saw her reach for the knob, he suddenly remembered. God, he *had* been obsessed with Dakota his whole life, hadn't he? It *had* been love, even then.

Knowing what he would see, Kai trailed his mother outside, and the others followed, looking around the empty expanse of dirt lot for something spectacular.

"This one pretty much sealed the deal, Kai," his mother said, still standing by the open door. Everyone turned back to her as she closed it and there was a collective gasp from the group loud enough to be heard by the locals still milling about in front.

Dakota's face collapsed into astonishment, and Kai eyed him with obvious worry plastered to his face. The entire backside of the house, just like the front, was covered by a mural, but not a wolf this time. It was a boy. A young teen boy, Lance noted, no more than twelve or thirteen. And not just any boy. It was clearly and unmistakably Dakota's face gazing back at them. His regalia and feathers and face paint were rendered with striking perfection, but the eyes were what held Lance's gaze. Those eyes were so lifelike, so penetrating, even down to the little squint Dakota retained to this day. The face was young, but the expression old and serious, yet hesitant and poignant all the same. To Lance's untrained eye, it was the most remarkable painting he'd ever seen in his life.

Kai sighed heavily. "I was fourteen when I did this one," he said quietly, to Dakota alone, even though everyone else was present. "When you didn't show to the powwow that year, I was so sad I came home and started on this."

He fell silent then, eyeing Dakota to gauge the other boy's reaction.

Dezba broke the silence. "And he barely stopped long enough to eat until it was done."

Dakota finally pulled his eyes from his past and fixed them upon the young man beside him. "You make me look so, I don't know, so noble and handsome. I'm not like that."

Kai offered a shy smile and a little shrug. "You are to me. You always were." He reached out a hand and Dakota took it, intertwining their fingers, and Dakota shook his head in amazement.

But then his features darkened with guilt. "I feel like shit, Kai," he whispered pathetically. "When my friends made fun of you, I did too. I'm such a jerk."

He lowered his gaze to the dirt beneath his feet.

Kai reached out and placed a hand under his chin, gently lifting the young man's face so they could make eye contact. "You worry too much, Cloudy Boy, about stuff that already happened. Can't we just be together now and go on from here?"

Lance inadvertently glanced over and found Ricky eying him with a look much like the one Kai directed at Dakota, and knew Ricky often thought the same about him.

Dakota smiled and nodded, turning his gaze back to the lifelike painting before him.

Lance also nodded to Ricky, indicating that he, too, would work on leaving the past where it belonged, and focus on the here and now.

Everyone stood silently for a few more moments, staring at the magnificent mural. It was easily as good, if not better, than the one of Lance back in L.A.

Finally, Reyna broke the silence. "Your talent is incredible, Kai. You should be in a gallery somewhere, like Beverly Hills."

Kai grinned at that. "Yeah, but who'd want pictures of Cloudy Boy 'cept me."

Dakota looked aghast for a split-second until everyone busted up, and then he shoved Kai playfully away from him. "*Gnaye*."

Kai laughed, but his mother frowned.

Dakota looked sheepish, which made Kai laugh all the more.

"What's that mean?" Lance asked.

Kai grinned. "It's Lakota for 'fool'."

Now Lance, Ricky, and Chris laughed too. Even Arthur found it amusing, having long ago given up on cleansing his knights of that rather impolite word. They were all simply too fond of it. He glanced at Jenny and shrugged.

That was the cue for everyone to board the bus for their short trip to the hotel. They would get cleaned up and return that evening to the Many Farms High School gymnasium for the communal gathering and feasting. The meeting with the tribal council would occur in the high school's library the following morning. Despite the poverty he'd seen so far, if the rest of the Navajo were as cool and accepting as Kai's mom, Lance thought as he climbed back onto the bus, this should be a drama-free visit.

†††

The hotel was modest and simple, sufficient to meet their needs, but not in any way showy or ostentatious. Lance and Ricky talked about the severe conditions they saw on the reservation, and Kai's mural tribute to Dakota, which still left both boys breathless when they pictured it.

Showered and shirtless, standing before their bathroom mirror and brushing their blow-dried hair, the boys looked shyly at each other with equal parts desire and affection.

Finally, Lance asked, "If you could draw me, Ricky, how would I look?"

Ricky smirked a moment. "Like a dumbass."

Lance laughed, but then turned serious. "I mean besides that."

Now Ricky turned serious too. "I'd draw you like one of those Greek gods, Lance, all buff and manly and powerful and beautiful. Always beautiful." He stopped and looked bashfully at Lance in the mirror.

Lance's mouth hung open, making him look like a dork. But he couldn't help himself. "That's how you see me?"

Ricky nodded, offering a small smile. "And that's on a bad day."

Lance blew out a breath, the hand holding the hairbrush dropping to his side, and he turned to Ricky with a look of astonishment. "God, I am *so* lucky to have you."

Ricky grinned now. "Damn straight."

They both laughed and finished getting ready.

†††

In one respect, Lance noted as their bus pulled into the parking lot, Many Farms High School looked like most high schools in L.A.—institutional, boring, almost prison-like.

As with everywhere else on the reservation, the grounds were devoid of landscaping and vegetation—just dirt lots cut with concrete walkways. The single-story buildings looked to be made of redwood of a new vintage. Despite the intense heat, the wood did not appear beaten or weathered.

Nearly everyone from Many Farms would be present in the gym, Arthur had been told, just like they always gathered for basketball games. The entire community was curious about the Round Table and their local boy's adventures therein.

Lance noted that the gym looked typical, much like the one at Mark Twain, except these kids were the "Lobos" and their mascot was a wolf. Bleachers rose up toward the ceiling on either side of the court, with "Lobos" painted just behind both baskets in maroon and white and a wolf's head adorning the walls at strategic points. Courtesy of *ABC News*, an enormous video screen covered one of the backboards and Lance saw with a start his own face large as life on the screen as he entered. Obviously Charlie was already filming. Helen had been given permission by the tribal council to film the event because the council felt showing solidarity with Arthur might bring awareness of Indian issues to the rest of America, and the council had also asked for video highlights of Arthur's crusade to show to the locals.

The stands were packed with Indians young and old and everyone rose to politely applaud as the group entered. A man stepped forward and introduced himself as the Many Farms tribal council representative and shook hands with Arthur, who proceeded to present his team. The rep led everyone to a podium that had been set up at the far end of the basketball court. Two other men stepped forward to introduce themselves as Tribal Council members. Both wore jackets and ties, but Native strings of beads and other traditional accoutrements adorned their dark jackets. Both looked middle-aged to Lance, with jet-black hair, but one with a receding hairline.

These men were especially pleased to see Kai in his mix of knightly attire and Native regalia, and welcomed him back to the home country after acquitting himself so admirably as a Knight of the Round Table. Kai seemed surprised they knew of his exploits, and the men grinned proudly. They'd not only seen and heard everything Kai had been about, the men told him, but they planned to show video so all the gathered Navajo could celebrate their Native son.

That made Kai turn red and a laughing Dakota slapped him on the back playfully. "That's my native son," he said, and Kai tossed off a lopsided grin.

The three tribal representatives were especially excited at meeting Lance and congratulating him on all of his achievements. The president said, "You have shown the world that we Natives are a people to be reckoned with."

Not certain how to accept that compliment, Lance did what Edwin advised when dealing with any politicians. He smiled and said, "Thank you, sir," in as polite a voice as he knew.

The floor of the gymnasium had been set up buffet style with tables lining its edges, and the center left open for dancing. At least, that's what Kai told them. Navajos never got together like this in such numbers without dancing. "That means you and me, Cloudy Boy, doing our thing."

Dakota grimaced. "You mean, you doing your thing and me looking like a dumbass trying to copy you."

Kai laughed. "Yup."

Once they were seated in a row of chairs laid out behind the podium, and before the feasting began, the tribal council president offered a prayer for the safe return of Kai and the success of the Children's Bill of Rights.

"We hope and pray this bill will help our Native children, so they will no longer be stripped of their heritage."

That drew thunderous applause and cheers, and Lance realized once again how big a problem that must still be. Shuddering at the thought of foster homes being wantonly shoved on children, he forced himself to focus on the president's remarks.

The man introduced Arthur and Lance and the entire team, all to a standing ovation, and then asked everyone to sit. When they did, he said, "Our own Kai Begay, raised right here in Many Farms has, as you all know, been gone these near two years to represent our people at New Camelot, as an honored Knight of the Round Table. King Arthur has spoken most highly of our local boy and we are proud to call him one of our own."

He turned and pointed to Kai, who sheepishly stood after being nudged by Dakota on one side and Lance on the other. The crowd went even wilder with applause than before, and Kai looked abashed. He'd never been known for anything on the rez but his artwork, and that hadn't gotten him much attention. Sports were considered more important, especially basketball, and those guys had always been the big heroes.

He resumed his seat and the president announced to the crowd, "Witness now some of King Arthur's crusade in action, and Kai's heroic deeds since leaving the reservation."

He seated himself and the lights dimmed slightly. On the enormous screen, images flickered to life, video clips of Arthur's entire campaign, including Lance's death and return, but mostly featuring events after Kai joined up that highlighted his heroics as much as possible. Kai sat beside Dakota, stunned that his people were so proud of him, sadly realizing that people should be proud of each other just for being good people and not because they did something big or heroic.

Everyone silently watched the footage. They became especially animated during Kai and Dakota's race through Griffith Park with Lance and Ricky, and then even more excited by the cell phone footage of the Washington D.C. incident. They watched in awed silence as Kai and Dakota were knighted, and cheered at Kai's words to the Arizona state legislature. When the montage concluded, the crowd whooped some more and Kai looked embarrassed. But then it was time for food and that broke the spell for everyone.

As honored guests, Arthur's group served themselves first. There was a stew called *atoo'* which blended mutton with corn, potatoes, celery, squash and onion. Of course there was fry bread, and Kai kept trying to teach Lance and Ricky how to say its Diné name, *dahdiniilgahazh*, because he loved hearing the boys twist their tongues into knots trying to pronounce it. There were numerous toppings set out for the fry bread -tomato, lettuce, beans, and cheese. Corn was served, as well as baked squash. Among the other vegetables were wild onions, chilis, potatoes, and beans. For dessert there was peach pudding and corn ice cream. Lance loved the former and thought the latter tasted "Weird, but not terrible." That made all the locals around him laugh.

Arthur, Jenny, and Merlin sat with the elders, the president, and Dezba, enjoying the festive atmosphere and hospitality of the people. Despite the hundreds present, the mood was cheerful and family-like with food passed back and forth, drinks shared, laughter and buzzing conversation abounding. Arthur found the entire event delightful and these people endearing. He could tell Ryan and Gibson felt the same way. Even Merlin enjoyed the experience, developing a keen interest in Native culture.

After everyone had eaten their fill, locals in colorful regalia moved to the center of the court to perform traditional dances. Young Indians provided the drum and flute accompaniment and the dancers moved with a grace and fluidity that impressed Lance and Ricky. Despite all their accomplishments thus far, learning how to look cool while dancing wasn't one of them. Thus, when several local girls broke from the circle to grab their hands, as well as those of Kai and Dakota, the boys at first balked.

Kai laughed. "It's okay, guys, just follow my lead," he said cheerily. "It's in yer blood."

Lance scowled. "If it is, I haven't found it yet."

That drew another laugh from Kai and suddenly all four boys were out on the dance floor, in the circle, and moving along with the others. Of course, Kai was fantastic, as good a dancer as he was a painter. Dakota, too, knew the footwork required for these tribal dances. But Lance and Ricky stumbled along feeling like idiots as they attempted to replicate the moves, at least until the rhythm of the drums settled into their minds and souls. Once they stopped feeling self-conscious and simply felt the music, the dance steps became easier, began to flow, and both boys settled into a decent rendition of each traditional dance that was presented.

After a few large group numbers, several local girls approached with bows and quivers of arrows for Kai, Dakota, Lance and Ricky. Slipping the quivers over their shoulders, the boys smiled their thanks and the girls retreated along with the other local dancers. Lance looked quizzically at Kai.

"They want us to perform the bow and arrow dance," Kai told them happily. "It's really easy. Cloudy knows this one."

Dakota nodded. Rather than feel intimidated, Lance and Ricky both smiled. Kai had been right – this kind of dancing *was* in their blood and they were having a blast. So following the lead of their Indian brothers, once the drummers began, the two boys found themselves dancing forward and back, side to side, waving their longbows and bowing to one side of the auditorium and then to the other. It was a short dance, probably not more than a few minutes, but the moves were simple and both boys easily kept pace with their more experienced brothers. When they finished, the crowd roared its approval, with Reyna hooting and cheering the loudest.

Arthur turned to Dezba with a grin. "Your son is a remarkable young man, Lady Dezba. He has proven a godsend to me. You must be proud of him."

She smiled, her leathery skin crinkling with pride. "As I'm sure you are of your boys."

"That I am. Our own Lady Reyna has dubbed the four of them the Native Knights."

She laughed, and the king instantly knew where Kai had acquired his own. "And so they are," she replied with a grin.

When the dancing finally concluded and the affair began to break up, Arthur and the other knights mingled with the Navajo locals as they slowly departed, shaking hands and chatting with the people. Justin and Darnell had the odd sensation that some of the kids who greeted them had never seen an African-American before, or at least so infrequently as to make them a curiosity. Both knew they were a long way from the hood, and this world was as foreign to them as they must be to these people. Still, for a couple of city boys, they enjoyed the laid-back attitude of the Navajo and rather wished city folk could adopt it too.

Of course, as The Native Knights, Kai, Dakota, Lance, and Ricky were the biggest celebrities amongst the people, especially the kids. It seemed everyone wanted to shake their hands or just stare at them in awe before departing the gym for home. Lance and Ricky felt different after the dancing than they had before, as though they were now a part of this culture and these people, despite being of a different background, and happily thanked and greeted each and every person who approached. These people weren't asking for anything like crowds often did in the city, but merely wanted to extend their greetings or just commune with the boys a moment before leaving. Lance knew they saw him as The Boy Who Came Back, but they didn't act all whacked-out and crazy like so many people around the world had done, which made him feel almost normal for a change.

After everyone had dispersed and only Arthur's group and the tribal council remained, Arthur turned to the three men and directed that all of his knights do the same. Then he bowed and said the word Kai had taught them all, *ahéheé*, which meant "Thank you." Lance followed suit, and then all the rest simultaneously.

The tribal council members looked very pleased and the president replied, "*Ahéheé*" right back. Then all three bowed respectfully.

Lance followed Arthur and Jenny and Chris outside into the hot summer night, Ricky, Kai, and Dakota beside him. Kai's mother stood just outside the double gym doors awaiting them.

"A word, son," she said to Kai, who stopped, causing the others to stop too.

Arthur nodded to Kai. "We'll await you at the bus, Sir Kai."

Kai nodded and watched as they all followed the king. Dakota turned to look back and held Kai's gaze a moment before the darkness swallowed him up with the rest. The rez didn't have much in the way of street lighting—just the twinkling mass of stars overhead that looked like a gigantic blanket of glitter waiting to engulf the world.

Kai stepped to his mother's side and looked uncertainly into her aging face. The merciless desert sun had wreaked havoc on her once youthful features, but she still possessed a beauty Kai had often sketched as a boy. "Yeah, -*má*?"

She gazed upward at her tall, lean, handsome son with a twinkle in her own eyes to easily rival the stars overhead. "Does Dakota know you want to marry him?"

Embarrassment assailed Kai and he blushed furiously, grateful for the dark of night to cover it up. "-*Ma*!"

She just smiled in that way only mothers could. "What? I see it in your eyes."

Kai looked away, uncomfortable talking about such things with his mother.

"You *don't* want to marry him?" she prodded playfully.

He turned back to her aghast. "Course I do." Then he paused as a horrifying thought shot through him. "If he'll have me, anyway."

Dezba laughed. "Son, he had you at six." She shook her head and chuckled. "A Shaman told me years ago that you two were connected at birth, that your spirits were destined to come together."

Kai's face crumpled into shock. "He did? When did he say that?"

She laughed again. "When you were six."

His eyes widened in surprise, and then he laughed too.

"Such a serious boy, Dakota, even then," Dezba went on wistfully, thinking back to the first powwow Dakota had attended, the one where his eyes had latched onto Kai and never let go. "Always trying so hard to be a man. And now he probably wants to be a boy again, doesn't he?"

Kai shrugged. "Kinda. But he's a great man, -*má*."

She nodded. "I know. So are you, *shiyaah*. Your father would be proud."

Now Kai felt the old inner doubts and fears flood back in, the ones before he'd left the rez to join Arthur. "You think so, I mean, with me being Two-Spirit and all?"

His mother looked like she wanted to slap him for a split-second, but Kai could see it was a look of exasperation rather than anger. "Did you see yourself in that video tonight?"

He nodded, suddenly feeling like that little boy she'd caught sneaking extra fry bread from the kitchen before dinner.

"What does being Two-Spirit have to do with greatness like that?" she asked firmly, but with a loving tone nonetheless. "You are an amazing man, Sir Kai Begay of the New Camelot clan."

That brought a huge smile to his face and he leaned in to hug her. "I'll always be of your clan, -*má*," he said warmly. Public displays of affection, even between parents and adult children were frowned on, he knew, but it was so dark he figured no one would notice anyway. They separated and his mother gave him that knowing look.

"So, do you and Dakota wish to sleep in your old room tonight?"

He saw at once what she was suggesting and probably turned purple he was so mortified. "-*Má*!"

She laughed. "Well, you are a grown man and he is almost your *ach'ooní*, and I could stay with your aunt. I figured you probably don't have much time alone with all the adventures you've been having."

Kai couldn't make eye contact with his mother. He couldn't believe they were even talking about this! Sure, he was grown and all, but this was his mother talking to him about sex!

"He's, uh, not my husband yet, -*má*, and you're right, we don't get to be alone much."

She seemed to be enjoying his flustered state and chuckled again. "Then it's settled. I'll tell your—"

"Wait -*má*," he said, cutting her off just as she started to turn away. "We can't."

She eyed him expectantly, awaiting the reason with her old motherly patience still intact.

"We made a vow, Cloudy and me, a solemn vow to protect Lance and Ricky, to not leave 'em till we find the guy who's after 'em. We swore, -*má*, and you know we can't go back on our word."

He felt so helpless under her penetrating gaze, but then her middle-aged face broke into an enormous grin of admiration. "Like I said, son, greatness," she said quietly, but with authority. "You make me ever proud to be your mother."

She leaned in and rose on her tippy toes to kiss him on the cheek. As she stepped back she said, "But your Dakota is troubled. I see it in his eyes, in the way he walks."

Kai nodded, suddenly feeling the invisible weight of Dakota's pain and guilt wash over him and drag him down. "It's private, -*má*. You know the Indian way."

"I also know he's my son now too," Dezba went on with a sigh. "And I think he needs a mother. Send him to me before you leave."

Kai smiled. His mom never ceased to amaze him with her intuitive nature. A true soul whisperer like Lance. "I will, -má."

Then with a wave goodnight she was gone, swallowed up by the dark and the unearthly quiet surrounding them. Having lived so long in the city, Kai had almost forgotten how eerily silent it got out here. Feeling good, and yes, proud of himself, Kai strode back to the bus and found Dakota awaiting him by the open door. The rest had boarded.

Dakota's cloudy face threatened to storm with worry. "Is everything okay, Laughs A Lot?"

Kai reached out and took the other boy's hand and just held it a moment. "It's perfect."

He glanced around to make sure the coast was clear, leaned in for a quick kiss, and then they boarded the bus, bringing the day to a happy conclusion.

†††

The interior lobby of Many Farms High School was simple, but beautiful, Lance noticed as he entered the following morning with Ricky, Kai, Dakota, and Arthur to meet with the tribal council members. The others had gone off with Jenny to sightsee around the reservation. Kai had already pointed out some of the amazing rock formations and mesas visible in the distance, and the others wanted to explore them. A large number of Navajo youth had volunteered to show the visitors around.

The floor of the entryway to MFHS was an enormous circle, cut into four red sections like giant pizza slices split by a pattern of yellow and orange with green arrows pointing toward the center. Kai had previously explained how the four directions were central to Navajo tradition, and Lance surmised this circle a visual representation of that belief.

The meeting took place in the school library, a small, but brightly lit and newly apportioned facility with towering bookshelves in back and numerous round and rectangular-shaped tables scattered throughout the center. Mobiles displaying dangling animals hung from the high, sloped ceiling and a long, colorful mural stretched above the entrance.

The meeting proved fruitful, and the council members expressed their gratitude to Lance and Ricky for specifically mentioning Native children within the CBOR. Their hope was that giving their children specific rights under the Constitution would help bypass the loopholes in the Indian Child Welfare Act. It saddened both boys to hear story after story of Indian children removed from their homes and tribes by social service agencies for reasons of poverty alone, when the same standards were not applied to other children.

The council also assured Lance and Ricky that every child in every school within the Navajo Nation participated in the August Surprise the boys had planned for the U.S. Government. Knowing that most, if not all, the children throughout America had done the same gave the Indian kids a feeling of solidarity with their non-Native peers and they hoped that by teaming up to gain passage of the CBOR, Indian children wouldn't be thought of as "separate" anymore.

The meeting concluded with a prayer, both in English and Navajo, for the success of Arthur's crusade and the passage of the CBOR. Then lunch was brought in and everyone relaxed in the company of each other. Lance and Ricky felt comfortable with these men, in part because they knew the Navajo did not look down on them as Two-Spirit the way so much of the country did, but also because they felt oddly at home in this place, despite never having been there before.

As they said their farewells to the council members, Kai told Dakota that his mother wanted to see them before they left the reservation. Lance and Ricky bade them good-bye and trailed after Arthur in search of Jenny and the others. Dakota sheepishly followed Kai along the dusty roads to his mom's house, nervously asking, "Do you think your *iná* likes me now that she knows about us?"

Kai grinned. "-*Má* loves you. She told me so."

That seemed to put Dakota at ease for the remainder of the walk. Though wanting to, he did not reach for Kai's hand, but let their fingers brush gently against each other as they ambled side by side beneath the pelting sun and cerulean blue sky. Despite his love for his family at New Camelot, Dakota missed the wide-open spaces and vistas of his home state, and knew Kai did too. But unlike Kai, he couldn't return to *his* home, and knew there would be trouble when Arthur tried to bring him onto Pine Ridge. He shuddered just picturing his mother's face, especially the way he'd last seen it, accompanied by her final words to him before he'd left.

When they arrived at Kai's house, Dakota insisted on entering through the back so he could once more marvel at the amazing mural Kai had created. Just seeing his thirteen-year-old self looking so noble and proud gave Dakota a boost of confidence that maybe, somewhere deep inside, he *was* those things rather than just a drunken kid who stole his brother's life away like a thief in the night.

Dezba welcomed both with a hug and a big smile. Her long gray-speckled black hair was tied back in a single braid, and she offered the boys fry bread and *Chilchen* and they sat together in the small living room chatting about the trip ahead and other mundane matters. But Dakota felt the weight of Dezba's eyes on him the entire time, and he knew she wanted to talk of more serious matters.

"Kai," she finally said casually, "if I may speak with your *bich'áayaa íí'áhí* alone."

Dakota blanched at hearing the word "boyfriend" from Kai's mother's mouth, but wasn't surprised when Kai instantly stood up, as though this moment had been pre-planned. Kai looked at Dakota, still seated in a wooden chair gazing up at him uncertainly. "I'll wait out back." And then he was down the hall and out the back door before Dakota could respond.

Dakota pulled his gaze from the now empty hallway, the click of the back door cutting off his sight of Kai, and looked back at Dezba. He knew what she wanted to talk about.

She smiled, crinkling the creases around her mouth into a pleasant kaleidoscope. "You love my son and he loves you," she began, her voice soft and soothing, the exact opposite of his own mother's. "And that makes you my son too. I know you're troubled, Dakota. I see it in your eyes, even in your walk. Such a proud boy you used to be. What happened?"

Dakota looked down at the handwoven rug at his feet with its southwest pattern of oranges and yellows and browns. "It's family."

"And I'm not family?" she asked gently, causing him to look up into her loving brown eyes.

He gazed into those eyes a moment longer, and then confessed everything, his voice hitching and cracking as he described his brother's current, and permanent, condition.

Dezba listened, stony faced, but accepting, and made no comment until the boy who loved her son said, "She hates me. My mother hates me."

Dezba shook her head. "A mother can't hate her son, Dakota."

Dakota felt the weight of his near-nineteen years and fought back the tears. Lakota men didn't cry. "You wanna know the last thing she said to me 'fore I left the rez?"

She nodded.

Dakota paused, his heart hammering at the memory, his breath stuck in his throat and nearly choking off the words. "She said, 'I wish it was you instead of him'."

Despite his fiercest efforts, a lone tear forced its way out and rolled silently and heavily down his cheek. Dezba's face registered momentary shock, and then she rose from the sofa, grabbed his hands, and pulled him to his feet into a hug. He gratefully hugged her back, wishing it were his own mother he held in his arms.

"She's angry and hurt, Dakota," Dezba said soothingly. "One day she'll remember she has another son."

He swallowed and fought to control his voice as he said into her ear, "She always loved him more than me. When I met Kai and knew I was different from other boys, I figured that was why. Or maybe it's just cuz I never smiled much. But he was always her favorite."

She pulled back to make eye contact. Dakota viewed her through blurred, distorted vision. *No more tears!*

She smiled sadly. "One day she'll remember. Mark my words."

He nodded, wishing her words to be true, but knowing they were not. He knew his mother. She'd hate him for the rest of her life. "Thanks," he said anyway, grateful for her love and support.

She smiled and released him, eyeing him up and down as though appraising him for new powwow regalia because he'd outgrown his old. "What you did was a tragic, stupid teenaged thing to do, Dakota, but you have since brought great honor and prestige to all our people through your heroics with this Round Table you joined. And you are the best thing to ever happen to my son. Please don't let the worst thing you ever did become your whole life. You've too much to give."

He gaped at her, openmouthed and stunned. No one in his own tribe had ever spoken to him like that, no one in his own *family*. His father had the drinking problem too, and often fought with his mother when he wasn't off the rez for months at a time doing who knew what. Dakota had heard them praise Chayton as the "better son," but never him. Even when he'd become the best rider on the rez. Even that didn't warrant a compliment.

"Thanks... *iná,*" he said with a small smile of gratitude.

That drew another smile and more crinkles to her mouth and cheeks. He bade her farewell and walked down the hall to the back door. Feeling like part of his burden had been lifted, he turned the knob and pushed open the door. Then his breath stopped. Gazing at him was the one person who made him feel human.

Kai tilted his head in a scrutinizing way, and Dakota said, "What?"

Kai laughed the laugh Dakota loved. "You're just as noble-looking now as you were at thirteen."

Dakota smiled and shut the door, stepping down off the raised back porch to stand beside Kai. Together they stared at the mural. Without turning his head, Kai said, "Everything go okay with –*má*?

"As Lance would say, your *iná* is amazing."

Now Kai turned his head, and Dakota turned his. Their eyes met, and their hands came together. Kai grinned. "Ready to go?"

Dakota nodded. "Time to kick more white man ass." He smirked and Kai laughed again. Then, hand in hand, they sauntered off in the direction of the bus.

†††

Chapter Two

Dad, What Did That Mean?

The journey from Many Farms to Las Vegas took seven hours, with most of the terrain flat desert, but a few mountains, rock formations and mesas came into view to break up the monotony. For the city kids, the novelty of wide-open vistas had worn off and most welcomed any real city, especially the famous and supposedly glamorous Vegas, which only Reyna had visited before.

Breaking from their standard tradition of staying in ordinary hotels or motels, in Vegas they would be staying, per the manager who'd personally emailed Arthur with a "Deal you can't refuse," at Excalibur Hotel and Casino. The publicity factor of having the real King Arthur and his Knights of the Round Table stay for two nights easily offset the carte blanc treatment the king and his knights would receive. It would be a win-win for everyone and provide great visuals for both the hotel and Arthur's crusade.

Despite wanting to spend every moment at Ricky's side, Lance knew it was his responsibility to move amongst his team to chat and assess any issues, because as Arthur's son and heir it kept him in touch with the needs of his fellow knights. So he took the opportunity during this seven-hour drive to do just that. He found Techie and Justin deeply missing Ariel and Bridget, which he could understand. The couples Skyped every place there was Wi-Fi, but that hadn't been since the Grand Canyon. Many Farms had no such modern conveniences except at the high school. Ariel was taking summer school courses at Santa Barbara and prattled on about campus life, which made Techie all the more anxious to join her.

Justin quietly told Lance that he'd never cared about any girl like he did Bridget, and Lance laughed. He knew too well how awesome Bridget was, despite the drinking and partying, which thankfully she'd toned down since entering college, at Justin's urging. As head of security for New Camelot, Justin had a high-profile position that gave him the strong possibility to embarrass Arthur if things got out of control in public.

"You know about that, right, Lance?"

Lance scowled and laughed. "Oh, yeah."

The two fist-bumped and Lance moved on to chat with Darnell. As usual, his hair was done up in cornrows, which Lance had always thought looked cool, but figured would never work with his long hair. The young man lounged in a seat staring forlornly out the window. Lance sat beside him and punched his shoulder.

"Hey, man, what's up?"

Darnell pulled his gaze from the rugged terrain outside and eyed Lance uncertainly. "Ah, nuthin', man. Just thinkin'."

Lance searched the other's brown eyes. "About what?"

Darnell shrugged. Where Justin was big and muscular, Darnell was tall and lanky and good at basketball.

Lance offered a smile. "C'mon, man, give. You okay?"

Darnell didn't smile, but then he seldom did. "Guess I'm feelin' kinda lonely."

Lance frowned. "Why? You got all 'a us."

"Not what I mean."

"Then what?" Lance searched those lost-looking eyes, soul whispering the boy to find the truth. And then he saw it. "Cuz you got no girl, like the others?"

Darnell nodded, suddenly looking embarrassed and small and a lot younger than his nineteen years. "Everybody gots somebody, Lance," he said quietly, not wanting Justin and Techie to overhear. "You and them other Two-Spirits got your boo, Este gots Reyna, and the others gots a girl waiting on 'em and worrying over 'em. I don't go no one, man. If I disappeared tomorrow, nobody'd even miss me."

Lance felt momentarily stunned. Darnell had always been the cocky, "I got everything covered" sort of guy, and Lance had no idea the young man even had such feelings. A moment of panic hit him as he once more recognized that he was falling into the same trap Arthur had, the one that had led to all the initial tragedy in the first place.

"What about your mom?" Lance asked, realizing he'd never met Darnell's mother. She hadn't ever visited New Camelot and he seldom spoke of her. Lance only recalled seeing her that one time on TV being interviewed by Helen.

Darnell shrugged again. "Yeah, she loves me and all, but shit, Lance, that's my moms. All the girls I knew 'fore were hood rats. You know the kind."

Lance nodded. He did know, his mind seeing a younger Darnell, growing up like Este in the gang life where hood rats were welcomed because they put out and didn't expect much in return. But now Darnell was older, more mature. Now he wanted something real, like Este and Reyna, or Justin and Bridget.

"We're not gonna be on the road forever, Darnell," Lance offered. "You'll find somebody when you get home. Maybe even one of those same girls. They can change same as you, especially the ones we got in the Table. They already changed, and seem pretty cool to me."

"Yeah, I guess, and I dated some of 'em, but none did it for me, you know? Anyway, it'd just be cool to have a female to talk with along the way."

Lance considered. "Have you asked Reyna, or even Ariel or Bridget if they know any girls who might be interested? I mean, you are, like, super famous, man." He grinned.

Darnell considered the idea. "You think they know any black girls?"

"Only one way to find out."

Darnell grinned. "Thanks, man. You got smarts."

Lance laughed. "Long as I stay off the booze."

Darnell laughed, too, and they bumped fists before Lance moved on to Reyna and Esteban. The two sat huddled together, Reyna's head on Este's shoulder, Este's eyes roaming the empty landscapes outside the bus. Lance saw it in his eyes even then – Este was still brooding over the encounter with his father.

"Hey guys, how's it going?" Lance offered cheerily as he stood in the aisle.

Reyna smiled, but Esteban merely grunted. Lance eyed him, but then looked at Reyna. She gave a slight shrug.

"Is Vegas cool, Reyna, or just crowded as hell?" Lance asked conversationally.

Reyna laughed her airy laugh. "Both, actually."

Lance chuckled. "How's Excalibur? Will it make Dad laugh?"

"Oh, yeah. Cheesy as hell."

They shared another laugh, but Esteban didn't even seem to know they were conversing. Lance's instincts told him to leave well enough alone for now.

"Cool," he said to Reyna, flashed that smile she adored, and then moved on to where Sylvia and Edwin sat together playing games on Edwin's iPad. It still cracked Lance up to see the beautiful, delicate-looking Sylvia get so bloodthirsty while playing. Sure she was a crack shot with the bow and arrow, but blowing away aliens and zombies and even enemy soldiers didn't seem to fit her normal persona.

Edwin "died" on screen and grinned up at Lance. "This girl kicks butt, Lance," he said, elbowing the smirking Sylvia as he did. "I've finally met my match."

Lance laughed. "Any heads up for me, Edwin, 'fore we hit Vegas?"

"Yeah, stay away from the bars," Edwin retorted with another grin.

Lance chuckled. "Still underage, remember? I meant for the state legislature."

Edwin was resetting the game to start another battle and glanced up at Lance with a serious expression. "Their senator in Washington 'talks the talk' on child welfare matters, so play that up. Push the state to walk the walk too."

Lance nodded. "Got it. Thanks."

Right behind them sat Ryan in one seat with Gibson across the aisle in the other. Gibson was sound asleep, head lolling against the window, snoring. Lance eyed him before turning to Ryan, who looked up from the book he was reading to smirk. "That's my partner, all right."

He chuckled and Lance grinned. "How you doing, *nino*?"

Ryan placed a bookmark where he'd left off and looked appraisingly at his godson standing in the aisle. He shook his head as though to clear it.

"If you'd told me five years ago I'd be heading to Vegas with my godson and a guy named King Arthur to help them get a children's bill of rights passed, I'd have arrested you on the spot and dumped you in the psych ward at County USC."

Lance laughed. "If I'd even imagined all this five years ago I'd have *wanted* to be in the psych ward."

Both of them laughed, and Ryan once more assessed this remarkable boy who'd snuck into his life and captured his heart the way no kid ever had. This boy had opened his eyes to just how great having kids could be, and Ryan would be forever grateful.

"I'll say it again, Lance," the older man said, his crinkly face scrunched with uncharacteristic emotion. "You are the best thing to ever happen to me, hands down, and I'm so proud you picked me to be your godfather."

Lance's mouth dropped open in shock for a moment as he looked into the man's eyes and saw pure sincerity. And then he did what he always did when complimented – he looked down in embarrassment. "Thanks, *nino*," he said quietly to the floor before lifting his eyes and fixing them on the rugged face of this man he'd come to love and respect. "Coming from you that means the world."

He raised a closed fist and Ryan raised his. They bumped and the older man smiled. Lance returned it before moving on to sit beside Chris in the next bench. The smaller boy sat playing *Madden Football* on his iPad and beating the computer every time.

Chris looked up when Lance scooted in beside him and frowned. "This game's too easy, Lance. I win at every level."

Lance laughed at the petulant look in his brother's blue eyes, as though it was the game's fault that he kept winning. "I think the problem, little man, is that you're just too good."

Now Chris laughed and set the game down on his lap. Once more, Lance saw the boy in a new light, the light of a child growing up fast. The smaller boy had vowed never to cut his long blond hair as long as Lance never cut his, and his blue eyes had somehow gotten bluer, deeper, more like Mark's.

"I can't wait to play real football on a team, Lance," Chris said excitedly. "You think Mom and Dad'll let me when this trip is over?"

Seated in the bench seat right in front, both Arthur and Jenny turned their heads as Lance replied, "I'm sure they will."

Jenny frowned. "Isn't he a little young for football, Lance?"

Lance shrugged. "Naw. They got teams for kids his age."

Jenny smiled and looked at Chris. "We'll see, honey."

"Mom," Chris said petulantly. "I'll be ten in October and I'm big enough."

Jenny glanced at Arthur expectantly. "And so you are, Chris," the king agreed. "If there is a team for youth your age near to New Camelot, we shall explore it together. Deal?" He held up one clenched fist over the back of his seat.

Chris broke into a huge grin and bumped Arthur's fist with his own. "Deal!"

Lance met his father's eye. There was something in Arthur's look that gave him pause, his soul whispering talents kicking in big time.

Then Arthur smiled and the moment faded. The king turned back around to gaze out the window.

But Lance had seen something in those eyes, something painful, and that something sent him into an emo mood for the rest of the trip, one even Ricky couldn't pull him out of.

†††

Las Vegas proved to be what Lance suspected – loud, crowded, busy, glitzy, glamorous, and sleazy – everything he hated. Growing up he'd always hated crowded places, especially malls during the Christmas season, because he felt everyone could see into him the way he could see into them, and they'd figure out his deepest, darkest secrets. Fame had only increased his aversion to crowds and noise and "big" places. Alas, he had to force that aversion far down inside for the success of the crusade, but places like Vegas didn't make it easy.

Ricky sensed the problem right away as the bus and its entourage cruised down the strip with everyone planted by a window gaping at the immensity and tackiness of the place, so he held Lance's hand and squeezed it from time to time as Lance scowled at New York/New York, Circus Circus, the Luxor, or the faux Eiffel Tower, not to mention staples like the Bellagio and the MGM Grand.

It was all beyond Ricky's experience as a poor kid growing up, but crowds didn't bother him as much as they did Lance. He knew he'd need to stay extra close to his boy lest the emo part show its face again as it had the past few hours. He knew something other than Vegas had triggered the mood swing, but hadn't pressed the issue because he knew Lance would confide in him eventually. With Lance, you had to ride out the emo moments to sail on to the blissful ones.

Arthur chuckled with amusement at the sight of Excalibur, just across the strip from the MGM Grand. The colorful turrets and cupolas in particular made him laugh as he pointed out that the original Camelot was built of rough-hewn stone and handmade bricks and was without color or fancy adornment. Over the decades it had grown and become more ornate, but nothing like what he now saw before him. Still, he pronounced the place "A faint reminder of home" and looked forward to seeing the Tournament of Kings show he'd been told about.

Lance thought the place looked "Kinda cool," with the castle set between two towering V-shaped buildings which he presumed housed most of the rooms. The bus and secret service cars had been given a special location to park, back where the talent entered and exited, so Arthur and his group could avoid being mobbed.

Everyone piled out of the bus, flanked by the omnipresent agents as well as Ryan and Gibson, and filed into the hotel through the talent entrance, where the manager met them. The effusive, middle-aged man in the bright blue suit personally escorted them to their rooms to get cleaned up, thereby avoiding the lobby all together. The halls were elaborately ornate and medieval-looking with pillars, enormous chandeliers sporting faux candles, long, stained glass windows, battlements overlooking both outdoor and indoor areas like the main entry hall. There were tapestries and medieval-style paintings hanging everywhere. Arthur enjoyed his walk through the place, proclaiming a slight homesickness for the castles of ancient Britain.

Their rooms were oddly modern, with funky wicker chairs, flat screen TVs, weird lamps with skinny round shades that looked like lighted car tires, and fancy-looking bathrooms with massive mirrors spreading across the length of the room. The sleeping arrangements were the same as always, and everyone quickly settled in to shower and get cleaned up after their long, dusty ride across the desert. They would take in the Tournament of Kings show that night and get to eat dinner with their hands, without any chastisement from Jenny.

"The perfect place for boys to eat," Lance proclaimed to his mother when he'd learned no utensils were allowed, and she'd laughingly agreed.

Arthur was looking forward to seeing how he was portrayed in the show, but Merlin grumbled, "The wizard is always the joke character these days," and suspected he wouldn't like it at all.

Unbeknownst to all but the management of Excalibur, Arthur and his knights were scheduled to "perform" after the regular show, which had been shortened to fit in the real king and his Round Table. The kids would spar with swords and shields, and engage in archery duals. Arthur, Dakota, and Kai would perform moves on horseback, and the entire group would reenact key moments from the early days of the movement. Since the event would be filmed by Charlie, Arthur and Lance felt it would be a great opportunity to show America the beginnings of the Round Table, which no one but the participants had witnessed, and it would visually demonstrate just how far they'd come in four years.

Once everyone had cleaned up and dressed in their knightly tunics and pants, Brooks and another secret service agent supervised the unloading of weapons from the bus so everyone could practice in the arena before dinner.

✝✝✝

The arena was massive and oblong shaped, with a faux castle, replete with portcullis and battlements, at one end, and rising tiers of spectator seats along the other three sides. Arthur and his company were seated early, before the general public was allowed in. The king and his knights were given the place of honor directly across from the castle, down closest to the field so when it was their turn, they could easily enter the performance area. Their swords, shields, bows and arrows rested beneath their tables, left in place after the earlier rehearsal.

The kids felt giddy with excitement, even the ones who were no longer kids like Reyna, Darnell, and Justin, and all looked forward to performing for the crowd. Esteban managed to pull himself from his funk during rehearsal and Lance felt he would do so again when the two reenacted their first sword fight.

As the two youngest, Chris and Sylvia would also demonstrate their accuracy with the bow and arrow, and Edwin jokingly prodded Sylvia, "Just pretend they're zombies and you'll hit every target dead-on." She laughed.

As the crowd trickled in for dinner, heads turned and people gasped as they recognized the storied guests. Children pointed and everyone couldn't help but stare. Arthur and Jenny and the knights waved and smiled and even signed autographs as people, mostly kids, approached excitedly. Arthur noted once again just how popular Lance was with the youngsters. Every one who approached wanted to talk to him, pose for a picture, get his autograph - far more than with any of the others.

Ricky kept smirking each time a pretty girl asked for a picture with Lance, but some wanted pictures with both boys, and that earned Ricky a return smirk from Lance. The food was simple and tasty, and everyone had the exact same menu: Pepsi, tomato soup, a full Cornish game hen that had to be ripped apart to be consumed, potato wedges, broccoli, and a dinner roll. The dessert was apple strudel, which Chris loved. Beer, not ale, was also served upon request, but Arthur and Jenny did not partake. Merlin, fearing the worst for his portrayal in the show, downed at least two that Lance observed.

After dinner, the show began. It was fun and well acted. Merlin had proved prophetic again in his fears about how he would be portrayed. The character wore big blue robes and the usual wizardly conical hat, with a phony white Santa beard and hair, and overacted shamelessly while conjuring fire and the like.

The jousting by knights was excitingly staged, as were the sword fights. The actor playing Arthur looked older than the real thing and wore brightly colored robes with a large crown on his head. It was all done with smoke and fire and pounding music to add to the excitement, and the audience ate it up. Arthur commented to Jenny and the kids that the performance brought back found memories of the first Camelot.

During the show, Helen sent Charlie off to get in position to film "The real Camelot in action." Charlie grinned and slunk off to his prearranged spot with a perfect vantage point to capture all the action.

After the show ended and the actors took their bows, the one who played Arthur spoke to the crowd as the others wandered offstage.

"Ladies and gentlemen, we have a rare treat for you tonight only here at Excalibur Hotel and Casino," the man began in a deep voice that easily carried out to all spectators. "As you all know, we have been graced by the real King Arthur and his Knights of the Round Table."

The audience burst into thunderous applause and much table slamming with their mugs.

"But they are not merely our guests for dinner, no," the actor went on in that side show barker kind of voice, "for they have graciously agreed to demonstrate their own skills with the medieval weapons that we, as actors, merely play with."

That sent up another rousing cheer of approval from the rowdy dinner crowd, causing the faux Arthur to grin widely.

"I give you the real King Arthur and his noble knights!"

The man bowed and vanished offstage beneath the portcullis.

Taking their cue, Arthur stood to more clapping, mug slamming, and foot stomping. The king grinned and offered a bow to the crowd. Then he gestured for the kids to join him in the arena. Everyone rose, gathered up their weapons and stepped out of the eating area onto the dirt floor.

The show horses were brought back out for Arthur, Dakota, and Kai. Earlier, the three had befriended several of the splendidly gorgeous animals, especially the Indian boys with their innate horse whispering talents. Arthur had chosen the white because she reminded him of Llamrei, Dakota the black and Kai the brown. Kai laughingly chided Dakota that the boy had chosen black "To fit your cloudy spirit." To everyone's surprise, Dakota laughed right back. The fourth show horse remained tethered to the drawbridge.

The only knights sporting bows and arrows were Reyna, Chris, and Sylvia. Everyone else carried a shield and sword and all had been outfitted earlier with wireless lavaliere mics to project their improvised dialogue to the excited crowd. Arthur spoke briefly to the audience, welcoming them to this modern version of Camelot. He proceeded to introduce everyone, saving Lance for last. As he'd expected, Lance got the loudest, most rousing cheer of all, which caused Lance to look surprised, and Ricky to playfully shove him in response.

The stagehands had set up some archery targets at the far end of the arena, right in front of the open portcullis. The group sat themselves around on the ground as Arthur took his seat in the throne stagehands had rushed into place. A separate chair had been brought for Lance to sit beside the king. They "acted out" some of their early gatherings within the storm drains of Los Angeles, with first Chris showing off his archery prowess, and then Sylvia. Both got perfect bulls eyes to great cheering from the crowd.

Then Reyna stood and mad dogged Lance as she had in the beginning. "You expect me to take orders from a boy who's younger and prettier than me?" she challenged haughtily, drawing a huge laugh from the crowd.

Despite his best efforts not to, that laughter made Lance blush again, just as he had that night in The Hub when Reyna first uttered those words.

As before, Reyna whipped out an arrow and fired straight across the arena, hitting her target square in the center, turning back to Lance with a smug expression. The crowd "Ooohhed" their appreciation of her skill.

Arthur turned to Lance and nodded. The boy stood and strode forward, snatching the bow and quiver from her hands angrily, putting on a show for the crowd and enjoying himself after allowing that initial laughter to spook him. Glaring at her smug expression, he briefly thought how much she was getting into her part and should take up acting for a living. Then he slipped out an arrow, nocked it, took aim quickly and seemingly without care, and let loose. The arrow sailed true, striking hers from behind and splitting the shaft. The audience went wild with approval.

Reyna gave him the head nod of respect and reseated herself. Arthur looked out amongst the others, asking if anyone else wished to challenge Lance's authority as First Knight. That was Esteban's cue. He laughed along with Justin and Darnell, and when questioned by Arthur said, "Well, he looks kinda girly to me."

Despite the fact that it was all pretense, Lance still hated hearing that word, his old insecurities never far from the surface. He unsheathed his sword and said to Esteban, "Grab any sword you want and let's see if I fight girly."

Justin and Darnell whooped it up and the audience started chanting, "Lance, Lance, Lance!"

Man, they're really getting into this, Lance thought as Esteban stood and picked up his sword from the ground. They moved to the center of the arena and squared off. Esteban put a hand over his mic for a moment and said quietly, "Go easy, Lance, you're not that little boy no more."

That startled Lance, but then he remembered how much Esteban had been sweating during their rehearsal earlier, much more than their first battle when he'd been fourteen. *Cuz I'm bigger and stronger now*, he thought proudly as he prepared himself for Esteban's first swing. The fight lasted but a few minutes, as had the original, and ended with Esteban on his back in the dirt, panting, Lance's sword point at his throat.

"Still think I'm girly?" Lance challenged.

"Hell, no!" exclaimed the overacting, panting Esteban to cheers from the crowd.

Lance reached out a hand and helped Esteban to his feet and then everyone in the "cast" bowed to the audience encircling them.

Justin and Darnell followed with a mock sword fight, displaying their talents to an appreciative crowd.

At this point, Kai and Dakota mounted their horses, trotted to the center of the arena, and staged a sword fight on horseback. It was excitingly choreographed – the boys had spent forty-five minutes earlier practicing their moves. Lance found himself caught up in the battle. The Indians hacked at one another with abandon, and the audience watched with bated breath to see if one would emerge the victor.

After five full minutes, the two boys declared a draw, bowed to one another, and trotted back toward the throne to bow before the king. Now it was Lance and

Ricky's turn. They stood in the center of the arena and Lance gave Ricky a hearty shove before speaking to the crowd.

"Ladies and gentlemen, this fool thinks he can kick my ass."

Ricky moved in and shoved Lance just as hard. "And I *can* kick it any way, any time."

Lance mock glowered. "Yeah, you and what army exactly?"

Ricky smirked. "Me and the army of Lanceisaweakassfool, that's who!"

The audience roared with laughter and applauded wildly.

Lance chuckled at Ricky. "Bring it on, little man," he said tauntingly.

And then they began. These two knew each other's moves and style perfectly, and fought in earnest, determined to give the audience a real show and get a much-needed workout in the process. They hacked and swung and parried, bodies spinning, hair flying, heads ducking. They slammed their heavy blades into their equally heavy shields. Under the bright stage lights the boys sweated profusely as they tucked and rolled and righted themselves with swirling hair and a clang of blade against blade. The mock battle was fast, furious, and thrilling. The audience "Ooohhed" and "Aaahhed" and gasped on occasion, but the boys kept right on fighting.

The battle had been raging for over five minutes when suddenly an arrow whizzed past Lance's head and struck Ricky full in the chest, lodging itself near the heart and sending the boy spinning backwards to sprawl in the dirt, where he lay unmoving.

Stunned, Lance's mouth dropped open, and he spun around to protect his back.

Hiding behind the faux battlements, someone lurked, shielding himself, bow and arrow ready for another assault.

Lance whirled back around. "Reyna! Up there!" He pointed behind him even as Kai and Dakota galloped over and the others came sprinting across the dirt to the fallen Ricky.

On his horse, Arthur was momentarily stunned, but then called out, "Chris, Sylvia, assist Reyna against the attacker."

The audience seemed to think the assault part of the show and clapped wildly as Reyna, Chris, and Sylvia pelted across the dirt toward the faux castle shooting arrow after arrow up at their attacker to keep him pinned down.

Ryan, Gibson, Brooks and the other three agents also sprang into action. They had been sitting back a few rows from Arthur and the team so as not to be a distraction, and now leapt from their seats to plow forward onto the field. Jenny was up instantly and chasing after them. Edwin sat frozen, looking stunned.

Heart pounding with terror, Lance dropped down beside Ricky and grabbed the head of this boy he loved and turned the face around. Ricky's eyes fluttered open and focused on Lance, who let out an enormous breath of relief.

"Oh my God, you're alive!"

Ricky sat up with a grin, eyeing the arrow sticking from his chest with amusement. He reached up and pulled it out. "Fool," he said to Lance in a chastising tone. "I got a vest on."

The audience cheered.

Lance allowed himself a second to smile. Of course, they were both wearing the vests Brooks had given them – thinner than the heavy-duty ones, but vests nonetheless. They'd become so accustomed to wearing them every day that Lance had forgotten.

"Fool," he told Ricky with relieved exasperation.

He stood and pulled Ricky to his feet while Kai and Dakota circled them with their horses and Arthur quickly joined in. Ryan ran over and blocked Lance and Ricky with his body, drawing his gun and aiming up at the battlements. Gibson followed the Secret Service agents through the drawbridge, quickly spotting the stairs leading up to the battlements. They split into two teams and began ascending the steps two at a time.

The archers continued to pin down their assailant with a volley of arrows when suddenly the man rose to his full height, pulled back his bowstring and let loose an arrow straight at Arthur.

"Dad!" Lance yelled, and Arthur spun on his horse to see the arrow speeding toward him. He raised Excalibur and struck the arrow, slicing it in half and sending the pieces skittering onto the dirt in front of his mount.

Lance and Ricky turned back to the castle battlements. The man looked to be clad in thick, possibly bulletproof clothing, with a ninja-type mask covering his face. Ryan raised his gun just as Gibson and the agents pelted up the side stairs and out onto either side of the castle. The man was now trapped between them, but he made no move to nock another arrow.

Instead, shouting the words, "*Sic semper tyrannis*," the assailant tossed a rope over the battlements and in one fluid acrobatic motion he was up and over, sliding down the rope, dropping to the dirt, leaping for the fourth horse and untethering it before Ryan or anyone else could act without endangering the crowd. Then he was up onto the horse and grabbing the reins. With a kick to its sides, the stallion bolted forward at an intense gallop, straight toward Lance and the others, scattering Reyna and Chris, who dove to each side and landed hard in the dirt to avoid being trampled. Off to one side, Sylvia nocked an arrow and spun to take aim at the fleeing assassin.

Arthur, Kai, and Dakota flicked the reins on their horses to move them aside, while Ryan shoved Lance and Ricky away, raising his gun but finding any shot he might take too risky with the audience in the background.

The man galloped past Arthur, nearly knocking Jenny to the ground as she stumbled out of his path, and then right up the steps into the audience. People screamed and others clapped. Most, it seemed, still thought this a part of the show. The stallion galloped onto the steps between sections and vanished from sight, heading into the hotel.

Furious, Arthur trotted to Jenny and extended a hand. She was dirty and had a few scrapes, but smiled anxiously up at him. "I'm fine, Arthur."

He nodded and then flicked the reins of his mount and pelted forward, following their attacker up into the stands and vanishing from sight into the hotel.

"Kai, Dakota!" Lance called out in a commanding voice, "Help Dad!"

Without hesitation, the Indian boys spurred their own mounts into frantic pursuit.

Lance suddenly realized the audience was clapping and cheering, chanting "Arthur, Arthur, Arthur" and "Lance, Lance, Lance" and understood they thought everything was staged. He glanced out at the people giving them a standing ovation. "Uh, we'll be back!" he said into his mic, grabbed Ricky and said, "C'mon!"

Then he scooped Chris up off the ground as the little boy clambered to his feet. "Let's go, Chris. Knights with me! Techie, Sylvia, stay with Mom!"

Then without waiting for anyone else, he pelted forward with Ricky and Chris flanking him. Reyna, Justin, Darnell, and Esteban scrambled to their feet and ran after them, up into the stands and into the hotel. Techie and Sylvia rushed to Jenny to make sure she was unhurt, and Edwin joined them from the stands.

Jenny's heart pounded with fear as she saw her entire family race off in pursuit, wondering if the attacker might be leading them into a trap.

✝✝✝

Arthur steered his horse through the double doors leading into the Fantasy Faire Midway, noting the people and children already scattering as the assailant crossed through the flashing, brightly lit arcade area toward an exit to his left. The panicked adults were clearly unnerved, but the kids playing games stopped to cheer and clap as Arthur galloped across the lush, colorfully patterned carpet in pursuit.

The assailant galloped out of sight, and Arthur followed. A moment later, as the gamers and their parents milled about in confusion, Kai and Dakota burst forth from the Tournament of Kings arena and pelted across the arcade without so much as a glance at the astonished patrons.

By now, all of the children had ceased their games to watch the spectacle unfold, and went wild with excitement as Lance and his knights, swords drawn and ready, followed by Ryan, Gibson, and the agents blasted into the midway and looked around.

"Which way did they go?" Lance asked breathlessly.

A boy pointed. "That way, Sir Lance."

"Thanks, man," Lance said, already on the run, his team close behind.

✝✝✝

Arthur emerged into an enormous open area dominated by a towering fountain with stone dolphins around its base. He heard shouting from the stairs and galloped around to the foot of them. People were scattering, one man even leaping over the railing onto the other staircase to avoid being crushed as the assailant deftly maneuvered his horse right up the stairs and into the casino.

Arthur's heart pounded, but his breathing remained steady. He had to keep focused to make certain no one got hurt because of him.

"Aside, if you please!" he called up the stairs at the growing crowd of gaping hotel patrons. They quickly complied and with a flick of the reins, Arthur guided his mount up the carpeted stairs in pursuit.

Immediately following, Kai and Dakota did the same, to much applause and picture snapping by the hotel patrons who seemed to be loving the entire episode.

The fleeing man scattered gamblers young and old as he galloped dangerously through the crowded casino, nearly colliding with an elderly, white-haired lady stepping away from one of the flashing slot machines. Arthur followed, but at a less frenetic gallop so as to avoid any possible injuries. He gave the shocked lady a smile as he passed and spotted the escapee rounding a large machine called the "Wheel of Fortune."

Arthur spurred his mount to follow, knowing that Kai and Dakota had closed the gap and trailed just behind him. But then the king realized the man was merely using the Wheel of Fortune as a way to double back along the opposite side of the casino and quickened his pace. People screamed in startled fear or clapped with glee as Arthur and the Indians rounded the same machine to follow. It occurred to Arthur in those frantic moments that in this town everything was artifice of some kind, so these people, startled though they may be, thought his pursuit part of a staged show, much like the one he'd watched downstairs. *What an odd place,* he thought, as he watched the fleeing man race for the next flight of stairs leading to the third level. One hand on Excalibur's hilt and the other gripping his reins, Arthur followed.

†††

By the time Lance and the others were out of the arcade and surrounding the fountain, no horses were in sight, but a substantial crowd of people had gathered to find out what was happening. He and the others stopped to assess the situation. Helen and Charlie, camera rolling, trailed behind and Charlie waved the camera everywhere, attempting to find the unfolding story.

Lance looked up and around, but there was no sign of his father or the others. "Where did they go?" he asked the crowd at random.

Some shrugged, obviously having just arrived. A few pointed up the stairs, gazing in awe at the world-famous knights. They especially gazed long and hard at Lance as he whipped his head up to take in the higher floors. Pointing at Justin, Esteban and Darnell, he waved them up. "You guys, all the way up. If dad's not in the casino go up to that castle thing and look around."

Without hesitation, the three young men bolted for the stairs on their right and took them two at a time.

Lance turned to Reyna, who stood tautly gripping an arrow nocked and ready to fire. "Keep your eyes up there, Reyna," he commanded. "If you have a shot, take it."

She nodded, and swung her long ponytail behind her out of the way.

Then Lance turned to Chris, who also stood at the ready, arrow nocked, arms tight with tension. "You, too, Chris."

The boy nodded, his deep blue eyes flitting about as he scanned the upper levels.

Lance turned to Ryan. "What do you think?"

"I think we need to get up top. Gib, you and Brooks with me. You other three stay here in case the guy comes back down. Don't shoot unless it's necessary. Too many people here." The other three agents acknowledged their orders while Ryan, Gibson, and Brooks took off up the stairs.

Lance looked at Ricky and their eyes locked a moment. He saw fear and love in equal measure, and offered a reassuring smile. "We got this," he said, and Ricky smiled back nervously.

He, Ricky, Chris, and Reyna scanned the upper floors carefully for any sign of the horses. Esteban appeared at the railing on the Casino Level and shouted down, "Not here. We're going up."

Lance raised his sword in acknowledgment and Esteban vanished from sight. And then Lance saw them. The top level was mostly faux castle battlements, mere decoration to add adornment and a sense of setting to the overall scene. But the largest portion, a semi-circular stone wall topped by standard-looking battlements jutted out and over the lower floors, and it was there that the assailant galloped his horse, rounding whatever was in the center, Arthur in hot pursuit. But the fleeing man was suddenly stopped by Kai and Dakota who trotted around from the other direction to cut off his escape.

Trapped now between the Indians and Arthur, the man quickly dropped his reins and threw up his gloved hands in surrender.

"I give up," Lance and the others heard almost four stories below. Every head craned upward and Charlie aimed his camera at a sharp angle to capture the action.

"I'm just an actor," the man shouted, his voice ripe with fear. "Please don't kill me!"

Lance exchanged a mystified look with Ricky. An actor? What did that mean?

"Off the horse, sir, and make no sudden movements," Arthur instructed, his deep voice strong and steady and easily heard from such a distance, Excalibur out and pointed toward the other man.

The man slowly and with great caution eased himself off the panting horse while Lance watched with his breath on hold. Something was wrong here.

Just then Esteban, Justin and Darnell arrived, their heads barely visible over the extreme angle of the battlements. The man raised his hands into the air and stood before Arthur. Kai and Dakota's horses nickered nervously as the Indians kept their swords at the ready.

Something was wrong. Lance knew it. He pulled his gaze from his father and scanned the crowds pooling around the various railings at the Casino Level. *Just tourists*, he told himself. *You're imagining things.* But he wasn't. He spotted a man in black partially obscured by milling people raise both hands and pull back on a slingshot.

Lance whipped his head back around and up. "Dad, look out!"

Arthur looked down and locked eyes with his son for a split second before something struck the rear flank of his horse. The animal brayed with pain and reared back onto its hind legs. Caught by surprise, and aided by Excalibur's weight, Arthur toppled backward, Excalibur flying from his grasp, as he went off the horse and over the battlements.

"Dad!" Lance screamed, vaguely aware that Ricky and Chris had cried out too. He watched in horror as Excalibur flew end over end through the air and his father toppled helplessly over the battlements as though in pursuit. Flinging out a hand, Arthur managed to grasp with strong fingers one of the cut out stones used for firing arrows. That stopped his downward plunge, but he swung dangerously back and forth, barely clinging to the stone with quickly slipping fingers.

Reyna had already leapt for the stairs in pursuit of this new attacker, and vanished quickly into the crowd.

Excalibur sailed down into the fountain point first and embedded itself into one of the stone dolphins, sinking six inches into the rock and wobbling with singing vibrations.

"Dad!" Lance called again, his heart in his throat as the man he cherished dangled precariously above his head.

Barely hanging on, Arthur turned to look down at Lance. "Lance, Excalibur!" the king called out.

But Lance was frozen at the sight of his father in peril.

Chris reacted first. "I got it, Dad," the boy called out, dropping his bow and arrow. He clambered up the tiled wall that held back the water and leapt in with a splash. Pushing his way forward, the small boy had to then climb up onto the open shell-like base of the towering, gargoyle-topped fountain to reach the now unmoving sword, which shimmered beneath the lighting from above.

Drenched from head to toe, Chris braced one foot against the dolphin head within which Excalibur had embedded itself, gripped the hilt with both hands, and pulled.

Lance's eyes never left those of his father, and not for the first time Lance considered what he would do if this man were killed. He couldn't even imagine it, even back in the beginning when R. had tried to assassinate the king. He'd never felt more helpless as he watched the man dangle, and him four stories below and useless. But then Esteban and Justin and Darnell were there, leaning over the battlements and grasping for Arthur's hand. Esteban got it first and used his prodigious strength to haul the man up high enough for Justin to grab his other arm.

Letting out the breath he was holding, Lance exchanged a look of relief with Ricky before noticing Chris, still struggling to pull Excalibur free. Anxious to return the fabled sword to his father's grasp, Lance handed Ricky his sword before clambering over the retaining wall and dropping into the water. He strode purposefully forward and climbed up into the dish to stand beside the sopping Chris, who looked red-faced from exertion.

"It's stuck, Lance," Chris said, his voice breathless and strained as he let go the hilt and gazed up at his big brother.

"Lemme."

Chris nodded, but looked dubious. "I think it needs Este's guns."

Lance's eyebrows flew up in surprise and he almost laughed. "We'll see. Step back, okay, in case it yanks out and I fall."

"Okay." Dutifully, Chris stepped to the side.

The area surrounding the fountain teemed with tourists and hotel guests, everyone now watching Lance as the boy pushed his wet hair back off his face and reached out to grip Excalibur's hilt with both hands.

A jolt struck him, like electricity, thrumming through his nerves and tingling his entire body. He nearly let go in startled fright. *What the hell?* But then the sensation died away and he attributed it to static electricity or something. Gripping the hilt tightly, forearms taut with tension, Lance pulled. To his amazement, the sword slid from the stone as though it were embedded in butter.

Chris gasped in surprise, and Lance frowned, knowing Chris was not weak by any means, seeing in his mind's eye the boy straining to free the sword mere moments before. Not sure what it meant, but just happy to be able to return Excalibur to Arthur, Lance turned and raised the sword over his head with his right hand.

"I got it, Dad!"

And then he froze. Arthur stood atop the battlements gazing down at him with an expression of wonder. Beside him stood Kai, Dakota, Esteban, Justin, Darnell, Ryan, Gibson, and Brooks. And every one of them looked like they were seeing a ghost. They looked like the people had that night Merlin brought him back.

A chill ran through his body, almost the chill of death, but he didn't know why. He suddenly realized that everyone had fallen completely silent. The only sounds were slot machines upstairs, a few arcade games, the splashing of the fountain water, but no people sounds. Excalibur still raised on high, he turned to scan the faces of the surrounding crowd. They had the same look of awe, of amazement. He spotted Edwin and Jenny at the fringe, both openmouthed. He saw Merlin beside them, his mysterious gray eyes fixed on him with a look of revelation.

And then Lance locked eyes with Ricky just outside the fountain. He also stood in gaping astonishment. Heart pounding with dread, Lance said, "What?" his voice barely a whisper.

Ricky's eyes flicked upward, above Lance's head, but no words came out of his mouth. Now Lance glanced up, and gasped. The hilt, his hand, and the long, sleek blade of Excalibur appeared to be… glowing.

Fear rippled through him and threatened to cut off his very breath. No! It couldn't be glowing! It had to be a trick of the light! Gingerly, hand trembling, Lance lowered the sword and gazed into the shimmering metal of its shiny, pulsing blade. His right hand still appeared enshrouded by a bluish light, and he felt warmth tingling throughout his body, but then the glow began to fade. No, not fade. It seemed to sink deep within the metal of the sword, and into the jewels of the hilt. In moments, Lance found himself gazing at his own reflection within the blade, and he saw not the young man he normally saw, but a frightened boy who suddenly knew the world had shifted, and would never shift back.

Still shaking with dread, Lance glanced upward and met his father's gaze once more. The man nodded knowingly, his expression equal parts joy and sadness.

And then the spell broke. The tourists all began talking at once, the Secret Service agents were up in the fountain helping Lance and Chris out and onto the carpeted floor. Ricky was there beside Lance, brown eyes wide with uncertainty, and Chris stared up at Lance with wonder.

"It was really stuck, Lance," the boy said quietly, as though maybe Lance might think he was lying. Lance tousled his wet blond hair as Jenny pushed her way through the crowd to engulf them all in a hug.

Helen and Charlie began interviewing hotel guests and witnesses to get their take on what happened. After that, everything was a whirlwind of activity. The Las Vegas PD arrived to arrest the man whom Arthur pursued, despite the man's claim of innocence. He told Ryan and the other cops that he was a stuntman hired to dress a certain way and wait in the casino for somebody to come along on a horse and then he was to switch places with the guy. After that, he was just supposed to flee from whoever was chasing him. He thought it was all a publicity stunt.

Ryan believed the man, but had the local police detain him for further questioning to make sure there wasn't more to his story. Reyna had returned to report that the real culprit had gotten away, disappearing somewhere in the crowd.

By the time Arthur and the others made it back down to the first floor, leading their horses carefully through the crush of people, the hotel manager was there with his staff helping to move people along and calm everyone down. When the manager saw Arthur he hurried up to the king looking fretful and afraid. "Oh, King Arthur, I'm so sorry for all this trouble. Please don't sue us!"

Arthur chuckled at the man's terrified expression and placed a gauntleted hand on his shoulder reassuringly. "Never fear, good sir, I have not become *that* Americanized."

Everyone around them laughed and the manger looked immensely relieved, promising Arthur everything on the house for him and his team for the remainder of their visit.

And then Lance was there, gazing up into Arthur's eyes with those intense green ones everyone loved. Uncertainly, his arm trembling, he held out Excalibur to the king. With a smile Arthur took it, returning the blade to its sheath around his waist.

"Thank you, son," Arthur said, noting the fearful look in the boy's eyes. He knew that look. He'd had it once himself.

Lance felt his whole body tremble, and it wasn't because he was soaking wet and dripping all over the carpet beneath his feet. He was afraid. "Dad, what did that mean?"

Arthur placed a hand on Lance's shoulder and felt the tremble. He smiled reassuringly. "Excalibur likes you."

Lance saw the twinkle in the king's eyes and knew his father was jesting, saying something to put his mind at ease. But Lance's mind was not at ease, and once again, gazing into the eyes of this man who'd been everything to him, he knew for certain that Arthur was hiding something, some deep truth of great significance, some truth he knew would bring him pain.

†††

Of course, Helen put her footage on the air immediately, though not before myriad tourists had uploaded cell phone videos of the episode to Facebook and YouTube. The footage of Lance pulling Excalibur from the stone and somehow making the sword glow got the most hits and comments from viewers online. As for the mainstream media outlets, some expressed the cynical viewpoint that the entire incident had been staged to gain more support for the crusade.

Getting ready for dinner, Lance had glumly sat before the flat screen in his room and watched the coverage. Every time he saw the glowing sword he kept telling himself it had to have been a trick of the light because any other explanation scared him too much. Ricky and Chris sat beside him, Ricky holding his hand and squeezing gently.

"Do you know how you did that, Lance?" Ricky asked, hesitantly. "You know, made it glow?"

Lance looked over sharply, terror clamping onto his soul. "I didn't do anything, Ricky. It was static electricity or something."

"It was stuck really hard, Lance," Chris said, causing Lance to turn to him. "I'm pretty strong and it was stuck."

Lance nodded. "Well, I *am* stronger, Chris."

Chris just gave him that wide-eyed look that said, "Don't BS me, Lance, I'm too old for that."

"Know what I think?" Ricky said, releasing Lance's hand and throwing an arm across the boy's shoulders.

Lance glanced over. "What?"

"I think Excalibur finally figured out what the rest of us already knew, that you're the most beautiful boy in the world."

Chris chortled with amusement and Lance found himself grinning despite his fear. He shoved Ricky back onto the bed and shook his head in dismay.

"Dumbass," he said with a grin.

Splayed out on the bed, Ricky laughed with delight. "And you looked even more beautiful holding up that sword."

Now Lance turned and pounced on him. They wrestled and laughed, while Chris watched with amusement. But the moment Lance's lips met Ricky's, Chris exclaimed, "No making out in front of the little brother!" Then he jumped on both of them and the three laughing boys rolled and wrestled for a few minutes before deciding it was time to get dressed for dinner.

†††

Dinner at the Camelot Steakhouse was a mix of raucous laughter and subdued silences, punctuated by other diners approaching for autographs, mostly from Lance. The restaurant was nicely apportioned, with soft-backed chairs rimmed with gnarled-looking wood frames, an enormous visible kitchen extending across one wall, live piano music throughout the night, and steaks cooked over a Mesquite Wood burning broiler.

For Lance, however, being once again the object of curious looks, often surreptitious ones when the others thought he wouldn't notice, unnerved him. It was like when he'd first become The Boy Who Came Back, only this time it was because he was now being called The Boy Who Made Excalibur Glow. It was bad enough having tourists gawk, and even his fellow knights eyeing him uncertainly, but the weight of Merlin's gaze on him throughout the evening set his heart to pounding. Lance would look up from his food to see the wizard's piercing gray eyes fixed on him in a way they never had before.

He felt Arthur's eyes on him, too, watching him, sizing him up and making him feel as small as when he'd first met the man and accepted the role of First Knight. As though knowing he made Lance uncomfortable with those looks, Arthur would always smile warmly whenever the boy caught him looking and raise his goblet in tribute.

Lance also knew the attack was once again his fault. Jenny had explained over dinner that what the assailant had yelled out were the same words, in Latin, that assassin John Wilkes Booth shouted immediately after shooting Abraham Lincoln and leaping from the viewing box at Ford's Theatre. In English, the words meant "Thus always to tyrants," which prompted Arthur to believe they were aimed at him. But Lance knew better.

"I'm the young Mr. Lincoln, remember?" He told his father quietly, and sadly. "You could've been killed and it was all my fault. *Again*."

Arthur and Jenny assured him the incident had not been his fault, but simply another attempt to rattle them and derail the crusade.

"You remain, Lance, one of my greatest treasures in life," Arthur assured him, his face creased with worry, his tone one of sincerity. "You exude greatness, my son."

Lance looked long and hard at the man's face. He knew Arthur to be somewhere in his thirties, but the man looked older than that and Lance accepted that most of the worry lines had come from him, from his childish behaviors at fifteen, and from fear over the dangers now confronting them. He offered the smile Arthur loved and raised his own glass of Pepsi in salute. "Thanks, Dad."

Despite his father's soothing words, Lance remained unsettled throughout the meal. Ricky tried to wrest the mood from him, joking about "The emo Lance" making a comeback, but none of it helped. The funk had settled over his soul and wouldn't be lifted. So Lance sat and ate, pausing now and again to gaze at his hands as though expecting them to start glowing. The ball of fear coiled around his heart was, he knew, there to stay.

†††

As a result of the "The Excalibur Incident," as CNN had dubbed it, leaving the hotel the following morning to meet with the Nevada state legislature proved far more difficult than anticipated. Arthur, and particularly Lance, were swamped by media personnel throwing questions at them right and left as they stepped outside the hotel.

Besides hordes of tourists and hotel guests craning their necks for a looksee, there were news vans and cameras and reporters everywhere. Brooks and the other agents, along with Ryan, Gibson, Dakota, Kai, and Ricky, surrounded Lance and Arthur like a circular shield as they made their way to the bus.

Arthur instructed his team to board the bus ahead of him, but Lance insisted on staying with his father. Once everyone was inside, and still flanked by the agents, Arthur agreed to answer a few questions.

No, the incident had not been "staged." Yes, it was another attack by their mysterious enemy. No, he had not been hurt and this latest incident would in no way slow down the crusade for children's rights.

Then rapid-fire questions flew at Lance. All had to do with Excalibur and what had happened and what he thought it all meant.

The scorching summer breeze blew his hair into his eyes and Lance lightly brushed it aside as he held up a hand for quiet. When the questions ceased coming, he said, "When I first grabbed Excalibur I felt an electrical shock run up my arm," he stated flatly, forcing calm into his not-very-calm voice. "And I think that's all it was, static electricity or something. Maybe cuz I was wet. But I didn't do anything to make it happen."

"Do you think it had anything to do with you being the boy who came back, Sir Lance?"

Lance scanned the crush of reporters for the questioner, but couldn't tell who had called it out. He drove his penetrating green eyes into the crowd and said firmly, "No." Then he turned and hurried up the steps into the bus, Arthur right on his heels. The doors closed as Lance slid in beside Ricky and grasped the other boy's hand like he never wanted to let go.

"Hold on to me, Ricky," he whispered fiercely, his voice tinged with near desperation.

Ricky locked eyes with him. "I got you, Lance," he said, his voice strong and laced with confidence. "I always got you."

Lance smiled weakly and laid his head against Ricky's shoulder as the bus pulled away and left the hotel behind.

†††

After all the drama at the Excalibur, the joint session of the Nevada state legislature was almost anticlimactic, and pretty much a piece of cake. The interior looked remarkably similar to that of Arizona, and even Washington D.C., with curved rows of end-to-end desks facing the two-tiered curved and raised bench areas for those speaking to the assemblage.

Lance gave his prepared remarks, which he'd reviewed briefly with Edwin prior to the session, and reminded the legislators that Nevada always seemed in favor of improving the lot of children in the state, re-iterating that the CBOR would do that for kids in every state. Despite having already done these kinds of speeches many times before large crowds, Lance felt nervous and distracted by the way many of the lawmakers gawked at him. Their expressions mirrored those he'd seen at the hotel the night before, and it was obvious they'd all seen the video of him with the glowing Excalibur.

Despite the stares and uncertain looks throughout the session, Lance felt he'd presented his case strongly, and then he and Ricky answered questions, which were few in number. It seemed, on the surface at least, that these people were already leaning so much in their direction as to have no real challenges, or they were so in awe of Lance after the previous night that they sat speechless in their seats. In either case, the session ran far shorter in time than had the one in Arizona, and Lance, for one, couldn't wait to get out of there and out of Nevada.

By the time they returned to Excalibur and snuck in through the back, the Las Vegas Police investigator dropped by to chat with Ryan and give him and Gibson an update. Yes, the actor's story panned out. No priors, no history of drug use, not even any misdemeanors, a certified stunt rider, as well. He'd been given a heavy fine for reckless endangerment and released that morning. As to the real perpetrator who'd escaped into the crowd, there'd been no sign. The police had found his "performance clothes" tossed into a corner of the casino behind some slots, but the clothes had thus far revealed nothing of substance. The guy had simply vanished.

Lance listened to all of this useless info because he'd already known what would be said. Whoever wanted him and Arthur dead was too slick to leave any clues. No, he knew that however the next few months played out, ultimately it would end up with him against his stalker, and all bets would be off.

That night Lance didn't want to go out with everyone and eat because he felt too much on display, and elected to stay in his room and order room service. Arthur and Jenny objected strenuously, but Lance insisted everyone else go out and have a good time. Ryan and Brooks took it upon themselves to provide protection, and Arthur convinced Jenny to reluctantly agree. Ricky insisted on staying with Lance, but Lance even more vigorously insisted Ricky go out with the others and spend some "Quality fun time with Chris. Play games with him in the arcade and stuff."

Neither Ricky nor Chris liked that idea, but finally agreed when Arthur insisted Lance needed some time alone. And so Lance sat wearing a tank top and workout shorts on his bed skimming idly through the TV channels looking for something other than news stories about him. Brooks lounged in a chair that looked fit for a hobbit beneath his prodigious size, and Ryan had stretched out on the sofa. They'd ordered burgers and fries from room service and awaited delivery.

After about thirty minutes, there was a knock at the door. "Room service," came a voice from the other side. Guns drawn, Ryan and Brooks rose and approached on either side. Ryan motioned Brooks behind him and yanked open the door with a flourish. A young man not much older than Lance wearing an Excalibur Hotel-emblazoned uniform blanched when he saw the raised weapons. In front of him sat a large cart heaping with food and another one right behind him.

Ryan frowned and lowered his weapon. "We didn't order all this," he said suspiciously.

"But we did," came a familiar voice and then Arthur stepped from where he'd been hiding to flank the relieved delivery boy. And then suddenly everyone was there, Jenny and Ricky and Chris and Reyna – the entire team poured into Lance's room and dragged the food carts in with them.

Shocked, Lance leapt off the bed and gaped at everyone. "What are you all doing here? I told you to go have fun."

"And so we shall, son," Arthur replied with a grin. "Right here with you."

"Didn't think we'd let your fool ass get away with being emo again, did you?" Ricky said with a laugh.

Lance still looked amazed and gawked at the carts practically spilling over with food.

"Compliments of the hotel, Lance," Reyna said with a huge grin, and then she threw her hands to her hips in that act of consternation Lance always loved. "Now start smiling and looking prettier than me or there'll be hell to pay!"

That finally got Lance to laughing and within moments everyone was spread out all over the room with food on their laps talking and joking and giggling. Some of the others had gone to their own rooms for extra chairs, but a few, like Chris and the Indian boys, sat cross-legged on the floor and ate happily. Without the crush of stares and unwanted attention, Lance relaxed and laughed and ate and shoved Ricky around and even joked with Merlin about his horrible taste in music. To his credit, the wizard took the jibes good-naturedly and no longer gazed at Lance with those peculiar looks, for which the boy was happy. All in all, it was a perfect night for everyone.

†††

Hoping to avoid another massive crowd pooling in the lobby and outside the hotel, Arthur and his team arose at four a.m. the following morning and made ready for departure. The hotel staff managed to sneak all their bags out the back and into the bus by five and then the team slipped out into the already hot, dry morning with the sun barely beginning to make its appearance. They filed quickly into the bus with thanks and salutations to the relieved-looking hotel manager, and then they were on their way for a projected six-hour journey north to Salt Lake City, Utah.

†††

Entering the city from the south the knights were not privy to the sight of the Great Salt Lake itself, which some were curious about due to the legend that you could float on the surface of the lake because the salt content was so dense. Jenny promised they would stop to check it out on their way to Idaho.

Salt Lake was a mostly low-lying city, nestled between the lake to the northwest and steep mountain ranges on its eastern and western borders. It looked picture-postcard pretty to the knights as their bus approached from the interstate. There wasn't much of a downtown in terms of skyscrapers, and the cityscape was dominated by the gargantuan Salt Lake LDS Temple that sprawled over ten acres and rose two hundred feet into the air.

The sky looked blue and the air clean. Gone was the brownish tint so common above the skies of Los Angeles. The air was hot and dry and the temperature in the eighties as the bus rolled into their hotel parking lot and everyone began to debark. Since their tour schedule had been posted on the website, the parking lot swam with hordes of curious spectators. But at least, Lance pointed out to Ricky, there weren't any signs condemning them to hell.

"Yet," Ricky added with a grin as they descended to cheers and applause and clamors for autographs. While Lance and Ricky and Arthur moved amongst the crowd shaking hands, smiling and offering gratitude for the welcome, Justin, Darnell, Reyna, Techie, Esteban, Chris, and Sylvia all passed out stickers and tossed others way back into the throng, setting the kids scrambling for the free goodies.

For Techie it felt like he was some kind of rock star. There were Asian kids in the crowd who specifically called his name and shouted things like, "You rock, Techie!" For a kid who'd been invisible in high school and not important to anyone before joining the Round Table, the attention was both flattering and empowering. He suddenly realized that he was a role model to other Asian kids, whether he wanted to be or not, and that they looked up to him. Naturally shy and reticent, he forced himself to grin at the kids who called to him, and shake the hands of anyone within reach. This trip had opened his eyes to the importance of New Camelot for kids everywhere because it made them all, the popular and the shunned, feel good about themselves.

For his part, Darnell was happy to see so many black faces amongst the crowd. He'd expected a place like Utah to be all white people and thought maybe he and the other dark-skinned kids would feel on display. But the people gathered here were diverse, and he spotted more than a few cute young ladies checking him out and even calling his name. Yeah, fame had its perks, he thought, as he shook hands and handed out stickers. After his talk with Lance, he'd taken a handful of the "Sir Darnell" stickers and written his cell number on the back. These he handed to several cuties that were giving him the eye. It wouldn't happen here, he knew, but he was sure Lance had been correct – he'd find someone to love who'd love him back and miss him when he was away, and then his life would be perfect.

For Lance, the experience wasn't as bad as he'd feared. The kids in the crowd thought "It was so cool the way you made that sword glow" and didn't seem spooked by it at all. The adults, however, eyed him warily. Twice now he'd been the centerpiece of something seemingly miraculous, and that gave many grown-ups pause as to how he should be treated. Fighting down his nerves and fears, Lance flashed his ingratiating smile no matter what expression was directed his way, and found himself changing most of those uncertain looks to smiles.

Despite his nervousness when speaking to large crowds, Ricky always found himself enjoying these encounters with the public. Because Lance was the center of his world, and the centerpiece of the crusade, Ricky always just assumed no one even noticed him much. But a lot of kids, girls *and* boys, clamored for a sticker with his picture on it and that made him feel good, made him realize that maybe he personally was inspiring kids out in the world, not because of the overall crusade, but just for being himself. And that felt pretty cool!

After navigating their way through the crowd and checking in, everyone did their usual clean up and showering after the long and dusty bus ride. Lance and Ricky helped the excited Chris get showered and dressed and, as always, stood side by side shirtless in front of the bathroom mirror drying their hair so each could admire the other's physique.

Now that they were nearing their eighteenth birthday, they had filled out in the shoulders and chest and their regular workouts had added a lot of muscle, which both commented on with regards to the other. As always, they were shy and playful when admiring one another, and as always the blood rush of excitement almost brought them together in an intense kissing session. But Chris's presence just outside the open bathroom door dampened that fire pretty fast. Still, Lance thought to himself, he was happy for his physical reactions to seeing Ricky shirtless, and for not once recalling Richard while having those reactions.

They went out to a local restaurant that could accommodate a large group, and once more interacted with the public throughout dinner. Lance and Ricky laughed and messed with Chris after a cute little girl who looked only ten or eleven crept up and shyly asked for his autograph. Unlike Lance and Ricky, however, Chris wasn't shy at all and enthusiastically signed the girl's napkin and chattered on about how pretty she looked and how he hoped she would talk to her parents about the CBOR.

When the happy girl skipped excitedly back to her family to show off the little note Chris had written, Lance elbowed his younger brother with a wink. "You're the smooth one in the family, Chris," he said jokingly.

Ricky nodded. "Yeah, the girls better watch out for you."

Now Chris blushed. "C'mon, guys, I'm only ten."

That got a laugh from everyone, including Arthur and Jenny.

A teenaged boy, blond and green-eyed and thin, approached Lance and Ricky during dessert, though both boys had noticed this kid eyeing them the entire meal from several tables away.

"Hi, guys, I'm, uh, I'm George," the kid said, extending his hand. First Lance, and then Ricky shook it.

When the kid didn't say anything for a moment, Lance filled the awkward void by asking, "So how old are you, George?"

"Fourteen," the boy answered quietly, as though fearful of being overheard. He glanced slightly back at his parents and multiple siblings, all of who were watching suspiciously. Then George leaned in with a napkin for Lance to autograph. As Lance reached for his pen, George whispered, "I'm gay, but if my family ever found out I'd get punished, maybe sent to one of those place to change me."

Lance froze in the act of signing, and Ricky gasped slightly, his eyes starting toward the boy's family.

"Don't look, please!" George said desperately, his frantic voice a whisper, and Ricky quickly pulled his gaze back to the boy's frightened face. "I just wanted to tell you guys how much I admire you and wanna be like you and not be afraid anymore."

Lance exchanged a look with Ricky, the pain in his eyes mirrored in those of the other. Then he leaned in to George surreptitiously. "Don't let them do anything to you, George," Lance admonished quietly, but with an intensity that barely masked his rising anger. "It's kids like you we're fighting for, and you always got a home at New Camelot if you need it."

He slipped George a sticker with his cell number secreted beneath the sticky paper, special editions he'd had prepared just for kids like this whose parents wouldn't want them communicating. "My number's inside the sticky part, George. If you need to run call me and I'll help. Don't let them make you hate yourself like I hated myself for so long, okay?"

George smiled shyly as he casually pocketed the special sticker, but kept a normal one Ricky gave him in his hand. "Thanks, Lance."

Then he darted back across the restaurant to his table, where, as Lance and Ricky watched, his parents held out a hand for the sticker Ricky had given him. George handed it over to his father, who eyed it and tossed it onto the table as they rose to exit the restaurant.

Lance sadly watched them go, his heart lurching when George turned his head to toss back a quick smile before being lost to sight around a corner. Lance turned to Ricky with a disgusted sigh. "I hate people like that, Ricky."

"Me too."

"Lance," Arthur spoke from the other end of the table. "It is just such as them we seek to win to our cause. We must never give up."

Lance eyed his father, his heart rate subsiding. "I know, Dad. It just hurts to see that crap."

"Yes, it does," Jenny added, her voice tinged with sadness. "Unfortunately, we'll never end it all. We just have to do the best we can."

Lance nodded, but still felt bad for that boy. Reyna, seated beside Chris, leaned over the small boy's head to kiss Lance on the cheek. Startled, Lance said, "What was that for?"

Reyna flashed her own astonishingly beautiful smile. "Just for being my amazing baby boy."

That brought a smile back to Lance's face. "Thanks, sis."

After that, the rest of the evening was upbeat, and when it was time to depart more stickers were passed out and they encouraged the patrons to support the Children's Bill of Rights, and to ask their representatives to do the same.

†††

The Utah State Capitol building looked to Lance like a cross between The White House and the U.S. Capitol. It was an enormously long, four-story stone edifice with a protruding portico, massive columns all along the front, and a titan-esque rotunda dome towering upward from the center.

"What's with all these capitol buildings and those rotunda things? They all look the same." Ricky said to Lance as the bus rolled into the parking lot designated for assembly members and senators.

Lance shrugged, his mind on the talk he planned to give, and the opposition Edwin had warned him was likely in this state. "Boring ass designers, I guess," he said in response, and Ricky laughed.

As always, Edwin hovered around Lance and Ricky with last minute advice. "These people will likely feel your CBOR undermines their parental rights," the intern told them in the anteroom as they awaited their appearance. "You need to hammer home the point you've made before that you're mostly worried about government agencies hurting kids, rather than parents."

Lance nodded, and Ricky gave his hand a supportive squeeze. Edwin eyed the gesture nervously. "Oh, and none of that, either."

Lance smirked. "Actually, I thought I'd just grab Ricky right in the middle of the session and kiss him till he can't breathe."

Edwin's mouth dropped open a moment in shock, while both boys chuckled. "Hey, I'm up for that," Ricky said, and then both of them shoved Edwin at the same time. The man laughed and visibly relaxed.

†††

The interior of the assembly chamber, while similar in design to the others they'd been to, looked closer to the one in Washington than any of them, Lance noted as he walked purposefully up the center aisle to polite applause by the standing lawmakers. There was a large upper gallery for spectators, and it appeared that every seat was occupied. All the copings and door frames were gold filigree, with paintings embedded within the curved-edges of the ceiling, and an enormous skylight raining sunshine down onto the dark wood rows of seats and the double-tiered speaker's bench up-front.

Because of limited space, everyone but Lance, Ricky, Chris and Ryan had to sit up with the general public, all in the first row of the gallery so they could have a good view of the boys down in front. Helen and Charlie, his camera recording the proceedings, positioned themselves dead center of the middle aisle, moving into place after Lance and the others passed by.

The three boys and Ryan stepped around the lower of the two front semi-circular benches and shook hands with the Speaker of the Assembly, who ushered Ryan to a seat and led the three boys up four carpeted steps to the upper bench, proceeding to introduce them as the lawmakers extended their polite clapping a few more seconds and then seated themselves. The Speaker sat down in his thick leather chair behind the boys after offering Lance the microphone.

As always, Lance greeted everyone formally and with great respect. He offered the mic to both Ricky and Chris so they could also thank the legislature for giving them this time. Once the mic came back to him, Lance launched into his basic remarks about the Constitution serving everyone in the country eighteen years and older, but essentially acting as though anyone seventeen and below didn't exist. He specifically re-iterated that the CBOR was not to undermine parental rights, but to give children the same rights against unlawful treatment that adults have always had, especially by government agencies like social services and the school system.

Once he'd spoken for about fifteen minutes, including yet another retelling of his own toxic experiences with social service agencies, Ricky and Chris chimed in by sharing bits of their own life stories and why the CBOR was necessary and long overdue.

It was when Lance opened the floor up to questions that everything went to crap. One of the legislators raised a hand and Lance called on him. Wearing a gray suit with a bland tie, the man stood and looked rather haughtily at Lance, who patiently awaited his question.

The man held up a piece of paper and then lowered his eyes to read from it. "In your amendment thirty, *Sir* Lance, you clearly state, and I quote, 'no parent may force a child to undergo psychological treatment for issues related to sexual orientation.' Is that a correct reading, young man?"

The man's tone dripped with smarmy elitism and Lance's contempt meter leapt into overdrive. Still, he replied calmly, "Yes, sir."

The man lowered the paper and glanced around at his fellow lawmakers with a smirk. "How is that *not* undermining parental authority?"

Lance's mouth dropped open, and he turned to Ricky as though to confirm he'd heard the question correctly. Ricky nodded in the affirmative. Collecting himself so as to not lose his cool, Lance calmly looked out at the man and forced their eyes to meet. "Forcing a kid to go through some kind of treatment when there's nothing wrong with him is a parent's right?"

The man met Lance's gaze straight on and didn't blink. "Yes," he said. "It's both a parent's right and responsibility to make their sick child well."

That sent a ripple of unease through the galleries as the public digested that statement. Lance spotted Kai leaping to his feet way up in the front row, but then saw Dakota and Reyna pull him back down. The legislator's answer was so out there Lance had to take a moment to believe he'd heard it right.

"Being gay is not a sickness, sir," he stated, his voice tight with emotion.

The man chuckled. "What would you know about it? You have the same sickness."

Now the public went crazy, chattering and protesting. Lance saw Reyna leap up and make for the aisle, but Esteban grabbed her hand and pulled her back. The speaker had to gavel for quiet and when he got it, he indicated that Lance continue.

Lance knew his mouth hung open stupidly, and that Charlie was capturing it all on camera, but he honestly couldn't believe the direction this session was going.

"I don't have a sickness," Lance said, forcing a calm he didn't feel into his voice. "The only sickness I see is the one called 'stupidity'. Sir."

Now the man lost his smug look as a large number of spectators in the gallery broke into wild applause. Again, the speaker's gavel had to calm them down.

When everyone had settled, Lance looked at the astonished legislator and said, "You may as well sit, mister, cuz this is gonna take a few." Without awaiting a response, Lance looked out at Helen. "Lady Helen, please bring Charlie closer. I'd like this part of the video to be cut separately and put on our website for everyone to see."

Grinning, Helen waved Charlie over. He had the camera professionally atop one shoulder and continued to film as both he and Helen moved into place just below Lance.

Lance turned to Ricky, who instantly gave him "the look." Only this time Lance didn't need it. He was fired up and needed no encouragement to go off. He'd prepared these remarks after his talks with Father Mike and Pastor Tom, hoping he'd never need to use them. But now he did.

Turning back to the nervously expectant group of lawmakers, he said, "I'm saying this to all of you here today, but also to everyone else in this country who might try to make our crusade about being gay. I will never talk about it again and if any of you anywhere ask anything about gay stuff you will be ignored."

He paused a moment as though daring someone to contradict him. When no one did, he went on. "Our crusade is for every child in America, from the poor inner city kids like me and Ricky to the rich kids of Beverly Hills, to the kids of every religion, every skin color, and yes, every sexual orientation, to gang members and the homeless and the mentally ill. Everyone. It's about us having real civil rights under the Constitution, rights that will protect us both from government and from corrupt, abusive, or just plain old stupid adults, *including* parents."

He took a breath and scanned the room, gratified that every face and every set of eyes were fixed on him as though glued. "Yes, Ricky and me are what you call gay. It is not a sickness and no, God didn't make a mistake. We're exactly how God wanted us to be. And no, we didn't choose to be gay. We both tried hard to be so-called straight. We had great girlfriends who loved us. We could've lied to them and kept on lying to them until eventually we'd marry them and have kids with them. But it would have all been a lie. And that's what so many of you so-called religious people out there want us to do. You want us to be sinners, because you decided that bearing false witness every single day is better than being gay. Well, it isn't."

He paused again to catch his breath and let his words sink in. Then he continued, "The stupid part comes in where you all think a boy like me is attracted to girls, but just wakes up one day and decides to fall in love with boys because it's so much fun to be hated, bullied, mocked, rejected, and pushed away by most Americans. What a great choice, right? Wrong. That would make me more stupid than you, and I'm *not* stupid. Being gay isn't a choice. Hate is."

Another pause to see if they were still with him, and their openmouthed looks of shock indicated they were. "Oh, and don't any of you anywhere in this country throw the Bible at me, either. No, Ricky and me haven't lain together like it says in Leviticus. That's a mistranslation, anyway, just like the other six lines in the Bible supposedly condemning gay people. But I do confess to being a sinner. I've committed abominations from Leviticus. I've eaten shellfish."

There was laughter from the gallery.

"And worse than that, I've had milk and meat together at the same time," he went on, drawing another laugh. "But I haven't kept anybody as a slave like it says is okay in that book, and I never hated on disabled people, either. Leviticus says God doesn't want disabled people near his altar. If you wanna believe that crap, fine. Your choice. Don't put it on me and don't make our crusade for all children into something *you* want it to be."

Lance paused again to catch his breath and let his words sink in. "And while we're talking religion, you people out there who think Jesus wants you to hate and condemn kids like me don't know the Jesus I met when I read the Bible and got baptized two years ago. Yeah, I know, I got baptized Catholic and to some of you other Christians out there that's the same as devil worship. Well, too bad. When I take the Eucharist I feel close to Jesus and I can *feel* how much he loves me. Jesus never said a word against boys like me, but he did tell us all not to throw stones unless we're without sin. Of course, all of you who hate boys like me are perfect, aren't you? The Jesus I know only condemned *one* group of people – those nasty-ass Pharisees. Why? Cuz they were hypocrites. They did the talk, but not the walk. Just like you. You talk Jesus, but you don't walk Jesus. At least I try my best. At least I'm not the one out there condemning people."

Then he offered a little smile for the camera. "And for those of you hypocrites who think you're a shoo-in to be with God after you die and us perverted disgusting fag boys aren't, I got news for you – you better start praying. Cuz I already died and I was *this* close to God." He raised his right hand and held his thumb and forefinger an inch apart. "God was right there in the light. I could feel him. I wanted to go. And he'd have taken me, too, if it had been my time, just like he took Mark and Jack. Two gay boys went to heaven because they were more like Jesus than most of you who hated on them. So go on with your hating and your stupidity, and we'll go on fighting for every single child in this country, especially the ones you try to poison with your evil." He glared at the no-longer smirking lawmaker, who merely sat in his seat and refused to raise his eyes. "Did I answer your question, *sir*?"

The adults both on the floor and in the gallery sat in stupefied shock when Lance finished, but every child and teen leapt to his or her feet clapping and cheering. Kai and Dakota whooped loudly, but Reyna's distinctive shout of support rang out loudest of all. It took the speaker gaveling for several minutes to restore order while Lance smiled angelically into the camera and waved to the kids in the galleries around him.

Ricky and Chris each leaned in and hugged Lance, who cast another solid, defiant look at the legislator who'd initiated the discussion. The man pretended to be reading something on the computer screen at his desk. His fellow lawmakers didn't know what to do, but Lance was gratified to see some of them applauding his declaration, as though happy someone finally told that guy off.

When order was restored, Lance lifted Chris into his arms and the three boys gazed out at the assembled lawmakers of Utah. "That video will be up on our website for anyone to view at any time because we're done with that topic forever. Now, does anyone have any *real* questions or comments to make about our CBOR?"

He scanned the faces of these men and women who dictated policy in Utah, and had great power over the citizens, and felt pleased that he'd rattled them. That seemed to be the problem with politicians, he'd long ago discovered - they expected everything to go their way and they hated being challenged. Well, he smiled inwardly, he'd brung it on and they were hereby challenged. And now they were silent. No one raised a hand so the speaker called the joint session concluded with a single slam of his gavel.

By the time everyone had exited, and Arthur's knights mingled with the public on the lawn in front of the capitol building, Lance had been invited to three senator's offices and five assembly members' to discuss possible support of the CBOR. Edwin admitted that Utah was likely a lost cause after Lance's "Performance in there," but he acknowledged that Lance was "Right on the money" and high-fived the boy with a big grin. Reyna had grabbed Lance in a huge hug, but he was too tall now for her to swing him around like she used to so she settled for a kiss on the cheek. "My baby boy rocks!" she shouted, causing him to turn red and Ricky to playfully shove him around.

The kids and teens who'd been in the gallery swamped Lance when he exited the building, not asking for autographs, but merely wanting to shake his hand and thank him for speaking out like they wish they could. Lance asked them if they'd "Spoken out in school" per Operation August Surprise, and every one of them had, which made him happy. He assured them that their support of the CBOR was the best way to challenge the status quo, and happily signed stickers for them.

✝✝✝

The next two days were taken up by public appearances, town hall-style meet and greets with Salt Lake City residents, and those meetings with senators and assembly members. Despite Edwin's suspicion that Utah was a lost cause, Lance felt he'd made a real connection with the people, and that ultimately it would be the people who would decide on the CBOR, not the more narrow-minded lawmakers who objected to it. The night before they were scheduled to leave, Lance got a call on his cell from a number he didn't recognize, but since it wasn't the nine zeroes he answered it.

A young male voice said, "It's George. Remember me?"

Lance instantly tensed, fearful that the boy might be in trouble. "Course, George. You okay?"

The voice on the other end spoke quietly, but with passion. "I'm okay. Just wanted to say thanks, man, for what you said to all those lawmaker guys and people like my parents. It's so cool to know a guy like you's got my back. Thanks, Lance."

Lance's breath hitched a moment in his throat, and he forced himself to swallow. "You're welcome, George," he answered quietly, his voice filled with emotion. "I always got your back."

"Cool. Gotta go. Bye." Then the phone went dead and Ricky gazed over at Lance from where he sat reading on his bed.

"Everything okay with him?"

Lance nodded, but couldn't speak. It still amazed him that a homeless kid who'd steered clear of everyone growing up could have such an impact on strangers. He'd never imagined such possibilities as a child when his only real dream was to win the X Games. Man, calls like that from George were way better than winning a medal!

The next stop, he knew, would be Pocatello, Idaho, Jack's hometown, and as the bus pulled out of Salt Lake and onto the interstate the following morning for the eight hour journey, he already felt the weight of emotion he knew he'd experience being where Jack had grown up, and from where he'd been driven away. Being where Jack walked, in the city that had rejected him, made Lance queasy with guilt and sorrow, and quickly consumed all of his thoughts. As the bus moved out into early morning traffic, the funk settled over him immediately, and Ricky knew the reason, so he just sat beside Lance and held his hand and loved him like always.

✝✝✝

Chapter Three

Have I Done Right By You?

Idaho looked lush and green with mountains and valleys to break up the landscape, and proved far more interesting to drive through than the other states thus far. The group stopped briefly at the Great Salt Lake where Esteban and Justin grabbed Darnell and carried him kicking and screaming to the water's edge threatening to throw him in to test the "floating" legend.

After swinging the lanky, protesting nineteen-year-old a few times, Esteban holding his arms and Justin his feet, while everyone else but Lance stood around and laughed, they let him down and busted up with glee at the look on his face. Then it was back into the bus.

Lance said not a word to anyone, and didn't make his usual rounds to "check in" with each of his team members. He sat and stared without seeing out the window, as forlorn and emo as Ricky had ever seen him. He knew the boy felt wracked by guilt and remorse all over again that Jack was dead because of him. It didn't matter that Jack had made the choice willingly. Lance would always feel responsible.

For his part, as he gazed longingly at Lance's long, luxurious hair with those perfect features turned away from him, Ricky felt an old fear gnaw away at his heart and soul, the deep-seeded fear that Lance wasn't over Jack after all, that he still loved the handsome older boy and that he, Ricky, was merely a poor substitute for what Lance could no longer have. He knew he shouldn't even entertain such thoughts, knew they were irrational and foolish, but he couldn't help himself. His own sense of inadequacy, especially compared to a guy like Jack, clutched at the core of his being and made him doubt his very worthiness to be with Lance. So he, too, sat for the entire journey lost in an emo funk easily as deep as Lance's, and even Chris couldn't pull him out of it.

Pocatello was nestled between mountains and valleys with old-fashioned light posts and period buildings in the downtown area. Hanging from every streetlight was a sign in bright yellow and orange proclaiming, "Proud To Be Pocatello." Techie had Googled the local demographics and had announced to everyone on the bus that the town was about eighty-seven percent white, seven percent Latino, and just scatterings of every other race.

"In other words, guys, we're gonna be a circus act," the Asian boy said with a wry chuckle, drawing laughs from the others.

Lance wasn't surprised by the news. Jack had told him during their clean up tour that everyone on his football team had been white like him and there'd been only a handful of minorities at his high school. That's why L.A. had been such a culture shock to the fifteen-year-old when he'd hit town in search of fame and fortune. He'd laughingly told Lance that at first he just stared at all the blacks and Latinos and Asians because they'd been such a novelty in Pocatello.

They drove through town to the inn where they'd booked rooms, and when they pulled into the parking lot Chris declared that the two-story lodging looked like a giant IHOP because of its blue tiled roof, and the comment drew nods of agreement from many. Once they'd gotten everything squared away and checked in, it was time to clean up before heading over to Leigh Bennett's house for dinner.

As they dried their hair side by side, Ricky felt oddly invisible. Lance didn't even glance at his pecs and abs, which he usually couldn't pull his eyes away from. Ricky eyed Lance's face in the mirror as the blow-dryer waved back and forth listlessly, at the lost and troubled look in those poignant green eyes, and his heart lurched with fear.

He finally cleared his throat awkwardly, his blood pounding with uncertainty. "You, uh, you gonna be all right with this?"

It took Lance a moment to respond, as though he only just realized Ricky was in the room. He lowered the hair dryer to the counter and sighed heavily. "I look in this mirror and I see me and I think it should be him, that he should be alive and standing here. Not me."

"Lance, you don't know how much you scare the shit out of me when you talk like that."

Lance blew out a breath. "I'm sorry, Ricky. It's just how I feel. Yeah, this stop will be the hardest of all and I really need you."

Ricky smiled now and took Lance's hand in his, placing it up against his wildly beating heart. "I got you, Lance, right here."

Lance smiled sadly, but his eyes shone with gratitude. "Thanks."

†††

Leigh Bennett's home was simple and small, resting comfortably on a quiet street lined with trees and single story houses. Hers was painted light yellow with a pitched brown roof and a large porch surrounded by white fencing. Again, because of their Internet schedule postings and updates, the arrival of New Camelot at her home early that evening was well-known to the locals, and the streets teemed with the curious as the multicolored bus with its multicolored occupants rolled into this small enclave of the country.

The looks directed at the bus as it passed were clearly noted by all its occupants – looks of curiosity and wariness mixed with bits and pieces of awe and wonder. In other words, Techie had hit it on the head – they were a circus act come to town to be ogled, and depending upon their "performance," might or might not be accepted.

Lance spotted Leigh framed in her open doorway before the bus even pulled to a stop, and his heart began pounding. And then Arthur was there in the aisle, a hand on Lance's shoulder, drawing the boy's eyes up to his compassionate face.

"Are you ready, son?"

Lance saw in his dad's eyes the same pain and guilt he knew his own reflected, and realized how difficult this visit would be for Arthur too. "Yeah, Dad. How 'bout you?"

Arthur looked faraway and tortured, his thoughts and feelings racing back with total clarity to that night of three years past when Jack had uttered those fateful words that continued to haunt his dreams: "I volunteer." He sighed heavily, and nodded as Jenny appeared at his elbow and smiled at the still-seated boys.

As they stepped from the bus onto the sidewalk outside Leigh's house, the knights eyed the silent crowd around them with uncertainty. Even the usually super-confident Reyna looked unsure of herself as she wrapped her arm through Esteban's and glanced at the spectators. The adults seemed especially wary, but then several teen girls approached and held out photos to Reyna - photos of her. "Could we get your autograph, Lady Reyna?" one of them asked hesitantly.

Reyna grinned with delight, her smile seeming to break the ice. As a smirking Esteban handed her a pen, suddenly all the neighbor kids surrounded them, making Brooks and Ryan a bit nervous, but buoying the hopes and spirits of the knights that perhaps they wouldn't be *too* much of a freak show, after all. Once everyone had signed numerous autographs, even Lance who did his best to smile and appear ingratiating, Arthur announced to the locals, "The Lady Bennett awaits us, but we thank you kindly for your gracious welcome."

He smiled and bowed courteously, and even some of the frowning parents in the street melted slightly and offered a return smile. Then Arthur was into the front yard and up onto the porch, bowing again to Leigh in greeting, Jenny right beside him extending her hand. Arthur stepped to one side and introduced each knight in turn as he or she stepped onto the porch, bowed to Leigh, and then entered the house. Arthur also introduced Sergeants Ryan and Gibson, as well as the four Secret Service agents. Leigh welcomed each one of them, but her eye continued to find Lance and Ricky, hovering nervously at the end of the line. Lance could barely look up at the house, or her. His eyes remained downcast until he heard his father's gentle voice say, "Lance?"

The young man looked up at his father's expectant face, noted Jenny's lovely features couched with obvious worry, and then he fixed his gaze on the woman beside them–the woman who'd allowed Jack's father to humiliate him and drive him away. Despite her confession at the funeral, Lance wanted to hate her for not standing up for that amazing boy he'd known, for not taking Jack and leaving her husband behind. But her gentle look of compassion, remorse, and deep abiding sadness sent an emotional knife slicing right into his heart.

Slowly, as though stepping into the tomb where Jack was buried, Lance strode up onto the porch and approached, Ricky trailing behind.

Leigh's face broke into a wide smile, spreading the laugh lines around her mouth as wide as they could go.

"Lance, how you've grown!" She stepped forward and enveloped him in a huge hug. He stiffened, at first, and then gingerly hugged her back. She stepped back and studied his face, looking him up and down and shaking her head. "What a handsome man you've become." Lance turned red, despite himself, and offered a half-smile. Leigh seemed to understand his reticence for she turned to Ricky and extended a hand. "And this is the world famous Sir Ricky, another handsome young man."

Ricky shook her hand, not sure what to say or even how he felt about her. Not having known Jack at all he felt mostly indifference. It was Lance he worried about.

Leigh returned her gaze to Lance and he met it. He saw in her eyes that she knew how hard this was for him. Her own guilt lay just behind the irises.

"Is this the house where Jack grew up?" Lance asked finally, his voice a whisper of uncertain breath.

Leigh shook her head. "No. I finally left my husband and took everything of Jack with me. The extra bedroom is his, or would've been had I the courage to take him away before it was too late. All of his things are in there."

Lance stiffened, and Ricky placed a hand on his shoulder. Lance nodded, and stepped past her into the house. Ricky followed and only the three adults remained on the porch.

"Thank you for bringing him," Leigh said sincerely to Arthur and Jenny. "It means the world to me to have him here."

"Thank you for inviting us," Jenny replied, and then Leigh ushered them both into the house.

The front door led straight into a living room with several modest-looking sofas, comfortable stuffed chairs, a fireplace, some shiny wooden end tables, and the entire crew sat or stood around waiting. But that wasn't what stopped Lance dead in his tracks. He vaguely heard the front door close behind him, and from far away picked up a slight intake of breath from Ricky at his side. But his eyes had fixed themselves to the area above the wooden mantle, to a poster-sized photo of Jack at fourteen or fifteen, wearing a blue football jersey with red sleeves and the name "Indians" in red-trimmed white lettering across the upper chest. His already thick, veiny forearms were folded across his chest, just beneath the team name and he gazed solidly and with great intensity into the camera.

Lance's heart began to hammer in his chest as he gazed at the young face staring out at him.

Jacky…

Jack's face looked so young and innocent, not as hard and traced with the degradations of street living as it had been when Lance first met him. Above Jack's head were the words: "Jack Bennett Memorial GSA of Idaho" accompanied by the rainbow logo of the national GSA network, which Lance had seen many times before. He could scarcely breathe, and his throat felt choked with every emotion he could imagine. No one spoke, not even Arthur or Jenny. They merely watched him, and waited.

Finally, Leigh broke the awkward silence by stepping around Lance and Ricky and stopping beneath the photo, her expression filled with regret. "Jack's legacy, Lance," she said quietly, "and my greatest accomplishment so far. Idaho's first ever GSA network, dedicated to the memory of my son. I've been pushing to get a GSA into every high school in the state," she went on, her voice filled with pride and remorse. "Starting right here in Pocatello, at Jack's own school. Since he'd become so famous with you they decided to capitalize on that and start a local chapter in his name. I hope in a small way to make a difference for other kids that I never made for my own."

She looked down at the thick, off-white carpet in shame. No one said a word. Lance couldn't take his eyes off that strong, handsome young face. The room and everyone in it had vanished and it was only him and Jack.

Arthur broke the awkward silence by stepping over beside Leigh and touching her arm gently. She looked up at him, eyes brimming with tears. "Jack would be honored by what you have done, Leigh," he offered in that gentle, disarming tone he had so mastered.

Leigh nodded, and then broke down. Jenny rushed over and wrapped her arms around the other woman, who sobbed into her shoulder. "I was a horrible mother, Jenny. I didn't deserve a son like Jack."

Jenny soothed her with words of gentle comfort while everyone else sat around awkwardly, a poignant silence filling the room.

Lance stood watching the woman cry, his own heart lurching with pain and guilt and remorse. He couldn't even look at Ricky for fear he might start crying too.

When Leigh finally calmed down, Lance stepped forward. He saw some napkins on the coffee table beside a tray of crackers and cheese, scooped one up and silently handed it to her. She seemed momentarily surprised, as though she wouldn't have expected Lance to do something nice for her, took the napkin and dabbed at her eyes so as to not overly smear her makeup. Jenny released her as Leigh composed herself, and the others exchanged uncomfortable glances amongst themselves.

Lance looked at Leigh with a kind of inner strength he didn't feel deep down and asked, "Can I see his room now?"

Leigh nodded. She led the way from the small living room into a narrow hallway, Lance following in silence. Ricky trailed behind and Jenny nudged Arthur to follow.

Leigh stopped in front of a closed wooden door, painted white and showing no signs of being opened much, not even discoloration of the white around the doorknob from fingertips brushing against it.

"In here," she offered with a heavy sigh that seemed to have a life of its own. "I tried to make it look just like it did in the old house, except I added more photos."

Lance turned to Ricky and his father sheepishly. "I wanna go in alone, okay?"

Ricky's hurt look pierced Lance's heart, but he ignored it and turned to his father.

Arthur's expression was one of understanding. "Of course, son."

Keeping his eyes averted so as to not see the pain in Ricky's, Lance turned back, gripped the knob and pushed open the door. Fearful of his reaction in front of the others, he quickly stepped inside and shut it behind him, sealing himself off from those who loved him. He nearly lost his breath as he scanned the room.

There were several posters of the Denver Broncos team or individual Bronco players adorning the wall above a twin bed sporting a royal blue coverlet. Next to the bed were a small bench press and a few dumbbells. Plates that looked pretty heavy to Lance lay stacked on the floor beside the bench.

Across from where he stood was a chest of four drawers with a mirror rising up from the back against the wall, and shelving was attached to the walls on either side of the mirror. On these makeshift shelves stood football trophies of varying sizes and quality. On the top of the bureau sat a number of framed photographs, and dead center rested a dirty, mud-encrusted football that had obviously seen a lot of use over a long period of time.

As though sleepwalking, Lance stepped cautiously forward, drawn to the photos on the bureau before him, to those images of that miraculous boy he had known. Stopping just short of the images, Lance's heart thudded and his blood pounded as his gaze fell on the first photo, set within a gilt metal frame - Jack at around Chris's age, maybe ten or eleven, wearing a colorful football uniform and clutching a full-sized football that made the boy's arms look small by comparison. Jack grinned rakishly from beneath the glass, the same rakish grin that had captured Lance's heart and endeared him to the older boy.

Feeling suddenly light-headed, Lance reached out to clutch the edges of the bureau, supporting himself as tears burned the backs of his eyes and threatened to burst forth with a passion.

"Jacky," he whispered to the picture, to all the pictures, to the room itself. Still supporting himself and feeling weak in the knees, Lance scanned the images before him. One showed Jack as a young boy playing on the shore of some lake, shirtless and already showing the kind of definition that would later blossom into the impressive muscularity of the older teen. There was one of Jack and Leigh together at some kind of amusement park when Jack was maybe eight or nine. The boy grinned happily at the expectation of getting on whatever ride they were waiting for. There were even a few with his father, but these were always sports related, and always with a football in the shot.

Lance studied the man's face. He seemed to be mad dogging the camera, his features cold and uncaring and uncompromising. Lance stopped breathing a moment. This was the man who'd driven Jack away, the man who'd humiliated him in front of his entire school, the man who'd rejected him cruelly and without remorse. An intense urge rose within Lance to spit on the image in hateful disgust, and he had to forcibly resist it.

There were images of Jack all the way up to his teens, the most recent showing Jack as Lance imagined him just before running away. Jack wore his Indians football jersey, hands in front clutching a football, biceps already bulging, chest much bigger than the average fifteen-year-old, his face one enormous, rakishly handsome grin. The number on his jersey was a "1" and the caption beneath read, "Poky Indians Varsity Quarterback."

With trembling fingers, Lance reached out one hand and clutched the photo, gazing deeply into the face of the boy who'd died for him, and tears forced their way from his eyes against his will. He tilted his head up to look at his own haunted face in the mirror.

"Oh, Jacky," he whispered as tears dribbled down his no longer boyish-looking cheeks. His breath caught and nearly choked off his next words. "Have I done right by you after what you did for me?" He lowered his eyes to the photo in his hand, and suddenly felt faint. Stepping back from the bureau, he plopped heavily onto the end of Jack's bed, the hand clutching the picture visibly trembling, and allowed the tears to flow.

Lance knew he shouldn't be crying at his age, but the image of Jack's happy face, the memories of that astounding boy and his ultimate sacrifice broke down any barriers he could even try to keep up, so he lowered his head and wept, awash in feelings of love and shame and sorrow.

So lost was he within his pain that he was startled to feel a hand gently alight on his shoulder, and looked over fearfully, only to see Arthur sliding lightly onto the bed beside him. Then the king's arm was encircling his shoulders and Lance leaned in to his father and cried quietly. Neither spoke. They simply sat together soaking up the ambiance that was Jack, allowing the boy they both loved to fill their hearts with his invisible presence.

Finally, Lance whispered hoarsely, "Did you do the right thing, Dad? Letting Jack die for me?"

Arthur turned his head sharply, but Lance's eyes were fixed on the framed photo in his hands. "It was his choice, Lance, and looking back I know for certain he made the correct one."

Lance looked up now, his face heavily streaked with dampness and guilt. "How can you know that?"

Arthur eyed his son with such love in his heart that he nearly cried himself. "Because of all you have accomplished, Lance, not for yourself but for the greater good. Jack was wise beyond his years, son, and he understood that the greater good would be served by you more than him. And he loved you, Lance."

Heart in his throat and threatening to bring on more tears, Lance digested his father's words. "Is this all part of God's plan, like people say?"

Arthur shrugged, his bearded face becoming thoughtful as he considered his response. "I do not know if it is God's plan, son, but the circle of life He put into motion seems to follow its own path and we are all a part of that path. Sometimes it takes tremendous pain and loss to bring about the greater good. There is no real way to know for certain until it is all said and done and we look back upon the results."

Lance considered those words and fell silent, his gaze once more lowering to the rakish grin and soft brown eyes looking back at him.

Arthur cleared his throat awkwardly. "You never showed me the letter Jack wrote to you, Lance," he said cautiously, his voice gentle and inviting. "Would you share it with me now?"

Lance looked up, surprised at his father's request, but even more surprised that he *hadn't* shown Arthur the letter. Shifting the picture frame to his left hand, Lance slipped his right around to the back pocket of his jeans and slipped out a battered looking leather wallet. There wasn't much in it except a little money and his California ID. And the folded letter from Jack. Fingers trembling slightly, Lance extracted the wrinkled sheet from its plastic holder and reverently unfolded it beneath the watchful eye of his father. He hadn't looked at the letter in some time, and just the sight of Jack's handwriting brought another burning sensation to his eyes. He handed the letter to Arthur without a word and returned his eyes to Jack's handsome face.

Arthur read through the letter, fighting back the emotional upsurge welling within him at Jack's heartfelt words to his son. He nearly choked with grief at one passage in particular: '*When I found out there was a way to keep my promise – I did promise to save you – and that the whole crusade, everything we'd worked so hard for, would collapse and die without you, well, the choice was obvious, but not easy. I didn't want to die. But given a choice between me and you, Lance, you would win every time.*'

Such an extraordinary boy, the king thought absently as he carefully read the letter twice. *Such strength of character in one so young.*

Finishing, Arthur refolded it carefully so to not damage the already weak and failing paper fibers, and sighed heavily with his own sad regret. "A boy like few others, Lance," he said quietly as he handed back the letter.

Uncertainly, Lance took it and cradled it within his fingers as he turned his head to make eye contact with Arthur.

"He exemplified my belief that in life we must do what is right rather than what is easy," the king went on. "You share that quality with Jack, son, a likely reason he loved you so deeply."

Lance's eyes widened in surprise, but then a cloud passed over his heart once more at the loss of his friend, and he whispered his biggest fear almost inaudibly. "Do you think Jack's proud of me, Dad?"

Arthur smiled sadly, but with genuine honesty. "I know he is."

Lance leaned in and hugged his father tightly.

After a few moments, Arthur pulled back and made eye contact with Lance. "Ricky waits without."

Lance nodded, his heart thudding anew. This was the moment both he and Ricky must come to terms with Jack and his place in their lives. "Tell him to come in."

Arthur rose to his feet and moved to the door. Lance watched him, momentarily distracted by the man's ordinary jeans and polo shirt, a sight he still wasn't used to. Arthur gripped the knob, offered one more look of encouragement, opened the door and stepped from the room.

Ricky entered, looking to Lance both beautiful and frightened, and closed the door behind him. He stood and stared uncertainly at Lance, and Lance gazed right back. He nodded for Ricky to enter and sit beside him. With obvious trepidation, Ricky stepped around the bed and sat gingerly beside Lance, glancing down at the photo in Lance's hand before scanning the room and absorbing the presence of Jack, the one boy he knew might have a stronger hold on Lance's heart than he did.

Finally, heart thumping with dread, he turned his head and locked eyes with the boy he loved.

✝✝✝

Arthur ambled back into the living room stroking his beard thoughtfully. Jenny hurried over, her face creased with worry.

"Is Lance all right?"

"I believe so."

Reyna let out an audible sigh of relief, squeezing Esteban's hand happily.

Leigh affected a cheerful face, and clapped her hands together excitedly. She scanned the upturned faces of all the men in the room and said, "So which of you young men wants to help me barbecue the hamburgers?"

Her question was met by a lot of blank stares from the guys, which made Reyna and Sylvia giggle. Darnell turned to Justin, who shrugged, while Techie and Esteban exchanged a confused look. Kai and Dakota looked mystified.

Finally Darnell cleared his throat awkwardly, "Uh, begging your pardon and all, Lady Bennett, but we don't do no barbecuin' in the hood, 'less it's torching a car when the Lakers win or somethin'." He caught the stunned look on Leigh's face and fumblingly added, "Course we don't do that stuff no more, you know, bein' knights and all."

He looked mortified and Justin tossed him a grin. "Smooth, bro."

Leigh laughed, and the other ladies joined in. "Reyna and I can help, Leigh," Jenny offered with a grin, giving an equally confused Arthur a playful shove. "The king doesn't barbecue either."

That drew a smile from Arthur, and everyone laughed.

†††

Ricky held Lance's gaze for as long as he could, and finally looked down at the picture in Lance's hands.

"May I?" he asked hesitantly, his heart pounding in his chest.

Lance handed over the framed photo wordlessly.

Ricky looked into the soft brown eyes, marveled at the perfection of Jack's young face, felt intimidated by Jack's rakish, confident grin and muscular arms. He finally released his breath, but couldn't bring himself to look up and face Lance again. He had to get this out in the open once and for all.

"I know I'm a shithead for even saying this, Lance," he said breathlessly, "but I hate how jealous I get every time you think about Jack." He heard Lance suck in a breath, but still couldn't face the scorn he knew he'd see in those eyes. "I know you love me, but I just feel there's just no way you can ever love me as much as him and I feel so—"

Lance's hands surrounded his in that instant, cupping the photo and cutting him off in mid-sentence. "No."

Uncertainly, Ricky lifted his eyes and fixed them on the perfect face before him, a face marred by guilt and pain. "No, what? No, you can never love me as much as Jack?"

Lance shook his head. "No, I can never love *anyone* as much as you."

Ricky's breath stopped, and his blood pounded even harder as his heart beat wildly with exhilaration. "Then why do I always feel so... feeble compared to Jack?"

"You're not feeble, Ricky," Lance said with assurance, still clutching the other boy's hands. "You're the baddest boy I know. It's just, well, Jack... died for me, Ricky. How would you feel if I died for you?"

"I'd wanna die too," came Ricky's answer without hesitation.

Lance nodded. "Exactly. But it's more than that."

"Tell me."

Lance looked long and hard into those wide, fearful eyes and struggled to coalesce his thoughts. "It's like, well, Jack was so badass that he made me start to realize it might be okay to like boys instead of girls, you know? If it hadn't been for him I probably would 'a just pretended to love some girl like Bridget and then..."

He trailed off, his breathing almost stopped as he considered the implications of what he was saying.

"And then what?" Ricky asked quietly, desperately.

Lance swallowed nervously. "And then I might never have let myself love you."

Ricky gasped, warmth suddenly suffusing his whole body.

"It's Jack who gave me you, Ricky," Lance went on, his voice almost a whisper because he could barely breathe. "That's why I get this way about him. He gave me my life, and he gave me you to make my life worth living. Do you understand?"

Ricky grinned then, his fears slipping away, the warmth encircling his heart and filling his soul with peace. All he could do was nod, but it was enough.

Lance smiled when he saw Ricky understood, and suddenly felt more at peace than he had in months. He looked deeply into Ricky's inviting brown eyes, felt Ricky's fingers entwined around his, and the picture of Jack wrapped up between them. It was like Jack was there in their midst, letting him go for good. And Lance let *him* go too. Jack, who had been everything once upon a time now seemed to be telling him good-bye once more, insisting that Lance let him rest in peace. And so he did.

The two boys sat together in silence, and then a knock at the door startled them, causing each to release the other's hand and turn quickly as Leigh stepped into the room.

"You guys getting hungry?" she asked cheerily. "I'm about to show you big city boys how to barbecue. Wanna join us?"

Lance and Ricky exchanged a look between them since neither had ever used a barbecue before. But the thought of Esteban flipping burgers brought a slight grin to Lance's face and he said, "Yeah, we're in."

Climbing off the bed, Lance reverently replaced the photo of the fifteen-year-old Jack where he'd found it, looked once more into those soulful eyes, and then followed Ricky and Leigh from the room.

†††

Leigh seemed to own a multitude of barbecue aprons because she slung one around the front of every male except the officers and agents. Even Arthur sported one. Jenny and Reyna couldn't contain wild bouts of laughter at the sight of these guys, especially Esteban and Justin, wearing aprons and gingerly reaching into the hot barbecue to flip over burgers and poke them with knives to test for readiness. Jenny's camera got a lot of use that night.

Lance and Ricky playfully jostled each other when it was their turn as cooks, and Arthur felt relieved that Lance seemed to have emerged from the darkness that had briefly consumed him. Chris, however, while working with his two brothers and seemingly having fun, had a distant look in his big blue eyes that Arthur well understood. Chris had loved Jack too.

After the food was cooked, amidst lots of jokes by Reyna at the guys' expense, everyone sat around the backyard and enjoyed the fruits of their labors. Leigh had even taught them how to grill onions and how to cook the buns "Just right so they're still soft."

With the veil of Jack mostly lifted, especially outdoors without any photographic reminders, the mood lightened. Lance slipped into a slight funk when Leigh told how them Pocatello High School had retired Jack's football jersey and put up a dedication to him in the administration wing for everyone to see as they entered the school.

She sighed and suddenly looked lost and faraway. "The same people who allowed kids to mock my son decided to cash in on his fame and claim they were sorry." She shook her head in disgust. "They even advertise on their website, the home of Jack Bennett, Knight of the Table Round."

Lance listened in stoic silence, but Reyna blew out a disgusted breath. "That's sick."

Leigh smiled sadly. "It is, but it allowed me to get the GSA started over there. How could they say no after getting all that publicity?"

"Is it helping?" Chris asked suddenly, the first words he'd spoken all through dinner. "Is it helping kids like Jack?"

Leigh nodded. "I have my sources among the student body," she said happily. "They clue me in on Facebook if there's any shit going down and I get right on it."

Jenny looked startled to hear Leigh cuss, but then Leigh flashed a disarming smile. "Well, it is shit, isn't it?"

That drew a laugh from everyone. Looking pensive, Chris absently brushed his blond bangs off his forehead and finished eating his burger.

Later, after all had eaten their fill and every one of the guys had tried his hand at the barbecue, it was time to return to their hotel. The following day Leigh planned to take them over to Pocatello High School, where the principal had arranged to give them a tour and to address a student assembly in the gym. Summer school was in session so the number of students would be far fewer than during the regular year, but that suited Lance just fine. He didn't know how he'd respond if some hater kid called him a faggot or made some nasty comment about Jack. He just might lose it, and that could be disastrous to the cause.

As everyone began leaving for the bus, Lance noticed that Chris was not in the living room or the backyard. He asked Leigh if she'd seen him.

"Oh, yes, he asked to spend some time in Jack's room," she replied, her face clouding. "It seems my son made quite an impression on that boy."

Oh, shit! Lance thought, turning to Ricky with mortification. "I was so caught up in myself I forgot how much Chris loved Jack. I'm such an asshole!"

Ricky blanched white, too, also not having thought of Chris in favor his own jealousy.

Leigh smiled sadly. "Don't be too hard on yourself, Lance. C'mon, let's go get him."

The boys followed her down the hall to the bedroom door, which sat partially open. The sound of soft crying could be heard wafting out into the hall.

Leigh turned to Lance and he nodded. His heart beat with sadness at the sound of the young boy's tears just beyond the door. Leigh pushed it open and they entered. Chris sat on the bed almost exactly where Lance had sat earlier. He clutched Jack's old football to him, arms wrapped around it like it was a life preserver. His hair spilled around his face, obscuring it from view as he cried.

Lance hurried around the bed to sit on Chris's right, engulfing the boy in his arms, wrapping him securely in a strong embrace, while Ricky sat on Chris's left and did the same. The three boys huddled together in silence, the poignant air punctuated by Chris's low sobs into Lance's t-shirt. Leigh stood watching them, her face riddled with pain and motherly concern for the sorrow of a child, her mind flitting back to all the times she'd comforted Jack in her arms, even when he'd been fifteen and the target of daily harassment at school.

After a few minutes of awkward silence, Chris raised his head from beneath Lance's arms. His milky-white cheeks streaked with tears, he said, "I miss him *so* much, Lance."

Lance's heart lurched and he nodded breathlessly. "Me too." More tears beckoned, but Lance blinked them back. He had to stay strong for Chris.

Leigh stepped over and stood before the three boys, her face motherly with love. "You know, Chris, that was Jack's first full-sized football and his greatest treasure. I'm sure he'd like you to have it."

Chris's blurred blue eyes bulged so wide Lance thought they'd fall right out of the sockets. "Really?" His breath seemed to catch in his throat and he hesitated. "I can… really have it?"

She nodded. "Really. It's what Jack would want. He always loved showing younger boys in the neighborhood how to play."

Chris glanced down in awe at the old, dirty, worn down piece of pigskin in his lap as Lance and Ricky released him and waited. Impulsively, Chris handed the football to Lance and leapt to his feet, grabbing Leigh in a hug that caused her to suck in a surprised breath. "Thank you so much!" the boy gushed into her light summer sundress.

Lance watched as the woman froze momentarily, her expression suddenly somewhere else far away. Then it softened and she wrapped her arms around the boy's shoulders and returned the hug.

When Chris released her and took the football back, Leigh glanced down at the seated Lance with a sad, thoughtful smile. "I have something for you, too, Lance."

His eyes widened with surprise as she turned to the bureau and opened the top drawer, slipping out a reasonably thick photo album. Turning back to Lance, she held it out. Hands trembling slightly, Lance reached out to take it.

"These are all the pictures I have of Jack," Leigh said quietly. "From infancy till he... well, till we drove him away." Lance's breath caught and he momentarily froze, hands on the proffered album. "I had copies made for you."

Swallowing dryly, Lance closed his hands around the album and pulled it to him, resting it in his lap as a chill washed over him. He glanced at Ricky, who nodded that it was all right. Then he raised his eyes to Leigh's expectant face. "Thank you so much for this, Mrs. Bennett," he said in a hoarse whisper. "I'll treasure it."

She smiled warmly. "Call me Leigh, and I know you will. From all I've heard, you and Mark meant more to my Jacky than anyone."

Ricky saw the tears ready to burst forth as Lance began slipping into that super emo mood of deep sadness, and quickly placed his hand on top of the other boy's, squeezing gently.

Lance turned to eye him gratefully, and then nodded at Leigh, not trusting himself to speak for fear the dam would burst once more.

†††

Everyone waved out the windows to Leigh as the bus pulled away from her house, and she waved happily back. Lance and Ricky sat together with Chris between them. Lance cradled the still-closed photo album while Chris hugged the battered football to his chest. Ricky sat in silence with both, knowing they needed time to process all the emotions swirling through them.

†††

That night in their hotel room, Lance sat with Chris and Ricky on his bed and they flipped through the entire photo album. Both Lance and Chris allowed themselves a few tears along the way, and Ricky held Lance's hand securely within his own, but the experience was cathartic and necessary. Though all three felt sad as that final shot of the fifteen-year-old, rakishly grinning Jack appeared on the last page, Lance closed the book with a feeling of putting the boy who'd given him everything into the proper place within his heart – alive and never forgotten, but not a heavy weight dragging him down to failure. No, for Jack failure was *never* an option, and it would never be for him, either.

Pocatello High School, the group was informed by the principal the following morning, had been built in 1892, but the original structure had burnt to the ground thanks to a boiler room fire in 1914. Once rebuilt, the school had been remodeled and added on to over the years, and it was probably the most beautiful school Lance or any of the kids had ever seen. Schools in California tended to look institutional, but this one with its towering front entrance, brick and stone exterior, enormous windows and fancy adornments along the top and front made the place look more like a cathedral than a high school.

As they stepped into the cavernous administration building, its walls lined with senior class pictures dating back almost a hundred years, one enormous portrait-sized photo leapt out to practically grab them as they entered. It was Jack, in a very similar pose to the one Leigh had over her mantle – rakish grin, muscular arms folded across his number, expression cocky and confident and handsome. But Lance didn't tear up, and neither did Chris. They stopped and gazed at the photo with reverence along with everyone else, noting the dates of birth and death with slight hitching of their breath and increased beating of their hearts.

The principal prattled on about how Jack's experience at PHS and subsequent heroic achievements within the Round Table had opened the eyes of many students and adults in Pocatello about gay kids and what it meant to be a man in this society. Lance only half-listened, losing himself once more in Jack's soft brown eyes, recalling the moments they'd shared, and cherishing those memories.

As they made their way to the auditorium, a chant could be heard wafting down the hall toward them, rising in pitch and intensity the closer they got. "We want Lance! We want Lance! We want Lance!"

Lance almost stopped dead as he realized what they were chanting. Arthur grinned at him, as though not the least bit surprised. Ricky shoved him playfully and said, "Your fans await" in a formal tone, eliciting a smile from Reyna.

The principal shrugged. "You're quite the celebrity among our student body, Lance. They've been excited about this visit for weeks."

With a sigh, Lance said quietly, "Wow," and then followed the principal to the big double doors and held his breath as the man shoved both doors open and stepped inside.

It looked like a typical gym with bleachers on each side packed with chanting, hand waving teens. More chairs filled the floor on both sides, with an open aisle straight up the middle ending at a podium already set up with a microphone. The moment the kids saw Lance they rose en masse to their feet, burst into thunderous applause, and changed the chant to "We love Lance! We love Lance! We love Lance!" Music began blasting from the speakers, music instantly recognized by Lance, Ricky, and Chris, who'd watched the film together after finishing the book – it was The Ivory Tower theme from *The NeverEnding Story*.

Lance stood frozen just inside the doorway, Ricky to one side, Chris to the other. Helen moved around in front with Charlie and his camera, capturing the stunned expressions on the boys' faces for the world to see. As with all appearances related to Round Table business, the knights had donned their tunics and leather pants and sported their swords, bows, and quivers of arrows. At Arthur's insistence, Lance wore the small crown the king had given him, his thick hair spilling down the back of his vibrant green tunic. Ricky looked equally majestic in red beneath his shimmering gold circlet. Chris had now taken to wearing Lance's old circlet to hold back the flowing blond tresses falling past his shoulders, and his sky blue tunic matched the color of his eyes.

Ricky laughed at Lance's frozen expression and lightly shoved him forward. Lance grinned back and started up the aisle, leading the others in a two-file procession. Lance waved to the chanting teens as he walked, and everyone else followed suit.

Arriving at the podium, Lance moved to one side and everyone else gathered behind him, clearly recognizing that he was the star of this show. The principal stepped to the podium and raised both hands for the crowd to quell. The Ivory Tower theme wound down, and after a few more moments of clapping and chanting, the hundreds of gathered teenagers resumed their seats, settling into a murmuring kind of quiet.

The principal grinned out at them. "Students of PHS, I give you Sir Lance of the Round Table!"

He stepped back and extended an arm toward Lance. The students erupted into another spate of clapping, punctuated this time with foot stomping. Lance stepped up to the podium, Ricky and Chris right behind him, and grinned at the crowd, creating yet another round of cheers.

When they finally settled down, Lance thanked them for such a warm welcome. He also thanked those who were supporting the passage of the CBOR and who furthered that cause in April. Another rousing cheer filled the auditorium, causing the principal to frown with the uneasy possibility that perhaps the students had done something he didn't know about.

Lance asked if anyone had any questions for him and one boy in the top row of the bleachers leapt to his feet immediately. "Sir Lance!" the boy called out in a challenging tone. "Are you gay?"

Lance blanched and felt his knees go weak. Ricky and Chris both stepped to either side of him looking furious. Reyna could be heard cussing under her breath.

But before any of them could respond, the entire student body rose to its collective feet and chanted in a singsong tone, "No, he's eemmmoo!" And then they all laughed uproariously and began clapping once more.

It took Lance a split second to realize what they had done, and then his fear eased into an enormous grin. He turned to Ricky, who also understood. Lance leaned into the microphone with a smile. "I guess you all saw our Ellen interview, huh?"

The standing students shouted, "Damn straight!" That set off another round of laughter and high-fiving amongst the kids, and drew an even bigger grin from Lance and Ricky. Chris stepped around between them and placed Ricky's hand within Lance's and then pushed both upward into the air. The assembled students cheered all the louder and Chris beamed up at his older brothers with pride.

When everyone finally settled back down, their message of acceptance clearly delivered, Lance released Ricky's hand and looked seriously out at their silent, expectant faces. "You guys are awesome for this and for supporting the CBOR. If we can get that passed it will help all of us kids everywhere in the country. So email your representatives and senators and push your parents to do the same." He paused a moment, took a deep breath, and continued. "But none of this would be possible without one amazing boy, and that boy isn't me." There were murmurs of surprise from the teens. "I might be the one behind all this, but one brave, selfless boy made sure I had the chance, and he's the one we must always remember and cherish, the one and only Jack Bennett!"

Lance's heart nearly stopped as the students rose to their feet and cheered even louder than before, clapping and whooping and stomping. The ovation went on for nearly five minutes while Lance and the others stood in awe of the response. It thrilled Lance with its vindication of Jack and his heroic efforts, but also enveloped him in a cocoon of sadness that Jack wasn't alive to see what he had wrought.

I hope you're watching, Jacky, he thought silently. *I hope you know what a difference you made down here.*

The rest of the Q & A went smoothly and delightfully, with students asking questions of all the knights, making everyone feel welcome and important.

Leigh stood behind the principal smiling sadly, light tears of joy welling in her guilt-ridden eyes.

†††

And so their short visit to Pocatello that laid to rest the ghost of Jack, and simultaneously celebrated his memory, came to an end. The trip to Boise, the state capital, would take between three and four hours and they wanted to arrive before nightfall. The following day would be yet another in a seemingly endless series of "pitch" sessions to the state legislature on the CBOR. Just the thought of it made Lance groan with dismay, and he once more vowed to Ricky as they sat on the bus rolling through the green, open countryside, that once this campaign ended he was done with politics forever. Ricky just smiled knowingly as if to say, "Yeah, right."

†††

The joint session of the Idaho state legislature went smoothly the following day, with not a single question directed at Lance or Ricky about a "gay agenda" or an "anti-parent" agenda. The questions were thoughtful and indicated that many of these lawmakers had given the matter some real consideration. Most indicated they had discussed the CBOR with their own children and teens and were taking the idea seriously.

Curiously, the amendment that seemed to be of the most interest was number thirty-one about children receiving just compensation for their own labors, and how the money earned would not be under the control of parents or guardians. Lance was asked specifically why that was in there and could he give a good example of a situation to which that would apply.

"I can," he answered with a nod. "Every summer you see on TV that Little League World Series where a whole bunch of twelve year olds are put on the spot to make their hometowns look good by winning the thing. The TV network makes money, commercial companies make money, and Little League Baseball makes a ton of money. But the kids who're being all stressed out to win or they'll embarrass their hometowns and stuff? They don't get a dime. And it's not like they're gonna go on to a career in baseball. Only twelve kids in history have ever done that. So these kids work their butts off, put in all the effort, and earn nothing except the *thrill* of being exploited on TV. That's wrong, and that's only one example. Kids in commercials or modeling or acting don't get control of their own money – their parents do. It's not right and it just tempts adults to pimp out their kids."

That response seemed to satisfy the questioner, and the rest of the session proceeded in like fashion.

The real drama occurred that evening. They were all sitting around a large table at Sizzler laughing and yucking it up and chatting with the locals when Esteban received a text on his phone from Sir Phillip back in L.A. The message included a link to a TV news video and Phillip told Esteban he should watch it.

Esteban seemed mystified by the message, and Reyna shrugged before pulling her iPad out of her purse and powering it up. Arthur and Jenny were seated across from them and Arthur asked Esteban if there was a problem.

"Dunno," the young man said. "Sir Phillip said to check something out."

Arthur and Jenny exchanged a look of concern. They had been in regular contact with the teen knight since leaving New Camelot, but only to post updates and status reports. Never had Sir Phillip contacted them with anything approaching a problem or concern.

Seated next to Arthur, Lance eyed his father anxiously as Reyna opened the link Phillip had sent and gave Esteban her ear buds so he could hear above the din of the noisy restaurant.

The table grew silent as everyone watched Esteban, curious as to the nature of what he was looking at. Even Kai and Dakota, who didn't know him as well, saw instantly that something was wrong.

Esteban's face went from curiosity to a frown to disbelief and then to fury as everyone watched the transformation. Reyna, looking over his shoulder at the video, gasped in shock, but said nothing because she couldn't hear the audio. But she recognized the victim's photo displayed on-screen.

Lance nervously awaited Este's response. It wasn't long in coming. Apparently the video had ended because Esteban yanked the buds from his ears and slammed his thick fist down on the table hard enough to knock utensils to the floor.

"Fuck!" he spat before leaping to his feet and bolting through the startled crowd toward the exit.

"What?" Lance asked in shock, but Reyna just shook her head, shoving the iPad across to him and jumping up to go after the man she loved. Lance looked at Ricky and then at Arthur as everyone left his or her seat to crowd around them. Lance disengaged the ear buds, returned the video to its start, and pressed the "play" arrow.

A local story from *Channel 7 News* came onto the screen. The scene was an alley of some kind and the legend on screen proclaimed, "Man Found Murdered Execution-Style." The camera captured the medical personnel covering a man's body. The man lay on one side, his face bloody, and was quickly covered by a sheet.

As the body was lifted onto a stretcher, an on-camera reporter said grimly, "As you saw in that quick glimpse, the man's face was almost unrecognizable because, we've been told by the police on the scene, he was shot point blank through the back of the skull in an apparent execution-style murder. The man has been identified as one Rafael Gallegos, known gang member and wanted fugitive of many years."

A photo of the man appeared on screen, and Lance gasped. It was Esteban's father! Then Esteban's photo appeared right next to his father, though it was clearly a screenshot taken from the Internet.

"As you can see, the man had in his pocket this image of the young Sir Esteban of King Arthur's Round Table, a former gang member who left the gang life to join New Camelot."

A large pool of blood splattered on the ground remained clearly visible behind the reporter. The man continued in a sober voice, "It appears the victim had his phone on video record in his pocket and captured the conversation that transpired between him and the murderer. While the police have not yet released the recording, they did reveal that the murder of Gallegos senior was apparently committed in place of killing Gallegos junior, who had what gangs call a green light, presumably for leaving the gang and encouraging other youngsters to leave with him. It appears Mr. Gallegos had been ordered to kill his son or be executed in his place, and chose the latter. More details on this potentially explosive story as they come in. This is Jimmy Martinez reporting from East L.A."

The video ended and Lance froze the image, his heart beating with sick dread as he turned to look at Arthur. The king's face had lost all color and he looked stunned.

"Shit," Darnell whispered with a shake of his head.

"The ole man was righteous after all," Justin said quietly.

Even Techie looked shocked that anyone would do such a thing, especially a guy who'd ditched his kid so long ago.

But Lance recalled the man's words back in Arizona just before he disappeared into the crowd, and told them to Arthur now. "Dad, he said 'the business with the homies has to do with you, but I got your back'. Something like that."

Ricky whistled in surprise. "He knew all along. He saved Este's life." His own heart pounded with emotion. His birth father would never have done that for him.

Jenny leaned in to Arthur. "You need to talk to him, Arthur."

The king sighed heavily, the weight of the moment visibly slumping his broad shoulders. "I know. Excuse me."

He rose and left the table. Everyone watched in silence as he crossed the crowded restaurant, acknowledging greetings from patrons with a nod and a half-smile, and then disappeared out the exit to the parking lot.

†††

Arthur found Esteban and Reyna inside the bus, he with his shoulders slumped, staring sightlessly out the window, clenching and unclenching his fists while she sat by his side and attempted to soothe him with loving strokes of her hand along his bare forearm. But the corded muscles and bulging veins in that forearm told Arthur that she was not succeeding.

Esteban had always been known for his ability to remain calm in a crisis, but Arthur knew this situation was different. This was about guilt and regret and wanting to go back in time and say something left unsaid.

Reyna glanced up as the king stepped into the bus. Her face had dissolved into anguish at the uncertain state of Este's emotions and her own helplessness at being unable to make him feel better.

She knew instinctively that this was something Este needed to work out with Arthur, the man he thought of as his father, so she rose from the bench and slipped passed him to exit the bus.

Arthur sat beside the young man, eyeing him cautiously, noting the tightness of his muscles, the coiled stance of his rigid body, even the veins in his thick neck bulging with anger. He saw their faces reflected back at him in the bus window, one young and handsome, the other older and bearded. But both wore the exact same expression – regret.

Shifting awkwardly, and keeping his voice calm and steady, Arthur said, "The words we fail to utter, like the choices we fail to make, haunt us the most, Este. I should have learned that lesson over the course of my first life, but I did not. I repeated the same foolish mistake in this one. It cost me Mark and Jack, and nearly cost us all Lance."

Esteban turned his anguished face toward the king. "Yeah, but you figured it out, Arthur."

"After two lifetimes, yes. We men are slow about such things, Este. Do not berate yourself for an understandable mistake."

Esteban turned his whole taut body and kept one fist clenched in his lap, as though he might punch out the window at any moment.

Arthur hadn't seen the young man so angry since Lavern was murdered.

"I dissed him, Arthur," Esteban said quietly, his deep voice filled with shame. "I should 'a known the older homies wouldn't let me just walk away. My father came to kill me, Arthur, that's the code. Kill me, or die for me." He stopped, lowered his eyes and shook his head in anger. "And I dissed him."

Arthur shook his head. "No, Este, you didn't."

The young man looked up in surprise.

"As a father who has made numerous mistakes," Arthur went on sadly, "I can assure you your *jefe* did not expect forgiveness from you, nor should you have been expected to give it. He chose his homies over you, an error I nearly made with Lance. He merely wished to let you know that he had not forgotten you."

Esteban's eyes widened with shock and comprehension.

"Honor his final choice, Sir Este, not the careless young man he once was, and always know that his loss was my gain." Arthur offered a smile. "You are a son any man would be proud of."

Esteban fell into a dumbfounded silence, choked with emotion, unable to speak or even to breathe. Arthur patted him on one brawny shoulder, rose from the seat and exited the bus.

Esteban looked almost shell-shocked when Reyna cautiously reentered the bus and approached him. Never the least bit shy or uncertain, she felt uncharacteristically nervous as she stopped and gazed down at him. He looked up at her. The anger was gone, though the regret remained. She offered her most sincere smile.

"I love you, Sir Este of the Table Round," she said breathlessly.

Despite his pain, her declaration thrilled and humbled him in equal measure, as it always did whenever she said those words. He couldn't help but return her smile. "I love you more, Lady Reyna of the Table Round."

She slid in beside him and threw her arms around his thick shoulders. He embraced her and pulled her in, and they sat in solitude.

The table remained quiet and somber while Arthur was gone, despite the boisterous tumult of the crowded restaurant. Everyone sat picking at their food, lost in his or her own thoughts about what Esteban's father had done. Lance had sunk into a funk rather quickly, causing Ricky great concern. Death always had that effect on Lance, no doubt reminding him how close he, himself, had come to its permanence. Knowing Lance better than anyone save for Arthur, Ricky sat and allowed his bare arm to brush up against Lance's, allowed only that basic human contact to remind the other boy that he was there when the need for talk arose.

Lance had indeed sunk within himself since watching that news broadcast. The sight of that dead body, the dead body of Este's father, had sent terrifying visions through his mind and heart, horrific images of Arthur dead, gunned down in a pool of blood, Excalibur lying useless by his side. The image had blasted through his consciousness like an IMAX movie with vivid colors and emotions, and then segued directly into remembrances of Arthur's face back in Las Vegas, when he'd stood atop those faux battlements gazing down on Lance holding Excalibur aloft in triumph. His dad's expression had been one of almost fatalistic acceptance.

Lance sat beside Ricky, grateful for the warmth of the other boy's arm against his, hoping it would gradually seep into his soul and push back the intense cold wrapping itself so tightly around him. *Am I becoming like Merlin*, the boy wondered, as he flicked a glance across the table at the old wizard, whose eyes were fixed on him with curiosity? *Is this some kind of vision or premonition about the future?* The thought chilled him even more, freezing his heart in the midst of a beat, and he fought to shake off the disconcerting feeling.

At that moment, Arthur slid into his chair beside Jenny, nodding affirmatively to her unspoken question, and then turned to all the expectant faces awaiting his report. He sighed, and Lance noted that the worry lines on his once unmarred face had deepened, become more permanent.

"Sir Este is well," the king announced calmly, "but will need time to adjust to this new reality about his father. Be supportive, my knights, but not intrusive. As you well know, he is a young man who wears his pain in silence."

There were relieved murmurs and head nods from everyone. Lance sighed, and then felt eyes fixed on him. Thinking it was Merlin again, he turned in that direction, only to find it was Ryan, not Merlin, studying him intently. He frowned.

"Everything okay, *nino*?" he asked, his voice tentative.

Ryan smiled tightly, but even that sent deep crevices into his weathered face. "Yeah. *You* okay, godson?"

It freaked Lance out how Ryan seemed to sense his mood shifts almost as easily as Arthur and Ricky. "Yeah, *nino*. Just thinking about stuff."

Ryan nodded, his expression revealing his awareness that whatever Lance was thinking about was significant. But he asked no further questions and resumed eating.

After finally escaping the restaurant and handing out stickers to everyone as they left, the group moved somberly across the parking lot to their bus. As always, Ryan, Gibson and the agents walked along the outer perimeter of the group scanning the darkness for impending danger.

As the knights began filing into the bus, Reyna shushed them, indicating Esteban beside her in the seat, head slumped against her shoulder in sleep.

Lance stopped Arthur before the king could enter the bus. Ricky hesitated, but one look from Lance told him he wished to speak with their father alone. Ricky nodded and stepped up into the bus with Chris in tow.

"Yes, son?" Arthur asked, when only he remained, with Ryan, hand inside his jacket, standing guard nearby.

Lance looked up at his father's shadowy face. The uneven parking lot lighting made the king's expression not quite readable. "I been wondering, Dad."

When Lance paused, Arthur prodded, "Yes?"

"If whoever is out to kill me would take you instead and leave me alone, would you do it?"

Arthur didn't even flinch. "In a heartbeat," he stated with a firmness that even caught Lance by surprise.

Lance swallowed fearfully, his green eyes searching for his father's brown in the darkness. "Even if I told you not to?"

Arthur nodded. "Even then."

Lance sighed heavily.

"We have had this discussion before, Lance," Arthur reminded him quietly. "There is no one on this earth I love more than you."

Lance's eyes widened into saucers. "Really?"

"Really."

Lance fell into one of his pregnant silences, and Arthur placed one hand on the boy's shoulder. "Why are we speaking of this, Lance?"

Lance shook his head, not because he didn't want to answer, but because he didn't *know* the answer.

Yet somehow Arthur, as always, seemed to. "Has it to do with what happened in Las Vegas?"

Lance's eyes widened even further. "Kinda. Well, yeah. It still scares me, that whole thing with Excalibur. I just feel it means something I'm not gonna like."

Arthur offered a sincere smile, his gleaming teeth visible in the dim overhead lighting. "Life is filled with what we don't like, Lance, and rife with what we do. But what we *must* do is always of greater import than what we'd *like* to do."

With that, Arthur withdrew his arm and ushered his son into the bus.

Lance eyed him once more, struggling to fathom the meaning of those words, but seeing nothing further forthcoming, stepped up and entered the bus.

Arthur turned to Ryan soberly. "If any harm should befall me, James, protect him as though he were your own."

Ryan's heart lurched, especially after overhearing their conversation. But he didn't even hesitate in his response. "You know I will, Arthur."

The king smiled and then both men entered the bus in silence.

†††

Chapter Four

Do You Still Wish It Was Me?

Esteban spoke with his mother that night from his hotel room and her response was short and to the point: "Better him than you, *mijo*." Esteban thought her tone harsh given the circumstances, but was his own when he'd spoken to his father any different? Like mother, like son.

At first, Esteban felt compelled to return to L.A. for the funeral, but between his mother, Reyna, Arthur, and Gibson, they convinced him to pay his respects at the gravesite when they all returned to the city. Gibson, in particular, felt the scene could be too volatile given the execution-style nature of the killing and that Esteban could still be targeted, but the young man knew better. His father had made a deal and the price had been paid. He was as safe as he could be from his old homeboys. Former enemies, however, might take it into their heads to gun him down at such a gang-related event and take a few others with him. So Esteban's cooler side prevailed and he relented, much to Reyna's intense relief.

"I'd die if anything happened to you, Este," she'd whispered into his ear, startling him because it made her sound almost dependent, a quality she seldom, if ever, displayed, even when it came to him.

Both the death of Esteban's father and "The Excalibur Incident" remained Internet staples for the next several weeks as the tour continued. Many still poo pooed the glowing Excalibur as a Las Vegas/Hollywood style special effect to bolster Arthur's campaign, while others saw it as yet another omen that The Boy Who Came Back was special and had a great destiny to fulfill.

While they had already spent a lot of time together on this trip, the business with Esteban's father seemed to bring Justin and Gibson even closer. After Boise, they were practically inseparable, as though the death of Rafael Gallegos had reminded both men of the instability of life and the need to cherish every moment possible.

Likewise, Lance, Ricky, and Chris clung more to Arthur, as they had when they'd first become a family, and whenever there were opportunities to sightsee, the boys stayed close to their parents and shared precious family moments that, deep down, Lance felt might never come again. The emo part of him kept forcing its way to the surface with ill omens and bad feelings, but he continually squelched it. Like Justin, he intended to cherish every moment, and just let the future be a mystery for now.

The tour moved up into Helena, Montana and then down to Cheyenne, Wyoming where both state legislatures graciously welcomed them. Kai and Dakota, in particular, loved the wide-open spaces and gorgeous mountains, and even the city kids had come to appreciate the lush beauty America had to offer.

From Cheyenne, the knights rode into quaint Fort Collins, Colorado, for a rally of young supporters at Colorado State University. Kids of all ages, including a huge number of college students, attended the rally to pledge their support for the CBOR, and to push their state representatives to vote for it.

Denver was their next stop, and a joint session of the state legislature, which went surprisingly well considering Edwin had proclaimed Colorado an "Odd state politically speaking." Lance wasn't sure what he meant, exactly, but the lawmakers proved friendly and affable enough–for politicians, anyway. They did some Town Hall-type get-togethers in Denver before sailing on through Colorado Springs with its amazing Garden of the Gods rock formations that kept the kids in a constant state of awe.

The four Native Knights wished they could stop and enjoy the outdoors and its beauty, vowing to take a vacation one day together and spend quality time seeing places they'd rushed through in order to remain on schedule.

The four of them, in particular, loved Santa Fe and Albuquerque, New Mexico, because of all the Native Americans they encountered and the plethora of Native culture they could partake of. Lance and Ricky, who'd always thought of themselves as sort of generic Latinos of Mexican descent, found the artwork and culture of Native tribes fascinating, and felt a pull toward a past they'd never known before.

Both Lance and Dakota were visibly disturbed to hear that New Mexico was the drunk driving capital of the country due to the high alcoholism rate amongst Native Americans there, and talked on the bus rides about what more could be done to prevent Indian kids from getting hooked. It would be a future project, they decided, after the CBOR. The group took time along the way to celebrate, with loud dinners and cake, Dakota and Kai turning nineteen, including raucous renditions by all the knights of "Happy Birthday to You" that embarrassed both young men, but generated rousing applause from the other restaurant patrons.

In late July, the bus and accompanying Secret Service cars pulled into San Antonio, Texas, where a rally had been scheduled for the following day at The Alamo, the sight of an historic battle between some two hundred fifty defending Texans and the invading fifteen-hundred-man Mexican army under Santa Anna. Lance had chosen the sight precisely because of the pride that battle still held for Texans, and because he wanted to make yet another point about why kids in America had more than earned equal rights under the Constitution. Edwin warned him that Texas was likely a lost cause, that these people were too rigid and would never approve rights for children that might in any way reduce the control of parents. Lance smiled cryptically and said, "We'll see."

†††

San Antonio at the end of July had weather Lance thought more appropriate for one of those places where they cremated bodies. The coolest it got the morning of their Alamo rally was seventy-eight degrees, with the high projected at one hundred three. And man, was it humid! None of the Angelenos were used to such moisture in the air and instantly felt their baggy tunics filling up like hot air balloons and sweat streaming down their torsos.

The Alamo had been rebuilt with a roof that curved upward, and stone walls that used parts of the original structure. The front entrance remained intact with the exception of a modern locking door to keep out trespassers when the landmark wasn't open to the public.

There was a bright green rectangle of roped-off lawn directly in front of the entrance with a plaque explaining the significance of the site. A wide, cobblestone-style walkway around this lawn was used to access the front entrance, and the area surrounding the structure was lush with large shade trees and open grass.

For today's event, folding chairs had been set up along both sides of the roped-off lawn and behind it, with the street area off the curb barricaded and made available for attendees who had to stand. A podium had been set up in front of the dark brown, double front doors. Folding chairs had been placed behind the podium for Arthur's group and those dignitaries who'd chosen to attend.

The mayor of San Antonio surprised Lance with his youth, and the man laughed because everyone always commented on how young he was. He welcomed Lance, Arthur and all of the team with hearty handshakes and a big, camera-ready grin. But unlike the manufactured grin former Mayor Villagrana used to flash back in L.A., this one seemed genuine, even gushing, as the man excitedly introduced his wife and several city council members.

They had gathered inside the Alamo itself in order to make a "Grand entrance," as the mayor laughingly put it, for the huge crowd massing outside. "Seems everyone in San Antonio wants a look at the boy who came back, Lance," he told the boy, "and at the famous King Arthur."

The king smiled with amusement as Ricky shoved Lance like he always did and said, "Mr. Popular strikes again."

Lance shook his head bemusedly and shoved him back. "Dumbass."

That drew a laugh from the mayor and his wife. He went on to explain to the team that many kids in San Antonio looked up to the youth of the Round Table, especially since most were minority themselves and saw the young knights as role models.

Lance rolled his eyes at Ricky without the mayor seeing them. The mayor was a nice guy, that eye roll said, but still played group politics like most. Ricky grinned back in complete understanding. They were always so in sync that words were hardly ever needed between them.

As they waited, everyone felt an almost otherworldly reverence fall over them in this hallowed spot where so many people had died. There was a large chandelier hanging from the high, curved and beamed stone ceiling, a wooden information booth set up along one wall, and flags lining the other. For the most part, the building was dark and shadowy and empty, devoid of any modern trappings that might distract tourists from the true meaning of the site.

The thick air felt hot and sweltering, with Lance, Ricky, and Chris shifting uncomfortably as sweat dribbled down from their underarms into their pants. Finally, the mayor announced that it was time. He stepped outside with the city council members and his wife, and the knights heard a loud cheer rise from the crowd gathered outside.

Guy must be popular, Lance thought, which made him wonder for a brief moment what might be happening in L.A. with Mayor Soto running New Camelot in their absence.

When he heard, "And I'm proud to present King Arthur and his noble knights," Lance stepped up beside the king, who smiled at him, as did Jenny, and then he followed his parents out the open double doors into the harsh, sweltering late morning sun, Ricky and Chris at either side, the rest following.

The crowd clapped, but the applause was not thunderous like the kids in Pocatello had displayed. It was courteous and respectful, but wary and reserved. The kids in the crowd were much more enthusiastic, but not ecstatic.

Yep, Lance thought, *Texas must be a hard sell, just like Edwin said.*

But he had a plan.

All of the knights waved and smiled as they always did no matter how a crowd received them. Courtesy was a prime directive of chivalry, and the young people had learned it well.

Once everyone had seated him or herself, and the crowd members who had chairs also sat, the mayor introduced Arthur, who rose with a sweep of his cloak and stepped to the podium. Lance knew his dad must be dying in the heat, especially since Arthur had told him the Britain of his day usually had gloomy, cool weather.

Arthur thanked the mayor and city council members and all of the people for attending. He reminded them that, as a non-native-born American, he could not vote and had little influence on the politics of the nation. But he respectfully asked every adult present to keep an open mind on the CBOR. Then he introduced his three sons.

To stronger applause from the kids in the vast crowd, Lance, Ricky, and Chris rose from their seats and moved to the podium. Arthur placed a hand on Lance's shoulder and squeezed encouragingly before resuming his seat.

The sun beat down mercilessly as Lance stood before the microphone gazing out at all these people who looked like they might want to be won over, but weren't sure. He spotted numerous TV news crews in the back alongside Helen and Charlie, both local and national, filming everything that happened and, Lance knew, hoping for some kind of gaffe on his part, something they could use to goose their ratings. He didn't plan on making any gaffes, but he did suspect what he had to say would make the top of that night's news shows.

"Good morning, Texas!" he shouted excitedly into the mic, throwing a fist high into the air.

That got a cheer from the kids in the crowd who shouted back, "Morning, Lance!"

Lance grinned broadly, excited about what he planned on saying. "I've heard that Texans are straight shooters," he said. "You say what you mean, none of that PC crap like we got in Cali. That true?"

Now the entire crowd erupted, adults along with kids, with a resounding, "Damn straight!"

That made Lance smile even more broadly. Reyna and the others sat behind the podium exchanging looks of uncertainty since none of them knew what Lance was up to. Even Edwin didn't know. He sat beside Sylvia squirming in his light blue jacket and tie.

Ricky and Chris exchanged a quick smile since they did know where Lance was leading this conversation.

"I'm real happy to hear that," Lance told the crowd when they'd settled, "Cuz I have a question for you. I've seen online lots of comments from adults that us kids haven't paid our dues to this country enough to have earned any real rights under the Constitution, that we should just be grateful to live in the greatest country in the world. Some of those comments came from Texas." That got a laugh. "So tell me the truth, you grown-ups out there, how many of you agree with that?"

Most of the hands rose quickly into the air.

Straight shooters, Lance thought to himself with a smile.

"That's okay by me," he said, not turning when Reyna gasped behind him. "But I wanted to share some info with you that I found on the Internet. I never learned it in school and probably you kids out here didn't learn it either. I guess it just wasn't considered important."

He smiled sweetly and slipped a folded sheet of paper from his pocket, tantalizing the curiosity of the crowd by slowly unfolding it and spreading it onto the podium. Then he looked at the expectant, suddenly interested throng before him.

"We all know the historical significance of The Alamo behind me," he began. "Hell, I even heard it mentioned once in my eighth grade history class." That drew a big laugh. "Two hundred fifty brave men holding off an invading army of fifteen hundred. But did you know there were brave kids fighting here, too, fighting for Texas?"

There were murmurs from the crowd, especially amongst the kids, which emboldened Lance.

"Now we don't know the exact ages of everyone who fought and died here that day," he said somberly, "but we do know that at least two boys my age fought on this very spot for the Texas you all know and love. And one boy was only a little older than my brother here." He put a hand on Chris's shoulder. "Just eleven years old." He paused to gaze out at their keenly interested expressions. "Of course, those kids just fought for Texas. Nothing to do with the Constitution, right?"

The confused reactions of the crowd heartened him.

"But wait, I have more useless info that schools don't think us kids need to know. In World War II, at least two hundred fifty thousand boys my age or younger fought against Germany and Japan, fought *for* the Constitution. A lot of 'em died. There was even a twelve year old named Calvin Graham in the Navy who got a Bronze Star and a Purple Heart for valor, but his medals were taken away when the government found out he wasn't of age while defending that Constitution."

There were gasps of surprise from the crowd, and the kids sitting on the chairs and standing around the perimeter were riveted, their eyes big as boiled eggs.

"What about World War I?" Lance continued, on a roll and feeling confident, wondering what his mom thought of his "teacher mode." He glanced at his notes before continuing. "The draft started in 1917 for men twenty-one to thirty, but there was a bad flu bug that hit that age group hard, so the congress decided to lower the age to eighteen, where it stayed. Suddenly, us teenagers were real important to a country whose main document didn't include them. Amazing how that happens, huh?"

He grinned sweetly again. His voice remained steady, without a trace of sarcasm or snark. No, this one he needed to play straight, the way Texans liked it.

"Now the Civil War, that was a biggie for us kids. It was even called the Boys War cuz so many of us fought and died. These are the numbers for the Union side. Oh, for anyone out there who went to L.A. public schools, that was the side fighting *for* the Constitution."

There were a few chuckles, but more of the people looked awed as Lance went on.

"During those four years, eight hundred thousand boys seventeen and under fought, and many died. Two hundred thousand sixteen year olds fought, one hundred thousand fifteen year olds, three hundred aged thirteen or under and there were twenty-five who were ten – Chris's age -- or younger." He paused a moment, his intense green eyes almost shimmering beneath the hot sun. "I didn't know any of this, did you? Course I went to school in California so…." He shrugged and let the thought trail off.

The adults in the crowd were glancing around, especially at the children scattered in amongst them, as though seeing those kids in a new light. Lance hoped and prayed that's exactly what they were doing.

He grinned again. "Hopefully you don't find all this history stuff boring? Do you kids?"

"Hell, no!" came a shout from way in back, and that got a big laugh from the crowd.

Lance laughed, too.

"Cool, cuz the War of 1812 was amazing. There was this nine-year-old in the Navy named—" he checked his notes "—David Farragut, who was a midshipman appointed by President Madison. He fought in the war, commanded grown men, got taken prisoner by the British and finally ended his Navy career at the age of twelve. Pretty cool, huh? A nine-year-old given a Navy ship by the president. Wow!"

He heard lots of murmuring amongst the kids in the crowd, and also noted that their parents' eyes were as wide as the kids'.

"But none of these kids count for much, right?" Lance asked, letting the question hang in their air like a storm cloud. "I mean, they were just fighting to defend the Constitution. They didn't help create it."

He paused yet again for dramatic effect, thrilled that heads craned closer to hear every word.

"Except they *did* help create it. The American Revolution. Did you know there was no age limit if a boy wanted to fight, though fifteen was the preferred one? George Washington had so much trouble keeping grown men in the army he took anyone who was willing, including thirteen year olds. And a lot of us kids were willing. A lot of us fought to create this country, and yet when that amazing piece of paper called the Constitution was written, we were just property again. Man, you grown-ups have worse memories than us kids. We been here all along, defending this land with our blood, sweat, and tears, but we still haven't earned the right to be real human beings under the *law* of that land." He scanned the silent, stunned faces. "*Now* how many of you think we haven't paid our dues?"

Not a single hand went up this time, and Lance turned to Ricky and Chris. Both boys beamed with pride. Then he turned to cast a look back at the others. Reyna blew him a kiss, Arthur and Jenny nodded proudly, Ryan and Gibson both grinned, Edwin nodded with stunned approval, and the mayor sat with his mouth hanging open. Lance threw him a thumbs up sign and grinned. The mayor couldn't seem to help himself and grinned right back.

Lance turned to face the crowd. The kids were grinning at him, many flashing a thumbs up, while their parents and the other adults looked at him with a combination of wonder and bewilderment. Lance decided to ignore Edwin's advice and go for broke.

"Since you've all been so cool and so straight up with me today, I'm going to give my political adviser Edwin a heart attack right now." He paused as he heard Edwin suck in such a sharp breath that the sound wafted out over the silent gathering, drawing the eyes of many toward the young man in blue seated behind the podium.

"From what I know of Texas," Lance went on, "most of you are probably pro-life. Am I right in thinking that?"

The crowd was clearly caught off guard a moment, but only a moment. The Texan aplomb quickly kicked in and this time the adults shouted, "Damn straight!"

Lance nodded in acknowledgment. "And what is the main argument people on the other side use for wanting every kind of abortion to stay legal?"

A woman seated in the front row vigorously raised her hand and Lance pointed to her. "Yes, ma'am?"

The woman stood and said in a voice laced with anger, "They claim that a woman can do what she wants with her own body. But the baby in her womb isn't her body, it's a human being made in the image and likeness of God."

Much applause greeted her comment and, obviously feeling vindicated, she resumed her seat.

Lance pretended to contemplate her statement, though he'd expected something like that. "So you're saying that the child inside her *isn't* her property?"

The woman stood again. "Hell, no!" she spit out to more enthusiastic applause before she sat again.

Lance once more appeared to mull over her words. "Then why is the biggest objection to our Children's Bill of Rights that children are essentially the property of their parents and the CBOR takes that ownership away? If, like you said, ma'am, we're not property *before* we're born, then why are we property *after* we're born?"

He stopped, pleased that he'd rehearsed that part the night before. One wrong word on such a controversial subject could lose him the entire state. From the stunned, but wide-eyed, looks on the faces of almost every adult present, Lance knew he'd not struck out or even hit a triple. He'd hit it right out of the park.

The same woman stood, grinning from ear to ear, and looked at Lance with such admiration he nearly blushed. He knew Helen and Charlie were recording him and fought back the urge. He was way too old for such foolishness.

"Sir Lance," she said with probably more deference to a teen than she'd ever shown before. "You are exactly what some people on the Internet say you are, a gift from God. I don't know about everyone else here, but you are right on the money and your bill of rights has my vote."

She began applauding. That broke the stunned silence of the crowd, and then everyone was up and clapping, vigorously and wholeheartedly this time. The kids whooped and pumped their fists into the air.

Lance beamed.

Ricky leaned in and whispered, "Young Mr. Lincoln strikes again."

That caused Lance to laugh and shove Ricky playfully, with Chris joining into the tussling. Their playful antics charmed the crowd, and the gathering effectively came to an end. The mayor gave Lance a look of amazement as he concluded the appearance, but assured the crowd that Lance and the others would be mingling amongst them to chat, so if people wanted to hang around they could feel free.

Amidst the chaos that followed, Lance, Ricky, and Chris found themselves surrounded by Dakota and Kai, Ryan, Gibson, and Brooks as the crowd swamped the three boys for autographs or stickers or just to shake their hands. The remaining Secret Service agents surrounded Arthur and Jenny as they made their way among the people accepting congratulations on their success. More than one parent complimented them on "That fantastic kid you got there." Arthur and Jenny wholeheartedly agreed with such sentiments.

Lance signed hundreds of autographs, shook so many hands his own felt like he'd been swinging a broadsword for three straight hours, chatted with admiring adults and gushing kids, and even accepted umpteen kisses to the cheek from fawning girls, which embarrassed him but amused Ricky to no end. Kai and Dakota also found the attention from girls flattering and funny. The four posed for numerous photos as The Native Knights, and many an admiring kid would ask for pictures with one or more of them, especially Lance. But Ricky had a Team Ricky following of his own, and many a girl wanted a shot with him alone, which made Lance happy to see. Finally, after what seemed like hours, the four rejoined their fellow knights near the front entrance to The Alamo and Lance found himself face-to-face with Edwin.

The young man eyed him curiously from behind the designer glasses, causing Lance a moment of hesitation, almost like Edwin was angry at having his instructions ignored. But then the moment vanished, the mild-mannered Clark Kent reappeared and Edwin grinned broadly. "I'm still having that heart attack you gave me, Lance," he said with a laugh, clutching at his chest dramatically.

The awkwardness of the moment before gone, Lance laughed too. "Still think Texas is a lost cause?"

Edwin shrugged. "We still have the legislators in Austin, but let's just say you may well have out-Lincolned Lincoln."

Ricky grinned at Lance, who grinned right back. For all he'd heard about Texas, Lance had almost been afraid he'd be shot on sight. But these people were straight up and welcoming. And not a peep about "the gay thing." So much for media accuracy, he decided. But then, he'd learned about media bias the hard way in L.A. and didn't need any reminders.

†††

Lance had been correct in his thinking that his remarks would make the top of the news, especially those about abortion. Of course, he had not come out as pro-life or pro-choice and didn't intend to, as he told the reporters who interviewed him before the group departed the Alamo. It was too contentious an issue, he told them. When prodded by Helen for some kind of stand, Lance answered, "I'm pro children not being property. You can read into that whatever you want."

And read into it the pundits and the public and the various political factions did with a vengeance. Each side tried to co-opt him and his words to their cause, but his statements had been so purposely ambiguous that they engendered more debate than they did any actual commitment to a particular viewpoint.

However, his historical lessons on the contributions of kids to the protection of the country during wartime had galvanized even more children and teens to the cause than before, and quite a large number of adults. Commentary raged on the Internet and talking head shows about the whole "Children as property without real rights" concept, inspiring many a pundit to bring up slavery in their passionate defense of Lance's position.

All in all, it had been a stupendous day, in Lance's estimation, with support for him and the cause more increased than decreased. And they hadn't even hit the state capitol yet!

Dinner that night at a big, family style rib place in downtown San Antonio turned into a raucous affair. Patrons swarmed around the group all evening, shaking hands, wishing them well, having pictures taken with their favorite knights or ladies. Esteban glowered every time some hotshot young cowboy wannabe cuddled in close to Reyna for a picture, but she just flashed her lovely smile and told him to stop being so jealous. That got a laugh from everyone but him.

Given that this was Texas, country music abounded, playing in the background almost everywhere the group went in San Antonio, and Merlin was in country music heaven, eliciting mocking jibes from the young people. He smilingly ignored their comments and absorbed the country atmosphere around him with intense pleasure.

The response of Texans was overwhelmingly positive toward Lance and his message. However, after one large group had swarmed the table, gotten pictures, been given stickers and encouraged to hit up their legislators, Lance discovered one of the restaurant napkins had been left on the table near where he and Ricky were sitting. On it were scrawled the words, "Faggots go home!"

Ricky instantly glowered and swept his fierce gaze around at the patrons, almost daring anyone to fess up. This time Lance remained the calmer, gently touching Ricky's arm in a soothing gesture and saying, "There's an asshole in every crowd." He casually tossed off the beautiful smile that practically melted Ricky every time he saw it, and all was suddenly well once again.

The remainder of the dinner passed in a fun, uproarious fashion as everyone joked and ate, and Techie sent phone pix of the event to Sir Phillip for posting on their website and Facebook pages. Even Dakota laughed and goofed around with Kai, stealing food from his plate, stealthily pulling his braids so Kai would think Lance was doing it. Kai laughed and shoved Dakota's long, freely hanging hair into his face whenever he tried to put food into his mouth.

Arthur felt good as he sat with his wife and his family, a sense of pride and deep success wafting over him that this Camelot would thrive, unlike the first one. He marveled to himself at how far Lance had come from that skinny, wary boy he'd met in a dark alley one night, and how masterful Lance had become at uniting people to his way of thinking. *He's better at forming coalitions than I ever was*, the king thought, turning to look at Merlin. The wizard seemed to sense Arthur's eyes on him, and met them with his own. As though he knew what Arthur was thinking, he raised his glass of wine toward Lance in tribute. Arthur grinned and did the same. Lance didn't even notice.

†††

The group packed everything up the next morning for their hour and a half trek to Austin, the state capital, where Lance would address the state lawmakers that afternoon. The mood on board the bus was jovial and spirits remained high. Since they were nearer to big cities, most of them could get Wi-Fi on board, so Techie and Justin chatted with Ariel and Bridget during the journey, excitedly sharing details about the trip and getting updates from back home in the process.

Lance and Arthur kept up a regular contact with Sir Phillip and Mayor Soto about New Camelot business and were continuously assured by both that everything was "Just fine." The mayor indicated he and Sam were working on "A big deal," but couldn't say any more just yet. That piqued Arthur's curiosity, but he trusted both men and didn't worry in the least.

The session at the Austin State Capitol building with both houses of the legislature went surprisingly well, thanks to Lance's speech at the Alamo. Apparently, from what Edwin and some of the lawmakers told him afterwards, his remarks in San Antonio had satisfied many of the objections the representatives personally felt toward the CBOR, and after a couple of Town Hall meetings with citizens the day after, Lance smirkingly shoved Edwin as the last of the crowd filed out and said, "Still think we don't have Texas?"

Edwin laughed and playfully shoved Lance right back. "I'll never underestimate you again."

The group piled back into the bus for yet another happy dinner filled with glad-handing and photo ops. This time, there were no nasty notes slipped Lance's way, for which he and Ricky were grateful.

Since Dallas was en route to Oklahoma, Reyna had booked them lodging for a one-full day, two-night stay in the famous city. The journey was a scant three hours, and Dallas boasted some historic sites, like Dealey Plaza where President Kennedy had been assassinated in 1963. Once checked into their hotel, the group traveled to this landmark and took a tour of the Sixth Floor Museum. Standing at the window from which Lee Harvey Oswald had shot the president, Lance felt a chill envelop him from head to toe, so much so that he pressed in close to Ricky for warmth and security, but was careful not to make it look like a PDA.

Ricky glanced over uncertainly, but Lance just shook his head, meaning they'd talk about it later. But what was there to talk about? Many a politician he'd met along the way had adopted Mayor Soto's nickname for him - Young Mr. Lincoln. And, of course, Lincoln had been assassinated. Now here he stood gazing down at the spot where another president had been murdered, and his mind swirled with the attempts already made on his own life and the promise to end it before November. He hated these premonitions, but couldn't stop them from coming. Turning quickly from the window, Lance hurried to another part of the museum, Ricky and Chris trailing him with concern.

Their town hall meetings the next day proceeded with great success. There were as many kids as adults at the get-togethers, and many a question reflected his comments made in San Antonio, or even his previous remarks about Little League World Series players not being paid. For all of the media posturing about the people of Texas being hard-nosed cowboy types, Lance found them to be friendly and welcoming.

Suddenly their sojourn in the Lone Star State came to an end as they packed up and headed north into Oklahoma.

†††

As a direct result of Lance's well-publicized comments from Arizona, Utah, Idaho, and Texas, the meetings with state legislators in most subsequent states went smoothly and without incident, largely because Lance had already addressed in earlier appearances many of the questions these people had concerns about. Over the next week and a half, the knights received warm welcomes in Oklahoma, Kansas, and Nebraska, both from the legislators and the people.

Lance and Ricky noticed random people staring at them oddly in all of these states, and it didn't occur them until later that most likely those people were watching to see if the boys did anything "gay" with each other, which made them laugh. The fact that most of the people they met loved them and never even mentioned "the gay thing," even when they attended mass along the way, buoyed his hopes that maybe by simply being themselves they were breaking down some of those barriers of ignorance that still infected many parts of the country.

While no one outside the Round Table knew that Dakota and Kai were also a couple, the two Natives got curious looks from people for being Indian because they wore feathers in their hair and some article of tribal regalia, even when dressed in knightly attire. Kai always laughed these off, and Dakota had, too, until the tour moved closer and closer to South Dakota. As that state drew nearer, Dakota's mood grew darker, his face more cloudy, his demeanor one of dread and anxiety.

As Lance continued his regular check-ins with all the knights whenever the bus was in transit, he began paying special attention to his Native brother because of the obvious funk he'd sunk into, and because he knew Dakota might soon start looking for alcohol to calm his unsteady nerves.

During the three-hour drive from Lincoln, Nebraska to the Pine Ridge Reservation, Lance switched seats with Kai for a while so he could chat with Dakota. Kai slid in next to Ricky and they instantly began laughing and playing around, which slightly bothered Lance in an irrational way. The two boys were much more alike in temperament than he and Ricky. His emo moods better suited Dakota. And yet, Ricky complimented him just as Kai's sunny spirit complimented Dakota, and Lance knew Ricky loved him more than anything. So why did it irk him to see them having such a good time without him?

Shoving aside his annoying anxieties, he turned to the silent Dakota, a boy who'd grown into a man before his eyes, a troubled man who'd accomplished so much greatness, and yet wallowed in the single worst thing he'd ever done because that 'thing' was forever.

Dakota's steely eyes remained fixed on the flat, boring landscape outside the bus window and he didn't turn his head until Lance said, "You really want a drink, don't you?"

Dakota's eyes fell on him and pierced Lance to the soul with their pools of pain. "A whole bottle," Dakota whispered, bowing his head in shame. Like Lance, he hated displaying a hint of weakness.

"I get that," Lance replied quietly, for once not sure what to say. Dakota's guilt couldn't be assuaged because there was no way to fix what he'd done.

"They won't let me on, Lance," he said soberly, with a sigh.

Lance frowned. "On what?"

"The rez." Dakota met Lance's gaze. "I am dead to them."

Lance put a hand on Dakota's shoulder and squeezed slightly the way Arthur always did for him. "If you don't enter, none of us will. Trust me on that."

Dakota nodded, but didn't look any more appeased. Lance distracted Dakota for a while with questions about tribal customs he was likely to see on Pine Ridge, and then went back to Ricky so Kai could be with Dakota for the rest of the journey.

†††

Lance spotted a large, handmade wooden sign with carved white letters proclaiming "Entering Pine Ridge Indian Reservation, Land of the Oglala Sioux" before seeing the standard green and white state-issued sign declaring the same. He glanced over at Dakota, who face looked drawn and tight, his hand gripping Kai's with knuckle-whitening intensity, his eyes narrowed and filled with fear. Lance nudged Ricky, who pulled his eyes from the sparse, empty landscape outside the window and looked over at his two brothers.

Kai attempted to quietly soothe Dakota with inaudible words and the warmth of his body pressed against him, but Dakota looked like one of those old dime-store wooden Indian statues Lance had seen on TV sometimes, except he was real, and frozen with terror. The sight of him looking so scared and diminished touched Lance's heart with deep sadness.

The empty, brown grasslands surrounding the bus seemed to go on forever until finally another official state sign declared "Pine Ridge" in bold white lettering against the standard green background. Everyone craned their heads to see as much as possible out the windows, everyone but Dakota who stared straight ahead as though mesmerized.

Lance spotted some outlying buildings amidst the continued sprawl of brown grassland, and looming just ahead was an enormous white water tower on stilted legs that reminded him of the aliens in *War of the Worlds*. Painted in huge black letters across the face of the water tank were the words, "Pine Ridge Indian Village."

As more of the village came into view, all chattering on the bus ceased, and mouths dropped open in shock. The dilapidated dwellings, most of which looked like they'd been built from the kind of junk the kids used to collect from the city dump, made any ghetto in L.A. look like Beverly Hills. To call these homes ramshackle would be to compliment them. Lance glanced at Ricky and saw the same look of appalled stupor on his face. He glanced around at his stunned fellow knights, most of who grew up in city-neglected squalor. But nothing this bad.

Like Many Farms, paved roads were absent – only the one they were presently on. The rest was dirt, with homes and businesses scattered haphazardly around. There was no sense of organization or planning, almost like everyone had just been dumped there and told to make their homes from whatever junk they could find. Old cars, rusting and beat up, sat in the hot blazing sun in front of this crackerjack-box home or that one. Old tires and trash lay strewn about.

They cruised past what looked like a new children's jungle gym sitting amongst overgrown weeds and garbage, including the back seats of an old car that Lance surmised people had put out so maybe they could sit and watch their kids at play. Or maybe it had just been tossed away because there was nowhere else to put it. Bringing back memories of his own childhood in poverty, Lance felt heavy of heart and soul, especially when he saw graffiti scrawled all over the play bars and on the walls of run-down businesses they passed. Gangs on the rez? Dakota hadn't told him that. Next to one house they spotted a man sprawled on the ground, arms splayed out, either drunk or dead. No one was around to notice.

"This is way worse than anything in L.A.," he suddenly heard Darnell say in an awed voice, but one filled with such empathy Lance had to make sure it was Darnell who'd said it.

"That's fer sure," Justin added, just as quietly and with the same amount of reverence.

"I never knew people lived like this," Reyna whispered, her hand in Esteban's, her head resting against his shoulder. He nodded silently. Yeah, he thought he'd grown up with nothing, but he'd been a millionaire compared to the kids living here.

Suddenly the bus came to a halt in what could have been the middle or the end of town – it was hard to tell without any organization to the layout. Agent Andrews, driving the bus, turned to Arthur seated behind him. "Looks like a welcoming committee, Arthur."

The king stood and Jenny stood beside him. They gazed out the dust-covered windshield at a large group of Indians gathered in front of the bus. Some were old, some middle-aged, some teens and some children. The youngsters carried bows nocked with arrows. All of them stared at the bus with hard, intimidating looks, their sun-drenched features impassive and cold.

Jenny turned to Arthur nervously. "They invited us, didn't they?"

The king nodded. Then suddenly, silent as a cat in a graveyard, Dakota was beside him, Kai, Lance, and Ricky close on his heels.

"It's cuz 'a me, Arthur," Dakota said quietly and shamefully, as though disrespecting the king was the worst thing anyone could do. "I told you."

Arthur turned to face the young man and offered a gentle smile. "And so you did." He turned toward the others standing and awaiting his orders. "The rest of you remain on board. The native knights shall accompany me." He gave Jenny a quick kiss, squeezed her hand, and then nodded to Andrews, who swung the big handle that popped open the collapsing door.

Arthur dropped down the steps and onto the dusty, cracked pavement. He'd been forewarned by Dakota about the reception they'd likely receive because of him, and so he'd had taken the unusual step of ordering his knights to dress in their Round Table attire, despite the extreme heat. He wished to make the strongest impression possible on Dakota's people. Thus, he was dressed in a light purple tunic, brushed brown leather pants and his knee-high boots. He wore a circlet to restrain his hair, rather than a more ostentatious-looking crown. The Native Knights were similarly attired, save for the scattered feathers tied to Dakota's flowing hair and the dangling feathers Kai had strung around his braids.

At Kai's insistence, and because they thought it looked cool, both Lance and Ricky, in addition to their normal gold circlets, had taken to tying two feathers in their own hair, one at each side of the face. At first Lance objected when Kai pushed the idea, saying he and Ricky were not really of any particular tribe and didn't want anyone to think they were mocking Indians. Kai insisted, however, saying they may not know which tribe they sprang from, "But you're native. My *má* said so, and if *má* said so, it's true."

So now the four boys stood behind Arthur as the king stepped toward their welcoming committee. Kai, Lance, and Ricky surrounded Dakota for protection, just in case.

"Greetings from New Camelot," Arthur offered with a respectful bow.

One of the elders, a man with skin like old boot leather and long, gray-white hair stepped out in front. He wore a flannel shirt, jeans and boots and Lance had no clue how old the guy might be. He had that ageless look to him, sort of like Merlin if he'd gone the aging hippie route.

"*Taŋyáŋ yahípi*, King Arthur," the man said, his voice sounding like sandpaper, as he offered a slight bow in return. "You and your knights are welcome here." Then he pointed one gnarled finger straight at Dakota. "But not that one. He must leave."

Several of the teen boys in the group raised their bows, which made Lance flinch and silently curse himself for stepping off the bus unarmed. He glanced at Dakota, whose eyes remained downcast, hair covering his face, his body taut with tension.

Arthur acknowledged the man's words, and the youths' threatening gesture, with a nod. "I understand. However, Sir Dakota is an invaluable member of my company and has personally, on more than one occasion, saved the lives of my sons at the risk of his own. Thus we shall all be leaving. Thank you for inviting us."

He turned and ushered the boys back toward the bus. Dakota's eyes flew to the king anxiously and he looked like he wanted to protest. But a voice from the crowd of Indians stopped him where he stood, froze his heart and nearly ceased his breathing.

"Let him in," the voice said coldly, without inflection or emotion. It was a woman's voice. As Arthur turned back, Lance caught sight of a small, wiry-looking middle-aged woman with long, gray-streaked hair standing at the edge of the crowd, arms folded tightly across her chest, eyes squinting with a mix of emotions he couldn't quite pin down. The youths with the bows lowered them deferentially.

Dakota turned, too, and met the gaze of his mother from across the space between them. Her face, so hard and impassive, and so like his own, froze him in place. Then without another word, she turned and started down the dusty street alone, long hair trailing behind like a horse's tail, and never looked back once.

Dakota resumed breathing as he felt the warmth of Kai's hand gently brushing against his, but his eyes never left the retreating back of the woman who had given him life, and who now wished him dead.

Lance turned from Dakota to Arthur, awaiting the man's decision. As though nothing untoward had occurred, Arthur bowed again. "In that case, we shall be honored to join you. *Philámayaye.*"

The old man seemed surprised Arthur knew something of their language, but his face remained so impassive that only Lance caught the flicker of approval. Of course, Dakota had taught Arthur some key words, like the "Thank you" he'd just offered, and the king seemed especially adept at picking them up.

The old man said, "We have arranged for your company to be housed amongst us for the night. Villagers have offered their homes so that each one of you will have a roof over your head. Except him."

He didn't have to point this time. Everyone knew who "him" was.

Impulsively Kai stepped forward to Arthur's side, keeping himself between Dakota and the tribe. "Don't worry about *him*. *Him* and me can sleep outside. We're Indians."

The old man squinted at Kai, but made no response. An elder woman stepped forward to the man's side and gazed at Kai intently before offering a crinkly smile of recognition. "Is that young Kai Begay, the boy who dances like a dream spirit?"

Kai frowned, his anger still near the surface. "Yes, *winuhcala.*"

"Your mother is my friend," she said, as though that was all Kai needed to know. And apparently it was all she would reveal. He couldn't tell from her inscrutable expression if she thought he was a disappointment to his mother for siding with Dakota, or a likely source of pride.

The old man invited Arthur and his entire team to the Billy Mills Hall to meet with the villagers and the tribal council of elders. There would be refreshments and talk about their bill of rights.

Arthur thanked them and looked over at Lance, his eyebrows raised, asking the silent question Lance already knew – did he wish to add anything?

Lance stepped forward, bowing respectfully. "We look forward to meeting with your tribal elders, but we will not accept your kind offer of shelter for the night. As the brotherhood of the Round Table, we stand by our own. If Sir Dakota sleeps outside, we all sleep outside."

The green of his eyes almost glowed in the harsh sunlight as he pinned them to the elder.

"As you wish," the old man said quietly.

But Lance caught something in his tone, a flicker in his hard eyes. Admiration, maybe? He wasn't sure, but bowed again and returned to stand beside Arthur. Dakota cast him a look of gratitude and Lance tossed off a quick grin that almost made Kai laugh.

At this point, Lance waved the other knights on out of the bus. Everyone exited and followed the silent group of Indians up the cracked pavement, through the squalor of their village, to an area that almost looked like paradise by comparison. Here sat a few newly built homes resting lazily amongst the brown grass, and a large complex painted red and green, with the name "Billy Mills Hall" in big letters above the entrance.

Dakota walked stiffly with Kai on one side and Lance on the other, his head bowed in shame. As other Indians joined them, no doubt out of curiosity, Lance felt all of their eyes falling on them, and knew Dakota was the object of their intense interest. To distract Dakota from the scrutinizing, he leaned in to him and whispered, "Who's Billy Mills?"

Dakota glanced up at him, slightly startled at the interruption to their silent procession. Then he smiled ever so slightly, and Lance knew he understood why the question had been asked. His body posture relaxed a bit as he leaned in to Lance's ear and said, "The most famous of us. He won a gold medal at the Olympics in 1964 and later became a Marine."

Lance nodded, his mind considering the degradation behind him in which these people lived. Such was the gratitude, he supposed, of America to a people who brought them such prestige, and for a man who had served his country with honor. No matter how long he lived, he would never understand politics, or adults in general, even as he fast approached adulthood himself. Once more he silently vowed to never take people for granted.

Everyone gathered inside the basketball gym, notable to Lance and the other city kids for its white floor, rather than the standard brownish color they'd always seen in every other gym. There were lots of high windows letting the punishing sunlight into the facility, a strip along the walls depicting triangles aimed in both directions, and high on one wall hung what looked like a tapestry of a circle with ten triangles extending out from it. To Lance it looked like a crown had been pressed flat and mounted. Above this was painted in black, "Oglala Sioux Tribe."

Four long fold-out tables had been set up corner to corner to form a large square, and plastic chairs with the letters BMH painted on their backs surrounded these. The bleachers were extended as though for a game. Most of the villagers, Lance noted, headed for these bleachers, including all the children and teens, while the elders moved to join other elders already seated at these center tables.

The older man who'd initially addressed Arthur indicated which seats had been designated for the king and his wife. Arthur indicated the seat on his other side to Lance, who immediately stepped forward, Ricky at his side. Dakota held back, and Kai with him. Lance paused at his chair to look back at them. Dakota's eyes were on the elders, and their eyes were pinned to him with a cold detachment that chilled Lance's heart and almost made him shiver. Throwing protocol to the wind, he stepped back to Dakota and gently took his arm, leading him to the seat right next to Ricky, and near to the elders who would conduct the meeting. There were muted gasps from the villagers in the bleachers, and Dakota's brown face paled instantly. But Kai was there at his other side for moral support, and Lance offered a smile of encouragement. Reluctantly, Dakota sat as all of the other knights took empty chairs around the tables and awaited whatever was to come.

The elders introduced themselves to Arthur and seemed only interested in speaking with him. Lance didn't mind not being the center of attention for a change, for it allowed him to study the elders' inscrutable faces and the unreadable expressions of those in the bleachers, including kids his own age. He was shocked to hear that over sixty-one percent of the kids on Pine Ridge lived below the poverty line and that life expectancy for males was only forty-eight! Yeah, that seemed ancient to Lance at his age, but he knew well enough it wasn't very old compared to the rest of the country.

Dakota kept his head bowed the entire meeting, never once lifting his eyes from the table. His hands remained in his lap, Kai's hand resting gently atop them. Lance felt anger well up within him at the way these people were treating Dakota. Especially when they bragged about how many of their kids at Red Cloud High School had gotten Gates Millennium Scholarships over the past few years. Those scholarships were hard to come by, and would fully pay for any university or college the winning kids wanted to attend.

That achievement was awesome, Lance knew, and worth bragging about, but sitting right beside him was a member of this tribe who had done incredible, heroic things and had, in his own way, accomplished much more than winning a scholarship, because his deeds were aimed at helping others, not himself. Yes, Dakota had done something terrible, but it wasn't on purpose and he'd been an alcoholic kid who was drunk at the time. Lance knew from sharing a room with him how much Dakota's brother haunted his dreams and caused him to toss and turn with anguish.

The elders thanked Arthur for amending the CBOR to specifically forbid the government taking Indian children away because of poverty alone. As he had on several occasions throughout the meeting, Arthur assured them it was Lance and

Ricky who'd made the changes, that it was them who'd conceived and written the CBOR, that he and Jenny had little input in its creation or the campaign to get it passed.

The elders nodded and exchanged looks, but did not address either Lance or Ricky directly. Often Lance caught one or more of them casting a baleful glare toward Dakota, and more than once he made to stand in defense of his Native brother. Each time, Ricky grabbed his hand and gently tugged him back down, giving him the look that always calmed him.

Jenny reminded the elders that the CBOR would only affect children at the federal level, that the state of South Dakota could still enact its own laws. Admittedly, it would be more difficult to restrict children's rights under the CBOR, she assured them, and Lance would address that issue when they appeared before state lawmakers in Pierre.

Finally, as the meeting neared its conclusion, Arthur turned to Lance. "Is there anything you'd like to say to these people, Lance?"

Lance was certain his father knew exactly what he wanted to say, and he caught both Merlin's and Edwin's looks of caution from across the table before he stood. On his feet, he looked the elders straight in their squinting eyes. "Is there any chance you guys have a TV and DVD player in this place?"

Arthur swallowed his smile, though Jenny looked mystified, as did the elders. Apparently, that wasn't the question they expected.

The elders exchanged a look, and then the one who'd originally spoken to Arthur in the street nodded to a man at the end of the table. He wore a white polo shirt with the letters "BMH" emblazoned across the left chest. The man rose and quickly exited the gym.

Lance stood at his place and said nothing. He imitated the impassivity of the Lakota people surrounding him and gave away nothing of his intent. A few awkward moments passed until the man returned, rolling what looked like a fifty-inch flat screen on a cart into the auditorium. He rolled the cart over to where the elders and those in the bleachers could see the screen, then unrolled the cord and plugged it into a socket on the wall.

Lance glanced down at Ricky and smiled slightly. Knowing what he wanted, Ricky reached into his pocket and slipped out a homemade DVD he'd grabbed before they'd abandoned the bus. He handed the DVD to Lance with a smile of encouragement that seemed to say, "Go get 'em."

Lance turned and silently strode to the television. All eyes were on him, even those of his fellow knights who, like the villagers, had no idea what he was doing. Reyna attempted to get his attention, like he dared to do something without informing her, but Lance merely smiled in her direction before turning on the DVD player and inserting his disc. Then he faced the elders and the people. From the corner of his eye, he caught a glimpse of Dakota peeking at him uncertainly from behind his hair.

"I wanna thank you all for hosting us today," Lance began, his voice strong and clear and deep. "But I especially wanna thank you for a great gift you gave me. This video I'm gonna show might bother some of you, so if it does I got no problem with you leaving. But I'm showing it so you kids my age and younger can see what a true hero looks like. We kids make mistakes and do stupid, dangerous stuff. I bet most of you have, just like me and Ricky, and everybody here in the Round Table who was a kid when we started this crusade. But kids always deserve a second chance, and the one in this video has more than earned his. Like the chaplain at juvenile hall once told me, we're better than the worst thing we ever did, because if we're not there's no hope for any of us."

Without another word, he turned on the TV and pressed play. As the video began to unspool, Lance caught a movement as the door to the gym opened and Dakota's mother entered, gazing expressionlessly at the assemblage before her eyes were drawn to the television.

Lance had asked Techie to edit together every bit of cell phone and/or newsreel footage of Dakota in action, and these scenes played out before a stunned and silent group of stoic Indians. There was cell phone footage of Dakota pushing Lance to safety as the window-washing gondola crashed to the pavement behind them; there was some footage of the chase through Griffith Park, most courtesy of a camera hidden within the remote-controlled copter that had pursued them; there was footage from the chase through the streets of Washington, capped off by Dakota's feat of heroic strength that saved Ricky from toppling off the Arlington House roof.

Lance noted that Dakota instantly looked down when he realized what was unspooling, but everyone else in the auditorium was riveted by the images. Despite their reticence about showing emotion, Lance could tell the teens and children felt excitement, even awe, at what they were seeing. It was obvious they knew nothing of what their tribal member had been doing since leaving in shame.

As Lance turned off the TV, a deep and heavy silence fell over the entire gym. He glanced over at Dakota and saw the boy's eyes fixed on something behind him. He turned to see Dakota's mother locking eyes with her son. Then without a word, she exited the gym.

With an inward sigh, Lance turned to face the people, not the elders. "I know Dakota the boy did something horrible by his drinking. I'm a drunk, too, if I let myself drink."

Some of the kids reacted visibly, especially the teens, and Lance knew instinctively that many had already started down the same path.

"But Sir Dakota the man is one of great honor and strength, a man I'm proud to have at my side, a man I'm proud to call my brother."

With that, he bowed to the people, and then bowed to the elders before resuming his seat.

Dakota's normally impassive face looked ready to dissolve with an equal combination of gratitude and mortification, and Lance merely smiled at him to remain calm. He turned back to the silent elders, noting with some measure of pride that the kids in the bleachers were murmuring excitedly, despite efforts by the adults to quiet them.

The chief elder stood, a signal for Arthur and his knights to stand, as well. The elder stared long and hard at Lance for a moment before sweeping his squinting eyes onto Dakota, pinning the boy in place and causing him to squirm with unease.

"Your DVD was most enlightening, Sir Lance," the man said in his gravelly voice, revealing not a shred of emotion within those words. "May we keep it?"

Lance eyed him right back, determined to be respectful, but not cowed. "Yes, sir."

"Thank you." The man called the meeting adjourned.

†††

Outside Billy Mills Hall, the elders went on their way, leaving only the locals and the kids hovering about. The young children seemed fascinated by Lance, no doubt because of his miraculous resurrection, and many just touched him shyly before running off toward one of the many hovels they called home.

The teens, all of whom dressed in standard t-shirts, jeans, and bandanas, with quite a few boys looking banged out, surrounded Lance and the other young knights, eyeing them with the same hard, mad dogging glare as the elders.

Justin and Esteban shook their heads sadly, and Esteban said, "You guys oughtta lose the gang shit. It won't work any better out here than it did in the city."

He took Reyna's arm and they started back to where the bus was parked. The Indian boys, and a few girls, said nothing in response to Esteban's remark, but anger flitted across one boy's tatted face.

"He knows what he's talkin' 'bout," Lance said with a sigh. "Best way out 'a the slum is to fix it up yourselves, like we done in L.A. Don't wait for the old folks to act. Just do it, and they'll follow *you*."

The teens opened their eyes wide with surprise at his words, the first real show of emotion Lance had witnessed on this reservation. He offered a tight smile before nodding his head toward the others and they all followed after Esteban and Reyna. As they walked, Dakota kept his head down, Lance surmised, so he wouldn't have to look any passing Indians in the eye.

Suddenly, Dakota stopped, nearly causing Lance and Ricky to crash into him.

Kai stopped and turned back, a look of concern on his face. "You okay, Cloudy?" he asked breathlessly, the worry he clearly felt slipping into the tenor of his voice.

Dakota kept his head lowered. "I gotta see my brother."

Ricky sucked in a startled breath, but neither Lance nor Kai reacted. They both knew Dakota couldn't leave the rez without seeing Chayton.

"I'll go with you," Kai instantly offered.

"Me and Ricky too," Lance added firmly, as though arguing was out of the question.

Dakota looked up in stoic gratitude, expelled a deep breath, and then began walking again, this time crossing the street toward a dilapidated one-story home smaller than Kai's back on Many Farms, and way more run-down. Nothing but weeds and dirt and several truck tires covered what Lance assumed was the front yard. There were several stairs leading up to the front door, with an old and rotted wood bannister that looked ready to give way at any moment.

Dakota climbed those three steps as though ascending the gallows to be hanged. He stopped before a dirty, splintered door that looked like it had several bullet holes through it. Expelling another breath of fear, he gingerly raised one fist and knocked three times.

Lance and Ricky exchanged a nervous look as Kai placed one hand lightly on Dakota's trembling shoulder. The door suddenly swung inward, and Dakota's mother stood framed within it, long hair streaming down the front of her stained work shirt, flinty brown eyes scrunched with instant animosity.

"You are not permitted here." Her voice was ice and fire rolled into one.

Dakota hesitated, and Lance saw with shock that the boy was terrified.

Dakota could not meet her intense gaze, but kept his eyes lowered to the hard, rough-hewn floor beneath her feet. "I just wanna see my *sunkaku*."

Her eyes narrowed even more, and the hate poured forth from her mouth like vomit. "You mean what's *left* of your little brother, don't you?"

Dakota nodded slowly, head still bowed in shame. "*Yé / Ičhé, ina.*"

Lance remembered that word from when Dakota was teaching Arthur some basic phrases – it meant "please." Dakota's mother glared at her son so severely that Lance was certain she'd slam the door in his face. But she stiffly stepped to one side. "Five minutes."

Dakota hurriedly stepped through the door. She glared at the other three as they followed, making Lance feel uncomfortable and unwanted. But Dakota needed his brother and his brother needed him.

The interior of the house looked even more squalid than the exterior. A ratty stuffed chair rested against one unfinished wall. The table beside it was made up of some kind of stand with a sheet of plywood on top to set things on. At the moment it was covered with coffee mugs, a few plates, some candles, and part of a lamp that Lance suspected didn't even work anymore.

Beside the chair on the other side was a pile of bricks on which rested a CD/tape playing boom box that looked older than him. It was scratched and dented, with wires sticking out, and Lance surmised it only worked as a radio, if even that. The unfinished walls were scrawled with childish drawings and stick figures, no doubt created by young children, Lance thought, maybe even Dakota as a little boy.

He allowed Kai to follow Dakota past a dirty kitchen with plates and pans piled in the sink, while he and Ricky brought up the rear. Dakota stopped outside a battered door covered with scratches and more childish scrawls. He kept his eyes fixed on that door, never once turning to look at Kai or him or Ricky. Lance could read the body language well enough, even without his soul-whispering skills. Dakota looked ready to break.

Gripping the knob with one trembling hand, he turned it, pushed the door inward and stepped inside. The others followed. The bedroom was tiny, with only a beat-up twin bed sporting a ripped mattress, a little table with one leg slightly shorter than the rest atop which sat an ancient table lamp with no shade. To keep the lamp from sliding off the table, Lance noted, it had been duct-taped down.

But what caught and held his eyes was the pajama-clad boy in the wheelchair. The wheelchair looked like something a hospital might have discarded years before, so torn up and dented it appeared, and the teenaged boy was strapped into it by a belt around the waist. Unlike Dakota, his hair was short, though whoever cut it didn't take much care with the clippers, as it was uneven and ragged.

The boy tilted his head up when they entered, and Lance almost gasped. He looked so much like Dakota it was eerie. Same angular features, same prominent nose and cheekbones. But what instantly distinguished this boy from the young man trembling before him were the eyes. Chayton's eyes looked dull and without light, and drool slipped unheeded from his grinning mouth as he clearly recognized his brother.

"Kota," he said in a childlike voice, the very sound piercing Lance's soul and forcing his hand quickly into Ricky's.

Kai gazed with horror at this boy who he hadn't seen in over five years, while Dakota stumbled forward and dropped to his knees before his brother. His face a mask of pure anguish, Dakota barely managed to croak out, "Hey, Chay."

The torment in his voice yanked Lance's heart into his throat, but he couldn't pull his gaze away from the reunion.

The younger boy grinned foolishly, the lack of intellect written all over his slack face and dull eyes.

"I missed you," Dakota said, struggling to get the words out, obviously fighting to maintain control.

The grin grew bigger. "Missed Kota."

Dakota sucked in a breath, fisting his tunic desperately to keep from cracking. "I brought Laughs a Lot," he managed to get out. "He's still a dope."

Lance watched as Kai leapt to Dakota's rescue. "Hi Chay," Kai said as cheerily as he could, flashing a big smile. "Good to see you again, man."

Chay grinned back and Lance was sure the boy didn't even recognize Kai. Seeing that Dakota was losing it, he quickly stepped forward.

"Hi Chay, I'm Lance," he offered with his own bright smile, "and this fool is Ricky." He tugged Ricky forward and the two boys both smiled down at him. Lance knew Chayton had to be at least seventeen or eighteen by now, from what Dakota had told him, but the face and soft body indicated a much younger child.

It must've been the simple-minded grin and bare realization that people were even in the room that finally broke Dakota. Lance was shocked to see tears dribbling down the normally stoic face of his Indian brother.

Chay noticed too. "Kota cry?" His voice sounded soft and innocent and gentle.

Dakota nearly gagged as more tears began to flow and his hands flew to the arms of the wheelchair, gripping them like he wanted to snap them right off. "Just happy to see you."

Chay laughed. "Happy. Big brother."

Lance thought Dakota would break in two he looked so brittle. But the young man fought desperately for control. "I never told you, Chay, back when you could understand," he said haltingly, pausing a moment to blink back a fresh round of tears. "But I love you, bro. I love you so much!"

Lance didn't think Chay's smile of delight could get any bigger, but it did. "Love Kota," he said and clapped his hands together excitedly.

Lance's breath nearly stopped, and tears burned his eyes.

Dakota gagged audibly, more tears leaping unbidden from his puffy eyes to roll unheeded down his face. "I'm so sorry for what I did, Chay, I'm so sorry! I know you don't understand me, but if I could do what Jack did for Lance, if I could switch places with you, I'd do it in a second."

Now Kai choked back his own impending sob as he fixed his wide, fearful eyes on the one he loved. But Dakota couldn't pull his gaze from the feeble remains of the brother who'd once been so strong and vibrant.

"You'll never have a life cuz 'a me, Chay, never get married and have kids and be happy," Dakota went on in a voice filled with intense sadness and regret. "I know you don't hate me like everyone else, but I wish you would. I deserve it."

Chay just looked at him uncomprehendingly. "Hate?"

Dakota nodded. "I hate myself, Chay, but I promise you I'm never drinking no more." He paused as another sob worked its way up from his chest into his throat. "I'm gonna help our people, Chay, so no drunken piece of shit like me can ever again hurt kids like you. I promise."

Chay grinned more broadly. "Love Kota," he said, and spread his arms wide for a hug.

Lance almost lost it and gripped Ricky's hand so hard it hurt them both.

Dakota gagged and more tears fell to the dirty, unfinished floor at his feet. He opened his own arms and enveloped the boy in a fiercely tight hug, and Chay lovingly returned it.

They remained that way a few moments while Kai, Lance and Ricky looked on, all of their eyes watery, their breathing heavy with pain.

A cleared throat startled Lance and caused him to whip his head around toward the door. Dakota's mother stood there like a statue, cold and hard and unflinching. "Your five minutes are up. Now get out."

Dakota released his brother and turned to face their mother. She showed not the slightest emotion at his tears, even though Lance suspected she'd been there the whole time.

Dakota nodded silently and stood. He gazed soberly down at the boy in the chair, and then lovingly wiped a string of drool from his chin. Leaning down, Dakota kissed Chay gently on one cheek. "Love you, bro."

Chay smiled so broadly that Lance thought Dakota might faint from weakness. But the young Indian turned back to face his mother, who raised one hand to usher them out of the room.

Ricky and Kai exited the house first and stopped just outside as Lance followed close behind. They walked part way out into the street to give Dakota some space as he exited, but Kai and Ricky were ahead of Lance when Dakota finally stepped onto the porch and down the three creaky steps to the dirt lot.

Lance turned and moved back toward the house instinctively, watching as the young man turned to face his mother, who stood framed in the doorway like a macabre painting.

Dakota wiped tears from his face and looked at his silent mother. He said quietly, "*Ina*, do you still wish it was me instead of him?"

For her part, her flinty, hard eyes didn't even waver. "Yes."

Dakota's heart nearly stopped, his breath hitching in his throat. He nodded. "I know I don't deserve to have a life after what I done, but Laughs a Lot loves me and makes me happy." He hesitated, as her squint grew more pronounced. "When we get back to L.A., I'm gonna marry him." He fought to maintain his gaze. "You're invited."

Then he turned and walked toward Lance standing a few feet from the house. Behind Lance he could see Kai and Ricky standing together watching him uncertainly. Dakota shook, his whole body trembling with need. When he reached Lance he looked desperately into the younger boy's eyes.

"I need a drink, Lance," he hissed breathlessly. "More than ever. I need a whole fuckin' liquor store, man!"

Lance grabbed him by the shoulders and forced their eyes to meet. "No, you don't," he asserted calmly and fiercely. "Everything you need is standing over there, right next to everything *I* need." He forced Dakota to look past him at Kai and Ricky. "He'll share your pain, like Ricky shares mine. Let him."

Dakota turned back to Lance, his eyes wide with comprehension. He nodded, and turned to walk haltingly over to the man he loved.

That was Ricky's cue to leave Kai and walk to Lance's side. Together, they watched as Dakota stopped before the anxious young man, and Kai patiently stood there, taking his cue from the other.

"I need to ride, Laughs a Lot," Dakota finally said, his voice harsh and quiet at the same time, the voice of pent up energy and rage needing an escape hatch. "Ride with me."

"You got it." Kai held out a hand. Dakota eyed it a moment before taking it, and the two walked purposefully down the street.

Ricky turned to Lance, and then stopped up short, something behind the boy catching his attention. Lance turned to find Dakota's mother staring intently at him from the doorway. There were maybe five feet between them, and Lance felt the intensity of that gaze like a laser beam.

"So you're the boy who came back," she said, her voice flat and devoid of emotion.

Lance nodded uncertainly. "Uh, yes, ma'am."

"I heard you do miracles," she said, never taking her piercing eyes off him.

Feeling shame at his impotence, Lance shook his head sadly. "I wish I could," he said quietly, but earnestly. "I wish I could help your son."

Never breaking eye contact, she said, "You already have." Then she turned to re-enter the house, closing the door behind her.

Lance and Ricky exchanged a surprised look, both realizing that she wasn't talking about Chay after all. She was talking about Dakota.

†††

By the time Lance and Ricky got back to the bus, everyone had already hauled out sleeping bags and other camping accoutrements they'd brought from home, having anticipated that they might hit some remote areas and need them.

A few of the younger Indians were hanging around chatting with Esteban and Justin and Techie when the boys arrived. The Indians, wearing flannels and bandanas, looked to be around fifteen or sixteen. Lance gave them the chin nod and said, "You guys see Dakota and Kai? They said something about riding."

One of the teens, the older, harder-looking one, smirked. "Yeah, we seen 'em. They took a couple of horses from Uncle Billy's place." Then he snorted. "Never figured Dakota for a homo."

Lance bristled instantly, Ricky tensed up, and Esteban took a step forward in case of trouble. "It's Two-Spirit, not homo," Lance said sternly, but with more calm than he felt. "You got a problem with that?"

Lance's eyes blazed with fire and he must've looked scary because all the teens backed up a step. The one who'd made the slur glowered, but said nothing more. The younger one spoke this time. "It's cool. You wanna go find them? I can get you some horses, show you which way they went."

Lance nodded. "Yeah, that'll work."

"I'm going too!" Chris said quickly, leaping around Arthur and Jenny and running to his brothers.

Now the adults stepped in, first Ryan, then Gibson, with Arthur and Jenny right after. "Not so fast, Lance," Ryan said quickly. "You boys aren't going anywhere without protection."

Lance and Ricky both pulled faces. "Out here? Who'd try to hurt us out here?"

Gibson scowled at the Indian boys with their sagging jeans. "How about a bunch of gangbanging Indians who hate Dakota's guts?"

The young Indians at first looked offended, but then just shrugged and looked at Lance. "He's right," said the one who'd offered the horses.

Lance sighed and looked at Arthur and Jenny. They bore the same resolute expression, and Lance knew there was no point in arguing. Then he grinned and eyed the two sergeants with amusement. "You guys ever been on a horse before?"

The two men exchanged a sudden look of startled realization.

Lance smirked. "That's what I thought."

"Plus," Ricky put in, "we figured we'd grab our bows and arrows and sleep out all night with them, you know, real Indian stuff." He winked at Lance, who grinned broadly.

The two middle-aged men looked so comically flummoxed that even Arthur laughed, and the Indian teens simpered derisively. Lance crossed his arms over his chest, eyeing the two men, and fought back his laughter. Ricky, he knew, could barely hold it together, either.

"Go for it, Pop," Justin said out with a laugh, slapping his father on the back good-naturedly. "It'll be fun." Then he busted up and high-fived Darnell with glee.

Gibson scowled and turned to Ryan defiantly. "We got this, right?"

Ryan, Lance noted, looked nauseated at the notion, and nodded unconvincingly. "Absolutely." He cast Lance a look that almost made the boy lose it completely, but he suppressed the burst of laughter. He couldn't even look at Ricky or he'd bust up for sure. After the painful experience with Dakota at his mother's house, it felt good to laugh. Perhaps, Lance thought to himself, the presence of the two obviously-out-of-their-element cops might even bring a smile to Dakota's sad face.

"Okay, guys, let's get our stuff and roll," he said with a big grin. "Horses are waiting, right guys?"

The Indian boys, mere moments ago seemingly antagonistic, were now suddenly one with Lance and Ricky, in on a joke at the expense of grown-ups. "You got it, man," the youngest one said with a grin.

Lance, Ricky, and Chris leapt up into the bus to grab their bows and quivers of arrows, and Ricky snatched up a small backpack and stuffed snacks and bottles of water into it. Ryan and Gibson, dressed in slacks and short-sleeved button down shirts, still stood by the bus, unsure about what to do or even bring. It amused Lance that both men, always so together and on top of things back in the city, could be so confounded out here in the country.

Chris handed Gibson a sleeping bag while Lance tossed another to Ryan. He clapped the man on one shoulder reassuringly and in a dead-serious voice said, "Don't worry, *nino*, us native boys'll take care of you."

Ricky laughed and Ryan flashed a nasty smile. Lance, Ricky, and Chris laughingly hugged both parents, kissed Jenny and told her "Don't worry," and then followed the chuckling Indian teens up the street, leaving the others behind.

†††

They found Dakota and Kai sitting on a raised outcropping of rock gazing out over the most amazing sight Lance had ever witnessed, even more incredible than the Grand Canyon. Rock formations of staggering beauty and variety and color rose before him as far as the eye could see, and the rocks glowed reddish gold in the light of the setting sun. He looked at Ricky and Chris and saw the same expression of wonder on their faces. It felt like they were on another planet. The air was hot, but a slight breeze wafted Lance's hair and cooled the sweat on his neck and chest from the ride out.

The local teens had saddled up horses for all five and didn't even attempt to restrain their laughter when Ryan and Gibson awkwardly struggled into their saddles after several failed attempts. Lance tried to show them as Arthur had shown him with Llamrei, that you mount from the left and swing your right leg up and over, but the two men were more accustomed to patrol cars than four-legged animals. Lance would rib both men for days thereafter about how comical they looked, especially since he'd captured their antics on his cell phone for the rest of the team to enjoy.

Lance and Ricky hadn't been on horses since that time in Griffith Park a year and a half before, but took to the animals rather quickly, and the horses to them. Rather than give Chris a horse of his own, the smaller boy rode behind Lance on his, causing both of them to momentarily flash back to the night they'd first met in Long Beach and returned to the storm drains in a similar fashion.

The Indian teens pointed to the north and explained that Dakota and Kai should be visible if the group kept in that direction. They did warn, however, not to stay out after dark if they didn't find the other two, but to head back into the village.

Between them, Lance and Ricky got lots of pictures of Ryan and Gibson haltingly kicking and flicking the reins and attempting to get their horses to cooperate. Gibson, especially, kept grumbling, "Damn horse doesn't like me," which made the boys laugh every time.

Lance spotted two horses tethered to an old, gnarled thing that maybe had been a tree once upon a time, but there was no sign of Dakota and Kai. He dismounted with Chris, and the others followed suit. After all the horses were loosely tied to something and left to forage for the meager bits of available grass, Lance led the group forward into this amazing wonderland he'd never known existed.

They found their two brothers sitting together, heads resting against each other, watching the setting of the sun in all its reddish-gold splendor. Lance cleared his throat and the two turned in startled terror, leaping to their feet and grabbing for their bows. Upon seeing Lance and the others, Kai laughed and playfully shoved an embarrassed Dakota.

Lance grinned and approached them, Ricky and Chris in tow. The two cops hung back awkwardly, eyeing each other and scanning the surrounding terrain for possible threats.

Lance stopped before Dakota and locked eyes with him. "How ya doing?"

Dakota slipped one arm around Kai's waist, pulling the young man in closer. "You were right, like always. He took a lot of it."

Lance understood. "But it'll never go away. So keep him close and remember what I said to your elders. You're better than the worst thing you ever did."

Dakota eyed Kai a moment, the two men pulling in so close they were practically one, causing Lance to soul whisper that something significant had happened between the two Indians. And he was pretty sure he knew what.

Lance smiled and said to Kai, "Did he ask you yet?"

Kai grinned and nodded.

Lance smiled. "So, you're gonna marry this fool when we get back to L.A.? Wow."

Kai laughed like always, but unlike most of his laughter this was one of joyful expectation. "Damn straight!"

That drew a laugh from all three boys, and Chris let loose a whoop of joy. "All right!" he called out, his voice echoing back slightly from the surrounding hills and rock formations, and then he high-fived both Kai and Dakota.

Dakota looked at Lance with deep respect and admiration. "Will you stand with me, as my best man?"

Lance broke into a grin of pure delight and gushed, "Hell, yeah."

Dakota smiled and his face lit up beneath the reddish gold dusk like a painting.

Kai eyed Ricky with a grin. "So how 'bout it, Ricky? You up for being *my* best man?"

Ricky looked momentarily surprised, but then grinned happily. "You got it, bro."

Lance found his eyes drifting to the almost alien landscape spreading out before him. The setting of the sun only enhanced its beauty. "This place is badass!"

The Indian boys chuckled. "It's Bad*lands*," Dakota said with reverence.

"No," Lance reiterated firmly, his eyes still on the horizon. "It's badass."

Dakota laughed then. "No, that's its name, Lance. The Badlands."

"Good name," Ricky said, and all of them stood in silence, Ryan and Gibson, too, as the sun dappled the rocks and ridges and outcroppings with soft, glowing blues and yellows and reds as it slowly settled down past the horizon, leaving behind the beginnings of a star field such as the boys, and the older men, had never seen before. They must have stood, and then sat, in that same place for an hour as the sun retreated and the stars exploded onto the canopy above like magic.

Ricky held Lance's hand and Lance held Chris's while Kai and Dakota cuddled against one another. Ryan and Gibson, too, remained speechless as the majesty of nature took their voices and made it seem almost irreverent to even breathe loudly.

Ricky finally whispered, "Now I've seen two things more beautiful than you, Lance," to which Lance responded by a gentle push of shoulder against shoulder.

Once night had fallen and the grandeur of creation had made its mark, the boys rose to set up camp for the night. Dakota and Kai showed the city boys "The Indian way," and they delighted in this new knowledge. All five went hunting with their bows and arrows while Ryan and Gibson struggled fruitlessly to start a fire the way Dakota had instructed.

Lance, Dakota, and Chris all managed to target rabbits in the dark, and these were brought back to their camp where a laughing Kai took about a minute to light the fire the two sergeants had futilely failed at for an hour. The Indians showed their brothers how to skin and cook the rabbits, and then all of them ate the cooked meat with their fingers. Lance marveled at the taste, having never eaten anything so fresh before, and he could tell even the older men enjoyed the unusual fare.

After eating, everyone sat around the fire and the Indians told stories of the old days, of their ancestors, mostly sad stories because so much injustice had been done to them. But there were funny tales, too, and tales of undying love that touched Lance and Ricky and pushed them closer together as the night wore on. When it came time to sleep, Lance, Ricky, and Chris all cuddled up together near the fire, while Dakota and Kai did the same. Perhaps feeling awkward around the kids, and not liking the hard ground, Ryan and Gibson slunk off a few feet distant to find a less rough "bed" on which to lay out their sleeping bags. The night air felt warm and comforting, the stars soft and soothing, the fire warming, and it all combined to lull the boys into a quiet, dreamless sleep. The two sergeants, however, hated every minute of the experience, and Gibson, in particular, now knew why he'd never taken Justin camping as a kid.

†††

Arthur and Jenny were up and getting organized early the next morning for their journey to Mount Rushmore, which Jenny insisted the kids should all see once in their lives. She'd been there as a girl with her dad and had never forgotten the astonishment she'd felt that such a feat as carving gigantic faces into a mountainside could be accomplished.

Everyone had slept outside, some in sleeping bags, but others on blankets spread out on the ground. The warm night air had felt soothing, and everyone slept well beneath the shimmering blanket of stars above.

None of the villagers had bothered with them during the night, but Jenny had been amazed and touched when numerous ladies dropped by at dusk with food and drink for them. Everyone had thanked these women, but they merely nodded in response as though this kind of silent hospitality was an expected part of the culture and no thanks were required. The food had been delicious and everyone had his or her fill. Even the bigger men like Arthur, Justin, and Esteban could eat no more. Full stomachs also aided them in a peaceful night's sleep.

They had the bus loaded by the time Lance, Ricky, Chris, Dakota, and Kai came bounding down the street, high on youthful energy and excitement. Jenny's heart lifted at seeing them, and especially at seeing them happy. It must've been a good night for all of them. But then her eye caught Ryan and Gibson limping painfully behind the boys, grunting and groaning in pain, their faces displaying every emotion *but* joy.

She nudged Arthur and the king stood with her and the other knights as the boys rejoined them. Jenny saw Arthur's happiness upon seeing his sons safe and sound and obviously content, and slid her arm into his.

Gushing with enthusiasm, Chris prattled on about their adventures and how he'd caught a rabbit and about Dakota and Kai teaching him how to be a "Real Indian." Lance and Ricky laughed, echoed their brother's sentiments, and enthused over the unbelievable beauty out in the Badlands.

That was when the wincing, grimacing sergeants joined them. "Well, James, Robert," Arthur said, barely able to restrain a grin. "How was camping out beneath the stars?"

The two men exchanged a look of utter disgust, and Gibson said, "I haven't been to Hell yet, so I don't have a good comparison."

That made Justin bust up and approach his father gleefully. "C'mon, old man, I'll help you into the bus."

Gibson glared so harshly at his son that everyone cracked up, and Justin threw up his hands dramatically. "Hey, I tried."

As Gibson limped toward the open door to the bus, Lance threw an arm around Ryan's neck, causing the older man to grimace in pain. "Well, my *nino* had a great time, didn't you *nino*?"

Ryan looked at Lance sideways, and sighed heavily. "Is there a retirement age for this godfather gig?"

Lance grinned and shook his head. "Nope. You're stuck with me for life."

Ryan nodded exhaustedly. "I thought you would say that." He patted Lance on the back and trudged tiredly after his partner, stepping painfully up into the bus and out of their sight.

Lance looked at Arthur and shrugged. Arthur laughed.

The villagers showed up to bid the group farewell shortly thereafter. They moved so quietly, Jenny noted, that she had no idea they were all there until she exited the bus and saw them. Even Dakota's mother was there, standing in front with the elders.

Jenny's heart lurched at the look of pain and loss in the woman's hard brown eyes. Lance had told her what happened between Dakota and his brother and she couldn't even imagine what the woman felt each and every day as she cared for her brain-damaged boy.

On impulse, she approached, while Dakota's mother stood rigid and impassive as always, no emotion of any kind dancing across her stoic features. Jenny knew words were worthless in such a situation, and she didn't have any anyway. So she gently leaned in and hugged her. At first, the woman stiffened as though Jenny's touch was forbidden. But after a few moments her body began to loosen and her arms came up and she returned the hug. They stood that way for several moments, sharing a feeling only mothers can share, and then Jenny pulled back. She was astonished to see dampness glistening in the other woman's eyes.

"Take care of yourself," Jenny offered with a sad smile. "And thank you so much for the gift of your son. I'd have lost mine if it wasn't for him."

She smiled again and then turned to walk back to the bus. Dakota stood in front with Kai, his gaze fixed on the woman who'd given him life. As Jenny returned to Arthur, she looked back at Dakota's mom in time to see the woman offer a slight nod to her son that Dakota gratefully accepted.

Arthur thanked the elders and they thanked him, and all the knights bowed in gratitude for the villagers' hospitality. The big Indian boy who'd called Dakota a homo stepped over to Lance and said, "We're gonna do like you said. We're gonna fix up this shithole, no matter what anybody says."

Lance smiled and extended a fist. The boy bumped it with a look of admiration in his squinty eyes.

Then everyone was into the bus and on the road again for the next leg of their journey. Lance had caught the head nod from Dakota's mother and felt that tiny gesture was their greatest accomplishment.

†††

The drive to Mount Rushmore took about two hours, during which Ryan and Gibson lay sprawled in their seats sound asleep.

The plan was to stop for lunch, check out the carvings of Washington, Lincoln, Jefferson, and Roosevelt, and then drive the rest of the way to the state capitol, Pierre, situated along the Missouri River. While all the city kids expressed gushing excitement at the massiveness of the carvings, even jaded boys like Esteban, Justin, and Darnell, Dakota and Kai hung back scowling slightly, drawing Lance's attention. While Ricky lifted Chris onto his shoulders to carry him around, Lance listened as Dakota explained that the Black Hills belonged to his people and they had never appreciated having the faces of their oppressors looming over them.

Lance sighed sadly as he saw the weight of Dakota's ancestry mirrored in the boy's hard eyes. He'd never thought of it like that, but the Indian perspective made sense from their historical vantage point. He knew from studying history that human progress always seemed to trample on somebody. It had always been that way, and human nature wasn't likely to change any time soon.

When Ricky rejoined them he set Chris down and they stared up at the startlingly detailed carvings, in awe of the artistry and engineering prowess that had created them. Ricky turned to Lance with a smirk.

"What say we petition Congress to put your face up there?" he said, grinning. "At least then one of them would be beautiful."

Lance blew out an exasperated breath and shoved Ricky hard. "Fool."

After a leisurely lunch in the picnic area, everyone piled back into the bus for another three-hour drive. Justin couldn't help ribbing his dad at every opportunity as the man limped and groaned his way around the memorial and then back into the bus.

Ryan had paired up with Merlin and the two of them explored the memorial together. When Lance kept playfully razzing Ryan for being old and out of shape, the detective sighed and shook his head wearily. "Did Arthur wear you out as a boy?" he asked the old wizard.

Merlin's eyes twinkled with amusement. "You don't know the half of it."

Ryan chuckled and they rejoined their fellows at the bus.

†††

The statehouse in Pierre was one of the nicest Lance had seen yet, though its basic design mimicked all the others: huge dome in the center, enormous colonnaded entrance, elongated rectangular three-story buildings spreading out from the center. What set it apart were the more elaborate, ornate touches to the dome and the fancy carvings in the stone facade.

The interior of the house chamber resembled the others except that it was long, rather than round in shape, with rolltop desks and cloth chairs for the lawmakers. There was even a row of desks up the center aisle. Lance, Ricky, Chris, and Dakota entered in the usual fashion, but from up front this time rather than from the back. Everyone else had been seated in the upper galleries all around the perimeter of the chamber. Lance had insisted Dakota accompany them because this was his home state and much of what he wanted to talk about involved the Indian population. As always, Helen and Charlie stood near the front so Charlie could record whatever Lance had to say.

Once he'd been introduced by the Speaker of the Assembly, Lance launched into his prepared remarks about the need for children's rights and in particular, Indian children's rights.

He looked out at them with passion, his voice filled with intensity. "The CBOR is going to pass, with or without South Dakota. We'd love you on board, but whatever. What I really want to know is, why is Pine Ridge worse than any slum in any city in this country? You mean to tell me that there's not even left over wood and nails or furniture or tools and any volunteers among all your people out there who could help fix that place up and make it look like humans live there instead of rats? Hell, we take care of L.A. better than anyone takes care of those Indians. And don't tell me it's about jurisdiction or some crap like that."

He saw eyebrows shoot up in surprise and scowled. "Yes, I know that word. I'm not stupid. And jurisdiction has nothing to do with people stepping up to help their neighbors. That's called kindness, and last time I looked, *kindness* was free."

The lawmakers and spectators who filled the gallery sat in stupefied silence, obviously flummoxed by Lance's remarks. Finally, one female representative raised a hand and Lance pointed to her. "Yes, ma'am?"

She stood and glanced around at her stunned colleagues before meeting Lance's gaze. "You're one hundred percent right, Sir Lance. Thank you for saying that." Then she tossed a defiant look toward a middle-aged man one row over who, Lance surmised, must be her main rival on the issues, before resuming her seat.

That's when the spectators in the gallery stood and began applauding, giving Reyna an excuse to whistle and cheer. After everyone finally settled back down, the lawmakers began asking serious questions, especially directed at Dakota about the needs of Pine Ridge and his people. Lance gladly stepped aside to allow his Native brother access to the microphone, at first fearful Dakota would faint dead away from being in the spotlight. But after he began talking about his life growing up on the rez, about his own alcoholism and poverty, Dakota relaxed, and Lance was heartened to see real interest on the part of many lawmakers in the chamber.

All things being equal, Lance felt good about the meeting and felt these adults took him seriously. That was a start, especially with Operation August Surprise ready to hatch very soon. Then, he knew, *every* adult would stand up and take notice.

†††

Chapter Five

I Thought It Was Called Politics

The next three and a half weeks were a whirlwind of travel that effectively ate up the month of August and gave the California kids a valuable appreciation for their temperate L.A. climate. It got hot in Los Angeles during the summer, but not swelteringly humid. Some of the knights had to change their shirts three times in one day because they'd gotten so wet! They hit North Dakota, Minnesota, Wisconsin, Iowa, Missouri, Arkansas, Louisiana (where all the kids felt both awed by and nervous about the fact that they were below sea level in New Orleans), Mississippi, and then into Memphis, Tennessee where, in addition to their usual political stops, they got a tour of Graceland. Lance and Ricky loved oldies and so seeing Elvis's home was fun.

During these weeks, both Dakota and Esteban would slip into funks because of what had happened with their parents, and Lance knew well those kinds of dark and brooding moods. Reyna and Kai were a great comfort to the men they loved, but Lance also knew guys needed action, something physical to do when such moods came over them. So he'd taken to arranging "duels" for the general public at many of their stops.

These mock sword fights would usually occur in public parks or in front of City Hall, somewhere that was monitored by city authorities. These "battles" provided the local populace a great opportunity to see the knights having fun and being physical, as well as disciplined, and rapidly became the most popular feature of these Middle America stops. And they always brought Dakota and Esteban back from the brink by engaging their muscles and clearing their heads of painful memories.

The stop in Springfield, Illinois served a twofold purpose: meet with the state legislators, as usual, and see the birthplace of Abraham Lincoln. Most thought it because everyone called him "Young Mr. Lincoln" that Lance felt such an affinity for the sixteenth president, but it was more than that, as he'd told Ricky back in Dallas. It was the fact that he'd been targeted for murder that he felt bound to the long dead chief executive.

They toured the Lincoln Presidential Library, saw the house where Lincoln lived before starting his political career, and even made a stop at the Old State Capitol where Lincoln had so successfully debated Stephen Douglas on the issue of slavery. But it was the president's grave that touched Lance most deeply, and everyone could tell the sight of it plunged the boy who led them into a dark place.

Lance stood in reverent, thoughtful silence gazing at the mausoleum that housed the president's body, oblivious to curious looks from tourists, barely even aware of Ricky beside him. The structure was shaped like a stone version of the White House, with stairs leading up on each side and a gigantic Washington Monument-like obelisk rising from the center. At the base of this obelisk, a metal statue of Lincoln stood looking out at the world, and a large bust of the president rested majestically in front of the entrance.

Even Arthur and Jenny knew not to intrude upon Lance's melancholy, and the milling tourists must have sensed the same, for none even approached the most famous boy in the world. When it came time to board the bus and return to their hotel, Lance allowed Ricky to lead him by the hand, despite their previous decision to avoid public displays of affection. Ricky, however, knew instinctively that Lance needed that basic human contact and didn't give a rip if anyone was offended or not. If anyone was, they said nothing and the group boarded their bus without incident.

The joint session with the state lawmakers went well. Lance had slowly come out of his funk as the previous evening wore on and became his usual combative self the next day. He reminded the lawmakers how unpopular Lincoln's stance on slavery was because so many Americans of that time believed black people were less than white and should rightfully be considered property.

"Now we kids are the new property, ladies and gentlemen, and it's time to change that," he announced at the conclusion of his remarks.

From the enthusiastic response and the large number of legislators who wanted pictures with Lance after the session, he felt good about their chances of winning Illinois. However, they still had a stop planned for Chicago, and that one could prove dangerous. Given the high rate of gang violence and killings in that city, Justin and Darnell, in particular, wanted to meet with local gang leaders and try to convince them that "Might for Right" could work in Chicago just as it had in L.A. Since most of these gangs were made up of African American youth, the two young men felt the need to try something. Arthur and Lance wholeheartedly agreed.

By the time they rolled into Chicago, the entire country, from sea to shining sea, was in the proverbial uproar. As they checked into their hotel amid a flurry of excited hotel guests flitting around snapping pictures and hoping for autographs, Helen pulled Lance aside to warn him that every major news outlet in the country was converging on the hotel within the hour looking for a statement from him.

Without even having checked the news, Lance knew what this was about. "So Operation August Surprise isn't a surprise anymore," he said with a chuckle.

Helen frowned at him for the first time since the crusade had formally begun with her interview in Eucalyptus Park.

"Lance, this is no joking matter," she said sternly, sounding more like a typical grown-up than ever before. "Not only is the United States the laughingstock of the world, educationally speaking, but you've jeopardized the educational futures of millions of kids."

Against his will, anger roiled up within him, and Lance nearly impaled her with his eyes. "I thought you were on our side, Lady Helen," he said tersely. "I thought you knew we're more than those bullshit bubble tests they make us take in school. And we are. I bet as a group we kids are smarter than most adults."

He knew he shouldn't be raising his voice against her, but he couldn't seem to control himself. She clearly looked hurt by his tone, but maintained her professional aplomb.

"You know I'm on your side, and I agree with you about most adults. But we're talking about kids' futures here, Lance. There must've been another way to make your point."

He folded his arms across his chest in a huff and snorted. "There wasn't. You didn't hear those arrogant senators and that house speaker blowing me off, acting like adults always act toward kids, like we don't matter. Well now they know who runs the school system, and the reputation of this country. Maybe now they'll take me and my CBOR seriously."

Helen frowned again. "*Your* CBOR?"

Lance flinched, but stood tall and rigid. "Yeah. I thought of it."

"And a lot of others helped you create it," she added softly, hoping to calm him.

His face fell slightly under her intense look, and he looked down at the floor in shame.

"What's wrong, Lance?"

He looked up and saw in her eyes how much she cared for him, even though it was in her job description not to, and sighed heavily. "Dunno, Lady Helen. I'm just tired of being ignored by those guys in Washington. Tired of them thinking they're hot shit and kids like me and Ricky and the others are nothing but street trash or worthless kids who shouldn't be seen or heard. I'm just, you know… tired."

He paused and sheepishly lifted his head to meet her steady gaze. "I'm sorry I got rude with you, Lady Helen. You've been the most awesome friend I had since the beginning."

She smiled then, which lit up her face. "I still am."

He grinned. "I know. Don't worry about the kids, Lady Helen. The kids'll be all right. Best to worry about the grown-ups."

That got a laugh out of her.

†††

By the time Lance and the others were checked into their rooms, Lance had received ten calls from the Senate Majority Leader's office and eight from the Speaker of the House of Representatives' office, all of which he let go to voicemail. He was learning this game of political one-upmanship better than he ever wanted to, and letting them stew in their anger could prove to be a useful tactic.

Once everyone had settled in, they gathered in the room shared by Lance, Ricky, and Chris so Lance could "return" their calls. Techie hooked his laptop up to the flat screen TV standing atop the bureau of drawers, and Lance used Skype to call the Speaker of the House.

Thus far, neither Arthur nor Jenny had said anything to Lance about the uproar, or about what he should say to these two most important of men. They trusted him to handle the situation as he saw fit, and merely stood back with the others to observe. Lance did notice a slight grin on Arthur's face as the connection was being made, and he returned it. Edwin, however, stood nervously bouncing on his heels, having warned Lance that a "Compromising tone of voice was needed at this stage of the game."

Almost at once, the screen filled with the images of the House Speaker and the Senate Majority Leader and a lot of other lawmakers Lance didn't recognize hovering in the background. These two men, both middle-aged and slightly graying, looked livid with rage upon seeing Lance's face.

"How dare you do this to the country!" the Senate Majority Leader spat. With his thin, weasely face he looked comical in his rage.

Lance remained calm. "Do what, senator?"

The man looked apoplectic and the House Speaker blurted, "You know perfectly well what! Don't pretend you're not behind this!"

Lance folded his arms casually across his chest and stood tall and regal, not cowed and not the least bit nervous, but not haughty either. "If you mean was it my idea, yeah, I take credit for that."

The senator said in a huff, "Thanks to your stupid prank the United States has fallen to number fifty-four among the fifty-seven industrialized countries in education."

"You have made the children of this country the laughingstock of the world!" the House Speaker spat like venom.

Lance calmly shook his head. "No, Mr. Speaker, we, the young people of the United States of America have made you and yours the laughingstock of the world, because everyone knows those tests are about you people, not us."

"By telling the children of this nation to fail those tests, especially those in high school, you have endangered their chances of going to college," the senator put in furiously.

"Like you care about our education?" Lance tossed back, his anger visible, but completely controlled. He knew how to play for the cameras just like these guys did. "All you care about is the money you make off of us when we go to college, and don't tell me different. Those tests mean nothing except how good we can memorize stuff, and we never asked to take them in the first place. You're gonna tell me the colleges will run on empty cuz they don't have those stupid test scores? Yeah, right! They might have to actually find out what we know before admitting us, but trust me, senator, they'll admit us."

The speaker shook his head. "You have no idea what you've done."

"Yes, I do. We've shown you who's really in charge of education in this country – us. The kids. The only people who have no Constitutional rights. What's crazy is you give Constitutional rights to illegal immigrants cuz you want their votes. But us, *we're* still property. Trust me, gentlemen, Operation August Surprise is only the beginning. The new school year is just starting and so are we, unless you give us what we want."

The lawmakers behind the two men chattered loudly and with great indignation, and Lance thought the senator and the Speaker might have coronaries right there on camera.

"This is blackmail, young man," the Speaker said with disgust.

Lance smiled for the first time. "Really? I thought it was called 'politics'. I look forward to meeting with you both when we hit Washington in October, and I can't wait to watch the voting. That should be cool. Bye now."

He flicked his eyes at Techie and the Asian knight killed the Skype feed, cutting the man off in mid-response.

Lance turned to the others behind him and found everyone looking at him in open-mouthed awe. "Well, how'd I do?"

Arthur grinned, Jenny smiled broadly, and the others started clapping and whooping, slapping Lance on the back and praising his "balls" for "Standing up to those assholes." Edwin's face looked uncertain, and Lance could tell the young intern thought he'd gone too far.

Reyna hugged him and stood back with a huge grin on her face. "Remind me not to get on your bad side, baby boy," she said laughingly. "You just out bad-assed me."

Lance laughed and turned to Ricky, who stared at him so adoringly, with so much love and admiration that Lance could barely restrain his hands. He felt an intense desire to grab his boy and kiss him. It must have been obvious in his eyes because Chris piped up with, "Oh, no, they're gonna kiss again. Watch out."

That drew a laugh from everyone, and it got Chris snatched up by both boys and tossed onto the double bed where he was tickled without mercy.

After a few minutes of roughhousing, Jenny broke up the three boys and told everyone to get cleaned up for the press conference. Helen had gotten the hotel to open up one of its conference rooms to admit the press corps now converging on the hotel, and Lance needed to get ready.

†††

The small conference room was not well suited to a national invasion, but that's essentially what it got. Admittedly, only national news outlets and those within the surrounding Chicago area could get to the hotel on such short notice, but the room looked jammed from wall-to-wall when Lance and the others entered.

Camera operators and reporters jostled for position as Lance calmly strode to the hastily erected podium amidst a frantic flurry of desperately tossed out questions. He turned to Ricky, who grinned and gave him "the look," and then back to the reporters who acted more like a junior high class than adult professionals. He stood and calmly waited until everyone settled down, a trick he'd first learned from Jenny way back at Mark Twain High.

Once everyone realized he was ignoring them, the reporters ceased their frantic pitches and stopped waving their arms like performing monkeys.

"Good afternoon," Lance began in a steady, strong voice. "I think I know why you're all here."

That got a laugh from the reporters and seemed to break the ice. Lance told them what he'd told the Senate Majority Leader and the Speaker of the House, knowing that his words were being carried live throughout the country. Unlike the angry tone he took with the men in Washington, however, here in his address to the American people he kept his voice and facial expressions even and calm.

Had the president called him yet, he was asked? With a smile he said, "No, but I expect him to any minute."

That got another laugh. They asked him how he managed to convince so many kids to participate and he said, "I didn't convince them. The politicians did, by ignoring our bill of rights."

"What's next?" came the obvious follow-up from a CNN reporter.

Lance looked straight out at all of them, and right into their cameras. Long gone were the days when he felt shy around television cameras. "More civil disobedience, just like Henry David Thoreau said to do. You kids out there watching, take note. School is just beginning. Don't do anything you don't want to do, so long as you stay civil and don't get crazy or violent. If teachers give you busy work that you already know how to do, don't do it. Make the teacher give you a real test, not one of those stupid bubble things, but one where you actually have to write something or compute math problems. If you pass their tests, you don't do their busy work, and you demand something more challenging."

He paused to catch his breath, sweeping his eyes across the sea of faces. "Try the silent treatment like we did in Cali if you think it'll help. Refuse to take any more bubble tests. Do what you have to do. Remember, we're not real people in this country and the school system doesn't make us look good or bad. We know we're smart. That system exists to make adults look good, and I say screw 'em. Don't give 'em what they want till they give us what we want. You guys out there want a sound bite, a headline, that's it. Message to Washington: give us what we want and we'll give you what you want."

Another hand flew up and Lance pointed to a reporter from Fox. "But the damage has already been done, Sir Lance."

Lance shook his head emphatically. "That kind of trivial damage can be undone real quick," he stated flatly. "Grown-ups wanna play with bubble tests and crap like that, fine. Give us what we want and we'll retake those tests. No problem." His eyes burned and his voice tightened with ferocious intent. "The kids of America have served this country in wartime since before the country even began. We've worked in factories, we've put up with the crap dished out by social services and schools and government in general. We've done everything except become real citizens under the Constitution, and we're gonna raise holy hell until we are! Any more questions?"

The facial expressions before him convinced Lance that his performance must've looked genuine because they all gaped and seemed reluctant to enrage him further. Except he wasn't mad. This business of the standardized tests was the tipping point, he knew, the point at which the country would bite the bullet and approve the CBOR or hunker down for a long fight. He had to look like he and his fellow youth meant real business. And he'd apparently succeeded. Even Helen's mouth hung slightly askew.

Tossing off a thin smile, Lance thanked the reporters for their time and questions, then turned to exit the room without a backwards glance, Ricky and the others scrambling to follow.

†††

Lance had not been far wrong. No sooner had he, Ricky, and Chris entered their room to get ready for dinner than the president called. Lance hadn't spoken to the most important man in the world since The Excalibur Incident, and even then, as always, it was on Ryan's phone since the two men conferred weekly on security matters regarding the tour.

This time, however, the president called Lance direct to his own phone. He exchanged a quick look with Ricky before answering the call on speaker mode. "Yes, Mr. President?"

The man's voice came out testy and annoyed. Lance was glad they weren't on Skype so the president couldn't see him and Ricky grinning like fools. "I'm disappointed in you, Lance, *very* disappointed."

"Why, Mr. President? Because your own kids wanted to participate except they go to private school?"

"They did?" The man sounded shocked, but then quickly recovered his political poise. "You've hurt the children of this country, Lance, which I didn't expect from you."

Lance sighed. He was tired of all this political posturing, so he just said what was on his mind. "Mr. President, the only people who got hurt are you and the congress and the other adults who want to use those tests to brag about how much good you're all doing. Those tests have never been about us."

There was a long pause, which Lance and Ricky calmly waited to end. *No way am I gonna offer the man anything*, Lance thought as he waited.

"We need to fix this, Lance," the president finally said quietly, his tone indicating he was ready to deal.

"That's easy, sir. Help us get what we want and we'll retake those tests and ace 'em, if the questions are actually about stuff we learned, anyway."

"I have no say in the amendment process, Lance," the president said cautiously. "You know that."

"True. But you got lots of friends in Congress who *will* vote. You're the president. They'll listen to you."

Lance and Ricky eyed one another, awaiting the man's response.

"You're a canny kid, Lance," the president finally said. "Smarter than most."

Lance chuckled. "I'm almost a man, Mr. President," he said proudly. "And there are tons of smart kids in this country. Adults just don't wanna see us that way."

Another pause. The boys waited patiently.

"I'll see what I can do." Then the call ended and silence filled the hotel room like a vacuum.

Lance and Ricky turned to one another, grinned broadly, and then high-fived with abandon.

"That's the boy I love," Ricky said with gleeful pride. "Just served the president of the United States."

Lance laughed and they high-fived again. "Correction," Lance added smugly, "the *man* you love."

Ricky laughed too. "You got that right. The most beautiful, buff-ass man in the world."

Lance couldn't help but smile as he shoved Ricky. "Fool."

And then they were kissing. It wasn't even a conscious decision. Their lips simply came together the way they were supposed to, and stayed together until Chris came out of the bathroom and chucked a towel at them.

"Break it up, guys," he said sternly.

Reluctantly, they did.

†††

The meeting with the gang leaders was set for the following day at noon, on the Southside of Chicago in a public park nestled within some city housing projects. Ryan and Gibson had insisted on broad daylight since they could easily be ambushed in the dark in unfamiliar territory.

As the bus trundled through the streets of downtown Chicago, Lance marveled at the beauty of the city. He'd known there were high-end neighborhoods, but when they passed into the poor sections of Southside, he felt horrified at the run-down tenements, the trash-strewn streets, the grafittied storefronts and homes. This area looked worse than most neighborhoods in L.A. that the crusade had cleaned up. But, he knew, if they could do it in L.A., the kids here could do the same.

Since they had no idea how many gang leaders or shot callers, or even just regular runners might show, Ryan and Gibson had gotten clearance from the mayor of Chicago for the meeting, and backup from the police chief. Justin had already alerted the gangsters that there would be armed protection, but it sounded like the young gang members, at least, wanted to meet the knights and hear them out. Lance did not expect any adult gangsters to attend, and that was fine with him. The adults were the problem, after all.

Despite it being summer, hot and humid, most of the gangsters wore solid color beanies and long-sleeved shirts. Their pants sagged and many sported numerous tattoos. Lance glanced at Esteban, Justin, and Darnell, the three ex-gang members, and could see they looked comfortable, back on familiar ground, as it were.

Justin stepped forward, Darnell to one side and Lance to the other. Esteban lurked behind them with Ricky, Reyna, and the others. Arthur and Jenny stood to the side of Lance, Jenny clearly looking more nervous than she had in ages as she clutched tightly to Arthur's arm. Ryan and Gibson and the Secret Service agents formed a semi-circle behind the group and other uniforms lurked in the shadows of the tenement across the street.

The smallest and surliest-looking boy stepped forward, the others forming a semi-circle around him. Lance flashed back to that night so many years ago in Griffith Park when Esteban had stepped forward in the same surly fashion to confront Arthur.

"So," the kid began, his voice filled with the boyhood his demeanor eschewed, "you come to tell us we a bunch a dumbass niggas who need a white man to make us smart?"

That caught Lance off guard, but he knew enough not to show it.

Justin, however, just smirked. "Hell no, cuzz. You don't need nobody to tell you what youse already be knowing."

The glowering boy, who Lance surmised couldn't be much older than fifteen, folded his arms across his rather unimpressive chest and said, "Yeah? And what that be?"

Justin shrugged, and then spread out his hands to indicate the Round Table. "That all us here used to be enemies, just like you all right there. We used to be killing each other and makin' the mayor and the cops real happy, cuz then they didn't need to do shit. But this man back here-" he tossed a thumb in Arthur's direction without breaking eye contact with the sullen youth "-he taught us some cool shit, ideas that work, like chivalry and might for right. And ya know what? Now we's all brothers and sisters here and we got real juice in L.A. We gots the mayor and city council calling *us*, we takin' charge 'a our hoods and workin' to keep 'em safe. Our little brothers and sisters don't need no cops walkin' 'em to school every day like you got here. *We* keep 'em safe. Youse all can thumb yer noses at them ideas cuz they come from a white guy, but last time I checked good ideas didn't have no color."

Lance found himself eyeing Justin in awe, and realized everyone else in the group was doing the same. He'd never heard the older boy say so much at one time, and now realized just how much Justin had grown up and how much of a leader he'd become. And his easy return to the street language he used to use when Lance first met him was also impressive.

The hostile teen eyed his enemies and homies gathered around him, and Lance could see a light dawning in their eyes, just as he'd seen it dawn in Esteban's in Griffith Park. Then the kid turned back to Justin, and the surly look morphed into one of hesitant uncertainty. "How we gonna do what you all been doing?" he asked. "You got somethin' we don't."

"What's that?" Justin asked.

The teen pointed. "Him."

At first, Lance thought the kid was pointing at Arthur, but when he looked again he realized the boy meant him.

"You gots the boy who come back," the kid finished, his tone that of an awed child.

Justin turned to look at Lance, who stepped out-front. He scanned the uncertain faces gazing at him from across the space of the small park, and smiled. "I *was* the boy who came back," he said sincerely. "Now I'm just a boy like you guys. If you need my help, even just to drop by and assist sometimes, all you gotta do is ask. But right now I'm focused on getting us kids our own bill of rights so we don't get kicked around so much anymore. Once I win this fight, and trust me, I'm gonna win, you give the word and I'll be back."

The kids exchanged more looks, and this time there were head nods of approval.

"But," Lance went on, "in the meantime you don't need me. Everything we did to take back L.A. is up on our website. Just copy us. You don't need me for that. You—" he pointed to the kid who'd done all the talking "-don't look much older than me when my Dad put me in charge. Pick your people, smart kids like you, to organize and bring all your neighborhoods together. Get with the Latinos and everybody else and start cleaning this place up. Remember, it's not us against them that works. It's just 'us'."

That light of revelation bloomed brighter now in the boy's wide brown eyes, and he tossed off a half-grin. Lance grinned right back. Though it had never been planned to get up close with these gangsters, Lance's soul-whispering skills kicked in, and on impulse he crossed the concrete space separating him from the black youth. He heard gasps from behind and Ryan's voice cracked like a gunshot, "Lance!" But he kept going and stopped right in front of the suddenly tense boy. His homies and their enemies in the semicircle had instantly moved their hands to their pockets or inside their baggy shirts.

But Lance wasn't afraid. He tossed off that ingratiating smile that no one seemed able to resist, and stuck out his hand. "Name's Lance."

The kid hesitated a split second before he grinned. "*Shit*, everybody knows that, man." Then he shook Lance's hand with a strong grip. "Jamil."

Lance pulled back his hand. "Member what I said, Jamil. You need me after the bill of rights gets passed and I'm here."

Now Jamil nodded. Then he turned, snapped his fingers, and the black youths slithered out of the park and into various shabby dwellings along the perimeter. Jamil followed, and just like that the meeting ended.

Lance turned and strolled back to his fellows with a big grin on his face. The Chicago police officers approaching from their observation posts looked stunned, but Ricky grinned in admiration, as did Arthur. Jenny grabbed Lance in a tight hug of relief, but Lance focused his attention on Justin. He sized up this brawny young man who'd once threatened to kill him, and liked what he saw.

"You did good, man. Gotta have you do more talkin' from now on." He grinned.

Justin laughed and they high-fived. Then Gibson proudly threw an arm around his son's shoulders. "Got all his smooth social skills from the old man."

Justin turned and pulled a "wtf" face, which got a laugh from everyone.

Then it was into the bus and back to their hotel.

Of course, the mayor of Chicago wanted a photo op with Lance and Justin and Arthur, with everyone else in the background. He publicly thanked the knights for hopefully jump-starting something with the gangs similar to what happened in L.A., and invited them back to his city at any time.

✝✝✝

The month of September flew by with reports coming in from all over the country about teens and younger children engaging in civil disobedience at school. From kids giving adults the silent treatment and refusing to do any homework that wasn't beneficial to mastery of the material, to refusing to sign up for the SAT or

ACT standardized tests or filling out any government-issued forms asking for race or ethnic information, the movement continued to accelerate.

After Chicago, the tour traveled to Michigan, both to Lansing the capital, and Detroit where there was much of the same gang strife as in Chicago. The legislators and most of the adults they encountered were far more hostile than before due to America's terrible worldwide educational standing, and the current state of countrywide civil disobedience by the children. Some legislators complained to Lance that their own kids weren't speaking to them and wouldn't until after Michigan voted for the CBOR.

As in Chicago, due to the predominance of African American gang members in Detroit, Justin and Darnell again set up the meetings and did most of the talking. Darnell spoke this time and proved as powerful a persuader as Justin had in Chicago. Lance had to do little but promise to make himself available as needed.

The remainder of the states had similar reactions to Lance and the entire movement. They sailed on through Indiana and Kentucky, and then back into Nashville, Tennessee, where Merlin felt like he'd gone to heaven with all the country music he encountered. He made everyone laugh when he bought a large cowboy hat and proceeded to wear it whenever the group was outdoors.

Both Alabama and Georgia tried to bring up "the gay thing" to distract Lance from his agenda, but it didn't work. Instead, Lance focused on the racial equality within the Round Table and how it should be a model for every state. In Florida, Lance lit into the justice system which put kids as young as ten on trial as adults, insisting that the CBOR was desperately needed by the children of this state to protect them from a clearly out-of-control system. Many people in Florida responded with great passion in favor of the CBOR, and even some of the legislators privately told Lance they would support it, but they also warned him that as a whole Florida was a likely toss-up.

The Carolinas and Virginias liked Lance's points about how the CBOR would give more weight to the argument that an unborn baby was not property any more than a child born was property, or at least wouldn't be if the amendments became law.

From there, they wound through Ohio and into Harrisburg, the capital of Pennsylvania. Mostly due to anger and frustration over the school situation, Lance found the lawmakers in both states ready to vote in favor just to get their kids to cooperate again. Maryland and Delaware also expressed similar sentiments. Then it was back into Pennsylvania to visit Independence Hall in Philadelphia because Reyna had arranged a rally there, and Lance wanted to get the kids of Philly fired up at the spot where the Declaration of Independence was signed. And fired up they were too. An enormous crowd filled the grounds of the landmark chanting Lance's name, waving American flags, and carrying banners with his face on them. Kids called out from the crowd what they were *not* doing in school and then other kids would high five them.

Lance must've signed four hundred autographs that day, but it was worth it to be part of such excitement, to know that because of what he'd put into motion the kids of this country had become passionate about the future, a future in which they might soon have a real voice, instead of continuing their status as passive puppets at the beck and call of grown-ups.

After Philly it was across the Delaware River into New Jersey and Trenton. In addition to meeting with the legislators as usual, Lance wanted to visit the site of George Washington's famous Christmas Day victory that had been the turning point in the Revolutionary War. Techie compared Lance to Washington, which prompted Reyna to chortle with amusement. "He's already Young Mr. Lincoln, Techie, don't make him Washington, too. His head will get too big."

Lance scowled as Techie laughed, and Reyna grinned. But, Lance realized as they toured the historic site, he *was* a little like Washington, leading his ragtag group of cast-off kids on what had once seemed a next-to-impossible crusade, but was now gaining momentum with each passing day.

New York City filled everyone with awe at its majesty and sheer height. Lance felt like his head would fall off his shoulders as he looked up and up and up toward the top of the Empire State Building. Its spire seemed to touch heaven itself. They all traveled to the top and stood out on the observation deck, stunned at the view and the magnificent beauty laid out before them, including the imposing Statue of Liberty standing guard at the entrance to Manhattan. Ricky got a huge laugh from tourists, as well as his fellow knights, when he declared, louder than he'd intended, "This is beautiful, Lance, but not as beautiful as you."

When the boys realized they'd been overheard, they looked sheepish, with Lance shoving Ricky as usual. They visited One World Trade Center and the 9/11 memorial, standing in silent reverence for the lives lost that day.

After NYC, they traveled to Albany to meet with the state lawmakers, and found them eager to vote in favor of the CBOR, which pleased Lance and Ricky immensely. All the New England States seemed to be in their corner, too, so the group just enjoyed the sights and had fun meeting and mingling with the local people.

Finally, it was the end October and the tour headed back toward Washington D.C. from Maine, after throwing Chris a little birthday party to celebrate his tenth. Everyone had fun and Chris loved being the center of attention, as always.

All along this last leg of the tour, Edwin had kept Senator Cairns abreast of what was going on, and the young intern had done his best to "Keep Lance under control" as he told the senator just before the group left Maine to head south. Cairns had merely laughed. They were Skyping on Edwin's iPad and Lance watched the senator over Edwin's shoulder.

"That's not true, Senator," Lance protested, giving Edwin a quick shove. "I had to keep *him* in line. This man likes clubbing, let me tell you."

"No thanks, I'd rather not know," Cairns returned with a chuckle.

Both Lance and Edwin shared a laugh at that.

The trip from Maine to D.C. would take ten hours in the bus if they went straight through, so they spent another two nights in New York City on the return trip and got to ride the subways some more, something the young people enjoyed.

Since Vegas, there hadn't been the slightest hint of trouble, and the Secret Service agents had clearly become bored with the entire journey. All except Brooks, who loved messing with Lance and Ricky. In New York he insisted they apply for the job of replacing the two stone lions guarding the Metropolitan Museum since they were a better looking matched set than the ones already there. He did lots of playful stuff like that, and the boys, in turn, would hide his shades and the little earpieces he was required to wear.

Perhaps it was the absence of anything threatening for the previous two months, or maybe it was due to the excitement everyone felt that eventual passage of the CBOR looked imminent, but when Reyna suggested that they all stop and have a picnic lunch at South Four Corners Park in Silver Spring, Maryland, just outside of Washington D.C, Arthur and the men guarding him agreed at once. It was a warm fall day and a picnic would feel like a true family event before heading back into the dark world of politics. Whatever the reason, that picnic turned out to be the biggest mistake they ever made.

✝✝✝

It was a small park in a quiet community, away from the big city crowds they'd been surrounding themselves with, which was why Reyna chose South Four Corners in the first place. It had lots of trees, picnic tables, open fields, and it was early enough in the day that school would still be in session, so they'd likely have the park pretty much to themselves. Much later, after the cleanup, authorities cited the time of day as the prime reason the carnage wasn't greater and many more lives weren't lost.

Once the bus had parked and everyone scrambled off for a look around, Lance's eyes instantly went to a modern, freshly painted and sturdy looking swing set off in a sandy area next to slides and other climbing apparatus for small children.

Arthur moved to stand beside Lance and eyed the swings wistfully. The two men exchanged a look, grinned, and then took off running toward the swings, catching even Ricky off guard. Lance reached his swing first and leapt into the curved leather seat, his long legs dragging in the sand, while Arthur plopped down into the swing beside him. With a laugh of pure joy, Lance walked back as far as he could and kicked off into the air, bending his now-adult legs as far beneath the seat as he could to keep them from dragging in the sand and slowing his momentum.

Not to be outdone, Arthur placed Excalibur on the ground and followed suit. Within moments the two men, one nearly of age and the other ageless, flew high into the air amidst laughter and trailing hair. All the cares of the world and the crusade vanished within the transitory period of childhood gone, but never forgotten.

Ricky and Ryan stood just outside the sandbox gazing in wonder at the two in the swings, both with wispy memories reflected in their eyes, until Lance and Arthur joyfully slowed to a stop and almost reverently slipped out of the swings to stand facing one another.

Lance looked into his father's laughing eyes, seeing the man not as a boy sees him but as a man does, almost eye to eye and with an understanding that can only come with maturity. Still, the little boy within wouldn't relinquish itself and he enveloped Arthur in a gentle hug, which the older man gladly returned. Lance glanced Ricky's way, saw the look of longing in those big brown eyes, and waved him over. He gratefully joined in the hug and the three stood quietly a moment, simply relishing each other.

Reyna had made sure they stopped along the way for food and picnic supplies and they probably had enough to feed the U.S. Army, Lance thought when he saw it spread out over several clean, white wooden tables. There was chicken and potato salad and green salad and fruit and soda and water – you name it, Reyna had bought it. And so everyone sat down for a fun-filled lunch of laughs and congratulations and reminiscences of their journey, which everyone knew was nearing its end, not just the physical one, but the ideological, as well. As usually happened when kids kept demanding and demanding and demanding something, eventually the adults gave in. And that seemed to be happening now with the CBOR. By Edwin and Lance's accounting, they had thirty-nine or forty of the states on their side - more than enough. Now all they needed was the two-thirds of the U.S. Senate and House of Representatives, and Lance determined this final push in Washington would garner him both.

Esteban grew wistful as talk of the cross-country trip dredged up memories of his father, and Lance slipped downward, as well, thinking of Jack and Mark, John and Michael, even the episode with Excalibur that still haunted him. But Chris saved the day by insisting all the "men," as he put it, obviously including himself in that group, just *had* to play a game of touch football. It was a sunny day and perfect for having fun.

The ladies laughed, including Helen, who sat with the group eating and chatting as though they were family, which in a sense they were. Sylvia volunteered to cheerlead for one side and Reyna for the other. Since Chris appointed himself one team captain and Esteban the other, Reyna had to root for Este's team. He laughed when she said that, and she blew him a kiss.

Chris selected Lance, Ricky, Kai, Dakota, and Arthur for his team, supremely confident that speed would win the day over brawn. Esteban and Justin flexed huge biceps and grinned.

Esteban's team consisted of Justin, Darnell, Gibson, and Techie, even though Techie proclaimed himself "Lame at football." Esteban told him not to worry, he'd tell him everything to do and that the Asian boy's head for strategy was more important than his running ability. Techie reluctantly agreed.

Because they were one man short, Esteban convinced Brooks to join them, which made Lance and the others groan in mock pain, especially when The Rock stripped down to the tank top undershirt he wore beneath his suit and everyone, even the bigger guys, gaped at the man's musculature.

Edwin sat the game out, preferring to watch with Jenny and Helen. Ryan and the other three Secret Service agents hovered around the perimeter of the playing field, just in case, but no one expected anything bad to happen.

Helen instructed Charlie to film the game as part of the tour coverage so footage could be used in the documentary she was planning on this historic event.

Because it was unseasonably warm, all of the guys except Techie stripped off their shirts and donned workout shorts for the game, even Arthur, which both amused and thrilled Jenny to see her husband's strong upper body, honed to a fine shape from years hefting swords and shields as a youth.

Most of the guys were athletic looking, some like Justin and Esteban thick and powerful, others like the Native Knights toned with flat, wiry muscles and prominent veins. Jenny and Helen exchanged a look between them before turning to watch the game unfold. These two different ladies had come to like and respect each other along the way, and Helen "got" Jenny's message: don't exploit my boys on TV.

Of course Helen realized the sight of so many famous guys playing football would be welcome eye candy for any TV station to run, especially since so many girls, and boys, regularly "hit" on Lance and Ricky, and on some of the others too. Even Reyna had her steady suitors. Some of these kids making the advances, Helen had observed along the way, were young, twelve or thirteen. Being "out" to the world, Lance and Ricky got propositioned by a number of these young boys. She recalled one Latino boy who couldn't have been over twelve slipping Lance a note at one of the public gatherings that said, "I want you to sex me up."

Helen hadn't known what the note said at the time until Lance shared it with her later. But she did see how the older boy handled the situation. Rather than become angry or annoyed, he'd gazed into the eager eyes of the boy and gently said, "Don't try to grow up so fast, especially when it comes to sex. Trust me, I know." Then he'd smiled and given the boy an autograph and moved on through the crowd.

That encounter replayed itself now in her mind as she watched the men and boys, some still minors, and lamented how low this country had sunk during her lifetime in its exploitation of kids as sex objects, thereby sexualizing younger and younger children who shouldn't even be thinking along those lines until at least puberty, if not beyond. Sad. Her own childhood had been much easier.

Sylvia cheered whenever Chris's team scored a touchdown, and Reyna for Este's. Esteban had been correct about Techie – the young man had a head for strategy and had learned a lot getting his butt kicked over and over again by Chris on the *Madden Football* game. But even with Brooks, who'd played the game briefly in college until a knee injury put a professional career out of reach, Esteban and Techie were no match for Chris's acumen and almost mathematical understanding of the game.

As Arthur was the biggest player on his team, and knowing his father had no experience with this game except on the iPad, Chris mostly used him to guard against Brooks stopping any of his runners or receivers. The four Native Knights were swift as deer, even Lance and Ricky who'd grown up in the city, and Chris was an outstanding quarterback, despite his small size. If he managed to get the ball to one of his receivers, which was most of the time, a touchdown was scored. Amidst sweating torsos and flying hair, the four Native boys easily darted past the much bigger and slower competition to score.

Gibson had also played ball in high school, but even he was no match for Chris's coaching talents. Esteban as quarterback managed to get the ball to both Gibson and Justin several times, but scored only twice due to the speed of the others.

The score was thirty to twelve in favor of Chris's team when Chris snapped a pass to Lance, who snatched it deftly from the air and pelted in a zigzagging pattern toward the goal line. Esteban and Techie had changed their strategy, however, and now it was Brooks bearing down on Lance like a runaway locomotive. Lance felt a moment of blind panic as he pictured himself slammed into by the man, and started to veer around him when suddenly, without warning, Brooks' entire head exploded like a cherry-bombed pumpkin in a shower of blood and bone and brain, and Lance stumbled to a horrified halt as the body, like the ones in those zombie movies, twitched and collapsed to the grass amidst copious sprays of blood from the shattered head.

Then all hell broke loose. The other three agents dropped quickly from shots to the head fired from trees surrounding the field, but from which direction Lance couldn't even tell because everything happened so fast. The only thing that saved Ryan was leaping face first into the grass and lying flat and useless. Instantly both his gun and his phone were out. He swiped the phone and punched in a single number the president had given him for emergencies. Then he raised his gun and scoured the trees for targets.

Arthur unfroze. He whirled around. "Lance, Excalibur!"

Lance whipped his head around toward the picnic area in time to see Helen dragging Jenny underneath one of the tables, with Edwin sprinting for the bus. Excalibur stuck out of the ground nearby, its hilt glinting brightly in the sunlight. He spun back around and spotted Ricky, caught between Arthur and Chris. "Ricky, get Chris to the trees!"

Ricky screamed back, "Which ones?"

Lance felt stupid and frustrated since he didn't even know where the bullets were coming from. And none of them had their vests on.

How could I be this stupid?

"I don't know!" And then he was sprinting frantically toward Excalibur, his father's only protection.

Dakota and Kai reacted with the reflexes of cougars. Both leapt to the fallen agents, snatched the guns from their holsters, rolled around on the ground and began firing into the trees from the apparent direction of the shots, which stopped the shooting for a few seconds. Darnell did the same, his old street instincts kicking in from numerous drive-bys he'd experienced growing up. Techie planted himself flat against the grass and froze.

And then with a whupping and roaring of rotor blades, a helicopter rose up and over the trees bearing down on the field, machine gun turrets already spinning, kicking up dirt and grass with what Ricky knew were real bullets this time. He pelted toward Chris even as his younger brother sprinted toward him.

Esteban instantly ran for Reyna, grabbing her and shielding her with his body as they fell hard to the ground. Bullets strafed the ground right where she'd been standing as the helicopter flew on past and circled around for another pass. Then both were up and sprinting for the bus.

Dakota and Kai rolled onto their backs and fired some shots at the chopper, but couldn't hit anything vital. Darnell did the same. With bright sparks, the bullets seemed to bounce off, even from the windshield, as though the entire unit was bulletproof.

Lance grabbed Excalibur's hilt and plucked the sword from the ground. Just as he whirled around to head toward his dad, he spotted the copter heading straight for Justin and Gibson, spraying out bullets that bounced and kicked up the grass.

"Behind me, son!" Gibson shouted and shoved the boy behind him just as his chest sprayed open with bullets, blood splattering.

"Daaaaddd!" Justin screamed in horrified anguish as the man he'd come to love crumpled into a bloody heap at his feet.

Arthur was on the move to intercept Ricky and Chris. Both boys darted furiously toward him from different directions, even as Lance ran forward to intersect them. But then the chopper swung back around, more bullets firing, and suddenly Ricky went flying, spinning wildly out of control, flopping onto the grass and leaving a pathway of blood as he rolled onto his back and lay unmoving.

"Nnnnooooooo!" shrieked Lance.

"Ricky!" screamed Arthur, as he ran toward his son, heedless of his own danger. One of the snipers got him in the chest with multiple shots, flinging the king back and sending him into an unmoving heap beside Ricky's motionless form.

"Daaaddd!" Lance shouted even as he kept running, pounding frantically forward, heedless of the bullets singing all around him, despite feeling, or so he thought, a few strike him in the legs. But he realized later what he'd felt must've been clods of dirt striking his bare legs because no bullets touched him.

Hand still clutching Excalibur's hilt, he dropped to his knees before the unmoving forms of his father and Ricky. He reached out for Ricky's face, but heard Ryan's voice as he scrabbled forward on his hands and knees, "No Lance, don't touch them. You might make it worse." He still held the phone he'd used to call for help, but his gun was up and ready.

Charlie had been running around with the camera attempting to film, but seeing Arthur go down he lowered the camera and sprinted toward the fallen king. A sniper got him in the back and he spun wildly, the camera flying from his grasp and landing in the grass sideways.

Now Helen leapt up and out from under the table, despite Jenny's frantic call to stay, and raced across the field toward her fallen friend, apparently hoping to drag him to safety. She barely made it halfway before the copter cut her down in a shower of blood and bullets. Jenny screamed and screamed some more, fumbling with her phone to dial 911.

Techie and Darnell raced over to the fallen Gibson, where a sobbing Justin had his face buried in his father's bloodied shoulder. Sylvia darted from beneath a picnic table and sprinted toward Chris as the copter swung around, this time lowering that claw-like contraption that had previously been used to snatch Ricky off the ground at Arlington. Only now it was headed straight for Chris.

"Run, Chris!" Ryan shouted, drawing Lance's attention.

Chris turned and poured on the speed, zigzagging toward the nearest picnic table. Sylvia intersected him and grabbed his hand and together they kicked up dirt as they ran desperately toward Jenny, still beneath the far table and screaming for them to move faster. Her eyes widened with terror as the clawlike thing bore down on her son, and she leapt from under the table to sprint toward them.

"Faster, Chris!" she shouted breathlessly as she ran.

The panting, frantic children almost made it. Just as they were about to meet up with Jenny, the claw-thing grabbed at them both, closing around them and lifting them kicking and screaming off the ground. Jenny screamed.

"Laaannnceee!" Chris shrieked as he rose higher and higher toward the trees.

Lance was up and running, Excalibur in hand. No sniper bullets tracked him, but suddenly Edwin was there, panting and heaving as he shoved a gun into Lance's hand.

Lance flipped Excalibur to his left hand and raised the handgun in his right. He fired multiple rounds at the fleeing helicopter, and heard other guns behind him doing the same. Out of the corner of his eye, he spotted Merlin, Reyna and Esteban shooting one arrow after another in quick succession at any part of the chopper they could hit, while avoiding the dangling Chris and Sylvia. The enemy must've learned with the drone copter because now even the rotors remained undamaged by the arrows.

Lance was terrified of hitting the kids, but kept firing around them as best he could. Thanks to the shooting techniques Ryan taught him, his aim was good, but whatever he hit seemed unaffected by the bullets. And then with the same suddenness with which it had appeared, the chopper was gone, vanishing behind the trees, Chris and Sylvia vanishing along with it. Only the fading sound of *whupping* blades remained, and in moments it, too, had disappeared.

Approaching sirens could be heard in the distance.

Lance turned in anguish to a shell-shocked Edwin, and then sprinted back to the scene of the carnage. Ryan had gotten to his feet and stumbled over to Gibson, who groaned loudly enough for Lance to know he wasn't dead. Arthur and Ricky, however, hadn't moved, and made no sound, and Lance saw Jenny racing frantically across the grass to them.

Lance staggered past Gibson, whose bloodshot eyes were open and fixed on those of his son hovering frantically above him. The sergeant's chest was torn open from gunfire, ragged and bloody and bleeding profusely. Lance couldn't fathom how he was even still alive as he passed at a run to get to his father and Ricky.

Ryan's face was streaked with dirt and tears as he watched the life ebb from this man who'd been his partner and brother for so many years.

Gibson tried for a smile, but pain won out. "Take care of Justin, Ry... like you always... promised."

Ryan nodded sadly, feeling older and more useless than ever. "You know I will."

Gibson focused now on the grief-stricken visage of this boy whom he'd never understood until Arthur came along. "I never didn't love you, Justin," he croaked, blood dribbling from his mouth. "You're the... best son... a man could have."

"Dad..." Justin said, barely a whisper, his body wracked with sobs of pain.

"Tell your... mother," Gibson gasped with his last breath, "that I always... loved her." He tried again for a smile, and then he was gone. Justin keened like a wounded animal, and heedless of the blood, grabbed his father's lifeless body in a tight hug and rocked back and forth.

Lance saw Jenny scream as she dropped to her knees and desperately pressed her hands to the ragged holes in Arthur's chest in a futile attempt to staunch the blood streaming forth. Dakota and Kai were already crouched beside both of the fallen, eyes sweeping the area, guns ready.

Panting and panic-stricken, Lance reached them and looked down at his father, ashen and bleeding copiously from a jaggedly large wound. His own chest constricted so tightly he could barely breathe.

His breaths came in shallow spurts, his heart pounded harder than it ever had, as he let the gun slip from his grasp, stuck Excalibur into the ground, and knelt beside his mother and father. And the boy who was his soul mate. Ever so gently, he took Ricky's hand in his, pressing it lightly against his trembling chest. Blood had pooled from under the boy's back, the hand he loved to hold felt barely warm, and the beautiful face looked so pale that Lance felt overcome with despair. He placed a hand lightly upon Ricky's chest, and felt a weak and shallow heartbeat within.

"You can't die, Ricky!" he whispered, barely able to even speak, tears already forming behind the lids. "You can't! You promised me we'd be together for now and always! You *promised!*"

But Ricky made no move, no sound, no indication he was even in there. Lance looked from the unmoving Ricky to his father bleeding out beside him, and could take no more. He raised his eyes toward heaven and screamed with whatever breath remained in him, "Nnnnnnooooooooooo!"

And then he bowed his head and wept.

†††

For
Now
And
Always

Chapter Six

You'll Be Needing This

"Lance?"

He heard the voice and knew it was Reyna, but he didn't respond. The beeping and chirping sounds of machines filled his mind and heart, and his soul felt nothing but numbness. He sat between the two beds, now clad in a short-sleeved Team Ricky shirt with the boy he loved grinning outward from his chest, a photo taken when he was happy and life had meaning. He also wore gloves and a big mask over his nose and mouth because the Intensive Care ward demanded it.

Arthur lay in the bed to his right, Ricky in the one to his left. Both appeared to have every medical contraption known to science attached to them, monitoring every vital function.

Keeping them alive.

Both wore oxygen masks, and lay in critical condition. Only one visitor was allowed at a time, and then only for a few minutes. This was Lance's few and he didn't want anyone interrupting, even Reyna.

His eyes drifted to his dad, the man who'd saved him and raised him and taught him how to be a man. His larger-than-life face looked small and insignificant beneath the enormous mask keeping an even flow of oxygen going into and out of his lungs. His chest had a large dressing on it from the surgery required to remove three bullets, all of which lodged near his heart and damaged one of the valves, not to mention numerous arteries into and out of the organ. He lay unconscious, even though it had been eight hours since the surgery and he should be awake by now, according to the doctors. That wasn't a good sign. One of the many machines now in use acted like a sort-of exterior pacemaker, helping the heart beat with regularity.

His own heart pulled so tightly that he could barely move as he turned to gaze at the face of his beloved, the boy who had become his everything, the boy without whom he saw no reason to live. Ricky wore a similar oxygen mask, his amazing long hair that Lance so loved to caress splayed out across the pillow beneath his head, his features pale and bloodless. He'd been struck in the back by two bullets.

They had done extensive internal damage, with one lodged very near the spinal cord, and he'd lost copious amounts of blood prior to the arrival of the paramedics. The bullets had been removed, but there was no telling, the doctors had informed them, how much trauma there might have been to the spinal cord itself. If he lived, the doctors said, he might not walk again.

If he lived…

Those words had nearly caused Lance to collapse right there in the hospital corridor. Ricky, the most amazing boy in the word, the one who'd carried him, literally and emotionally, through all of his pain these past three years, the boy who he intended to spend the rest of his life with, had within a matter of seconds out on that field become the boy he might lose forever.

If he lived…

Lance sat as though his entire body had been shot full of Novocain, numb and exhausted and weighted down by a sorrow and despair such as he'd never felt before. He hadn't slept since all of this had happened, at least twenty-four hours now. But what was sleep when the two most important people in the world to him lay dying before his eyes and he could do nothing but watch helplessly?

And then there was Chris, and Sylvia…

"Lance…," he heard again, momentarily forgetting that Reyna was even there.

Very reluctantly, he turned his moist green eyes upward to see her gentle brown looking at him lovingly. She also sported the required face mask, but Lance didn't need to see her mouth to know the love and pain she was feeling. It was all there, written across those pretty eyes like the lines of a book.

"Lance," she said a third time. "You have to say something." When he merely squinted with incomprehension, she went on, "About this. To, well, the world. You're Arthur's son, you're in charge now. You have to say something."

Lance's tearful eyes narrowed with anger. "Say what, Reyna? That I fucked up? That cuz 'a me Ricky and Dad are dying? That cuz 'a me, Sergeant Gibson and Lady Helen and Charlie and Brooks and those other guys are dead? That Chris and Sylvia got kidnapped?"

Her eyes widened in surprise, and then narrowed with guilt. "It's not your fault, Lance. It's mine. I'm the one who insisted we stop for that stupid picnic!"

Her voice sounded riddled with remorse, and Lance reached out a hand to take one of hers. Despite the latex gloves, it was still the basic human contact both desperately needed.

"It's not yer fault, Reyna," he said with bitterness and rancor. "I'm the one this asshole is after. I'm the one he wants to suffer. And I'm the one who's gotta end it."

Her eyes widened and she shook her head, simultaneously squeezing his hand gently. "We're family, baby boy. We end it together."

Her voice carried such angry conviction that Lance felt momentarily better. This catastrophe *was* his fault, but he wouldn't have to bear it alone. He did have a family to share the pain, and to put an end to whoever was behind it.

He sighed and released her hand, swiping at the tears dribbling from his eyes. "Okay, Reyna, I'll say something. Where?"

"All the media are parked out-front," she said. "Hospital wouldn't let them in."

"You'll go with me?"

She nodded. "I told you before I'd follow you to the ends of the earth and I meant it. Este and the others will stand with you too. We love you, baby boy."

New tears threatened to pour forth, and to prevent that he stood to engulf her in a tight hug, relishing the feel of her arms around him, wishing they were Ricky's, but loving the fact that she cherished him. Which was good because he cherished her even more.

†††

The president had ordered that the wounded be taken to Walter Reed National Military Medical Center because it was the closest facility and could provide the best protection for Lance and the others, including the wounded Arthur, lest the attacker send someone to try and finish them off.

The facility was enormous, at least as much of it as Lance's pain-numbed mind was able to process the day before when he'd arrived in the back of the paramedic vehicle with Ricky. The paramedics originally said he couldn't travel with them, but Ryan flashed his Special Agent badge and the two men relented.

The centerpiece to the medical center seemed to be a gigantic tower, outside of which had massed hundreds of media personnel and their camera crews, kept at bay by soldiers standing guard at the entrance.

Stepping out into the corridor, Lance hugged Jenny and held her briefly before removing his mask and gloves and heading down the corridor with the others. Merlin stayed behind with Jenny to keep her company. She'd already cried more than Lance had ever seen her, and he saw in her eyes the fear that both Arthur and Ricky would die, and that she'd never see Chris alive again. Ryan had stuck close to a silent, grieving Justin since they'd arrived, and now accompanied the brooding young man as he followed Esteban and Reyna.

Lance could see the anger seething within Justin, the waterfall of grief the stoic knight refused to give in to, and he knew it would break sooner or later, as it would for all of them. The entire team was shell-shocked, even Dakota and Kai, both of who had stayed close to Lance since the attack. While he hadn't talked much with anyone, fearing his own voice would send him into an avalanche of sadness and emotion, he appreciated the presence of his Native brothers, especially Dakota. Lance felt that need for alcohol, as he still sometimes did in times of tremendous stress, and Dakota's eyes clearly revealed how much he understood the craving, and would always be there to prevent Lance from finding a way to give in to it.

The only one of their surviving group not still there was Edwin. The Congress had *finally* planned a vote on the CBOR to coincide with the New Camelot tour's arrival in Washington, though how that vote would turn out remained a mystery. No one in Congress would even talk to the press at this point. Since there was nothing he could do at the hospital, the young intern had returned to Washington to meet up with Senator Cairns and coordinate matters relative to this catastrophic development, possibly delaying the vote until word of Arthur and Ricky's fate became known.

As Lance and the others stepped out the front entrance, they were bombarded with camera flashes and frantic questions thrown their way from every direction. Lance had been told the surgeons who'd operated on Arthur and Ricky already spoke to the press corps and answered what questions they could, so he determined to entertain no such queries. He knew if he tried answering anything about the possibility of Arthur and Ricky dying he'd lose it, and he couldn't do that. His enemy would be watching – of that he was certain. Watching and gloating and hoping to see Lance break down.

Not this time, asshole, he thought as he stepped to the makeshift podium and microphone hastily set up by the hospital staff. *I'll only cry in private.* So he allowed his anger to rise, knowing it would keep the tears at bay.

He knew the president had issued a statement strongly condemning the attack and pledging all the resources of the federal government to bring Chris and Sylvia home safely, and bring the killer to swift justice. Senator Cairns, as the chief supporter of Lance in Congress, issued a statement of support for Lance, as did the Senate Majority Leader and the Speaker of the House. All pledged their thoughts and prayers for the recovery of Arthur and Ricky, their condolences to the families of those lost, and their support of Lance at this dark hour. Lance had watched it all with an emptiness that made their words sound even hollower than they actually were. He knew the only person the world really wanted to hear from was him.

So, as he'd learned so well how to do, he stood patiently, Dakota to one side and Kai to the other, until the questions ceased and the reporters realized he wasn't going to answer any. He scanned their faces. This was what they lived for, he sadly understood. This was how they made their living, feeding off the misfortune and pain of others. Sick.

He cleared his throat. "I'm going to make a statement, but I'm not going to answer any questions about my Dad or my—Ricky. The doctors already told you about that and nothing's changed. I also know you've been briefed by the Maryland PD, the FBI, and the Secret Service about the attack. I've seen it all on the news." He paused to collect himself. "We lost some amazing people yesterday, people who've done so much for me and for others. Sergeant Gibson was a great man, a cop who believed kids like me could amount to something in this world given half a chance. And Lady Helen gave your profession a good name. She always stayed a journalist and always gave me a fair shake, even when some of you didn't. I loved both of them and considered them family. Those brave agents were awesome, too, especially Brooks who joked with me and made me feel good about myself."

An image of Brooks standing up for him and Ricky at the prom flashed through his mind and caused him to choke up a moment. He paused to resume normal breathing, his eyes squinting with barely controlled rage.

"Do I know who did this? Not yet. But when I find out he'll wish he'd never been born." He looked straight out at the cameras, his face flushed with anger. "This is a message for the chicken shit who won't come out of the shadows and face me man to man. I'm coming for you. You think you're gonna kill me? Fine. You might. But trust me on this, I'm not going down without taking your sorry, piece of shit ass down with me! No one hurts my Dad, and no one hurts the boy I love. You're toast, asshole!"

Then he turned before he lost his cool and pushed past Reyna and Esteban to re-enter the hospital. He heard a few tossed out questions, and Dakota's voice saying, "Lance, wait," but he ignored it all. He needed to get inside. He wanted to sit in the chapel for a while, somewhere quiet and dark and peaceful where he could do what his dad had always taught him to do when he had no control over events – pray.

†††

The text message came through while Lance knelt before the altar praying. At first he ignored it, so lost was he in his uncertain questions to a God he didn't really understand, but who seemed to have set everything in motion. Was all of this, as his dad would say, happening as it was supposed to? That somehow out of all this sorrow something good would arise? How could it? He asked Jesus for comfort.

What if Dad dies?

Or Chris is killed?

Or Ricky...?

The phone vibrated again and Lance suddenly realized it could be his mom. But it wasn't. He peered at the now familiar 000-000-0000 number uncertainly before opening the text.

Multiple texts.

From him.

"Well, well, well, Lancey Nancy boy, how you feeling now? Your faggot boyfriend dead yet? He was supposed to die out there in the park, but maybe this is better. You'll suffer more watching that little pervert die slowly before your very eyes when you can't do shit about it. Ha! And the old man? He shouldn't last much longer either. Without his precious sword he's nothing.

Now here's the deal, Pretty Boy. I know you only care about boys so Sylvia doesn't mean much to you, but your little faggot-in-training does. You have thirty-six hours to get your ass here to me or else what your other boyfriend Michael did to those men will be tame compared to what I do to your little brother.

Are you getting the picture here, Pretty Boy? I know you have your Techie kid with you and he can use the link in this message to locate me. I also know you'll bring your pathetic modern-day knights for protection. Fine. I have lots of surprises awaiting you all. But if I see a single cop or federal agent or soldier headed my way, there won't be enough left of Chris for you to mail home in an envelope. Clear?

I saw your pitiful threats on TV. You're right about one thing, Pretty Boy. In the end it'll be down to you and me, and I'm gonna kill your sorry ass, just like I promised two years ago. So bring it on. I'm waiting."

Lance sat back, allowing the initial rush of anger to subside. That's what this guy wanted him to do – act like a stupid kid and react with pure emotion. He forced air into his lungs and calm into his heart, and then he opened the attachment. It was a Google map with a specific spot pinpointed and flashing. There were coordinates, too, coordinates Lance knew Techie could easily locate. He considered his options.

They were presently within a military hospital under heavy guard. Sneaking out would not be easy, but that's what he'd have to do. This would take some planning, and a private place where he and his team wouldn't be disturbed. He glanced around at the shadowy, peaceful pews and stained glass of the chapel surrounding him.

Thank you, Lord, he whispered in his mind. *This is perfect.*

With steady fingers and a calm determination, Lance sent out a blanket text to all of his team except Ryan. He asked Techie to bring his laptop, and inform Merlin. He instructed them to gradually slip away one at a time so as not to tip anyone off. They could say they wanted to pray or needed something to drink or whatever, but couldn't make anyone suspicious, *especially* Ryan.

Lance hated excluding his godfather, but the killer had been clear – no cops. Ryan was distracted in his grief over Gibson and was spending a lot of time with Jenny, helping her stay strong, and hopefully wouldn't notice the absence of the others until their meeting concluded.

After sending out his message, Lance sat back and waited. His grief over his dad and Ricky constantly threatened to overwhelm him, and he had to forcibly fight it off. Not now, he kept telling himself. Now was about Chris and Sylvia. Their lives were at stake and they needed his immediate help, and the help of the entire Round

Table. So he forced himself not to think of the two most important people in the world, but focused instead on seeing the man responsible dead at his feet. Not an image he knew Jesus would like, especially in a house of prayer, but it was the only image that kept the tears at bay and his head clear.

†††

"You know it's a trap, right, Lance?" Esteban said soberly after everyone had gathered and reviewed the message.

Lance eyed his fearless big brother just as soberly. "Course it is. And the place is probably booby-trapped up the butt. But we got Techie, and he's gonna figure out how to get in. Right, Techie?"

The young Asian looked up from the laptop before him and slid his drooping glasses back up his nose. Everyone in the room gazed at him expectantly. "I need a little time, Lance," he said apologetically. "I can hack into satellite data and get his security codes and shit, hopefully disarm some of his protections, but it'll take me a bit."

"We only have thirty-six hours," Reyna said quietly.

The others nodded. Lance looked around at their silent, grim young faces.

"None 'a you gotta go with me," he announced calmly and with conviction. "I'm the one he wants, and I don't want anyone else I love dying for me. Once Techie figures it out, I can go in alone."

"Like hell you are!" Justin spat with equal parts loyalty and anger. "That asshole killed my father, and shot my other father. I'm goin' in too."

"Me, too," Reyna said at once.

"And me," Darnell affirmed.

Esteban focused his intense gaze on Lance in that no-nonsense way that used to carry great weight out on the streets when he was a kid. "We're all going, Lance. We're a team, a family. We do this together."

Lance felt himself grow suddenly warm with love and pride in his fellow knights, his brothers and sisters who had stood by him all this time, who'd already given so much and yet were willing to give still more, even their lives. He nodded gratefully.

Merlin looked at Lance appraisingly, sizing him up as though assessing his potential for greatness. "Are you certain you wish to do this without your godfather, Lance? His expertise in such situations could be valuable."

Lance shook his head. "You saw the message, Merlin. No cops. And my *nino* would have to call in back up cuz that's what he knows." He eyed the wizard and then took in the whole of his team. Nine. That's all they were against how many?

"We gotta do this on our own. I'll let mom know to tell my *nino* where we went, say, ten hours after we leave, which should give us enough time to sneak in and get out with Chris and Sylvia. That's our top priority, guys, saving them."

"And keeping that asshole away from you," Esteban affirmed passionately. "No way he's gonna hurt *mi carnal*. And I still owe that fucker for Lavern."

Techie's fingers flew across his keyboard as he searched for a way into the security system.

"Where is this place, Techie?" Lance asked.

Without taking his eyes off the screen, Techie said, "Right here in Maryland, about fifteen miles away."

That sent a ripple of surprise through the group. Even Lance hadn't expected that. "Can you at least get a read on the place?"

Techie nodded, and waved Lance over. He hurried to stand behind the other boy, flanked by the others. On the screen appeared an overhead satellite view of an enormous compound of some kind, with a main structure and several outbuildings, all surrounded by empty fields and some type of fencing.

"Looks like a prison," Darnell said with a shake of his head.

"Yeah, but the kind you're not supposed to break *into*," Reyna added drily.

Techie's fingers tapped away with their usual lightening speed and accuracy. The image shifted to schematics of the buildings, with flashing red dots everywhere throughout. Techie studied the image carefully while Lance and Este leaned over his shoulders intently.

"Those red dots, booby traps?" Lance asked, though he was certain of the answer.

Techie nodded. "Maybe laser beams designed to trip something." Then he pointed to very pale orange glows scattered throughout the field surrounding the compound. "And these are heat signatures, Lance. Likely active landmines."

"Shit," Darnell whispered, shaking his head.

"Place is a fuckin' fortress," Esteban spat, cursing again and drawing Reyna's hand to clutch at his.

Lance stood to his full height, thoughtful as he absently grabbed his hair and gazed at it uncertainly.

"What is it, Lance?" Dakota asked, drawing everyone's attention away from the screen and onto their leader.

Lance tilted his head. "He called me 'Pretty Boy'."

Reyna shrugged. "So, everyone calls you that."

Lance eyed her. "Not anymore. Only...." His breath stopped a moment and his heart began to pound. "Ricky." Then he forced down the pain and returned his mind to the problem at hand. "Reyna, nobody's called me that since I got going with Dad. That was my street name. Before."

He swept his gaze over all their faces as realization dawned in each one.

"That means this asshole is somebody who knew you *before* Arthur," Esteban said quietly.

"Most likely. But Este, I didn't have no enemies, not like you guys. I wasn't affiliated. I ran my own. I didn't piss people off. That's how I survived out there."

Esteban nodded soberly. "I hear ya, *carnal*. But you did piss somebody off or all this shit wouldn't 'a gone down. No idea who?"

Lance shook his head, frustration and fear and guilt consuming him. He had to do something, to be active. "C'mon, let's figure out how to storm this asshole's castle."

Esteban and Justin and Darnell all exchanged a serious look.

"What?" Lance asked as the others leaned in closer.

"We been talking, Lance," Esteban began slowly, unusually timid for him. "Before, while we was waiting and thinking about the kids. I know how your dad felt and all, but, well… we're gonna need real firepower if we're gonna take that place."

That surprised Lance. "You mean guns?"

"Big guns," Justin said.

"The biggest," Darnell put in without a trace of humor.

Lance considered a moment what Arthur would do. "Dad hates guns," he said to fill the void.

Esteban looked soberly at him. "Lance, you know there's no man I respect in this world more than your dad. He's my *jefe,* too. But he's down, and you're in charge. It's your call."

Lance scanned their faces. All of them. He saw it clear as day – they'd follow his orders no matter what. "Where would you get 'em?"

Darnell and Justin exchanged a look. "We got a call from Jamil, you know, little homie from Chicago," Darnell said. "He's got homies in D.C. can hook us up."

"All you gotta do is give the word," Esteban finished, his intense gaze never leaving Lance's face.

Lance glanced over at Merlin, but the wizard remained impassive as always, his expression neutral. *No help there*, he realized. This call was his to make. His mind flashed back to the carnage in Four Corners Park, and his resolve hardened.

"Do it," he said with finality, his mind already moving on to the next decision, whatever that may turn out to be.

Darnell instantly whipped out his phone and wandered into a corner to make the call. The rest gathered around Techie and his computer to plan out their invasion, for that's what it would have to be – an invasion of the enemy stronghold to rescue their kidnapped fellows.

Their meeting lasted forty-five minutes before finally they began returning to the Intensive Care area so as to not make Ryan or anyone else suspicious. In his conversation with Jamil, Darnell had also been given an idea how to create the diversion necessary for them to sneak out of the hospital undetected, and Lance had to admit that Jamil was a pretty crafty kid.

During the entire planning of the operation, Merlin said not a word, nor did he offer any advice.

As the others dispersed, Lance asked Merlin to hold back. The wizard's silence when so many important decisions were being made worried him, and he knew the man's wisdom had served his father so well all those hundreds of years ago.

Merlin eyed the boy carefully. Lance gazed back uncertainly, his insecurities and childhood fears right there near the surface. "What do you see, Merlin, when you look at me?"

"Do you not recall our conversation in the library when you turned sixteen?"

Actually, Lance recalled every word of it. "You still see me as a hero?"

The wizard nodded. "Without doubt."

Lance sighed, his eyes drifting toward the altar and the large wooden cross suspended above it. Then he turned back to the man. "Did I make the right call, Merlin, about the guns, the invasion?"

Even in the shadows, the wizard's silvery gray eyes glinted ominously, and he shrugged. "Uneasy lies the head that wears the crown."

Lance's eyebrows shot up in surprise.

"Shakespeare's Henry IV, Part II," Merlin said by way of clarification.

"But what does it mean?"

The older man sighed and moved to sit right beside Lance, who'd remained in the pew from which he'd conducted the meeting. "It means that there's no way to know, Lance. You must do what you feel is right and let the chips fall where they may."

Lance nodded, and a pregnant silence fell between them. Then the boy locked eyes on those of the man. "I need you with me on this campaign, Merlin, just like my father needed you on his. I need your wisdom."

Merlin sighed heavily, for the first time sounding old to Lance, old and worn out. "Alas, my fighting days are over, I'm afraid."

Lance kept his gaze steady. "Not after what I saw in that park." He paused when Merlin didn't reply. "I could command you, you know."

Now Merlin's eyebrows shot up in surprise. "Indeed?"

Lance nodded, his heart heavy, but his resolve firm. "I know the code inside and out. The king's wizard must obey the king, and since I'm filling in for Dad...." He let the rest of the thought trail off, but the wide-eyed look on Merlin's face indicated the message had been understood.

After another pause during which Lance thought the older man might argue the point, Merlin sighed. "After all your rebellious antics a couple of years back, *now* you're a stickler for the rules. Ah, well, as you command."

Lance offered a nod of gratitude. "Thanks, Merlin. I'll be with Dad and Ricky. Let me know when it's time to move out."

The man nodded, and Lance hurriedly left the chapel.

†††

Jenny sat between the two beds, germ mask covering her nose and mouth, worry lines etching the corners of her eyes. The steady beeping and humming of machinery continued unabated, but there had been no change in the condition of either man by the time Lance returned to sit with her.

She looked up as he entered, and relief filled her as he slid into a chair beside her and wrapped his strong arms around her.

Lance held her tight while holding his emotions even tighter. He had a job to do, a job his father had prepared him for, and he had to stay strong to see it through to the end.

Even her quiet tears lightly dropping to his shoulder didn't bring a renewal of his own.

I'm a man now.

I need to stay strong.

"I love you, mom," he whispered into her ear soothingly, his voice slightly cracking despite his resolve.

"I love you, too, Lance," she choked through her tears. "So much."

He held her and she held him, and they sat together with their thoughts and the sounds of machinery keeping the men they both loved alive.

Finally, she pulled back and looked into his eyes for the first time since he'd entered the room. She must've seen his intentions, because she gasped. "What are you going to do, Lance?"

He sighed and glanced around the room, making sure they weren't being spied on or listened to. "We're going after Chris, Mom. And Sylvia. We're gonna bring 'em back safe."

It was then he showed her the text message, and briefly filled her in on their plans, including the part about the heavy guns they'd be toting. She sat numbly as he detailed what had to be done, and all the time Lance kept waiting for her protestations, her insistence that the police should handle it. But none came.

Looking him in the eye, as though searching his face for the boy he used to be, she said, "So like your father you've become, Lance, so strong and determined to do what's right."

"So you won't tell my *nino* until after we're inside?"

She shook her head as she took his phone and, with trembling fingers, slipped it into her pocket. "Oh, God, Lance, it scares me so much to think of losing you, too, when…." Her eyes drifted to Arthur's unmoving body with its shallow breathing. "But I know you have to go. For the children."

Lance nodded. "And for you, too, Mom," he added. "I've gotta end this once and for all or none of us are safe."

She returned the nod silently, taking his hand in hers and squeezing gently with trembling love. "Come back to me, Lance. Please. I can't lose you, too."

Lance squeezed her hand back, relishing that basic human contact with this woman who had become the most important woman in the world to him. "I will." He paused. "Can I, you know, say… good-bye… to them? Alone?"

She released his hand and nodded just as the door opened and Ryan entered. Lance didn't think the man could look older or more rumpled and hangdog, but he did. The loss of Gibson had struck him to the heart, and he looked broken.

"Any change?" he asked, though his voice indicated he already knew the answer.

Lance shook his head. "*Nino*, could you take mom down to the cafeteria for coffee or something? She needs a break."

Ryan nodded. "Course, Lance." He extended a hand to Jenny and she hesitantly took it, her gaze flitting back to Lance's green eyes watching them above the mask. She leaned in to kiss him through the mask, and he kissed her back. Then she stood and followed Ryan to the door.

"*Nino?*" Lance called out quietly.

Ryan turned back and in the shadowy light of the room Lance saw the guilt in the older man's eyes. "Yeah, Lance?"

Knowing this might be the last time he saw him, Lance suddenly choked up. "I, uh… I just, well, I love you, that's all. Thanks for everything you've done for me."

He knew he'd rushed the words, but too many emotions were pouring though him and he feared he'd lose control.

Ryan frowned and eyed Jenny, but she looked away, her eyes drifting back to the unconscious Arthur looking so small and helpless in the big hospital bed.

"Anything you need to tell me, Lance?" Ryan asked, his voice filled with law enforcement suspicion.

Lance gulped and shook his head. *Stay strong!* "I just wanted you to know that."

Ryan suddenly looked choked up and Lance thought for a moment that he might cry. "I love you, too, godson." And then he was through the door with Jenny and out of the room.

Lance held his breath a moment, his heart beating out of control, his stomach clenched with anguish. Then he stood and leaned over Arthur's bed, gazing into the face of the man who'd plucked him off the streets and made him the most famous boy in the world, the man who never cared that Lance liked boys or that he had long hair or that he always felt unworthy of love and honor. This man had given him everything, and now might have given his life, as well.

"Dad...." He stopped to collect his thoughts and calm the hammering of his heart. "I'm going to get Chris back, and I'm gonna save Sylvia. And I'm gonna stop this...."

He trailed off a moment and took a deep breath. Despite his desperate desire not to cry, a tear drifted from behind his eye to the front and down his face to drop onto the king's bare arm. "You picked me as First Knight cuz you believed in me, and you adopted me cuz you love me. You taught me how to be a man and how to take responsibility for my family and the crusade. So that's what I'm doing. I need you to hang on, Dad. I need you to keep loving me and being proud of me, okay? I need you to... not die...." He bowed his head then as more tears fell. "I love you, Dad, and no matter what happens I always will."

He leaned down to lightly kiss the man's cheek, feeling the bristles of Arthur's beard even through the face mask. And then he turned and looked into the face of the boy who practically stopped his heart every time he did.

Ricky lay breathing shallowly, his face so angelic and beautiful and perfect that Lance felt cramps of pain and anguish pull at his stomach and at the edges of his heart.

"Ricky...." It wasn't a name, or even a word. It was an emotion. A breathless, full-bodied expression of pure love, and Lance could almost say no more. "I love you, fool. Oh, damn, how I love you. You be here when I get back, you hear me? You *be* here!"

His tears dropped onto that most perfect of faces and Lance gently wiped them away with his gloved fingertips.

"You promised me, Ricky. For now and always. You *promised*. So don't leave me. This dumbass can't live without you."

He leaned down and kissed the soft, hairless cheek of the boy who completed him, and then knelt by the side of the bed, clutching the lightly warm hand, caressing the fingers, while more tears fell unheeded to the sterile white floor beneath him.

He didn't know how long he knelt that way, just him and Ricky and the machines beeping away, but finally a gentle hand on his shoulder brought him out of his memories to find Reyna looking down at him with deep compassion.

"It's time, Lance."

He nodded, gently kissed the hand of the boy he had once talked of marrying, and stood. They were all there, despite the rule about only one visitor at a time. His team. His family. All with compassionate eyes and determined expressions. Even Merlin stood with them, ready to take orders from him.

The wizard raised his arms and Lance saw Excalibur resting across them like the greatest of all treasures. "You'll be needing this," Merlin announced with quiet formality.

Appalled, Lance shook his head. "No way, Merlin. Excalibur belongs to Dad."

Without a word, Merlin stepped forward and held out the sword. "Excalibur... belongs to the king." He dropped to one knee, the sword resting reverently in his outstretched hands. "Your Majesty."

Lance sucked in a shocked breath, his eyes flitting to the other faces gathered around. They wore the same look he saw on Merlin's – this *was* how it was supposed to be, whether he thought it proper or not.

With trembling fingers, Lance reached out to grip the hilt, once more feeling a warm tingle skitter up his arm, just as it had in Las Vegas. He raised the sword before him, blade pointing toward the ceiling, light from the monitors reflecting off its shimmery surface like time itself.

And then everyone, even Reyna, dropped to one knee respectfully, pledging with that simple action his or her undying loyalty to him, the street kid with no name who'd come from so little to so much.

He looked at their upturned faces with determination. "Let's do this."

†††

Chapter Seven

He's Not A Boy Anymore

Ryan had been alerted to the ruckus out front by one of the new Secret Service agents the president had sent to replace those killed, and the aging cop struggled to come up with a name. Cortez? Was that it? Sighing, he followed the man to the chapel where Lance said he'd be praying. Poking his head inside the door, he found his godson alone, head bent reverently toward the suspended wooden cross.

"Lance, we have a problem."

Lance looked up, his green eyes vibrant even in the gloom of this place. Silently, almost as though he expected this interruption, Ryan realized much later, the boy rose and followed him out into the corridor.

The media remained encamped outside the hospital entrance like vultures waiting for death so they could feed on it voraciously and try to one up each other with their ghoulish coverage.

Yeah, Ryan thought with a sudden rush of anger, *waiting for the death of my best friend other than...* Just the thought of Gib pulled his heart tight and stunted his breathing.

Ryan had been told a large number of teens from D.C. had parked themselves outside with the media, determined to stay until Lance had spoken to them. As they stepped out the front doors, he instantly pegged them as gangbangers – beanies, sagging pants, tattoos up the butt, muscle shirts and team jerseys. All boys, and all African-American.

Great, he thought, *just what we need!*

The moment they saw Lance, the teens sent up a rousing cheer of support.

At least they don't wanna kill him, the detective thought as he watched Lance calmly address the crowd, sharing with them his father and Ricky's current condition and thanking them for their support.

That's when the fight broke out. Two boys, likely from enemy neighborhoods, started duking it out right there in front of the media. The reporters and camera people backed up, but excitedly filmed every single moment.

It didn't take but a few seconds before other boys jumped into the fray and suddenly what had been a calm, peaceful status update turned into a melee, if not a full-fledged riot. Ryan pushed Lance back inside and told him to wait in the chapel, simultaneously whipping his radio up to his mouth and calling for reinforcements. They streamed out of the hospital within seconds, Secret Service and military personnel, pushing past the calm and controlled Lance and diving into the brawling teens.

Ryan watched the battle, and the cleanup, but something seemed off to him. He'd had too many years working the streets not to notice. Something about the way the punches were being thrown, the epithets being hurled, didn't ring true. He squinted from the top step as the agents and soldiers gradually restored order, pulling boys from one another and separating the various groups.

That's what it was! Once separated, the fighters simply gave up.

Almost as if…

Suddenly, Ryan knew. "Shit!"

He turned and shoved angrily through the glass doors, quickly jogging into a sprint down the main hall and around the corner, drawing curious looks from the medical personnel he passed.

How could I have been so stupid?

He snatched at the chapel door and yanked it open, already knowing what he'd find.

Nothing.

It was empty.

"Shit!" he cursed again, and then started at a run to the ICU.

†††

He found Jenny seated between Arthur's bed and Ricky's, her face drawn and haggard with worry and fear, her clothes rumpled, her long blonde hair unkempt from lack of attention.

She looked up as he burst into the room shoving his mask into place, and simply held out Lance's phone to him.

Her calmness soothed him slightly and he took the phone from her trembling hand. Gazing at the text message Lance had received from their enemy, his face crumbled even more and his heart pounded with unaccustomed terror.

"They're walking into a trap, Jenny. You know that."

She nodded as Ryan searched for something on the phone.

"Where's the attachment?"

Without a word she tapped her head to indicate the info was there and no longer on the phone.

Ryan pulled up a chair with desperation and sat before her, setting the phone down on the small bed table and taking her hands in his. "Jenny, you know I love that boy like he were my own, and I respect no man more than Arthur, but this is too big. They'll all be killed. Please, tell me. Let professionals handle it."

Her face remained sad and introspective, but also resolute. "You saw the message. They'll kill Chris and Sylvia. This is the only way."

Ryan felt like cursing, but did not release his anger. He breathed deeply and looked at her more seriously than he ever had. "They're all going to die, Jenny, not just Chris and Sylvia. You saw what they came at us with!"

She looked like a woman resigned to whatever Fate had in store for her, Ryan decided, as though these past few years with Arthur had instilled that kind of calm within her. "Lance assured me they'd have plenty of firepower."

Ryan opened his mouth to say something, but she squeezed his hands gently. "He's not a boy anymore, James," she went on, almost as though realizing the truth of her words even as she uttered them. "Arthur raised him well. All of them. Their plan is to sneak in and find the kids. I'm to give them ten hours before giving *you* the location. Then you do what you have to do. But I trust him, James, and I'm giving him those ten hours."

Her tone, her words, and the sheer weight of it all told Ryan she'd made up her mind and there was nothing he could do to change it. Releasing her hands, he sat back with a sigh and gazed into the calm, unmoving features of this amazing man from the past who'd changed his life, and the world, for the better.

Yes, Arthur, he said to himself, *you did raise that boy well. And I trust him, too.*

But that realization did nothing to calm his fears, however, for he couldn't even imagine life without that boy. Listening to the *beep beep beep* of the machines, Ryan did something he hadn't done since he was a child – bowed his head in prayer.

†††

Jamil had been better then his word, Lance realized, after he'd snuck out of the hospital by the back exit while the fracas in front drew all the attention. Esteban waited in what Lance hoped was a borrowed van, and not one Jamil's homies had stolen. But he couldn't worry about that right then. Esteban told him the others were in back with the firepower.

"*Lots* of firepower."

Lance had merely nodded, no longer wondering if he'd made the right choice, his thoughts focused on breaching the enemy compound.

Secure in its sheath at his waist, and a little awkward within the beat-up and cramped shotgun seat, Excalibur's hilt rested comfortably within Lance's sweaty hand. He had his own bow and arrows in back, and knew Reyna had brought hers, too. Neither of them felt as comfortable aiming a gun, and Techie planned to use his smartphone as his chief weapon, hopefully hacking into the enemy's system and disabling at least some of his defenses.

They rode in silence through the woods north of Walter Reed and then further into the wilds of Maryland. Yes, Lance noted through the dirty glass of his side window, these were real woods out here, the kind you had to drive a long way to find in Southern California.

It was obvious that they'd reached their destination when the small dirt road they'd been traveling on ended at a closed gate with a bright, shiny sign proclaiming: "Private Property. Trespassers Will Be Prosecuted."

They'll be a lot more than prosecuted, Lance knew, but kept that thought to himself.

Esteban stopped the van and killed the engine, looking over at him soberly. Lance studied the face of his brother in the shadowy darkness and saw what he'd always seen from the moment Lance had bested him in that sword fight – unflinching loyalty. He wanted to say something, anything, even just to thank Este for that loyalty in case he didn't get another chance. But the words didn't come. He was their leader, their king, and Este knew the odds going in. They all did. That old line from *The Three Musketeers* came to him then: "All for one and one for all." That's how it worked for the Round Table, too. His team, his family, already knew how he felt, and he knew how they felt. Later, if they survived, would be the time for words. Now only actions counted.

So he acknowledged Este's look with a nod and then both young men exited the vehicle to join their companions unloading the van from in back. Lance gaped at the automatic rifles and semi-automatic handguns being passed around. They'd also thought ahead to retrieve their bulletproof vests from the bus when the bows and arrows were grabbed, and so that was the first order of business. Everyone strapped each other into those vests and covered them over with black t-shirts or sweatshirts. Since their Round Table pants tended to be light brown in color and might stand out more in the dark, everyone had opted for dark blue or black jeans and the best running shoes they owned. Lance wore the new skate shoes he'd gotten for his seventeenth birthday because they provided good traction, and because he might never get another chance to wear them.

He slipped his quiver of arrows over his head, as did Reyna, Dakota, and Kai. The Indians also took a handgun each. Techie refused a gun, feeling more confident with the smartphone in his hand. Lance watched as he located the compound's Wi-Fi signal and quickly hacked into it.

"That was too easy, Lance," he announced as the others strapped weapons to their backs. Even in the dark, Lance could see worry on Techie's youthful face.

"Of course it was, Techie," Lance replied with a heavy sigh. "This is just a game to him. Cat and mouse."

"Yeah, well I'm no mouse," Justin announced quietly, but firmly. "And that asshole's goin' down for what he did to my Dad!"

Lance nodded his way, and then scanned the faces gathered round him in the dark. "Everybody ready?"

All heads nodded in unison.

Lance turned to approach the gate. It was easily ten feet tall, as was the chain-link fence extending out from each side and surrounding the property. Not surprisingly, though the gate had a state-of-the-art electronically controlled locking mechanism, it stood open. They were expected, after all. Lance pulled it wide and ushered everyone through. Once they were all inside the grounds, he left the gate and joined his team.

With a whirring motorized sound, the heavy steel gate swung shut and clicked. They were locked in.

Everyone looked at Lance. He shrugged and turned to Techie. "Find the mines so we can go around 'em."

Techie studied the glowing screen of his smartphone intently. Lance moved to his side and eyed the screen, too. There was a sort-of infrared outline of an enormous, multi-building compound in the upper section of the screen. Techie ran his fingers over the glass to move the image. The buildings vanished and only empty land remained. He continued to scroll until the heat images of nine human bodies appeared.

But nothing else.

"I see us," Techie said, frowning, as the others crowded around, "but not the mines. I saw them on my laptop, but…."

And Lance understood. "But he did something so now you can't see them."

Techie looked up from the phone, swallowed hard and nodded.

"Shit!" Esteban cursed under his breath.

But Dakota and Kai had stepped forward and scanned the rocky terrain cannily, not even aiming their flashlights, just studying the ground intently. Lance paused to watch them, elbowing Esteban to look, as well.

Kai pointed about three feet in front of him, glanced over at Dakota, who nodded back and pointed off to his left about two feet.

Lance smiled. "You guys can see them, can't you?"

"We're Indian, Lance," Kai said proudly. "Born and raised trackers."

"You guys need to follow us exactly the same," Dakota said gravely. "You step the wrong way and…."

He let the thought trail off, but everyone already knew the punch line. Taking Reyna's hand in his, Esteban stepped up behind Lance.

"Let's go," Lance said quietly.

With Dakota in front and Kai slightly back and to his right, Lance queued up behind them and everyone else followed suit. Esteban reluctantly released Reyna's hand, leaned in for a quick kiss, and then placed her in front of him. With careful deliberation, tiny flashlights providing the only illumination, the group started forward. Lance kept his light trained on the feet of Dakota and Kai before him so everyone else could see clearly where to step, and where not to. Slowly, the line moved out into the field with extreme caution.

Dakota moved like a panther creeping up on its prey, Lance thought, each step calculated and cautious, some to the side and some at odd angles. But all in complete silence. Crickets could be heard, and Lance detected the clunky footsteps of his fellow knights behind him, but the Indians moved like ghosts across the field. Once, Dakota started to the right but Kai's hand on his shoulder paused his foot in midair. Kai pointed just a few inches to the right of where Dakota was about to set down his foot, and the Lakota boy nodded, moving his foot an inch to the left.

To Lance's untrained eye, all the terrain looked the same. But somehow the Indians could see subtleties in the dirt or shrubbery that indicated the earth had been disturbed and a mine planted.

I might be Native, he thought in amazement, *but I'll never be able to do that.*

The silence of the night creeped him out, and Lance knew his fellow knights would be feeling the same. Having grown up around constant city noise of some kind, this much quiet felt unsettling. He could not turn around, however, to offer any reassurance. His eyes remained fixed on the feet of his brothers just ahead, and he matched their movements with a precision that surprised him, placing each of his feet in exactly the spots where those of Dakota and Kai stepped first.

The going was slow. The moon provided their only illumination except for the tiny beams of light they carried, and chirping crickets kept them company. A cool night breeze crept up, wafting Lance's hair from side to side as he pressed inexorably forward. He wasn't sure he'd have had the patience a few years ago for this kind of measured stealth, but as eager as he was to get inside and save the kids, he didn't feel the old youthful rush of impetuousness threatening to overwhelm him. He remained calm and cool, listening to the cautious footfalls of his team close behind.

The vague outlines of buildings in the distance began to coalesce in the darkness up ahead, at the periphery of his vision, and Lance breathed a sigh of relief while forcing his eyes to remain on the cat-like feet of his Native brothers. Finally, it looked like something was going their way, that they would make it through the minefield unscathed. But then he heard the scurrying of small animals somewhere in the dark.

Dakota and Kai froze. Lance froze with them, knowing without looking that everyone behind him had done the same.

"What is that, Cloudy?" Kai whispered. "Can you tell?"

In the dark, Lance saw Dakota tilt his head, listening with intensity. "Small animals," he whispered back. "Gophers, maybe."

Suddenly Lance felt a chill grip his heart and freeze his breath as the sound flashed him back to his old life sleeping in dank, dirty alleys. "Not gophers," he whispered desperately. "Rats. A *lot* of rats." He met Dakota's steely gaze with his own. "Can you tell which direction they're coming from?"

Dakota titled his head again, and so did Kai. They looked at one another in horror. "From right behind us, Lance," Dakota answered with a sharp breath.

Lance's eyes widened with terror. "And they're gonna blow the mines."

Kai nodded solemnly.

"What'll we do?" Lance asked breathlessly, knowing the others behind him could hear. They needed a plan. Quickly.

Dakota met his look with an unflinching one of his own. "We run."

Lance's eyes grew even wider.

"Everyone," Dakota said more loudly, "Follow my steps exactly or–"

A mine behind them blew into the night, lighting up the field with a sharp orange blast and flinging clods of dirt into the air around them like brown snow flurries.

Lance gasped. The field writhed with hundreds of moving, slithering forms streaming desperately in their direction, squeaking and panicked from the blast.

A second mine blew, this one closer, spraying the group with more dirt and bits of rock.

"Now!" Dakota shouted, then turned and ran, his eyes never leaving the ground, his movements zigzaggy and seemingly erratic. Kai instantly followed, then Lance and then the others.

Lance practically held his breath as behind them mine after mine exploded amidst more frantic squeals and shrieks of terror from the desperate rodents. But he kept his focus, and prayed his team could maintain it too. His eyes remained riveted to Kai's feet directly in front of him and his old skateboarding skills served him well as he kept perfect footing and landed exactly where the Navajo boy previously stepped. The mine blasts grew ever closer, but none, Lance realized with gratitude, had been close enough to indicate a team member had been hit. And no one emitted a sound. Only their frantic footfalls came to his ears as he pelted onward.

Trees appeared at the edges of Lance's vision, with the buildings he'd previously glimpsed to the left of them, or so his mind envisioned the scene even as his feet landed each movement with the perfection of a figure skater. As the trees loomed larger, suddenly Dakota ceased his frantic running, and Kai stopped, as well.

Lance nearly collided with both boys. Kai held out his arms to guide Lance's body around behind him and then the three watched as the others leapt and gamboled and darted urgently forward, orange blast after orange blast illuminating the night behind them, punctuating the air with deafening explosions, and turning each member of his team into split second silhouettes. Dirt and rocks flew every which way as the frantic rats set off mine after mine.

"Do not move," Lance heard Dakota announce to the gasping and panting group of wide-eyed knights as the last of them left the minefield behind and they all gathered around the Indians, breaths ragged and hitching.

The explosions trickled to a stop, but suddenly Lance felt scurrying movements brushing against his legs and feet. He heard Reyna gasp, and Darnell whisper, "Oh shit!" as he realized the rats had surrounded them.

"Not a muscle," Dakota continued, his voice steady and calm.

So Lance froze, and saw his fellow knights do the same, the whites of their eyes wide and focused at their feet as hundreds of rats fled the minefield into the woods behind them. The rodents were clearly terrified, Lance could tell, and simply wanted to get as far from the carnage of their brethren as possible.

But just the thought of so many vermin brushing up against him made his skin crawl with revulsion, and he knew the others felt the same way. But he also knew Dakota was right. By freezing in place, the terrified rats would flee right past in their desperation to escape. If they moved or attempted to hurt the animals, the rats could easily turn on them and that would be that.

It seemed to take forever, but in fact the rats were past and into the woods within a matter of seconds. Lance released the breath he held and glanced at his team. Even the always-unflappable Reyna looked spooked by what they'd just survived, and he couldn't blame her. He lifted his flashlight and waved the beam over the now pitted and charred minefield. Huge holes gaped everywhere and the air was heavy with dust and grit.

Lowering his light, Lance said, "Everyone okay?"

All heads nodded. Techie looked especially distressed, and Lance was pleased to see Merlin place a comforting hand on the boy's shoulder.

"That was crazier than anything in the hood," Esteban muttered, and both Darnell and Justin nodded vigorously.

Lance turned to Dakota and Kai. "Thanks, guys. That was amazing." He offered a tight smile of gratitude, and Dakota nodded.

Kai, however, tossed off a strained laugh. "Nothing for us Indians, right, Cloudy?"

Dakota flashed Kai such a "wtf" look that Lance almost grinned. Then they looked around to reconnoiter their location.

Most of the trees were to the right as they faced the way they'd come, and the vague outlines of what looked like a massive two-story warehouse with a v-shaped roof rose out of the dark to their left. Like ninjas moving stealthily beneath a blanket of night, the group gathered around Lance to eye the building warily.

Lance studied the shape and outlines of the structure, focusing his eyes and letting them adjust to the dark again after the bright mine blasts had seared his retinas. So intent was he on the building, he barely noticed Darnell taking a step forward. The movement distracted him and as he glanced down he caught just the glint of a wire right where Darnell's foot was moving.

"Darnell, no!" he hissed.

But it was too late. The young man's foot caught on the wire and he toppled forward, arms outstretched to break his fall.

What happened next took only an instant. Lance heard a whooshing sound coming toward them and whipped his head to the right. Without understanding, he saw Kai leap forward like a deer on the run and plow into Dakota with both arms outstretched before him, shoving the other man hard to the ground.

There was a *thunk* sound and a grunt of pain from Kai, and then silence once more fell over them. Darnell scrambled to his feet as Lance raced to Kai, and a furious Dakota leapt up.

"Oh shit!" Darnell exclaimed as he rushed over and saw the arrow protruding from Kai's right side, right below the pec, blood already streaming out.

Kai looked momentarily stunned, as if in shock, as he gazed at a horror-stricken Dakota staring at the arrow.

"Why did you do that?" Dakota hissed, even as he reached out to keep Kai from collapsing. Lance grabbed his other side and eased him to the ground in a sitting position. Kai already looked ashen, even in the darkness, his pale face finding only that of Dakota.

"Cuz I love you, Cloudy Boy," he croaked, his breathing clearly impeded by the arrow.

Lance, suspecting the arrow had at least damaged one lung, watched Dakota fight for his customary composure, and not sure what to do, he glanced at Merlin.

"Set him up against a tree," the wizard said in a tight, but firm voice. "We don't want him falling over."

Lance nudged the stricken Dakota and glanced at the other guys. With extreme care, they gathered around their fallen comrade, gripping his feet and arms, and gently lifted him as best they could, duck-walking over to the nearest tree. Lance and Dakota held the wincing Kai by his right arm and thigh respectively, doing their best not to induce more bleeding from the wound. The arrow, Lance could see, had found its way through the seam between the front and back portions of the vest. Had Kai's arms not been outstretched toward Dakota, the arrow would likely have pierced the Indian's upper arm.

Easing Kai down and resting his back up against the tree, Lance stood up and everyone stepped back to give the wounded knight some space.

"Should we try to take it out?" Reyna asked, her voice taut with fear and uncertainty.

"No!" Dakota and Kai hissed simultaneously.

"Too deep," Kai added in breathless fear. "I'll bleed out." His eyes found those of his soul mate. "Shit, Cloudy, this hurts like a muther! Maybe we shouldn't be shooting animals with these things, huh?"

He tried for a laugh, but it came out a strangled gasp for air. Dakota dropped to his knees and took his hand gently, caressing it as though it were the most precious gift in the world to him.

Feeling sick, the cloud of failure already creeping over his soul, Lance turned to Merlin. "Can you do anything, Merlin?"

The wizard stepped forward and knelt by Kai's side, examining with squinty eyes the arrow and the ragged flesh where the head had gone in. He tilted his head up to Lance.

"I brought along some salves, some herbs, from the old days when such wounds were commonplace," he said as he stood. Slipping off his small backpack, the older man fished around a moment while everyone waited in silent fear. Lance eyed Darnell's guilt-ridden expression and tried to give him a look of reassurance.

Merlin pulled out a small satchel. "These will help slow the bleeding, and the infection," he said, gazing purposefully at Lance. "But they will not save him if we tarry too long on this mission."

Lance nodded and waved the wizard forward.

"We need to cut the shaft off," Merlin added matter-of-factly, like a surgeon about to operate on a patient.

"I'll do it," Dakota said at once. He released Kai's hand and slipped his hunting knife from its sheath.

Lance observed the two of them, his mind flashing back to Ricky lying near death in that hospital room, and knew exactly what both men were feeling.

Kai nodded to Dakota as he moved around to face the protruding arrow shaft. Kai gritted his teeth as Dakota reached out with steady hands. One hand grasped the shaft while the other placed the knife-edge against it, very close to the ragged skin and streaming blood. They locked eyes, and then Kai nodded.

Without hesitation, Dakota pressed the knife home. A *snap* ripped through the silence, and Kai grunted a moment in pain, and then quiet returned. Dakota eyed the shaft a second before tossing it away into the trees and stepping back to allow Merlin the space to apply his medicine.

Everyone watched mutely, with Lance feeling especially helpless, as the wizard removed some kind of paste from an ancient-looking container and applied it to the bloody wound. Kai's face instantly switched from grimacing pain to almost peaceful calm.

"Wow, that stuff works," he muttered, grinning over at Dakota beside him, who knelt once more to hold his hand. "Better than Indian medicine."

As Lance observed Merlin at work, his mind raced. They had to save Kai if they could. He held out a hand to Esteban. "Este, the van keys."

Obviously confused, Esteban reached into his jeans pocket and slipped out the keys, handing them over. Lance gripped them and turned to Dakota. "Dakota, once we get him patched up, you take him back to the van and get him to a doctor."

Dakota looked hopeful for a split second, until Kai's voice cut the night like a bullet. "No."

"What?" Lance said, mystified.

Kai shook his head. "Not our way, Lance," he said, his voice sounding raspy, but stronger. "We vowed to protect you till we dropped, and an Indian's honor is everything. Cloudy knows that."

His eyes found those of the man he loved, and Dakota hesitated for a split second, as though deciding whether to choose honor or love. For the second time since Lance had met him, the young Indian looked weak.

"He's right, Lance. I can't dishonor my people any more than I already have." He paused and looked over at Kai beside him. "Even for him." Those last words were barely a whisper against the cool breeze.

But Lance could tell Kai wasn't offended or upset. In fact, he looked amused.

"Besides, Lance," the wounded man rasped. "Cloudy can't drive."

Now Dakota appeared thoroughly embarrassed in addition to looking weak and afraid.

Lance exchanged a look with Merlin, who had finished dressing the wound with the salve, and then glanced at Esteban. He knew they couldn't spare or Reyna, and he also knew everyone in the group had known the odds, had known they might not come out of this alive. Now he began to understand the weight of leadership more fully, the almost impossible choices that had to be made, the heaviness of that crown Merlin had mentioned. But he had to do something for this friend who had saved his life on multiple occasions.

Stripping off his black t-shirt, Lance handed it to Dakota. "Quick, stuff this up and under both sides of the vest to slow the bleeding even more."

Dakota took the shirt, tore it along one seam, and set to work.

Then Lance startled everyone by unclasping his double-sided bulletproof vest, leaving him shirtless and exposed.

"Lance, what are you doing?" Reyna asked, her voice filled with alarm.

"I know what I'm doing. Este, your knife." He tossed the keys back and took the knife an obviously confused Esteban handed him.

Knowing time was of the essence, Lance squatted, ignoring the presence of everyone and their murmurs of concern. Using the knife, he sliced down the seam on each side of the vest, separating the front section from the back. He scooted closer to Kai's wounded side and eyed it a moment. Then he used the knife to dig a hole in the upper portion of one half of the vest, scraping and digging and removing some of the protective shielding that could save the life of whoever wore it.

Finishing quickly, Lance studied his handiwork and decided it would have to do. Looking up at the group, he said, "Who has pants that won't fall without a belt?"

All the guys looked at each other sheepishly, until Techie stepped forward. "I'm the nerd here. You need it?"

"Yeah." Lance held out his hand as Techie slipped off his belt and gave it over. Lance then handed half of the vest to Dakota and he kept the half with the hole in it. He slipped out his own belt and eyed Techie with a tight smile. "Guess I'm a nerd too."

He looped the belts together and handed one end to Dakota. "Put that vest against his side, covering the seam, and I'm gonna do the same with mine. Then we tie them together with the belts. That way he can't be shot at from the sides 'less it's a head shot."

Dakota's eyes widened in admiration and he nodded. "But why the hole?"

"So we don't push the arrowhead in any more," Lance replied, and he heard a sigh of understanding waft through his team.

Kai grinned. "Pretty slick, Lance. You *are* a great chief."

Lance grunted as he carefully placed his portion of the vest into place. "If I was such a great chief this wouldn't have happened in the first place. Shit, we're not even inside yet!"

He gently pressed his hand to Kai's back to ease him away from the tree enough to slip the belt behind him and then once more rested the man's head gently against the bark.

As he and Dakota secured the belts, Kai's eyes wandered over Lance's naked, sweat-sheened torso, and he smirked. "You just wanna scare whoever's inside with how freakin' buff you are, Lance," he said with a raspy, hollow laugh.

Lance knew Kai was trying to lighten his guilt, but Lance couldn't let himself be drawn in. Too much emotion would destroy him before his enemy ever could.

Once the operation was completed, Lance and Dakota stood. Lance looked down at the fallen boy, satisfied with their handiwork. Then he turned to ask Esteban for a gun. He froze. Everyone on the team stood staring at him, almost in awe.

"What?" he asked, wondering if Excalibur had begun glowing again. He glanced at the sword in its scabbard at his waist, but it looked normal. So what was with the weird looks?

It was Reyna who broke the silence. "Kai's right, Lance," she said quietly, her voice filled with respect. "You look so strong and noble and... well, to use your own words, toweringly beautiful. Like Jack with long hair."

Lance gasped at her words, and his own description of the boy who'd saved him.

"She's right, *carnal*," Esteban confirmed, his voice rife with admiration. "You look bigger than ever, like one of those Indian dudes from the movies, all fierce and warrior-like."

The others nodded in silent agreement, even Dakota.

Lance wasn't even sure how their comments made him feel. A warrior? That wasn't him. Except now it was, wasn't it?

Because I have to be.

But noble? Toweringly beautiful? Those things he didn't feel.

"But now you have no protection," Reyna added suddenly, the respect replaced by fear. "You may be buff, but you're not bulletproof."

Lance glanced at Merlin knowingly. "Yes, I am." He pulled Excalibur from its sheath and held its blade up in the moonlight, where it shimmered regally. Warmth instantly suffused his entire body, and suddenly the chill night air didn't bother him anymore. "Aren't I, Merlin?"

Merlin bowed slightly. "That you are, Your Majesty."

Lance heard Reyna gasp slightly, and uncertain murmuring wafted through the group. Obviously, they hadn't considered that possibility.

"Este, give Kai a gun with a lot of bullets," Lance ordered as he turned back to the Indian on the ground who'd become one of his best friends in the world.

Este hurried over with what looked to Lance's untrained eye like some kind of automatic mini-machine gun, and handed it to Kai. The Indian gripped it with ease and met Lance's intense gaze.

"You know how to use that?"

Kai nodded, coughing a moment before responding. "Este showed me how it works. No worries."

Lance's heart beat wildly, his chest heaving with near gasps for air. The emotional toll of this moment almost overpowered him, and he had to swallow hard and slow to regain control. "You hang on, Sir Kai of the Round Table," he said with purpose and force. "We're coming back for you. You hang on. That's a command!"

Kai tried for a grin, but the pain must've been too great because it turned into a grimace. "I'm not going… anywhere… Your Majesty."

Lance wanted to say a thousand things to this man in case he never got another chance. But all that came out was, "Thank you, Sir Kai, for being my friend."

Fearing he might lose his edge, every muscle in his upper body corded with pent up tension, Lance turned and waved to the others to follow. Dakota hung back, obviously torn between his duty, and the young man who'd stolen his heart at the age of six.

Lance paused after everyone had stepped carefully over the trip wire, and waited.

Dakota stood a few feet away gazing steadily at Kai, and Kai at him. Kai looked almost slumped over, his long braids tumbling down the sides of his chest, but his eyes still danced, even in the darkness, and he offered a sly grin. "Come back to me this time, Cloudy Boy. Okay?"

Dakota stiffened, and Lance wasn't sure what the taciturn man might do next. Dakota was anything but impulsive. But this time, impulse won out over reticence as he ran back and dropped to his knees before the wounded Kai, placed both hands on the pale cheeks and kissed him as hard and passionately as he dared.

Lance felt a wave of emotion engulf him, thinking of Ricky, wondering if he'd ever see that boy alive again, just as he knew Dakota wondered the same thing about Kai. He glanced over at the others beside him. They gazed at the two kissing boys with understanding and compassion, especially Darnell whose face revealed the guilt he clearly felt. Once upon a time, Lance knew, these "hard" guys would've looked away in disgust, and some would've talked shit or worse to kissing boys. But now it was different. Now they were brothers, *carnales*, the kind of *real* homies who looked out for each other. They were a family, and two of their own were suffering.

Dakota pulled back with obvious reluctance and locked eyes on those of his breathless soul mate. "On my honor, Sir Laughs A Lot."

That drew a warm smile to Kai's lips and then with a flourish of flying hair Dakota was up and running, leaping over the trip wire and rejoining Lance and the others, never once looking back.

Lance made eye contact one last time with the Navajo youth who possessed the infectious laugh and Da Vinci hands. Kai tossed him a handsome grin. Lance offered the chin nod, then turned and followed the others forward into the dark.

†††

Ryan sat slumped in his chair, exhausted, but not daring to sleep. Jenny sat beside him. They had remained in the Intensive Care room, masked and hospital-gowned, keeping vigil over their two loved ones. The silence felt heavy, like the air after a downpour, with only the beeping of machines for company.

Jenny looked up from Arthur's peaceful face and turned to Ryan. "Did you tell Sandra yet?"

Ryan looked startled a moment, pulled, as it were, from a deep reverie. Then he nodded, his aging face rife with guilt and remorse. "Justin talked with her, too, before he …." He trailed off, fighting, Jenny could tell, for his old stoic composure. "Jenny, if that boy dies too…."

She reached out and took his hand in hers, gently rubbing it through the latex gloves. "He's a man now, James. You couldn't have stopped him any more than I could've stopped Lance." She knew he already understood, but wasn't it always the way with adults to fight the fact that their kids eventually grew up and made their own decisions?

She sighed. "I'm so sorry about Robert. I know he was your best friend."

Ryan nodded again, and Jenny feared he might break down. She found herself wondering when he'd last cried? She'd seen him well up the night Lance had "died," but how many years before that had he shed tears? She squeezed his hand supportively.

"The irony of all this is my other best friend is lying right here in this bed," Ryan said, his voice raspy and choked with emotion. "A man I once thought was out to ruin my city. Times sure change."

"It's okay to grieve, James. Robert was a great man."

Suddenly, the stoic look returned to Ryan's face. "Can't grieve yet, Jenny, not while my boys are in danger." He looked pointedly at her and she knew what he wanted.

She shook her head. "They've only been gone two hours, James. I promised Lance ten."

He sighed and stood. "Time to make my report to the president." With one final glance at Arthur, and then a flick of his eyes toward the equally unmoving Ricky, Ryan exited the room, walking, Jenny thought, like the old man he was rapidly becoming.

In the dimly lit, but well-guarded corridor outside the room, Ryan stripped off his mask and gloves, eyed the two Secret Service agents on either side of the door, and then wandered away out of earshot. He whipped out his phone and speed-dialed the president, placing the handset to his ear anxiously.

"She still won't budge, Mr. President," he said heavily into the phone. "We'll have to wait the full ten. The men you sent are here on standby. Soon as I have the coordinates, we go in."

He listened a moment in nervous silence and shook his head, even though the president couldn't see him. "We did trace their phones, sir, and found them all right here in the laundry room. Sir Techie thinks of everything."

Another pause, then, "Yes, sir, that's what everyone calls him. I don't know even his real name. Yes, Mr. President, I'll check back before we deploy."

He paused again, and then sighed heavily. "No, sir, there's been no change. Both still unconscious. Good night, Mr. President."

He lowered the phone and hit the end button with his thumb. He'd felt helpless on more than a few occasions in his life, most notably that night he thought Lance had died and he'd been unable to do anything but watch the boy's life drain away into the asphalt.

Am I back there all over again, he wondered? *Will I have to bury that boy for real this time?*

He stared at the closed door with its thick glass observation window and armed agents to each side and forced resolve back into his heart.

Hell no! Not Lance. If anyone can pull this off, it's him.

Feeling slightly more energized, Ryan headed back to the nurse's station for a fresh mask and gloves. The vigil continued.

†††

Lance and his team crept cautiously along in the dark, carefully skirting the building, all of their eyes on the alert for more booby traps and trip wires. Beneath the moonlight, Lance spotted a door leading into the enormous structure. The door stood ajar, awaiting them. They were expected.

He glanced at Techie and found his friend staring at his sweaty torso with glassy-eyed admiration. Lance knew the other boy was very self-conscious about his body and had never taken off his shirt during any training sessions over the years. The young genius looked away in embarrassment as soon as Lance caught him looking.

"Obviously, we're expected," Lance said quietly. "What can you tell us about the layout, Techie, now that we're so close?"

Techie slipped out his large Nexus smartphone and powered it on. He'd long ago blocked his number from any and all prying eyes, which was why even the president and the NSA couldn't track it.

The crickets had quieted down after all the explosions, and the almost unearthly quiet reminded Lance of those cheesy Camp Crystal Lake horror movies he used to watch.

Techie examined the screen intently while Lance eyed Dakota. The Indian youth had his gaze momentarily turned back the way they'd come, though Kai had long ago been lost in the darkness. He must've felt Lance's eyes because Dakota turned quickly and looked embarrassed. Lance nodded with understanding.

As the phone sprang to life, they crowded around Techie. The same infrared-like grid re-appeared, clearly showing the contours of the interconnected compound buildings, with flashing or blinking indicators throughout marking the positions of something Lance didn't understand. But what he did notice was that the design of the interior reminded him of those pencil mazes he used to do in grade school, the ones where you entered at one end and had to find your way to the center in a set period of time.

The center of this structure was clearly visible with an odd, mildly pulsing orange glow within it. There were several other glowing blobs, Lance noticed, moving about the maze-like facility. And then he understood.

"Are those people?" he asked, pointing to one of the moving lights.

Techie nodded. "Yeah, heat signatures. Like I told you 'fore we left, I tapped into every satellite I could and used them to scan this place, hoping to learn whatever I could about the layout. I've also been trying to get into his computer system, and have got a program searching for the access code. So far no luck there. But this—" He pointed to the unmoving, slowly pulsing glow in the center section. "—is Chris."

Lance's heart skipped a beat and he heard Reyna gasp loudly. "Chris? How do you know?"

Techie eyed Lance nervously in the moonlit gloom. "I never told you, Lance, but when I was monitoring the computer lab to find, you know, the spy, I recorded everybody's heat signature with a program I found. That way I'd know for sure who came and went in case they used fake log-ins."

Lance's mouth dropped open in awe. He'd always known Techie was brilliant, but this was astounding. "That's so cool," he whispered. "And you're sure that's Chris?"

Techie nodded. "Yeah. I had Sir Phillip send me his signature."

Lance stared at the pulsing glow on the screen anxiously, his heart pounding with a mix of love for his brother and dread for what might have been done to him. "Is he okay? Can you tell?"

Techie nodded again. "The pulse is slow - that's his heart rate that makes the light pulse – like maybe he's asleep or unconscious? But he's alive."

Lance let out the breath he'd sucked in. Unconscious was bad, but alive was good. "What about Sylvia? Can you see her?"

Now Techie looked sheepish, almost humiliated. "I guess I forgot to record hers, Lance. Phillip couldn't find it. I thought I'd gotten everyone. Sorry."

Lance placed a hand of comfort on the young man's shoulder, thinking back to those few months before the tour. Had he even seen Sylvia in the lab? He couldn't recall. It seemed to him that she'd spent all of her time in the Training Centre.

"It's okay," he said with a confidence he didn't feel. "We'll find her. Shall we just walk in the back door or try to sneak in?"

Techie scanned the phone screen again. "Here's the thing. Right now, that open door is our only way in. All the rest have a key code to punch in and I haven't been able to crack the code. My program is still running, but—" He suddenly froze as the image on screen was replaced by a flashing message reading: "Success!" And then a seven-digit number popped up. "Bingo, guys, I just got it. Perfect timing."

He grinned and accepted some high-fives from his team, though Lance could tell all the computer talk was muddling their minds.

"So what does this mean, Techie?" Lance asked, his brows furrowed, his whole body taut with tension. "Can we sneak in now?"

Techie nodded from behind his grin. "But here's the thing, Lance. I can use the code to access any electronic door in the place. However, each time I do he'll know where we are."

Lance mulled that over a moment and said, "From what we know of this guy, he'll know where we are anyway. You all agree with that?"

He turned to the team and everyone nodded.

Then Justin said, "This guy seems to like booby traps, Lance. You know, Indiana Jones stuff."

Something jogged in Lance's memory, but he couldn't glom onto it. "You're right, Justin. Like this stuff out here, the mines and trip wires. Old school." He paused and considered while the team waited in silence. "I think if we walk through that door we'll be walking into more of those traps."

"I agree," Esteban said quickly.

"Me too," Reyna added. "Maybe if we sneak in and can stay off his radar for a bit we might get closer to Chris before he spots us."

"That means turning off my phone," Techie said, looking stricken. "We'd be blind in there."

Lance considered his options. Then it came to him. "Which of you can draw?"

Dakota looked sideways at him, obviously thinking of Kai.

But Darnell said, "I can. Sort of."

Now Justin looked over at him in surprise. "You *can*?"

Darnell nodded, looking embarrassed to be good at something so, in his worldview, unmanly.

Lance turned to Esteban, who wore a backpack of supplies and tools. "Turn around, Este."

The shorter man turned without hesitation and Lance unzipped the pack, fishing around until he pulled out a small pad and a pen. These he handed to Darnell.

"He wants old school, we'll give him old school. Darnell, copy what you see on Techie's phone, the whole layout, best you can."

Now realizing what Lance was doing, everyone grinned in admiration while Darnell quickly went to work.

Lance glanced at the wristwatch he'd "borrowed" from the hospital.

"How much time, Lance?" Reyna asked anxiously.

Lance felt his stomach tighten with fear. "Seven and a half hours till the troops arrive. We gotta move fast in there."

For a few moments, the only sounds were the scratchings of Darnell's pen against the pad of paper. The cold night air brushed against Lance's exposed, sweaty torso, but the warmth flowing into him from Excalibur prevented the chill from affecting him. Once Darnell had finished, Lance looked at an exact copy of Techie's screen, almost like a screen shot by pen.

"Wow, you *can* draw," he said, taking the pad and studying it. Darnell had even placed the glows were they'd been on the phone screen, as well as any electronic doors, and had clearly marked the computer room for Techie.

"Best way to gain control over the whole place," Techie told Lance, who tore off the paper and shoved the drawing into his jeans pocket.

"Our main goal is the kids," he told Techie and the group soberly and firmly. "But if we end up near the computer room it's all yours, Techie."

Techie nodded and re-examined his phone. "There's an underground bunker just ahead, Lance, on the other side of the swimming pool. It's got a hidden entrance, but I can see it here cuz of the electronic keypad my program picks up. We could try sneaking in that way."

"Let's do it. He'll have cameras all over the place, I'm sure, so even with your phone off he'll be able to track us."

Reyna held up her bow and grinned. "Don't worry. Old school works on them too."

Lance tossed her a small smile and told Techie to lead the way. He turned and moved parallel to the buildings, his eyes on the screen. Lance and Dakota followed close behind, their eyes roaming from the ground to the trees to the buildings looking for trip wires or other potential traps, even pits in the ground covered over with leaves. With this sick bastard, Lance knew, there was no telling what they might encounter.

The moonlight only heightened the horror-film atmosphere of the place, especially when they trooped silently past the empty swimming pool filled with scattered leaves that, once upon a time, Lance would've been hot to skate in. Now it just looked dead and desolate like everything else around him.

Skirting the pool, Lance followed Techie to the left where the young man suddenly stopped before an empty expanse of ground overgrown with weeds and brush. Everyone waited while Techie consulted his phone. Lance eyed Dakota and knew the Indian was thinking the same thing – wasn't this too easy? After the minefield and trip wire that had gotten Kai, there must be a lot more in store for them. But then Lance considered his foe – someone who liked playing games, who wanted to mess with him, but who *did* want him inside the facility.

Okay, asshole, bring it on, Lance thought bitterly, images of Arthur and Ricky splayed out in that field, bleeding and unconscious, filling his mind.

Techie tapped his sneakered foot onto the ground in a few spots, and then turned to Lance. "Here. There's a trap door leading into the bunker."

Lance nodded at the others and they all dropped to their knees, pulling away the weeds and brushing away dirt, finally revealing a metallic square embedded in the earth.

Lance stood and clapped the dirt off his hands. Forearm muscles bulging, every vein pulsing, he gripped Excalibur tightly in his right fist and held its gleaming blade out in the moonlight.

"Okay, this is how we go in," he announced in that tone which did not permit argument. "Techie unlocks this door and then turns off his phone. I go down first." Reyna opened her mouth to protest, but one solid look from Lance shut her down. "No arguments. I have Excalibur. If there's a trap at the bottom it's best I trip it. Only after I call up the all clear do the rest of you follow. Dakota first, followed by Este, Reyna, Techie, Merlin, Darnell, and Justin. You get down as fast as possible because we're gonna need to move fast. The longer we can keep him off guard about our exact location, the better. Reyna and Dakota, soon as you hit bottom look for cameras and take 'em out. He might know where we *were*, but not always where we are. Everybody clear?"

They nodded in the affirmative, but Reyna still looked more terrified than Lance had ever seen her. She stared at him uncertainly, and then turned to Merlin.

"Are you sure, Merlin, that he'll be safe? That's my baby boy over there." Her voice trembled, and Lance felt a gush of love towards this girl who way back in the day had mocked him.

Merlin placed a hand of comfort on Reyna's shoulder. "I'm certain, Lady Reyna."

Reluctantly, she nodded, but still eyed Lance fearfully.

He tossed her an off-hand grin. "Don't worry, big sis. I'm like a cat – nine lives."

She returned the grin, and Lance turned to Techie with a nod, hoping and praying he still had some of those lives left. Techie punched a code into his phone and suddenly, with a whirring of motors and a creaking noise, the metal door began to rise upward on hinges that clearly needed some grease. A square opening of pure blackness in the ground greeted Lance as the door swung up to a ninety-degree angle and stopped. The maw beckoned, and Lance didn't hesitate.

"Let's do this."

Threading the strap from his flashlight through and around one of his belt loops so the beam struck the ground at his feet, he swung himself around and stepped into the black, his feet finding the ladder rungs, and then his left hand gripped the railing. Still clutching Excalibur in his right, Lance began his descent into hell.

†††

Chapter Eight

None of You Are Supposed to Die for Me!

At first, Lance found himself engulfed in blackness. But the further down the ladder he climbed, the more he became aware of a dim light rising from below. Basic emergency lights, he surmised. Gripping Excalibur slowed his descent as he had to drop his left hand to each rung of the cold metal ladder cautiously so as not to fall. His flashlight beam swung crazily from side to side, revealing in kaleidoscope-fashion the ladder and the darkness beneath him.

He moved slowly, but with purpose. Time was not on their side, but he well knew the ladder, itself, could be wired to explode if he took a wrong step. Breathing rapidly, heart thumping, Lance lowered his legs into the dim pool of light rising from an obvious opening several feet below.

So far, so good. No tricks. No traps.

He looked down at the rectangle of light spilling into the shaft and knew it for a doorway. Probably leading into the bunker itself. Forcing his breathing to remain steady, he descended the final three rungs. He lowered his foot towards the metal floor, and paused. Everything seemed silent. He heard no approaching footsteps, no sounds of machinery. Nothing. It was like being inside a grave. Or at least as close to that as he ever wanted to get for a long time.

Steeling himself, Lance turned on the ladder so he was facing the open doorway. If anyone was there, his legs would already be visible so he might as well just go for it. He dropped to the floor, landing on both feet as lithely as a cat, his skating skills kicking in.

And then the machine gun began firing.

†††

Standing at the open trapdoor, staring down into the dark and seeing Lance's tiny light bob this way and that, Esteban wondered if any of them would come out of this alive. Sure, he'd gone on lots of missions as a kid, but gang members seldom did the sneaking around thing. They usually drove by or walked up and just shot you down. The cloak-and-dagger thing wasn't his style. He wanted to storm this place and take out the asshole that'd been stalking them. But this was Lance's operation, and Lance called the shots.

As Esteban and others looked down into the hole, Techie spotted something hidden in the bushes to their right. He scuttled over quietly and found a large wooden box. Glancing back at the others, he saw them all peering into the shaft, so he pulled up the lid on the box. Then he grinned.

Esteban observed Lance's light pause for a moment far down the shaft, and then drop a couple of feet. That's when the gunfire began. The shaft below him lit up with the flashes of automatic weapons fire, and suddenly he couldn't see Lance or his tiny flashlight anymore.

Reyna rushed to his side. "Oh my God! Do something, Este!"

Her face was etched with terror, the same terror he felt gripping his heart like a fist. The others crowded around, the gunshots echoing up the shaft into the quiet of the woods around them.

Dakota made a move for the ladder, but Esteban's outstretched hand stopped him.

Dakota glared fiercely. "I vowed to protect him."

Esteban nodded, his famous calm taking over. "We all did, Sir Dakota. But we have our orders. We wait till he gives the all clear."

"And if he doesn't?" Reyna asked anxiously.

"He will," came Merlin's voice from behind them, unruffled and self-assured.

Esteban turned and eyed the wizard a moment before returning his gaze to the gaping hole before him. The echoing gunfire continued.

†††

The moment the firing began, Lance instinctively dove for the floor and covered his face. It shouldn't have mattered. He'd seen the gun pop out of a panel in the corridor ceiling seconds before it opened fire and there was nothing he could use for cover. He should've been toast. But he wasn't.

He felt the electrical charge from Excalibur's hilt fill his hand, his arm, and then his entire body. And not a single bullet touched him. The noise in the small, tight corridor was deafening and he wished he could cover his ears, but that would mean letting go of the sword and he couldn't do that. So he endured. The dimness of his surroundings flashed in a rat-a-tat fashion as the sparks from the rapid-fire bullets lit up the air around him like fireworks. The smell of gunpowder nearly overwhelmed him.

But then the shooting stopped, and everything went quiet.

Cautiously, still gripping Excalibur firmly, Lance tilted his eyes up and out along the corridor. Smoke billowed amongst the glowing emergency lights lining the walls, but the machine gun, or whatever it was, had fallen silent.

Gingerly, Lance clambered to his feet and examined his torso and arms. He nearly gasped. He was completely untouched, as though the past minute had never occurred. The tingling was gone, and the electrical charge along with it. Excalibur rested in his grip like any other sword he'd ever wielded.

Except this wasn't any other sword.

This one had just made him bulletproof.

Looking back up at the weapon suspended from the ceiling, Lance now saw it looked more like an Uzi than anything else. But it wasn't moving or firing so he hurried over and slashed at the moorings with Excalibur's razor sharp blade, severing the gun from its platform and sending it clattering to the concrete floor at his feet.

He scanned the empty corridor with searching eyes, but there did not seem to be any other traps or trip wires in evidence. Of course, that one hadn't been evident, either, he knew. The pressure of his feet on the floor had triggered it.

Satisfied it was safe, he hurried back to the foot of the ladder and whistled loudly up the shaft. Instantly the moonlight above vanished as someone's body blocked it, someone rapidly descending. Lance stepped back as Dakota dropped to the floor beside him, gaping in stunned amazement at the hundreds of bullets scattered at his feet, and at the bullet holes in the walls around the ladder.

Esteban followed in quick succession, the others right behind him. Reyna gasped loudly at the bullet holes peppering the walls of the shaft. She quickly grabbed Lance and frantically scanned his torso for any damage. He couldn't help but grin. Seeing him unhurt, she pulled him into a tight hug.

"Oh my God, baby boy, I was so afraid for you!"

"There's gotta be hundreds of rounds here, " Darnell exclaimed. "Shit, man, how you still standing?"

Reyna let him go and Lance shrugged, noting the open-mouthed expressions on the faces of Esteban and Justin. Techie seemed unfazed. And Merlin smirked.

"The bullets never touched me," Lance said, his own voice filled with a slight amazement. "But that's not how Excalibur worked on Dad, Merlin. Mark told me."

Merlin shrugged nonchalantly. "Excalibur has a mind of its own, so to speak. How it chooses to protect each king from harm is a mystery."

Esteban tossed off a smirk. "So my buff-ass *carnal* can't do the Superman thing and watch bullets bounce off his chest. Too bad."

Lance gave a hollow laugh, but blushed slightly beneath the compliment, suddenly realizing he was half-naked in front of his peers, his team. Other than swimming, Lance had never been comfortable in front of others without a shirt, and he momentarily felt the discomfort of his situation. But then he shoved it away. Chris and Sylvia were in trouble, and his embarrassment wasn't important.

Turning to look down the corridor, he spotted a camera mounted high in the corner where the hallway t-boned into corridors branching off in either direction. He pointed it out. "Which of you wants to do the honor?"

Dakota and Reyna exchanged a look, and she waved a hand his way. Stepping forward, the Indian slipped an arrow from his quiver, nocked it, raised the bow and fired all in one fluid motion. The arrow struck the power cord running from the back of the camera into the wall, severing it cleanly.

"Good shooting," Techie said with a whistle of admiration. "They may just think the camera malfunctioned."

Lance tilted his head at Techie.

"What?" he asked as everyone gave him the same look.

Lance indicated the bullet casings and bullet holes surrounding them. "I think they know we're here, Techie." Then he offered a little grin to assure his friend it was a joke. Techie grinned back.

"But Techie does have a point," Lance said to the group as a whole. "Along the way, if we can disconnect these cameras they might not know for sure which ones we damaged and which just went down. So keep aiming for the power cords."

Dakota and Reyna nodded as Lance slipped Darnell's hand-drawn map from his pocket and examined it. "Looks like the computer room and the path to the center means a left turn from here. You agree?" He handed it to Techie, who nodded and started to hand it back. "You keep it, Techie. You'll be the navigator."

Techie rolled his eyes. "Another stereotype right out of Star Trek. The Asian navigator."

Lance shrugged.

But then Darnell piped up with, "He was the helmsman."

Everyone turned to the young man in surprise, and Lance was sure he saw him redden with embarrassment. "I was a nerd as a little kid, okay?"

Justin laughed and punched him, and the moment vanished. With a sudden soberness, Lance sighed and, gripping Excalibur firmly, started down the corridor. Wisps of white smoke from the gunfire still swirled around the dim lights, giving him the feeling of being in one of those mazes at Halloween where smoke machines tried to hide the monsters.

Monsters here, too, he thought as he neared the end where the corridor T-boned in both directions. *The human kind.*

Cautiously, he stopped and peered first to his right and then to his left. Both side corridors looked exactly the same as the one he was in – plain walls, emergency-style lighting, and cameras at each end. He waved Dakota forward silently and pointed. Within seconds, the cameras in both directions had been taken off-line.

Heart beating loudly, Lance started forward slowly. He knew the clock was ticking, but he also knew one false step could cost his team members their lives. For an instant he considered sheathing Excalibur and facing the threat with the same human vulnerability as the others. Why should he alone have such protection? But then he considered his position as king, as leader. By going first, he could trip any booby traps they stumbled upon, and Excalibur would allow no harm to befall him. He'd take the hits for his team, and that was a leader's job, after all.

He approached a heavy steel door that looked capable of withstanding a nuclear blast, which, Lance surmised, might be its purpose in an underground bunker like this. There was a keypad on the wall beside the door and he waved Techie over.

Techie punched in a seven-digit sequence of numbers, which Lance quickly memorized. With a click and turning of gears, the door popped open in their direction. Lance nodded to Techie to stand back and then he warily gripped the door and pulled it all the way open.

The comparison to those Halloween mazes didn't do justice to what lay before him. This was a maze, all right, with high walls and numerous branching corridors leading off in different directions. With a sigh, Lance glanced back at Techie, who studied the drawing in his trembling fingers.

Lance eyed those fingers a moment, realizing how terrified his friend must be. Techie had never been a fighter or even very physical in combat training. Sure, he'd learned to wield a sword to defend himself and stay fit, but he'd never mastered the bow and arrow and had early on settled for the tech duties he so excelled at.

Feeling a rush of gratitude to the young man, Lance placed a hand on his shoulder and squeezed gently.

Techie looked up from the drawing, startled momentarily, and then smiled back in gratitude. "We need to take the third branch on the right."

Lance nodded, glanced at his team, saw their looks of resolve, and pushed on ahead. He supposed the murky lighting was intended to unnerve him, and he had to admit it *was* unnerving. But his eyes, always excellent in the dark thanks to Arthur's extreme training within the storm drains of Los Angeles, quickly adapted, roaming the floors and walls and ceilings with purpose, anxiously seeking out any trip wires or false floorboards that might trigger an attack.

Arriving at the third branch, Lance turned to the right and started forward. The high walls and dim lighting looked identical which, he realized, must be the idea. One corridor looked exactly the same as the next, thus making it easy to get lost. But they had a map, thanks to Techie and Darnell, and Lance suspected most hapless victims their enemy may have lured down here hadn't been so fortunate.

A sound just ahead caused Lance to stop and listen. He felt everyone stop behind him. It sounded like something scraping along the floor, maybe a heavy desk or bureau being moved. And then it stopped. He turned to Techie and the others, eyebrows raised questioningly. Techie shrugged and Lance eyed Esteban right behind him. His big brother held up his own Uzi-style weapon to assure Lance he was ready. Lance turned and pressed on.

They passed through several more duplicate corridors with Techie constantly checking the map to make certain they were moving in the right direction. Lance's frustration was beginning to mount as the minutes ticked past with them seemingly no closer to the center, and Chris.

If you hurt my brother, asshole….

Suddenly they came to a dead end, and Lance turned to Techie with exasperation. "Are we lost, Techie?"

Techie's eyes squinted in confusion as they drifted from the map to their surroundings. The others shifted impatiently.

"Something's wrong, Lance," Techie announced, his voice a guttural whisper. "It's like… oh, shit!"

Lance's heart beat faster. "What?"

"He's changing the maze."

"Huh?" That came from a confused Esteban.

Techie cursed, a rarity for him. "It's like Hogwarts from Harry Potter, remember? How the staircases kept moving around all the time?"

Lance shrugged, his frustration growing. "So?"

"So he's moving the walls around so we get lost," Techie finished. "He's making our map useless."

"Shit!" Justin spat behind him, but Lance didn't even turn.

His head spun. "So we have no idea where we are?"

Techie shook his head, his expression one of failure and recrimination. "I'm sorry."

Lance turned to Merlin expectantly. "Any ideas?"

"None that come to mind," the wizard replied evenly.

Lance wanted to scream and shout and pound the walls.

Like a little boy.

Except he wasn't a little boy any more.

To calm himself, he asked, "No Dumbledore tricks in your little sack, Merlin?"

Merlin half-smiled. "Sadly no. Alas, Your Majesty, real life is far more complicated than fiction. The laws of physics and so forth."

Lance's mind raced frantically for an idea, something to get this mission back on track. He was the king. It was up to him to find a solution.

The laws of physics…

I wonder…

He leaned in close to Merlin and quickly ushered everyone in like a football huddle, just in case the corridor was bugged. "Merlin," he whispered. "Have you gotten any of your power back since, well, you know, bringing me back? It's been three years."

Merlin raised his eyebrows slightly. "As a matter of truth, Your Majesty, I have. But still limited. I thought to save it for an emergency."

The others reacted with surprise at the wizard's declaration, but said nothing.

Lance looked at the man dead-on. "This *isn't* an emergency?"

Merlin's gray eyes revealed nothing of his thoughts. "Most definitely. What did you have in mind?"

Lance turned to Techie. "Techie, if you can use your phone to get into the computer system, think you could control the maze, or at least direct us to Chris?"

Techie paused, biting his lip as he considered. "Yeah, I think so. But Lance, the phone will allow them to track us much easier than the cameras."

"That's where Merlin comes in." He turned back to the wizard. "Can you harness enough energy to mask Techie's phone, hide it from the sensors that would pick it up?"

Merlin raised his eyebrows again in surprise, obviously impressed with Lance's idea. "I believe I can, Your Majesty. At least for a limited amount of time."

Lance glanced at his watch. "We have about five hours before my *nino* gets here with the whole freakin' army. Is that too long?"

Merlin considered a moment. "It is a small device and should not require a large expenditure of energy to mask it. An excellent plan."

"Let's do this," Lance whispered with finality, nodding at Techie.

Techie slipped out his smartphone and eyed Merlin uncertainly. "What do I do?"

Merlin's expression remained unchanged. "Give me a moment and when I tell you, turn the device on."

Techie nodded, glancing at Lance nervously as though wondering if this would hurt. Lance offered a smile of reassurance.

Merlin did not close his eyes, but Lance could see the wizard staring ahead and seeing nothing in his path. Merlin had sunk into himself, channeling his power however he did it. Everyone waited, gazing silently at the older man until Reyna gasped slightly and pointed at Techie.

"Look at his hand."

Lance glanced down and noticed Techie's hand, and his phone, bathed in a slight glow.

Merlin spoke, his voice controlled and even. "Now."

Uncertainly, Techie used his thumb to press the power button, and his smartphone sprang to vibrant life in his hand. Gingerly, Techie dipped the fingers of his right hand into the energy field and opened some applications. The grid of the maze re-appeared, only this time it looked different than before because it had changed. Now the path to the control room was far more convoluted.

"Do you think you can take over the maze, Techie?" Lance asked hopefully.

Chewing his lower lip again, Techie played with the phone, inputting this code or that. "I think so, but it might take a little time, Lance."

Lance nodded. As frustrated as he was with their situation, he knew Techie was doing his best. "Okay. While Techie's trying to get in, we keep going. At least now we'll know if we're headed in the right direction."

Without another word, he turned and started back down the corridor after glancing once more at the phone screen for directions. Techie and Merlin followed right behind, with the others bringing up the rear.

The only sound besides the occasional sliding noise, which Lance finally figured out was the sound of walls moving, was Techie's voice as he kept his eyes on his glowing phone and directed Lance to turn left, then right, and then right again. Along each and every turn, either Reyna or Dakota disabled the cameras. To confuse their enemies, they also disabled cameras in corridors they *didn't* take.

Lance knew beyond a doubt that without Techie's phone they'd be hopelessly lost within this labyrinth. He turned to the left and pulled up short.

"Oh shit," he muttered as he gazed at what lay before them.

It was a pool of liquid, easily fifteen feet long and as wide as the corridor, with large stepping-stones across the center of the liquid.

Everyone gathered around Lance and stared at the pool in stony silence.

"We can't go around this somehow?" Lance asked Techie with a heavy sigh.

The tech genius shook his head, his eyes gazing fearfully at the liquid.

"How much you wanna bet that isn't water," Esteban said with a sour note in his voice.

Lance turned to Dakota. "Can I have one of your feathers?"

Immediately, the Indian pulled one feather from his hair and handed it over. With a knowing look at the others, Lance turned and took several steps forward, stopping at the edge of the pool. He looked around for trip wires or lose floor panels. Noting nothing awry, he dropped the feather into the liquid. It instantly sizzled and dissolved, leaving barely a trace of its existence.

He turned back to the others. "Acid."

"Very corrosive acid," Techie added soberly.

Justin eyed the stones with caution. "Looks like the stones will let us cross over, but...."

"But what?" asked Darnell.

"But why have the stones there in the first place if the acid's supposed to make us turn back?" Justin answered, titling his head from Darnell toward Lance.

Lance exchanged looks with Reyna and Esteban before turning back to Justin. "Only one way to find out."

He turned around and stepped toward the shimmering pool of deadly acid. Reyna's arm snaked out and grabbed his, spinning him back.

"Lance, you don't even have a shirt on!" she said fearfully.

Lance almost laughed at the absurdity of it all. "Like a shirt would protect me from acid? 'Sides, I got this." He held up Excalibur to Reyna, who eyed it uncertainly before stepping back.

Lance looked at all of them. "I'm gonna run across. If I make it to the other side without tripping any attack, the rest of you follow."

They all nodded except Merlin, whose concentration remained on the phone he was shielding, his eyes focused straight ahead.

Lance turned around once more, eyed the unmoving liquid, gauged the distance each stone sat from the previous one, and then sprinted forward. With the agility of a gazelle and the well-trained footwork of a seasoned skater, Lance practically danced across the stones, leaping nimbly from one to the next, not even thrown off balance by the weight of Excalibur in his hand. Within seconds he was across and standing on the opposite side gazing back at them. He glanced up and around himself, and even waved Excalibur over his head in case of any invisible triggers, but nothing happened.

"Okay," he said with a calm he didn't feel. That had been *way* too easy. "Come on over."

Without hesitation, Dakota stepped out onto the first stone, the corrosive acid still rippling ominously from Lance's run across. Nothing happened. He stepped to the next stone and the next. Nothing. Lance waved him over and Dakota broke into a flying leap from one stone to the next and within seconds landed beside Lance unharmed.

The Native Knights looked at each other soberly, and Lance knew Dakota had the same thought – which of their teammates would spring the trap?

Techie came next, leading Merlin by the hand. Lance watched with trepidation as Merlin managed to place one foot on each stone without ever once looking down. Techie was sweating visibly by the time they got to the other side.

Reyna came next, followed by Esteban, both at a run, nimble and surefooted. That left Darnell and Justin eyeing each other.

Lance watched and held his breath as Darnell placed a tentative step onto the first stone. Nothing changed. Darnell looked across the expanse of liquid and met Lance's gaze. Lance offered him a look of reassurance and waved him forward. With a sudden burst of energy Darnell flew from stone to stone and made it across unscathed.

That left Justin. He ran a nervous hand through his Afro, then clenched and unclenched his fists as he eyed the stones and the rippling acid fearfully.

Lance and the others watched and waited, Lance silently praying nothing would happen.

Justin backed up slightly, sucked in a huge breath, released it, and began to run. He landed hard on the first stone, leapt easily to the second, then the third.

Just when Lance felt an upsurge of relief, it happened. As Justin's foot made contact with the last of the stones, the flat rock dropped suddenly downward, plunging Justin's foot and ankle into the acid and sending the young man pitching forward.

A sizzling sound erupted from the liquid, like oil in a frying pan, and Justin shrieked in pain even as he flailed outward with his arms in a futile attempt to break his fall.

Since he was near the edge of the pool, Dakota and Darnell were able to lunge forward and grab for his flailing hands, snagging them and yanking him forward. Justin's other foot landed in the shallow pool and he shrieked again as the acid bubbled and sizzled around it.

And then Justin was out and onto the stone floor of the maze, his shoes and pant cuffs burned off, his feet and ankles bubbling and blistering with red blotches as skin peeled off and blood oozed everywhere.

"Oh, fuck!" he screamed, his voice anguished, his face scrunched with torturous pain as he rolled and pitched on the concrete in agony.

Lance stared in horror at the peeling flesh of the young man's feet and ankles and turned to Merlin.

"Merlin, will that cream you used on Kai help Justin?"

Merlin nodded, prompting Lance to dive quickly into the man's backpack and yank out the small satchel. The others stood around helplessly while Lance fumbled with the ancient jar and Dakota unscrewed the top. "Hold him," he told Esteban and Darnell with authority as he handed the jar to Dakota.

Esteban got on one side of Justin while Darnell squatted at the other, each grabbing an arm to steady the man's painful thrashings.

Lance hunkered down by Justin's charred feet, Dakota squatting beside him. With the Indian holding the jar steady, Lance dipped his left hand into the ointment while still clutching Excalibur in his right. Without hesitation, swallowing his revulsion at the peeling flesh and oozing blisters, Lance quickly rubbed the salve all over Justin's feet. Instantly, Justin stopped thrashing about, and his clenched teeth and painfully scrunched face began to relax. Whatever this stuff was, Lance realized, at least it eased the pain.

It also stopped the bleeding, he noted, as he covered both ruined feet and ankles with a thin coating. It did not, however, magically repair the damage. The feet were still hopelessly ruined, and would likely take extensive plastic surgery to fully repair them. Which meant Justin couldn't walk under his own power.

Pulling back his hand, Lance surveyed the shambles his operation had already become. One down, another hopelessly impaired. It would take two of them just to drag Justin along, which meant two fewer to fight at a moment's notice should the need arise.

Shit, he thought, *we're running out of time!*

His thoughts were interrupted by Dakota, who handed him a small rag to wipe the salve off his hand. As he did, Justin eyed him with gratitude.

"Thanks, Lance," he whispered, his voice soft and breathy, still laced with remnants of pain.

Lance stood and the others stood with him. Justin remained on the floor on his side, watching them. Lance looked at his team and sighed. "Este, Darnell, you guys support Justin. We gotta keep moving."

Even as they nodded, Justin said, "No" so quietly Lance wasn't sure he'd heard. He looked up from the floor, propped himself up on one elbow, and said, "Leave me, like Kai. I'm dead weight, Lance. Just slow you down. Just promise me you'll kill that fucker. For my dad."

Lance considered Justin's words and knew the man was correct. It was the smart thing to do, the strategic thing. But not the human thing. He shook his head. "You're coming with us." He flicked his gaze toward Esteban and Darnell, and both men understood.

"Lance—" Justin began, but one look from Lance cut him off at once. He sighed and awkwardly pushed himself to a sitting position as Esteban and Darnell grabbed him under the armpits and hoisted him to his feet.

Lance watched Justin put pressure on his ruined feet, saw the grimace of silent pain whisk across his stoic features, and also noted how much strength the other two had to exert to hold him up. He turned away.

"Let's go."

And so, with Techie giving directions, Lance led the group forward. Their pace, due to the carrying of Justin, had slowed to a crawl and Lance was becoming impatient, checking his watch every few seconds. Two and half hours. That may be all the time Chris had left to live.

The twists and turns of the maze irked Lance even as they ate up time, but Techie meticulously followed the changes the master computer made and adjusted their course accordingly. Lance rounded yet *another* corner and stopped suddenly. A slight whirring sound came to his ears.

"You guys hear that?"

They all nodded, eyes darting everywhere at once for the source of the mysterious sound.

"More walls moving, Techie?" Lance asked, his heart rate increasing.

Techie shook his head and looked up from his phone. "No."

"You sure?" Reyna asked as the sound stopped and then restarted, almost like gears shifting.

"Positive," Techie said with a slight grin. "Cuz I just got into the computer. I control the maze now, Lance."

Lance's heart skipped a beat. Finally a break! But his joy was fleeting. The gear-shifting sound came again and suddenly Lance heard behind him, "Look out!" He spun just in time to see Darnell shove Justin and Esteban hard away from him, sending both sprawling into the wall as a ceiling panel swung downward with a huge metal spike attached to it. The spike struck Darnell in the back just below the rib cage, piercing his body and protruding from the front, pinning him in a standing position to the fallen panel.

Darnell's eyes bugged out in startled bewilderment as blood spurted from his body. He grunted in surprise and the automatic weapon flew from his hand to skitter along the floor.

"Oh, shit!" Justin exclaimed even as Esteban and Dakota leapt to both sides of Darnell, holding him upright as Lance and Reyna rushed over to join them.

Reyna threw a hand to her mouth, and Lance felt like he'd been struck the fatal blow.

"Hold him up while we get this off!" he ordered, keeping one hand on Excalibur as he gripped the panel with the other. Reyna grabbed the opposite side and together they gently eased it back. The bloody spike pulled out of Darnell's body with a sticky, repellent sucking sound.

Este and Dakota eased the wounded boy slowly down and laid him out on his back. Justin crawled over to gaze into the face of his one-time enemy. "Why'd you do that, man?"

Lance watched Darnell's face, his own chest heaving with anger and guilt. Darnell looked to be in shock as his life quickly bled from his body.

"You got a girl back home, cuzz," Darnell croaked, his face pulled tight with pain. "I don't got nobody."

Lance could tell Justin was on the verge of losing it, giving in to rage or tears or both. "Shit, man, you got me," he told his fellow knight with sincerity. "We're brothers, cuzz."

Darnell smiled, and blood spilled from between his lips. "Lance…"

Justin scooted back as Lance dropped to one knee and faced his fellow knight. Darnell looked up at him with genuine gratitude in his eyes.

"You made me… somebody… special, Lance," he whispered, growing weaker by the second. "Thanks, man." He weakly moved one hand toward Lance and Lance grasped it in his, clasping it in solidarity. Tears burned the backs of Lance's eyes, but he knew he couldn't break. Not now. Not with so much at stake.

"You're a hero, Sir Darnell," he said in a strong, commanding voice, as though daring anyone to contradict him. "Thank you for all you did."

Darnell tried for a smile, but it came out a grimace. "Shit, it hurts," he mumbled. Then, eyes glazing over, he met Lance's gaze. "Tell my momma I… love… her."

Lance nodded, not trusting himself to speak. Then the hand clasping his went limp and Darnell's head lolled to one side. He was gone.

Lance released the hand, gently laying it down in the rapidly growing pool of blood from under Darnell's pierced body. Then with a snarl he leapt to his feet and slammed the flat of his fist into the nearest wall. "Fuck!"

He whirled around, flinging his trailing hair in all directions, like a lion shaking its mane. He pointed at Darnell's body with Excalibur. "*This* is why I wanted to come alone! None of you are supposed to die for me!"

Esteban stepped forward cautiously, Lance's wild-eyed expression clearly off-putting. "You're our king, and our *carnal*. There's no *you* anymore. There's only *us*."

Lance gaped at him, and then scanned the resolute expressions on the others' faces. Even Reyna's was set into one of determined resolve. She nodded to confirm the truth of Esteban's declaration.

Lance felt such an overwhelming rush of love for these people that he thought he'd faint away right there. How could they think so highly of him? A street rat gay boy who, but for a fluke of timing wouldn't even be here now! He saw Merlin turn and glance his way. The eyes still looked focused elsewhere, but the message came loud and clear into his mind – the wizard's words from two years ago, in the library at New Camelot: "Would that you could see yourself through my eyes, you would see a true hero, an amazing young man who is more real than most."

Lance breathed deeply, filling his chest with air and slowly releasing it. Their words, and Merlin's, shoved his doubts and fears aside.

They had a mission to complete.

"Thanks," he said in a whisper.

They all nodded and Lance was once more in command.

"Techie, get started. We're taking over this fucked up game."

Techie went to work. Lance waited anxiously until he saw a slight grin drift lazily across Techie's face, and then the sound of moving walls came to his ears. The wall just in front of them, currently blocking forward progress, slid and angled outward, revealing a previously unseen corridor. Techie waved Lance forward.

Clutching tightly to Excalibur's hilt, his torso and arms slick with sweat, Lance nodded and started down the new path at a brisk clip, eyes roaming everywhere for booby traps.

The others were caught off guard by his sudden move and scurried to catch up. Dakota and Esteban dragged the wincing Justin off the floor and had to practically pull him along to keep pace with Lance, who came to another dead end and turned to face Techie. Reyna snatched up Darnell's fallen weapon before trotting after them.

Techie examined the phone screen. "Computer control room is close, Lance. It's on the way to Chris. Shall we?"

Lance didn't even hesitate. "Do it."

Techie touched more keys on his phone screen. The wall in front of Lance shifted to one side, while the sounds of other moving walls came to his ears. In a moment, silence fell once more and Lance eyed Techie expectantly.

Techie looked proud of himself. "I got us a straight shot in, Lance."

Lance nodded and glanced at Justin, looking weak and in pain, dangling limply between the other two men. "You hanging in there, Justin?"

The young man grimaced. "I'm good. Let's get that bastard."

Lance acknowledged all of his team with a quick searching look, and then turned and strode forward into the newly opened corridor. The others, led by Techie, trailed after him.

The going continued to be slow, despite Techie having opened up the pathway, because Lance feared tripping more booby traps. He couldn't lose anyone else. He couldn't!

So another interminable thirty minutes passed. The air was hot and humid. Lance felt slick with grimy sweat, and occasionally had to switch Excalibur to his left hand to dry his right against his jeans. His eyes flitted every which way, and he knew without even looking that everyone else behind him felt equally on edge.

But nothing happened.

Then, just ahead, Lance spotted a door with a keypad on the wall beside it. This was the first door he'd seen since entering the maze, and he heard Techie say quietly behind him, "The computer room, Lance."

Lance stopped approximately ten feet from the door. His keen eyes studied the floor for loose boards, and the walls for any unobtrusive openings. The ceiling, too.

Quiet surrounded them.

Too much quiet.

Lance controlled his breathing as his eyes roamed. This still seemed too easy. The enemy had to know they were here; had to know they were controlling the maze. Was this all a setup? He knew his enemy wanted him alive, but also knew the others would be considered expendable.

If I continue to lead the way, he thought, *will this guy spring a trap with me in the middle of it? Does he know Excalibur keeps me safe? He must, after those bullets missed me….*

He felt momentarily paralyzed, uncertain what to do, thinking of his team, his family, and his desire to keep them from harm.

As though reading his thoughts, Techie stepped up beside him and gently placed a hand on his shoulder. Lance turned and met his determined gaze.

"Don't worry about us, Lance," he said quietly. "You focus on saving the kids." He paused then, suddenly shy and uncertain. "You're like, the best friend I ever had, and I mean that. I don't wanna sound, you know, well…."

He turned red and glanced down at the floor.

"Gay?" Lance finished for him, but with understanding, not anger.

Techie looked up, mortified. But he saw Lance wasn't mad and shrugged sheepishly. "Well, yeah, but I do love you, man. We all do."

Lance felt his chest constrict with a mix of love and gratitude and unworthiness. He made eye contact with every member of his team, and every one had the same look as Techie.

He didn't care if it made him sound weak, and he said, "I love all you guys too. You're the best family a guy could have."

He locked eyes with Reyna, and she blew him a kiss.

For some reason, that simple gesture relaxed him, and he tossed off a tight smile of gratitude before turning and approaching the door.

The others held back while Lance waved Excalibur around, hoping to set off any traps. Nothing happened. He waved them over. Techie hurriedly punched in the seven-digit code he'd previously obtained, and the door slid open into the wall.

Lance stepped in first. He found himself within a cavernous room with computer monitors across one wall and a large keyboard situated atop a console. An empty high-backed chair rested in front of the keyboard. The chamber was empty, another bad sign. The monitors showed various parts of the facility, but some were displaying just snow, obviously, Lance surmised, the ones where they'd taken out the cameras. Then he gasped.

On one monitor he spotted Chris, dangling from his hands, squirming, a look of terror on his face, with a huge buzz saw beneath him ready to slice open the little boy at the genitals. It wasn't spinning yet, but Lance knew it soon would be.

"What the fuck!" Lance spat, his anger instantly boiling.

"Oh, shit!" he heard Techie exclaim from behind, and then the knight was on the move, sprinting toward the keyboard controls.

Lance happened to glance down and sensed the slight anomaly in the floorboards before he saw it, and yelled, "Techie, jump!"

Physical training kicked in at once, and Techie obeyed, halting his forward momentum and diving to one side as fast as he could. The floor beneath his flying feet exploded up and out in a shower of yellow flame and smoke, and Techie shrieked in agony.

✝✝✝

Chapter Nine

I've Waited a Long Time to Kill You

He made his way smoothly and confidently through the corridors of Walter Reed, knowing his orderly's uniform and pushcart wouldn't generate a second look, even from those on guard. Being ex-military himself, he knew exactly how these people thought and how they would act at any given moment.

This assignment gave him that déjà vu feeling he didn't like. He'd almost killed Arthur once before, and the kid, too. Now it was like he was repeating scenes in a movie, going back to fix mistakes he'd made. Except they hadn't been mistakes, just unforeseen circumstances.

Well, he thought, *no unforeseen anything tonight.*

He preferred the elegance of his sniper rifle to this kind of subterfuge, but a job was a job.

He nodded in greeting to several passing nurses, making certain to continue his normal "rounds" before entering the intensive care ward. Once there, a quick injection into both targets and his work would be complete. Despite his usual nonchalance about killing, this mission unnerved him in a way even the heat of battle back in the day never had. The king and his kids, especially the one who'd already died and come back, creeped him out and hearkened back to the religious fervor of his grandmother.

Still, the boss wanted his revenge, and there was nothing for it but to finish the assignment and move on. Stopping at an open door, he pushed his cart into the room and began chatting with the wounded soldier occupying bed number one, glancing up at the clock with anticipation. Less than thirty minutes now, and it would all be over. He handed the soldier his pills and some water, and chatted amiably about the last Monday Night Football game.

†††

"Techie!" Lance shrieked as the screaming knight flew up and away from the blast in a shower of flame and crimson blood. Time froze for Lance as the floor in front of him erupted and what was left of Techie landed hard on the opposite side of the small crater, slamming into the computer chair and rolling over onto his back in a bloodied heap.

Lance's eyes instantly took in Techie's severed legs, tossed to one side and quivering like some radio-controlled Halloween prank. The tech genius spouted copious amounts of blood from stumps just below his knees, and Lance didn't hesitate. He shucked off his jeans, revealing the workout shorts he'd never removed after the park shooting. He held up the pants in his left hand and sliced them in half with Excalibur. Grabbing both halves, he leapt the crater in one smooth jump and skidded to a halt beside Techie, nearly losing his footing on the slippery floor.

The young man's eyes were open, but glazed, and Lance knew he was in serious shock. A low moan escaped his bloodied lips, and bits of the wooden floor had embedded themselves in his arms. Lance dropped to his knees in a vast pool of blood, lay Excalibur down, and rapidly began tying off Techie's left leg at the thigh with one half of his pants.

Reyna was by his side seconds later, snatching up the other pants leg and hurriedly tying it around Techie's right. Both of them pulled their tourniquets as tight as they could, and the bleeding slowed, but Lance knew from the enormous amount of blood around his knees that Techie had already lost way too much.

Then Esteban and Dakota were there, hovering anxiously and eyeing the wounded boy with anger.

"Shit!" Esteban exclaimed in fury, kicking out at the rolling computer chair and sending it crashing into the console with a hollow *bang*.

Lance glanced desperately over at Merlin. The wizard, no longer obscuring Techie's phone, fixed his gray eyes on the boy, and shook his head sadly. Lance nodded, and looked down at his friend, who was almost drowning in his own blood, his gentle, brilliant, loyal and soft-spoken friend, and wanted to scream to the rafters his hurt and frustration. This shouldn't be happening! Techie should be back home with Ariel doing what he did best. He should never have even come along!

"Hang on, Techie," he begged feebly, sounding, and feeling, weak.

I am weak, and I can't do this anymore! I can't watch my friends die anymore!

Lance nodded to Dakota and Esteban, who got behind Techie and helped prop him up, so his back rested against them both, and slipped the backpack off to make him more comfortable. Techie's glazed eyes focused on Lance and he groaned again. "Shit, Lance, it fucking hurts!"

Lance placed a bloodied hand on his friend's shoulder gently. "We'll get you to a hospital."

Techie shook his head, grimacing as he did so. "I'm done for, Lance."

Despite his best efforts to appear strong and manly, tears sprang to the backs of Lance's eyes and began to spill down his cheeks. "No, Techie, not you, man. You can't die."

Techie's eyes welled up. "I always wanted what you and Ricky had, Lance, you know… with Ariel. But she never…."

"She loves you, Techie," Lance said, his heart torn asunder. "Bridget told me. She was just too shy to tell you."

That brought a warm smile to Techie's pale, bloodied face. Then he frowned. "And I was too stupid to tell *her*." He looked up imploringly. "Lance, will you…."

More tears came. Lance couldn't help it. He didn't give a shit if they made him look weak. He was losing his friend, a great friend who was dying because of him, and that hurt worse than anything. "You know I will."

Techie smiled again, weakly and sadly. "Tell her to have a happy life, 'kay?"

"Oh, Techie…." Lance murmured again, his blood pounding. "This is all my fault!"

Techie reached out a hand and took Lance's in his. Lance glanced down at their clasped hands in surprise. "Basic human contact, remember?" Techie said, his voice filled with every emotion possible.

Lance nodded, gently squeezing the boy's hand in return.

"I volunteered, Lance," Techie went on, his voice raspy and weak. "I knew the odds. I did it for you and those kids, especially Chris. He's my little brother, too, you know? Save 'em. End this."

Lance nodded, anger welling up within him once more. "I will. I swear it."

Techie smiled sadly again and released Lance's hand.

Lance eyed his friend through blurred vision a moment. "Techie, I don't care if you think it's gay or not, I'm gonna hug you."

Techie offered a weak little grin. "You're not gay, Lance. You're my best friend."

He opened his bloodied arms and Lance moved in carefully to embrace him.

"I love you, Techie," Lance whispered.

"Love you, too," Techie whispered back without the slightest edge of embarrassment that would've been evident a couple of years back.

They held each other a few moments before Lance released him. Lance stood and Reyna dropped down to take his place.

Her own eyes awash in tears, she enveloped the boy in a loving hug. Pulling back, she kissed him on the lips gently and said, "You are amazing, Techie, truly the best of us."

Techie looked surprised by her words, and smiled gratefully. "Thanks, Reyna. Keep Lance safe."

Lance flinched at that, but said nothing as she nodded sadly and stood. Techie looked up at them. "Put me in the chair, Lance," he said, his voice weak, but his eyes blazing with intensity.

When Lance hesitated, Techie added, "I can control everything from in here. At least until...."

He let the rest trail off, his pallid face clouding over with inevitability, but Lance understood. He nodded to Esteban and Dakota. They gently slipped hands and arms beneath Techie and carefully lifted him. Techie winced in furious pain, but never cried out. Lance had to choke back a sob.

Reyna rolled over the chair and the men tenderly deposited Techie into it, rolling him and the chair over to the console. Reyna found his phone on the blood-soaked floor and placed it onto the console next to him.

Almost as though the keyboard were a blood transfusion, Techie's fingers began to fly with renewed energy as he searched through the mainframe.

Lance couldn't take his eyes off the silent image of Chris, dangling fearfully above the deadly saw blade, but took pride in the defiant glare his brother directed at something or someone Lance couldn't see.

"Okay, Lance, I'm in," Techie said, his voice sounding high and reedy, like not enough air was getting through to his lungs.

The camera on Chris pulled back to reveal a large chamber, some kind of central hub, just like it had looked on Techie's phone, but with more detail. Chris and the saw were encased in some kind of glass enclosure. There was desktop computer sitting on a small table, and a couple of high-backed wooden chairs, but not much else. The very center was a circular, dirt-filled arena like Lance had seen in old gladiator movies. No one moved. No one was within camera range.

Chris was looking off to the side past their camera view and Lance saw him mouth the words, "My big brother will save me." His breath caught in his throat, and Reyna gasped beside him. Obviously she'd understood too.

"Any guards in there, Techie? Any traps you can find between us and Chris?" Lance asked, fighting to control his breathing. That saw blade so close to his brother almost made him frantic.

Techie's bloodied fingertips slipped some on the keys and the smears of red looked ghastly beneath the overhead fluorescents.

While Techie searched, Reyna put her arm around Lance, eyeing his blood splattered torso and bare calves now smeared with Techie's blood, but he barely acknowledged her gesture or her look of concern. His focus was Chris.

"There are three more machine guns, or whatever they are, in the hallway leading into the control room," Techie finally said, breaking the awkward silence. He nodded toward a closed door off to his left. "Through that door. Soon as I open it, the guns'll start firing."

Lance nodded. "Any people?"

Techie's fingers kept moving, but Lance could see them slipping. Despite the tourniquets around each stump, blood seeped through to pool on the floor beneath the chair. His friend, he knew, didn't have much time left.

"I pick up three heat signatures other than Chris," Techie wheezed, his breathing becoming more ragged as he gazed at the computer monitor, and the grid displayed on it. One orangish blur was obviously Chris – Lance could tell from where it was positioned in the control room. There were two more within that control room, and one in the hall outside the hub, apparently guarding the door.

"Looks like only one guy between here and Chris." Techie turned weakly and looked up at Lance. His face was ashen, all color having left it. "Go get little man, Lance."

"Techie…." Lance stammered, wanting to say so much and knowing he never could. "I can't just leave you like this."

"No choice, Your Majesty," Techie said quietly, but with a strength of will Lance couldn't help but admire. God, the pain must've been excruciating and yet the boy still kept it together! "I'll do what I can here till somebody blocks me or…." He trailed off because everyone knew the rest. He turned stiffly to Reyna. "Grab my backpack and put it next to the keyboard, please?"

Uncertainly, she turned around and Esteban was already handing her the pack. She nearly dropped it. "Damn, this is heavy." She laid the bulging pack onto the console to Techie's left.

The computer genius unzipped the pack and turned to Lance. "I doubt I can shut this system down, and can probably only control it for a short time. But when I can't, you know, hold on anymore, I'm gonna take the whole thing out."

Lance furrowed his brows in confusion. "How?"

Techie pulled out a hand grenade and offered a bloody grin. "The old school way."

Lance sucked in a sharp breath, and heard Esteban whistle in surprise. The bigger man was rummaging through Techie's pack, pulling out more grenades.

"Where'd you get these, Techie?"

"Found 'em topside, while we were waiting for Lance. Figured they might come in handy." His pale face shown with painful pride, and he gratefully accepted Esteban's gentle pat on the back.

"Damn straight they might," Esteban said, slipping grenades into his pockets and handing some to Dakota and Reyna.

Techie grinned slightly at Lance, but Lance couldn't feel anything but a numb ache in his heart at the loss of his friend and brother. He placed a loving hand on Techie's shoulder as he glanced at his watch. "My *nino* should be here in about an hour. Hang on, Techie. We can still save you."

Techie smiled, his pale face filling with love and gratitude at the gesture. But his eyes told Lance the truth – he wouldn't last that long.

Lance pretended not to see that look because he couldn't bear any more heartache. He bent and scooped Excalibur into his right hand, wiping the blood off its hilt with his workout shorts. Gripping the sword with passion, he said to Techie, "I'm gonna stand at that door. When I give the word, you open it. I'll take care of those guns and the asshole keeping me from Chris."

Esteban instantly leapt to his side. "No, Lance. Let me and Dakota and Reyna. We got the weapons."

Lance looked at him soberly, without expression. His face, he knew, was still damp from the tears he'd shed, but his heart was resolute, and his will indomitable.

This would end.

Now.

"And I have this," he said in a regal, commanding voice as he held up the bloodied Excalibur before him. "You guys stay behind me till I take them out."

"But Lance—" Esteban began.

"That's a command, Sir Este," Lance said firmly. "From your king."

Esteban eyed him steadily, as though seeing him in a new light. "Yes, Your Majesty."

Without another word, or even a glance at the others, Lance strode to the closed door. He held out Excalibur before him, the fluorescent lights giving his blood-streaked, sweaty brown skin an otherworldly quality. He waved the others behind and to either side of him.

Dakota and Esteban carried Justin closer and laid him out on his stomach to Lance's left so he could aim his Uzi at the corridor beyond the door, and Esteban crouched beside him with an upraised automatic handgun pointing the same direction. Reyna had ditched Darnell's gun in favor of her bow and hunkered down with Dakota behind Lance's right side. He, too, had his bow out and nocked with an arrow.

Lance noted them in place and then turned back to Techie, knowing this would likely be the last time he'd see his friend alive. So he seared the memory of that pale, expectant, unbelievably brave face into his memory forever. He nodded, and whipped his head back toward the door.

With a click, the door slid open, and the gunfire erupted. Lance didn't even hesitate. He strode toward the barrage of bullets hacking and swinging Excalibur with reckless abandon. Bullets ricocheted off the blade and struck walls and ceiling and floor. But none struck him. He plowed into the first upraised gun and sliced it in two, knocking it from its turret. The second hung from the ceiling, firing round after round at the boy. But he spun and leapt, slicing through the muzzle and landing back on his feet. Then he turned to the third weapon as it popped up firing from a hidden chamber in the floor. Fearlessly, he strode to it and with a powerful swipe smashed it off its moorings, sending it hard into the wall where it fell silent. Suddenly, after such a cacophony of noise, the corridor fell silent, the air filled with the smell of spent gunpowder.

Then the armed guard came running. Lance heard his footfalls echoing before he saw the man round the corner and start firing. Every muscle taut, his breathing ragged, Lance gripped Excalibur so hard the veins in his forearms looked ready to burst. With a scream of pent up anger and frustration, he bolted from his spot toward the oncoming man, raising Excalibur for the killing blow.

He heard Esteban's voice shriek behind him, "No, Lance!" but paid it no heed. This man was a killer and a kidnapper and Lance had to kill someone, anyone, for what he'd been through.

The oncoming man kept firing, his face showing astonishment that even at point-blank range he hadn't killed, or even struck, the rampaging Lance.

The man tried to stop his headlong motion, but couldn't. Lance plowed forward and raised Excalibur higher, aiming for the head. With a scream of agony and fury, he swung down with the blade.

Gunfire erupted from behind him, and the man before him exploded in a shower of red as the bullets struck him full in the chest and he fell.

Lance's blade came down, but there was nothing to strike, for the man already lay dead at his feet, blood pouring from his ruptured body.

Furious, Lance whirled to find Esteban standing behind him, smoking gun upraised, his expression unreadable.

"I had him, Este!" Lance spat angrily. "I told you to stay back!"

Dakota and Reyna stepped into the corridor supporting Justin as Esteban closed the gap and placed one hand lovingly on Lance's shoulder. Lance shrugged it off, glaring at his brother and knowing he shouldn't. They were a team, after all, a family. Esteban had acted as a team member.

"I'm the killer, *carnal*," Esteban confessed quietly. "Not you. That was my life, what I used to do.

Suddenly Lance understood, and his anger slipped a notch. "You killed people before?"

Esteban sighed heavily. "Close enough, when I's fourteen."

Lance nodded, and Dakota remained impassive, but Reyna apparently hadn't known. There was something in her face that caught his eye, almost like pain. And she looked ashen, in shock even. Did she know nothing of Este's revelation until now?

"That didn't make me a man any more than sex did. Just gave me nightmares I still have." Esteban soberly and sadly locked his brown eyes onto Lance's wide green ones. "You're too good, Lance. I need you to stay that way. Please."

His look was so imploring, so desperate, that Lance nodded again, not wanting to let down the big brother he admired so much. For a split second his mind flashed back to what he'd almost become when they'd discovered a spy amongst them at New Camelot. The law of unintended consequences, as Michael had taught him, seemed to creep into every aspect of his life. Yes, he wanted to end this, needed to end it. That was his responsibility. But he didn't want to become his enemy.

"I'll do my best." That was all he could promise. "C'mon, Chris needs us."

He turned and pelted down the corridor. Esteban hurried after, with Reyna and Dakota slowed by the heavy weight of half-carrying, half dragging Justin. The young man did his best to walk, his face lanced with agony at every excruciating step, but he pushed on nonetheless.

Reyna winced painfully beneath the muscular arm draped around her neck, but she said nothing and forced her way along the corridor after the others.

When they rounded the corner, they saw another door with a keypad lock about twenty feet ahead. Lance and Esteban started toward it, but an agonized groan from Reyna stopped both in their tracks. They whirled in time to see the girl crumple beneath Justin's near-dead weight and collapse to the floor.

"Reyna, what's wrong?" Justin said anxiously as Dakota, every muscle in his arms straining beneath the effort, lowered him awkwardly to the floor beside her.

By that time, Lance and Esteban were there, and Lance's heart flew into his throat while Esteban let out a horrified gasp. Blood trickled from the area around Reyna's neck, between her right ear and shoulder. With obvious pain, but a strength of will Lance had always seen in her, she pushed herself up against the wall even as Esteban dropped to his knees before her, his face carved with shock and disbelief.

"Reyna, baby, what happened?"

It was obvious to Lance what had happened, and he knew Este understood, too. A stray bullet, one intended for him, had made its way between the folds of her vest and into the big sister he loved with his whole heart.

Reyna smiled. It was laced with pain, but still the most beautiful smile Lance had ever seen on any girl. "I forgot to duck," she said with a hollow laugh.

Esteban shook his head, clenching and unclenching his fists. "No. No. No."

"Reyna...." Lance began, his words choking up in his throat like vomit. His hand squeezed against the hilt of Excalibur so hard it looked like his skin would burst open, and his face fell into despair along with his heart.

Reyna flashed her radiant smile at him and reached up to take his hand in hers. "I love you, baby boy. It's been a wild ride and I'd do it again in a heartbeat. The ends of the earth and back. Remember that."

Lance couldn't begin to fight the tears that erupted, and he knelt to kiss her lightly on the lips, much like that time so long ago when she'd kissed him. He pulled back and searched her vibrant brown eyes for hope. "I love you, Reyna, and you won't die. I won't *let* you!"

She let go his hand and looked at the thunderstruck Esteban. Lance watched them both, so tough, so cool and collected, and was stunned to see Este crying.

"You can't leave me, Reyna, you can't," Esteban pleaded helplessly. "You're my whole life. I wanna marry you."

Reyna's eyes got wide and she slipped a smirk onto her face with ease, despite her obvious discomfort. "Now you ask," she said, rolling her eyes in consternation. "Great timing."

Esteban took both of her shaking hands in his. "Please, Reyna, please marry me. I'm begging you! Don't die. I can't live without you. I'll kill myself, I swear it!"

Lance watched the tears stream down Este's cheeks and thought of Ricky dying in that hospital bed. He might lose half his soul, just like Este, and his heart beat wildly with understanding and pain. He placed one hand on his big brother's suddenly weak and trembling shoulder and squeezed gently.

Reyna's eyes never left those of Esteban, and she shook her head in wonder. "Well, when you put it that way…." She pulled him in for a kiss and Lance blushed at the intensity of it, unwittingly feeling Ricky's lips on his and drowning in his own despair.

Esteban pulled back and locked eyes on those of the girl he cherished. "You hang on, baby, you hang on! We're gonna take down this fucker and I'm coming back for you. You hear me? I'm coming back for you!"

She laughed with delight, but then winced in pain. "I love it when you get like this, Este."

That brought a tight smile to Esteban's lips.

"I'll stay here with her," Justin said from behind Lance.

Lance turned and found Justin propped up against the opposite wall holding his weapon securely.

"I can't go no more anyway," Justin went on, his deep voice laced with painful agony.

Lance glanced again at the peeling skin and boils infesting his feet and wondered how the boy could even be conscious.

"Reyna and me'll keep watch out here," Justin added. "We'll take out any asshole who goes either direction."

"You got it," Reyna echoed from across the way.

Esteban looked up at Lance from where he knelt, and Lance nodded.

"Give Reyna a gun," the young king commanded.

Dakota quickly reached into Esteban's backpack and extracted an automatic handgun, handing it over to Reyna silently.

Lance glanced at Merlin, who stood quietly watching the unfolding events with his usual stoic indifference, and then back down at Reyna. "You want some of Merlin's pain stuff?"

She shook her head. "No. The pain'll keep me awake." She looked into Esteban's eyes again and must've seen reluctance to leave because she said sternly, "Get going so you can save those kids."

He swiped away the tears on his face, but made no move to stand. "I don't wanna leave you."

She mock shoved him and grinned. "Fool. You asked me to marry you. Think I'm gonna let you weasel outta that? Hell no!" Then she tossed off that lyrical laugh Lance loved. "So go already."

He still seemed reluctant. Lance again squeezed his shoulder. Esteban quickly leaned in and planted another passionate kiss on her all-too-willing lips and pulled back breathlessly. "I *will* come back for you."

"You better. Think I'm gonna marry Justin?" She winked over at the young man with the Afro, and he chuckled.

That seemed to convince Esteban that Reyna was still Reyna, still the fighter she'd always been. He stood and gazed at Lance. Lance saw in his eyes the same fear he had coiled around his own heart, the same fear he also saw in Dakota, who stood right behind Este – would any of them ever see his beloved again?

"I'm ready, Lance," Esteban announced, his voice stone-cold and hard. "It's time to finish this."

Lance cast one more longing look at Reyna, who smiled back at him, and nodded to Justin before turning and heading down the corridor. His three remaining team members followed silently behind him.

†††

He slipped up the long sleeve of his slightly baggy orderly's uniform and glanced at his watch. Almost time. Another ten minutes. Inject the kid, then the king. The drug, he'd been told, would take about fifteen minutes to act. Plenty of time for him to shuck off the costume, slip into his military duds, and stroll out the door with ease.

Piece of cake.

†††

Lance punched in the code Techie had given him and the door whooshed open. Within was another enormous chamber, larger than the computer room they just left, but circular, like it had appeared on camera. Dead center lay the old Roman-style gladiator arena packed with hard earth surrounded by concrete flooring. It looked to be about thirty feet in diameter. Big enough for two men to grapple in, Lance thought as he took in the rest of the chamber. There were two pillars made of an unusual-looking material embedded within the concrete beside the arena and separated by four or five feet.

He stepped hesitantly through the door, holding Excalibur out before him, every muscle taut and ready for action.

Merlin stepped in behind Lance while Dakota and Este flanked him, weapons at the ready. There was no one there.

Then he heard, "Lance!"

Turning to his left, Lance's heart skipped a beat. There was Chris, dangling from his wrists within the huge glass booth, fighting to keep his legs away from the razor sharp, but as-yet unmoving, buzz saw glinting in the overhead lights. Lance was so excited to see his brother he bolted across the room.

"Lance, wait!" Esteban hissed from behind him, but Lance paid him no mind.

He stopped before the booth and looked in at the bruised, tear-streaked face of his little brother. Chris looked so relieved to see him that he grinned mightily. Lance eyed the bruises on the boy's smooth, pale cheeks and the red welts around his wrists where the rope had dug into the soft flesh. He gazed in horror at the saw resting lazily on some kind of lift that, once activated, would rise and slice his little brother in half. What sick fuck would do this to a child?

Using Excalibur's hilt, Lance slammed it against the glass, but it just vibrated. He heard Esteban and Dakota running over to him and barely registered their presence on either side. Laying Excalibur onto the floor, Lance tried to feel around the edges of the enclosure for any purchase, anything to grab on to.

"Lance," he heard Merlin say sharply from somewhere behind him. "Don't let go of Excalibur!"

And that's when the gunfire erupted.

Lance spun around in time to see a small, rapid-fire gun of some sort mounted high in the rafters sweeping the room with bullets. Esteban dove for the ground and rolled while Dakota lifted his bow and fired an arrow.

The bullets bounced off the floor around them. One struck Dakota beneath his raised right arm and he went spinning onto the floor.

"Dakota!" Lance shouted, even as he dove for Excalibur. From the corner of his eye he spotted Esteban rolling over and over and firing upward at the weapon, and Merlin throwing himself flat to the floor and rolling to one side. Just as his hands reached for the hilt of his sword, Lance felt a sharp sting in his lower right side and pain arced its way throughout his nervous system. He'd been hit.

Fingers grasping wildly, Lance managed to get his right hand wrapped around the hilt before he could pass out. The moment his fingers touched it, the familiar tingle, that tiny electric charge surged up his arm and throughout his body. The pain vanished and he felt strong again. He knew the bullet was still there and that Excalibur only limited its damage, but he would need a doctor, and soon.

Jumping to his feet, Lance spun just in time to see Esteban take out the unmanned weapon with another barrage from his Uzi. Dakota rose to one knee and Lance hurried to him. Blood spilled from a small hole in the Indian's right pec, where the bullet had slipped between the front and back sides of the vest, and Dakota fought to mask the pain.

Lance helped him stand as Merlin raced over to examine the wounds. Esteban stood and flung his gaze everywhere at once, searching for more traps or weapons targeting them.

Lance glanced over at the desktop computer, which was on and showing various camera angles of the entire facility in slideshow mode. As an image of Techie flew past, Lance called out, "Techie, can you hear me?"

There was a momentary pause. Lance shooed Merlin away, who'd been trying to examine his back. "Help Dakota, Merlin. I have Excalibur."

Reluctantly, the wizard obeyed and began examining Dakota's wound when Techie's voice suddenly echoed all around them. "Yeah, Lance. I can see and hear you."

Lance felt a surge of relief to know that his friend still lived. "Can you disable that saw?" he yelled, pointing at Chris behind him.

Another pause. Then, "No, Lance, I'm locked out of that room. He must be on to me."

"Shit!" Lance spat, casting a furious look at Esteban as his brother strode toward him.

Just then, a hissing noise started overhead, like a giant gas leak. Esteban stopped suddenly, staggered slightly, gave Lance a wide-eyed look of stunned surprise, and then toppled forward to the hard dirt floor of the fighting arena, the gun clattering away to land beside the twin pillars.

Lance had barely a moment to register that the hissing was gas, and *not* the kind you cooked with. He saw Merlin and Dakota stumble, and began to feel light-headed, like there was no oxygen in his lungs or his brain. Not certain why, he used his last bit of strength to raise Excalibur, blade pointing down, both hands tightly gripping the hilt, and with every muscle in his arms and back plunged it downward into the concrete beneath his feet.

Releasing the hilt, Lance barely noted the sword wobbling slightly from the impact before everything in his line of sight vanished and he knew no more.

†††

Techie sat slumped in the high-backed chair, the pain in his legs having gone numb long ago, his life force bleeding forth from his body, and watched in anguished horror at what was being done to his friends on screen. And he couldn't do shit about it! With what little energy he still possessed, he frantically flew his bloodied fingers over the keyboard desperately searching for a way to regain control of the computer system.

Sweat poured down his face in rivulets and he had to keep swiping at his eyes as the salt and blood stung them and blurred his vision. He had no idea what Este had been chained to, but it looked automated, controllable, yet he couldn't get into the system to figure out how it worked. And the saw beneath Chris was also beyond his ability to control.

Other camera angles on the overhead monitors displayed various parts of the facility. He saw Darnell's torn and bloody body right where they'd left it. An exterior camera showed him Kai's inert form, head slumped slightly to one side, gun held listlessly in his lap. Was he dead already? And what about Reyna? He'd shed tears at her and Este's good-bye, thinking of Ariel and how he'd never get to tell her how much he loved her. There was no audio from the corridor camera, but Techie could see Justin's mouth moving, and Reyna pressed up against the wall motionless and unresponsive. Was she dead too?

Shit!

He knew he had little time left and sadly eyed the hand grenade he'd placed on the console. He'd die unable to help his friends. He'd die a failure. The only thing he could do was helplessly watch the end of the Round Table, and the end of the best friend he'd ever had. He admired Lance more than any kid he'd ever known and looked up to him like a god or something. Gay or not, Lance was everything he'd ever wanted to be, and more.

He'd seen the bullet strike Lance, had witnessed his strength of will in pulling himself upright with Excalibur, had gasped when the gas knocked them all out, and now observed the boy he'd tried so hard to emulate lying on his back on the concrete floor while Dakota fought to free himself. Like Dakota, Merlin was tied to a chair, but appeared unharmed, his head slumped in unconsciousness. Then Lance began to stir, and Techie pushed himself more upright in the chair to raise the volume on the speakers.

He desperately hoped he would die before Lance did. He couldn't bear to see that.

††††

Lance stirred. His head felt foggy and weak, like all the lights in the room weren't on yet. He almost floated, his vision blurring and un-blurring as he struggled to prop himself up on one elbow. Excruciating pain lanced its way through his side and forced wakefulness into his brain. He nearly collapsed, but pressed himself up onto his right arm. He saw Excalibur stuck into the concrete, unmoving. How had he done that anyway? He turned his head and spotted Dakota eyeing him. His Indian brother was tied to a straight-backed chair, hands bound behind his back, rope encircling his waist and pinning him to the wood back of the chair. Blood stained the right side of his shirt. Something stirred in Lance's memory, but his brain still felt cloudy and dull.

"You okay, Lance?" Dakota asked with obvious concern, even as he struggled to free himself.

Dully, Lance nodded, fighting back the pain in his side and struggling to get his bearings. He turned his head further and gasped. Este was just waking up, but that wasn't what shocked Lance. It was the man's position and condition. He was upright, and shackled at the wrists, the shackles attached to chains linking him to the two vertical pillars. The pillars looked both metallic and translucent at the same time, like they weren't made of solid metal.

Lance forced himself into a sitting position. "Este!"

His older brother shook his head to clear it, suddenly realizing the situation he was in.

"What the fuck?" he said in surprise, yanking on the chains. But the pillars wouldn't budge. He eyed Lance uncomprehendingly, and Lance looked back just as uncertainly.

The set up reminded Lance of something he'd seen in an old Hercules movie.

The traps, the trip wires, this gladiator pit, and now the pillars.

Old movie stuff.

What did it mean?

He spotted Merlin tied to another chair up near the desktop computer. The wizard had not yet awakened, but Lance could tell he was breathing.

Lance shook his head again and pulled his legs up and under him, sitting on them to catch his breath before rising fully. Then he heard a laugh. A chillingly familiar laugh, but one he couldn't quite place.

A shirtless, muscular man stepped out from behind the console wearing a Scream mask, designer pants, and Nike shoes.

Lance gasped. "Michael?"

The laugh came again as the figure stepped toward him. Lance felt rooted to the ground. His heart pounded wildly and he could scarcely breathe.

Michael was dead!

I watched him die!

"I've waited a long time to kill you, Pretty Boy," the figure said, stopping beside Excalibur and facing him with that creepy mask.

Lance gazed up at him in horror. The voice sounded familiar, as though the man was trying to disguise it. But it wasn't Michael. He knew every nuance of Michael's voice.

He heard Esteban behind him, "Let me outta here, Michael, and I'll rip your fuckin' head off!"

The figure laughed again. He reached for Excalibur and placed both hands on the hilt. Then he pulled. Lance could see corded muscles in his forearms and shoulders straining mightily, but the sword wouldn't budge. It held fast. With an exasperated sigh the figure released the hilt and stepped back, panting slightly from the exertion.

Then he laughed again. "I guess it won't be mine until you're dead, Pretty Boy. No matter. That'll happen soon enough. After I have my fun."

Lance forced himself painfully to his feet as the figure glanced over at Merlin, still slumped in his chair.

The figure laughed again. "Mr. Wizard and I will talk after the faggot king is dead."

The bullet, and however much blood it had cost him, made Lance weak and unsteady. He needed Excalibur. But the figure stood between him and his only hope. So, much like he did when confronting Michael on that train, Lance affected a bravado he didn't feel, and hoped his pounding heart wasn't too obvious.

"You're not Michael," he said calmly. "Who are you?"

The figure laughed again. "Oh, you do know your ex-boyfriends well, don't you? Most of your kind only remember the body parts and not the voice. Look at you – running around half naked like all homo boys do. Disgusting!"

That last was obviously thrown out to generate an emotional reaction, but Lance was too used to shit like that to rise to the bait. "What's wrong, not man enough to face me without a mask?" he said tauntingly. "Are you that butt-ugly?"

The figure paused and, even beneath the mask, Lance could sense a reaction. He'd hit some kind of nerve. "You pretty boys are always so fucking arrogant, think you own the world because everyone bows down to you. Well your pretty face won't help you any more."

One arm reached up and grabbed the top of the mask.

Lance held his breath.

The mask came off, and Lance almost choked in surprise.

It was Edwin!

He heard shocked gasps from his fellow knights behind him, but couldn't take his eyes off the smirking face of the young, unassuming, mild-mannered intern who'd been traveling with them all these months.

Who'd been their friend and supporter.

Who'd laughed and ate and played with them.

And who watched nothing but old movies on his iPad, Lance suddenly realized. *Who loved The Most Dangerous Game, a movie about a guy who hunted people for sport!* The trip wires, the booby traps – it all made sense now!

Lance almost couldn't speak he was so flabbergasted. He hadn't felt this dumbstruck since he'd first met Arthur. "How? Why?" was all he could blurt out. His voice sounded breathy and weak, but he almost had no air left in his lungs.

Edwin?

The young intern laughed. It was a cold, heartless laugh, again jogging Lance's memory. He'd heard that laugh before, but from someone else. Michael? No, even Michael's wasn't this cold.

"Fucking little pretty-ass fag boy like you never imagined a geek like me could be built, did you?" Edwin sneered. Then he shrugged and grinned. "Hey, the baggy dress shirts and glasses worked for Superman, right?" He reached up and snatched off the designer glasses, flinging them away with a chuckle.

Lance remained in a state of shock and utter despair. How had he missed this? Him, the soul whisperer? During all their time together how had he not seen such evil, such madness as he now saw lurking behind the man's eyes?

He heard Esteban from behind him, "Fuck you, Edwin, what's this shit about?"

Edwin glanced over toward Esteban the way one might observe a bug he was about to squash underfoot, and sneered. "Nothing to do with street trash like you, gangbanger. This is between Pretty Boy and me. An old score that needs settling."

"Edwin," Lance finally said, finding his voice. "I never even knew you before. What did I do to you?"

"You killed my father," Edwin stated bluntly and coldly. Those eyes, once laughing and seemingly carefree, now looked like something out of a slasher film – empty and soulless.

Lance's mouth dropped open and he heard Esteban spit out, "You fucking liar, Edwin! Lance never killed nobody!"

Edwin barely looked in that direction. "It's 'anybody', street trash, and I wasn't speaking to you."

Lance stood rigid, frozen with pain and fear and confusion. Este was right – he'd never killed anyone. Was Edwin just unhinged and imagining things?

"He's right, Edwin," Lance finally said, his voice as calm as he could make it. "I never killed anyone."

Edwin glared balefully, "Your pathetic excuse for a father did. Because you got in the way! You, a worthless, good-for-nothing street punk who only got where you are because you're pretty. Take a good look at the Indian faggot. Anything about his situation ring a bell, or are you all looks and no brains?"

Lance's mind reeled. The pieces were beginning to come together.

Because you got in the way.

He turned to look at Dakota, at the way his friend was tied to the chair, at how familiar it all looked, how it reminded him of… Jack! He whirled back around, his mouth hanging open in astonishment.

Edwin leered in triumph. "If I had my way I'd line up all the faggots in the world and shoot 'em. I learned that from the greatest man who ever lived."

Lance could barely speak, the revelation causing his mind to reel with disbelief. "You're R's son!" he blurted quietly and uncertainly.

Edwin's face grew dark and threatening in an instant. "That's *Mr.* R. to you, Pretty Boy. And yes, I'm the son of a god."

Even in his astonishment, Lance bristled and said, "Not much of a god. My father took him out pretty easy."

Edwin clenched his fists and stepped forward. Lance tried to raise his arms, but his weakened state slowed him down and he wasn't fast enough. One solid fist plowed into his gut and sent him crumpling to the floor. His solid abs, however, prevented even the wind from leaving his lungs, though he pretended it had for the sake of a feint.

"Fight *me*, you cowardly bitch!" Esteban spat in fury, pulling and yanking against the chains with enough power to rattle the pillars.

"Or me," Dakota said quietly and with perfect calm. "I owe you for Kai."

Edwin looked up from Lance, doubled up on one knee, and strode to Dakota in three quick strides. Without a word, he balled up a fist and slammed it into Dakota's face, splitting the boy's lip and sending blood flying.

Dakota said nothing, Lance noted from the corner of his eye. Like Jack, he didn't even make a sound. Just glowered defiantly up at the smirking Edwin as though daring him to do it again.

"I could beat you to death, Two-Spirit or whatever shit name you call yourself, but I'm saving that for the *pretty* fag boy. I want to lick his blood off my knuckles and then spit it out before it poisons me." He laughed again, that chilling, almost bloodcurdling laugh he'd gotten from his father.

Lance watched him turn haughtily and stride back to face him. He still couldn't believe how built the man was and how he'd never even noticed. No one had. He must've never taken his shirt off once in front of anyone, Lance realized, now recalling that Edwin had never even gone swimming with them at any of the hotel pools. Then another thought about the intern flitted through his brain as images of their travels flashed before his mind's eye, but he couldn't quite glom onto it.

Lance rose to his feet, pretending to be weakened by the blow, and glared defiantly at Edwin. "You might kill me, but you didn't kill my Dad. Or Ricky." He hoped he sounded strong and confident, despite his inner terror that they might yet die.

Edwin chuckled and glanced at his Rolex watch with glee. "I will have in about five minutes."

That caught Lance by surprise. "Whadda you mean?"

Edwin laughed again. "I'm giving Gonzalez a chance to redeem himself."

Lance eyed him questioningly.

Edwin smirked. "He's the hired gun who was supposed to kill your old man, but you got your faggot ass in his way." He spat in the dirt at Lance's feet. "Boy who came back, my ass! I don't know how you fooled the world, but you sure as hell didn't die and come back!"

Lance remained focused on Arthur. And Ricky. "What's he gonna do?"

Edwin grinned. "A little injection. Not as painful as I'd like, but still lethal. He'll call the moment it's done. I can't wait to see the look on your pretty face when he does."

Terrified, Lance turned to look at Esteban and Dakota, and both gazed at him with the same look.

Feeling bolder than he felt, Lance turned back and smirked. Knowing Techie was listening he said, "My Mom will kick his ass."

Edwin laughed and checked his watch again. Four minutes to go.

Jenny sat dozing lightly in her chair, the repetitive sounds of machines and oxygen tanks lulling her to sleep. Ryan had already left and she eagerly awaited what news he would bring, news on the fate of her other boys. The door clicked and Jenny opened her eyes in surprise.

She saw an orderly she'd never seen on this floor before, a man, middle-aged, older than any of the others. He nodded her way casually.

"Just checking his vitals, ma'am," he said politely. Too politely for Jenny's taste. And no one called her 'ma'am'. She'd made that clear. They were to call her Jenny, and everyone who worked this floor knew that.

Alarm bells went off in her head, and her heart began thumping. "You're new here."

The man appeared to be checking Ricky's heart and lung monitors, jotting a few notes onto a clipboard. "Yes, ma'am. Just filling in."

Well, she considered, that might explain the "ma'am" business. Just then her phone vibrated and she slipped it from her pocket. It was a text from an unknown source. Suddenly afraid, she glanced up once more and saw the orderly fiddling with something on his cart. Then she thumbed open the text. Her breath stopped.

'Lady Jenny, it's Techie. There's a man coming to kill Arthur and Ricky right now.'

She sucked in a tight breath, but refrained from the gasp of horror at the edges of her lips. Hands trembling, she texted 'okay' and slipped the phone back into her pocket. As causally as she dared, Jenny glanced over at the man and saw him preparing a syringe. Her heart flew into her throat.

She stood, resisting the urge to leap from her chair and charge the man. No, she had to catch him off guard. The two of them struggling might hurt the unconscious Ricky, and she couldn't risk that. So she stretched and acted like she just needed to move around a bit, strolling lightly around the foot of Ricky's bed to stand just behind the orderly.

He turned and eyed her suspiciously, but she would not be cowed. "What's that you're going to inject into my son?"

He smiled, but there was something off-putting in that smile, like it was something the man did so seldom it almost hurt his face. He was Latino, she could tell that much, weathered as though from long hours under a hot sun. But orderlies only worked indoors, didn't they?

He offered a shrug. "Just some meds the doctor ordered. See, it's here on the chart."

He handed Jenny a wooden clipboard with lots of data and scribbles on it she couldn't make head or tails of, but she took the board and pretended to scan it, all the while looking for something to use as a weapon. Her eye caught sight of a bedpan one of the nurses had left, just in case Ricky awoke and the catheter could be removed.

Forcing calm into her voice, she handed the man back the clipboard with a smile. "Go ahead."

He offered that forced smile as he took the clipboard and set it onto his cart. Then he leaned in toward the IV bag dispensing nutrients into Ricky through a tube in his forearm.

Jenny slid her right hand behind her and clutched the rim of the stainless steel bedpan. As the man prepared to insert the needle into the stopper, she swung up and over with all her might.

He must've spotted the move from the corner of his eye because he raised the arm holding the syringe to protect his face. The metal bedpan slammed hard into his forearm, sending the syringe flying and staggering the man back into his cart, knocking the clipboard and sundry items onto the floor with a huge clatter.

Just then the door flew open and the two agents burst into the room. The assassin glanced at them, and that's when Jenny struck. She swung the bedpan with all her might and slammed it into the side of his head. With a crunching sound and a grunt of pain, the man staggered back into the wall.

"Stay—" Jenny shouted as she slammed the bedpan into his arm—"away—" The man crumpled, obviously dazed. Jenny kicked out with one sneakered foot and connected with his groin. He screamed in agony. "—from—" She kicked him again, and his legs collapsed beneath him. "—my—" Then she threw the bedpan at him, connecting with his face and causing blood to spurt from an obviously broken nose. "—son!"

She must've looked so red in the face and out of control that the two agents merely stood in the open doorway gaping in astonishment. More men rushed into the room to check on the commotion and must've thought they'd entered the psych ward.

Jenny didn't care. She whirled around to gaze at Ricky's sleeping, peaceful face and sighed with relief.

"Get him outta here," she heard one of the men bark, and from the corner of her eye saw the agents lift the unconscious assassin and carry him from the room.

She turned to the agent in charge.

"Looks like you should be guarding us, Lady Jenny," he said with a grin, and then exited the room.

She smiled and returned her gaze to the perfect features of this boy she'd so come to love. Would he ever wake up? Then she heard something that nearly stopped her heart.

"You ladies always go to violence first."

She spun on her heels, and there was Arthur grinning at her with amusement.

"Arthur!" She rushed around Ricky's bed and practically threw herself onto her husband, pulling back at the last second so as not to hurt him. "Oh, thank God you're back!"

He chuckled, but she could see the strain his ordeal had left on his handsome face. "Well, someone had to tell my wife to stop screaming so loudly."

Her entire body filled with an onrush of joy, and simultaneous chills, and she bent down to kiss him desperately and passionately, a kiss he returned with gusto. She pulled back, her face flushed and her heart pounding. "I thought I'd lost you!"

"Not if I can help it," he replied, twisting his head to catch a glimpse of Ricky in the next bed over. "Ricky?"

She nodded, fear suddenly replacing her momentary surge of joy.

"How is he?" Arthur asked, struggling to move enough to get a better look at his son.

She shook her head. "Doctors said he should be awake by now."

She and Arthur exchanged a look of despair, the look of parents who know they might lose a child to death at any moment. Arthur's face clouded over even further. "I dreamt of Lance, Jenny. He's in grave danger."

She nodded again, more fear tightening its grip on her heart and soul. "He went to rescue Chris and Sylvia. They were kidnapped by whoever attacked us. The others went with him. Merlin too."

Arthur's eyebrows shot up in surprise.

Jenny sighed heavily. "He has Excalibur, and he's your son through and through. He'll bring them back. I have faith in him."

Arthur nodded. "As do I." But still he looked fraught with fear.

At that moment Arthur's doctor burst into the room with several nurses and Jenny had to step aside so they could examine the king. As she watched them check his vitals and perform other routine tests, Jenny slipped out her phone and checked the time.

It was already midmorning and James should be there soon. What would he find? Part of her desperately wanted to know, and part of her felt extreme terror at the possible answer to that question. She sighed and gazed down at the still unconscious form of her son.

"I love you, Ricky," she whispered, fighting the urge to cry.

No, I won't!

She'd gotten Arthur back and she'd have her sons back too. All of them. Lance would make sure of that.

†††

Lance watched Edwin glancing at the digital time readout on his computerized console with a slight flicker of concern on his twisted features. He checked his watch and quickly verified the time, his face scrunched with confusion.

Lance knew he had to buy Techie some time to regain control of the computer system. Then it hit him like a bolt of lightening – what if Techie was already dead and hadn't gotten word to his mom? No. He knew Techie too well. The man might not be a fighter, but he was no quitter. He'd have set off the grenade by now if he knew he couldn't continue.

So, in an effort to buy his friend a precious few minutes, Lance glared at the suddenly not-so-smug-looking Edwin. "Is Cairns in on this too?"

As though happy to be distracted, Edwin chuckled, sounding more and more like R. with each word or utterance. "He's a useful idiot, nothing more."

Like Villagrana, Lance thought, remembering what R. had said about the mayor. "So he doesn't know you're pulling the strings?"

Edwin grinned. "Oh, hell no. I created an alter ego, my Clark Kent, if you will. Super wealthy donor who bankrolled the senator's election and paid off his enemies. He does whatever I tell him." He glanced at the digital readout and Lance noted that it was ten-thirty in the morning. "And what he's doing right now is filibustering your childish bill of rights in the senate. He'll prevent it from getting an up or down vote and will continue to do so while I twist a few more arms to vote it down. Of course, I'll get on that *after* I kill you."

Lance felt blindsided anew. The deaths of his friends and now the death of his bill of rights? If he failed here, it would mean everything he'd done was for nothing, and everyone who'd died had died in vain. The weight of the world on his shoulders had never felt so heavy.

Edwin laughed again. "So you see, Pretty Boy, it's over. Your amendments are dead, your pathetic father is dead, and your latest faggot boyfriend is dead. And now it's your turn."

Lance felt defeated, a feeling he'd never given into in his life. Even when Richard had continued to hurt him, he'd never cried out after that first time. He'd never given in, just endured the pain and humiliation. But now everything did seem lost after all. Then a thought occurred to him, an unanswered question he wasn't sure he wanted answered.

"Where's Sylvia? What did you do with her?"

Edwin pulled a face of surprise. "Wow, so you do think about girls once in awhile."

"Where *is* she?" Lance repeated firmly, ignoring the dig.

Edwin shrugged. "Unharmed, if that's what you're asking."

Just then, as though on cue, Sylvia entered the chamber from behind the console. She appeared uninjured, and her clothes were different. Now she wore tight jeans and a t-shirt. Her hair looked washed and clean.

"Sylvia!" Lance exclaimed, both happy, and mystified, by her appearance.

She ignored him and strode haughtily up to Edwin. "The gook is trying to take over the computer system again. He also warned the faggot's mother that Gonzalez was on his way."

Her voice sounded cold and alien. Not the sweet, adoring girl who'd followed Reyna around like a puppy, who'd nurtured Chris, who'd mastered the bow and arrow with ease and excitement.

"What the fuck?" Lance heard Esteban whisper from behind him. But he didn't turn. He kept his eyes fixed on her smirking demeanor. His mind reeled with images – Sylvia attending every meeting within The Hub, her odd facial expression at Arthur's wedding, her chumminess with Edwin during their travels, her telling him she had an older brother, and the fact that Techie didn't have her heat signature on file. The blood suddenly drained from his face, and he knew.

"You're his sister," he said, his voice cold and dry and hopeless. Why hadn't he seen the resemblance before?

"What?" he heard from Esteban, but kept his eyes straight ahead.

Edwin chortled with delight, placing a loving arm around the girl's shoulders and giving her a perfunctory hug. "Blood of my blood," he said. "And a capable spy for our father. Until *you* killed him."

Sylvia's face clouded with hate. She broke away from Edwin and strode up to Lance in fury. He stood his ground, still unable to believe she had been the spy all along. She spit in his face and then hauled off and slapped him. The crack of her hand against his cheek echoed throughout the chamber. He was so stunned, he didn't even flinch.

"That's for my father, you fucking little bitch!"

Then she turned and strode back to her brother, turning to face Lance with a satisfied, but roiling, expression on her pretty face.

Lance reached up and wiped the spittle from his cheek with his hand, still in shock at this latest revelation. They'd played him. All along. R. Edwin. And Sylvia. And he'd been too stupid to see it.

Lance just stared at Edwin and Sylvia in silent shock. He decided to try one desperate plea, knowing it was fruitless. "Edwin, let Chris go. It's me you want. He's just a little boy."

He glanced over his shoulder a moment at the struggling, whimpering Chris. The blade still glinted ominously, silent and unmoving.

Edwin tossed off that heartless laugh. "He's already fucked, Lance, living with you faggots. He's just gonna turn into one anyway. I'm doing him a favor."

Sylvia laughed at that.

Lance felt numb and growing steadily weaker. The wound in his lower back trickled a steady stream of blood down his leg and into his skate shoe. He had to fight Edwin, but how could he win like this? The man was unhurt and obviously strong, and he was weak. And Excalibur stood out of his reach, silently embedded in the concrete, completely useless. He gazed at Edwin with an intense scrutiny, studying his size and muscularity.

Yes, the man was fresh and unhurt, but not *that* much bigger than him, Lance realized. He was a bit shorter and so looked more buff, but in truth Lance thought he might be stronger than the older man. When he was fresh, anyway. He'd never been much of a fighter on the streets. His small size and speed usually got him away from danger before it could physically assault him. But there was that one placement when he was ten where the staff used to make the boys fight each other and they'd place bets on the outcome. He'd learned some moves there, and of course Ricky had taught him all kinds of wrestling maneuvers, both legal and illegal.

Just the thought of Ricky sent a resurgence of strength coursing through his veins and tightened his muscles with anger. He had to get back to see his beloved's face once more time. And he had to save Chris. If *he* didn't, who would?

All of these thoughts raced through his mind in an instant as Edwin and Sylvia studied him mockingly. Despite his resurgence in strength and his indomitable willpower, Lance remained in a slightly slumped posture, the better to trick the enemy into letting his guard down.

"So here we are, Pretty Boy," Edwin said with a smirk. "When I get through with you, your face won't be so pretty anymore and no one will want an open casket at your funeral." He chuckled, obviously finding himself amusing.

Lance glared back. He felt no intimidation whatsoever. This man had terrorized him for years, had pretended to be an ally, was responsible for the deaths of his friends and the kidnapping of his brother. Because of him, Ricky and Dad might die! No, Lance felt such anger surge through him that it overcame the blood loss from his bullet wound. Edwin might make good on his threat, but Lance determined to take the man down with him.

Edwin extended an arm toward Esteban and Dakota, sweeping it over Lance's head to include Chris in his glass cage. "As you can see, I love old movies, especially those adventure films where the hero is put into some kind of contraption and has to get out before it kills him." He sounded giddy with glee, and Sylvia smirked by his side.

Edwin glanced up at the digital readout, and then back at Lance. "In ten minutes time, the computer will activate all three devices, one at a time. Your gangbanger friend will be ripped apart – something I got from your pathetic ancestors, Pretty Boy, since Indians used to use horses to do that to white people."

Then Edwin gestured toward a defiantly glowering Dakota. "Your native fag boy here will get a spear through the chest shortly thereafter. I can't wait for that one."

He pointed up into the rafters behind him. Lance followed his gaze and spotted a large wooden spear with a gleamingly sharp metal spike on the end. It was loaded into some kind of device designed to propel it forward, and Lance saw it was aimed straight at Dakota.

Edwin chuckled again. "And, of course, last, but not least, your whiny little faggot-in-training will be sliced in two, right through the balls. Appropriate, don't you think?"

Lance felt his blood boiling as he glanced back at Chris dangling like a slab of beef, wide-eyed and filled with terror. Fists clenched, but forcing control into his heart and mind, Lance turned back to face down his enemy. He would not be intimidated. Not by Edwin any more than he had by the man's father.

"Hopefully, you'll still be alive to watch them die, but I can't promise that. If by some miracle you should get the better of me, you might have a shot at shutting down the computer and saving your friends." Then he grinned. "Oh, and don't expect the gook or the others to save you either. While I'm killing you, my dear sister will finish them off."

He turned to Sylvia with a mix of love and madness in those wild eyes. "I'd say start with the other Indian faggot outside. Then the slut and the nigger. The gook'll probably be dead by then anyway. That way you can be back in time to see the grand finale."

Grinning with pleasure, Sylvia reached behind her and slipped a large serrated hunting knife out of a sheath beneath her t-shirt and held it out to Lance and the others. "This way I can watch them bleed out."

Despite his efforts at composure, Lance couldn't help but look appalled that this young girl, who he thought he knew, could be so cold and callous, so bloodthirsty. She laughed hollowly at his shocked expression, then turned with a flounce of her curly hair and vanished behind the computer console.

Edwin kept his eyes on Lance, grinning broadly. "Well, time for me to fulfill my promise, Lance. I did say you wouldn't see your eighteenth birthday, which is tomorrow, isn't it?"

That startled Lance because he'd so lost track of the days he'd honestly forgotten. Still, he held his composure and studied his enemy, seeking an opening to strike first.

"I told you it would end like this, one-on-one, man to fag," Edwin went on giddily, like a child who'd just pulled a fast one on his parents. "And now it will."

He stepped forward and Lance threw up his fists, using his arms to protect his midsection.

"You're a fucking coward, Edwin!" Esteban shouted from behind him.

That stopped Edwin and he cast a furious look at Esteban. "How's one-on-one, no weapons, *cowardly*, street trash?"

Esteban spat on the floor in disgust. "You can see he's hurt."

Edwin shrugged. "So, he'll be dead in a few minutes. What does it matter?"

"Cuz it isn't fair!" Esteban shouted, yanking on the chains so hard the metal poles rattled. "Let me fight you, you fucking pussy! I'll stomp your head into the floor!"

Edwin laughed that empty, soulless laugh he'd gotten from his father. "What does fair have to do with revenge?"

And then, thinking Lance was distracted, Edwin lunged for him. But all Lance's training with Ricky and Este over the years kicked in automatically. He leapt to the side and kicked out with one leg.

Edwin grunted as Lance's foot caught him in the shin and he stumbled, but didn't go down.

Lance tucked and rolled, landing on one shoulder and struggling painfully to his feet, staggering slightly as pain ripped through his lower back.

Edwin swung around and slammed one solid fist into Lance's upper back, forcing the boy to stumble forward. But Lance refused to fall. He pushed the searing pain into a small corner of his brain and turned just as Edwin threw a punch at his face.

The punch connected and Lance saw stars. His head snapped back and he pin wheeled with his arms as he tumbled and staggered backwards. Pain ripped through his face and into his brain. But he still refused to go down.

Edwin charged, and Lance dropped to a squat, causing the man to trip over him in a tangle of arms and legs. Lance stood and lashed out with one foot, connecting with Edwin's side and hearing a satisfying "Uugghh" of pain escape the man's lips.

Edwin started to rise, and staggered, but managed to spin back around very quickly. Lance didn't let him get all the way up before rushing him like a linebacker. He was vaguely aware of the frantic rattling and shaking of chains, and the straining of metal behind him, but his focus was on Edwin. His shoulder slammed into the man's midsection and he was shocked by how hard it was.

Edwin winced, but only stumbled back, grabbing Lance by the hair and yanking it viciously. Lance cried out in pain as his head snapped back, and then with his other arm Edwin drove a solid fist hard into his gut, again and again. Having spent so much time with Jack and Ricky working his abs, Lance found they could take the blows without even winding him. He focused on freeing his hair from the man's grip.

He reached up and grabbed Edwin's arm, and then spun around behind the man, pulling the arm up and back. Edwin cried out in agony and released his hair. Then Lance slammed a fist into Edwin's lower back, eliciting another painful grunt as the man stumbled away from him.

Edwin turned and glowered furiously.

Lance grinned beneath his panting. "Not bad for a pretty boy, huh?"

That seemed to enrage Edwin even more. He screamed and ran for him, but Lance was quicker. Employing a move Ricky had used on Michael, Lance dove for the man's legs and wrapped his arms around them, flipping back and up and throwing Edwin hard to the solidly-packed earth of the arena. The pain in his side and loss of blood were making Lance light-headed, and the air whooshed from his lungs as he also landed hard in the dirt.

He rolled and lurched to his feet, but suddenly felt overcome with dizziness and staggered back, allowing Edwin to regain his feet and charge. Lance's sense memory kicked in and, as Edwin dove for one leg to take him down, Lance executed another wrestling maneuver, turning into the move and using his upper body weight and strength to drive Edwin back to the ground. Not trusting himself to remain stable, Lance staggered away to put some distance between them. His eye caught the digital readout: only five minutes left.

He was running out of time. He started to turn when he heard Chris scream, "Lance, look out!"

He'd gotten about three-fourths of the way around when he felt Edwin's fist slam hard into his lower right side where the bullet had entered. Pain exploded in his brain and his entire body spasmed as though struck by lightening. Lance could hear Esteban shouting and the chains clanking with renewed vigor, but his brain felt clouded with dizziness and little dots danced before his eyes. He went down hard onto his back, another icy-cold stab of pain ripping through him.

And then Edwin was on him, straddling his midsection and pinning his arms to the dirt with both knees. Edwin cackled with glee at the helpless Lance pinned beneath him, and with measured control slammed his fist first into the boy's chest and then into his face. Lance could do nothing but take it. Pain arched through his chest and head with each fall of Edwin's fist.

He looked up through blurred vision to see Edwin crowing and raising both fists into the air triumphantly like the winner of a boxing match.

I'm finished. I lost after all.

Edwin glowered down at him and then grinned broadly, panting and heaving from his exertions. "Any last words, Pretty Boy, before I end your miserable existence?"

"Edwin!" Lance heard Esteban shouting, but the man ignored him. His victory was at hand and he clearly wanted to wallow in it.

Lance fought to clear his head. He thought of Chris, whom he'd failed. His father whom he'd disappointed. And Ricky, whom he'd abandoned. They'd promised each other. They'd promised. For now and always. But here he was giving up. He would lose the love of his life because he was too weak to fight back.

And then he thought of Ricky fighting Michael, how even when he didn't stand a chance he kept on going. And he thought of Michael, who'd loved him. What would Michael do?

He suddenly realized what it was about Edwin he'd been trying to recall.

And then he had it.

Through bloodied lips, he smiled.

The man looked surprised and lost the gloating smirk. "What's so funny, Pretty Boy? The fact you're about to die?"

"No. It's you, Edwin," Lance replied, hoping to talk long enough to clear his head. "You're obsessed with my looks and my body. That's all you talk about. You're hot for me, aren't you?"

Edwin looked like he'd been slapped. Then he tossed off a phony laugh. "You fag boys always think every guy wants to fuck you."

Now Lance laughed, though it sent ribbons of pain coursing through his midsection. "Not every guy. Just you. All the time we traveled you never talked about girls, Edwin. Not once. Why is that? No girlfriend?"

Edwin kept his cool, but Lance felt his whole body stiffen slightly. "I got all the pussy I want when I want it. No need for a girlfriend."

Lance smiled sweetly, hoping his battered face still retained some of the old charm people had come to love. "Yeah, I've heard that before from closet cases like you."

Now Edwin raised a bloodied fist. "I'm gonna shut that faggot mouth of yours, bitch!"

"Go ahead. You can kill every boy like me in the world and it won't change what you are." Lance's head had begun to clear, and he could see he was getting under the man's skin. If he could just carry out his plan before the fist fell....

"I am not a disgusting faggot like you!" Edwin spat, and the fist started to come down.

Michael's words flashed through Lance's mind and he said them, "That bulge in your pants says different."

Edwin's fist froze and his eyes flicked for a split second to his crotch. But it was all Lance needed. Using his strong abdominal muscles, he sat up and slammed his head into Edwin's, sending jackhammer blows of pain caroming through him and drawing stars. But Edwin cried out and grabbed his head, shifting his weight enough for Lance to drive a knee up and into his back. Now the man rolled off, clutching at his head in agony.

Lance had had enough. He would end this now. Drawing on reserves of strength he never knew he possessed, he lurched to his feet and flung out a foot, connecting with Edwin's crotch. Hard. The man screamed and grabbed for his privates, rolling and pitching and writhing in agony. Lance viciously stomped down on Edwin's thigh and heard a satisfying scream of pain. Edwin rolled and lurched in intense agony, and Lance threw himself onto the man, straddling him the way he'd been straddled. And he rained blow after blow onto Edwin's face, using every muscle in his powerful arms. He felt the nose shatter and blood spurt. He split the man's cheeks and pounded his mouth until the lips blew up like a balloon.

He could hear Esteban shouting his name but nothing registered. All he could see was the pain and death this man had caused, and he determined to end it. The face beneath him had become a bloody mess, and Lance's knuckles were red and slick. But his blood boiled with fury and he couldn't control himself.

Finally, Esteban's shouting penetrated his senses. "Lance, stop!" he heard as he raised his fist for yet another vicious blow.

And he stopped. His breath came in fits and stops, and his head spun. The man beneath him was almost unrecognizable, but Este's voice wasn't.

"Lance, *please*," he heard in that deep voice of the older brother he idolized. "Remember what I told you!"

Lance turned his head and looked at his brother. Este's wrists were cut and bloodied from the shackles, and he'd bent the pillar to his right. But it was the look in his eyes that would stay with Lance for as long as he lived, the look of someone who needed him to stay pure and unsullied, who needed him to be a hero.

Just then an explosion shook the building, and Lance's cloudy brain realized that Techie must've detonated his grenade. That meant Techie was dead. He didn't have even a second to grieve before the entire console of monitors, including the desktop computer, winked out and went dark.

And that's when the gears began shifting.

The pillars started moving apart, pulling Este's arms along with them. Shocked, Lance flicked his wide eyes over as Chris screamed in terror. The blade began slowly spinning. Lance stood on wobbly legs and spun his head around to look up into the rafters. The spear was also moving, loading itself into the launcher to impale Dakota where he sat silently struggling and fighting against his restraints.

He heard a chuckle behind him and turned back to the bloodied, battered Edwin. Despite his injuries, the man laughed. "Game over, Pretty Boy."

And suddenly Lance realized he'd been tricked. All of them had, even Techie. These killing traps had never been controlled by the computer. Probably not the maze, either. Edwin had given them that impression by allowing Techie to control things for a while. And blowing the computer was the trigger. Now his friends would die after all. Chris, too.

No fucking way, he thought, fighting the nausea and dizziness. He turned around and started lurching toward Esteban and Dakota.

Esteban had watched the fight with fear and desperation, especially when it looked like Edwin had the upper hand. But when Lance was ready to kill the man, he'd had to intervene. Now, as he fought and struggled against the pull of the pillars, he saw Lance turn and start toward him, and hoped he could hold off the pillars long enough for his brother to break these chains.

"Grab my gun, Lance!" he shouted. "Shoot the chains off."

Esteban was amazed Lance was still standing. His entire body was covered in blood, his hair matted and tangled, his face bruised and bloody.

Esteban felt his arms stretched almost to their fullest and he fought and struggled, the shackles digging into his wrists with unbearable pain.

Then he saw, like a wraith rising from a grave, Edwin somehow regain his feet behind the slow-moving Lance. There was a glint of something shiny and metallic in his hand as he lunged forward.

"Nnnnoooooooo!" Esteban shrieked in fury as Edwin plunged the blade of his knife into Lance's right side like Brutus had done to Caesar centuries before.

"Nooooo!" he screamed again even as Lance's eyes bulged wide with shock and surprise and he silently toppled forward to crash hard and unmoving into the dirt.

Edwin crowed with triumph.

Esteban went ballistic. With every ounce of his extraordinary strength he yanked his right arm and ripped the metal pillar from its concrete base.

"Este!" Dakota shouted, and Esteban looked over to see the Indian lifting his feet off the floor. "Get me free!"

In a hurricane of rage, Esteban swung his right arm, sliding the pillar along the floor. It passed beneath Dakota's feet and smashed the wooden legs of his chair, sending the Indian crashing hard to the ground. But Dakota didn't hesitate. His legs were up and through his tied wrists and then his teeth bit through the ropes within seconds.

Even while Esteban scrambled with his free hand for the Uzi he'd dropped, Dakota rolled out-of-the-way as the spear turned what was left of his chair to splinters. Then the Indian had his fallen bow and arrow in hand and rolled up onto one knee just as Esteban snatched up the Uzi.

Dakota let lose his arrow and it struck Edwin right in the heart, even as Esteban opened fire. Edwin's battered and bloodied eyes opened wide for a second in complete shock as his chest exploded and he flew backward into a bloody heap in the dirt, where he lay silent and unmoving.

Esteban whipped the gun around and shot through the chains binding his left arm to the bent, but still upright pillar, and then he and Dakota scrambled frantically forward to drop fearfully to either side of Lance.

Esteban eyed Dakota with a petrified look before gently placing his hands beneath Lance and lightly rolling this boy he loved over onto his back. Frenzied and desperate, he placed his ear against Lance's bloodied and bruised chest, and listened. He sighed with relief and lifted his head.

"He's still breathing," he whispered. "But just barely."

"Get him to Excalibur," he suddenly heard Merlin mumble behind him. He'd forgotten the man was even there. He whipped his head around to eye the waking, still-groggy wizard. "Hurry, Sir Este, before it's too late."

So Esteban and Dakota slipped their arms under Lance's own and lifted the dying boy to his feet, hurrying as fast as they could with his limp body between them to the spot where Excalibur stood waiting, firm and unyielding.

"Hold him up," Dakota said firmly, letting go of his side as Esteban slipped both of his arms under Lance's and held the boy against him, arms wrapped lovingly around his torso.

Dakota reached out and took both of Lance's blood-soaked hands in his, and gently pressed the fingers of each around the jeweled hilt. Excalibur instantly began to glow. Lance's eyes flew open suddenly and Dakota sucked in a shocked breath. He would later tell Esteban that for a split second he'd been certain Lance's eyes had also glowed, just like Excalibur. And then the moment faded.

"I'm all right now," Lance announced quietly, and Esteban released him. Lance stood strong and erect, his body suddenly surging with a power he knew was only temporary. It wouldn't save him from death, just stave it off for a brief while. He easily slid Excalibur out of its concrete tomb and raised it high above his head.

That's when Chris shrieked, "Lannnccee! Help meeeee!"

Lance heard Esteban mutter, "Oh, shit," but he was already running. He crossed the gladiator pit in a few strides, Excalibur raised high, his arms taut with renewed strength.

The blade was mere inches from Chris. The boy had his legs stuck straight out in front of him and was only able to hold that pose because of all the abdominal workouts he'd done with his brothers.

But Lance could see even from a distance the desperate sweat on his face, the shaking of his body as he fought the weakening core muscles. Lance never even hesitated. He slid to a stop before the glass booth and simultaneously swung Excalibur downward and across with every once of his strength.

"Close your eyes, Chris!"

Sword hit glass, and the booth imploded like a car windshield, blowing up and raining thousands of chunks of pebbled glass down on them from all sides. But Lance had become like Michael on that train, fierce and unstoppable. He leapt inside the booth and jumped up onto the platform housing the saw.

"Grab his legs," he ordered as Esteban leapt up onto the opposite side and grabbed for Chris's sagging feet. The boy whimpered in fear until he felt Esteban's hands swing his legs away from the rising, spinning death, and then Lance swung at the ropes binding his hands, severing them instantly and allowing Chris to drop safely into Esteban's strong embrace.

Turning, Esteban lowered Chris to Dakota, who easily grabbed on and held the boy in his arms until Lance was there. Still gripping Excalibur in his right hand, Lance enfolded his brother with his left arm, pulling the boy into a tight and desperately loving hug. The little boy clamped on to his brother like he never wanted to let go.

"I knew you'd come for me, Lance," Chris sobbed into his big brother's blood-splattered shoulder, "I knew it."

Lance turned and stepped out of the shattered enclosure, cradling Chris lovingly, Dakota and Esteban flanking him. Just then Ryan burst into the chamber from behind the console with a small army of men sporting weapons and flack jackets and helmets sweeping the room with the muzzles of their rifles.

"Lance!" he called out in relief at the sight of his boy across the vast room. Then he saw the carnage and the blood and Edwin's bullet-ridden and unrecognizable body twisted up in the dirt arena. "Holy shit!" He stopped a moment at Edwin's body as though to make sure he was dead before hurrying to Lance, his own gun waving frantically.

He stopped and stared agape at his godson - half-naked, bloody, bruised, hair tangled and twisted. "My God, Lance, are you all right?"

"I'm fine," Lance said quickly, "but Reyna and Justin and Kai need help." He turned to Esteban, suddenly terrified. "Sylvia."

Este and Dakota both turned and sprinted for the exit behind the console.

"*Nino*, send help with them," Lance ordered and Ryan instantly waved some men and arriving paramedics after the two knights. The group vanished behind the console and Lance swallowed his fear.

Please let them be alive, Lord, he thought desperately, hoping with all his might that his family was safe.

Paramedics in full military garb dashed up and gently extracted Chris from Lance's embrace. The boy refused to let go until Lance quietly said, "I'm right here, Chris, and I'm not letting you out of my sight."

Reluctantly, Chris allowed one medic to check him over while the other started examining Lance. Lance shrugged the man off. "*Nino*, there's no time for this. You need to get me to the capitol, now."

Ryan pulled a stunned expression. "Huh? Lance, my God, you're hurt, badly. You need medical attention."

"Most of the blood is Edwin's," Lance said impatiently, suddenly choking up. "And Techie's."

Now Ryan's face collapsed into shock. "Edwin?"

Lance blew out an exasperated breath, clutching Excalibur's hilt with a grip of frustration. "I'll tell you on the way. *Nino*, he sent somebody to kill Dad and Ricky, and Cairns is trying to fuck up our bill of rights!"

Ryan still looked confused, and almost dazed. "I didn't get any call about Arthur or Ricky."

That gave Lance a moment of blessed relief. It was true Edwin's assassin had never called to confirm the kill, so by the grace of God he'd been stopped. But Lance couldn't do anything about it in any case.

"Lance, you're seriously hurt," Ryan went on, waving another medic over to tend his wounds. "I need to get you to a hospital."

The young medic in the flack jacket carried a medical kit and nodded his head at Ryan, and for some reason that angered Lance.

He held up Excalibur so quickly that Ryan took a step back. "I won't die, *nino*. Not yet anyway. Not till I see my Dad and… Ricky."

"Lance," Ryan began hesitantly, but Lance jumped on his next word.

"*Nino!*" Noting the shocked and pained look in Ryan's eyes, he struggled for calm. "I've lost too much already," he said with a heavy heart and a voice weighed down by guilt. "I sure as hell won't lose the bill of rights too. I can't let them win!"

By now Merlin had been released from his captivity and stood beside Ryan. The weathered and old-looking detective glanced over at the middle-aged wizard. Merlin shrugged.

"Merlin can put his magic stuff on my wounds to stop the bleeding and Excalibur will keep me alive. Right, Merlin?" His fiery green eyes fixed on the wizard.

Merlin looked afraid, something Lance had never seen in those inscrutable eyes before. He chose to ignore that look. There was too much at stake and it wasn't all about him and whether or not he lived or died. "Both are stop gap measures, Your Majesty, quite temporary. They will not keep you alive for long."

"Long enough to stop Cairns and get back to my Dad and Ricky," Lance shot back without hesitation. "Now do it, Merlin. Your king commands you."

His fierce look left no room for argument. Merlin bowed with respect and hurried to fetch his backpack.

Chris grabbed Lance's hand and squeezed desperately. "Don't leave me here, Lance. I wanna go too."

Lance looked down at his brother with a ferocious and abiding sense of love and protectiveness. "Damn straight you're going with me."

By then, Merlin was back and tending to the dual wounds in Lance's lower back. From behind the boy he caught Ryan's eye and gave a solemn shake of the head.

Lance looked into his godfather's eyes. He saw pain mixed with fear and love, the desperate need of a parent fearful of losing a beloved child. But he wasn't a child any more, and Ryan would just have to accept that. He knew the man hated even considering this plan, wanted to insist on him getting medical care first.

"Lance, please—" Ryan pleaded, but Lance cut him off.

"*Nino!*" Lance barked so loudly even Chris jumped, and the medic who'd just started wrapping a bandage around his waist looked startled, too. "I *have* to do this. Please!"

Looking like it was the hardest decision he'd ever made in his long, complicated life, Ryan very reluctantly nodded.

✝✝✝

Lance sat in the back seat of the Secret Service vehicle with Chris while Ryan drove. He'd been in such a desperate hurry to leave that he'd refused to wait until some clothes could be found for him. One of the soldiers gave up his flack jacket, which Lance gratefully accepted. But he'd left it unbuttoned and there had been no available pants so he just stayed with his dirty, bloodied workout shorts and blood-splattered skate shoes. Most of the blood had dried anyway and, as Lance said soberly to Ryan on their way to the car, "I want Cairns to see what he did."

He fretted with anxiety the entire trip, clutching Chris's hand and squeezing, never wanting to let it go. When they'd first gotten on the road, Chris had lovingly used sterile cloths given him by the medics to clean blood off Lance's face. Even then, there were residual splotches mixed in with the black and purple bruises. That, coupled with his open jacket revealing the bruised, bloodied, and bandaged torso and his blood-splattered legs, made him look like something out of a war movie.

He didn't care. They'd left without learning the fate of Reyna and the others, so he had no idea if he'd lost more of his family. And, in their haste, Ryan had forgotten to grab someone's cell phone. He'd lost his own, he'd told them, when he'd nearly toppled into a spike-filled pit on the backside of the compound. He'd had the phone in hand and had to toss it to grab onto one of the soldiers accompanying him. Shining a flashlight into the pit after being pulled free, he'd seen his phone impaled on a razor-sharp spike. As a consequence, Lance sat in the back of the speeding car, its siren blaring, and thought about Arthur. And Ricky. Were they still alive? Would he see either of them ever again?

He glanced down at Chris, who sat staring out the window, clearly in shock. His disheveled hair was dirty and tangled, his clothes torn and soiled, and the eyes reflected in the glass of the window looked shell-shocked. Lance grabbed the boy and pulled him in, cradling him in his arms, and just held him. Chris pressed his head against Lance's chest and wrapped his arms around his big brother and they rode the rest of the way sharing that basic human contact.

†††

The Capitol Building rose up white and pristine in the bright November sunlight as Ryan raced into the Senate parking lot and met the senate police officers who'd heard the siren and spotted the car as it approached. Ryan leapt from the driver's seat, his ID already out and flashing. The officers took their hands off their guns as they saw the presidential seal and Ryan's security clearance. Several of them gasped when Lance stepped from the car. Even Ryan found himself staring.

Here, under the bright fall sun, in broad daylight, the blood, the bruises, the open jacket revealing the bandaged abdomen made the boy look like a wounded soldier fresh from the battlefield. The blood streaked Excalibur completed the image.

Ryan told four of the cops to accompany him as Chris joined Lance, and the group hurried forward to enter the Capitol.

Lance could hear Cairns' pompous filibuster from the hallway as they approached the senate chamber from behind the speaker's podium. Even with the door closed, the senator's voice boomed loud and clear to his ears.

"I was fooled by the maturity of that boy into thinking children needed rights under our magnificent Constitution, but of course they don't. They have all the rights and protections they need from us adults, especially those of us here in Washington who always have their best interests at heart."

Lance had heard enough. He nodded to Ryan and a senate police officer pulled open the door. Excalibur clutched tightly in one hand, and Chris's hand held securely in the other, Lance marched past Ryan and the cops without a word and strode into the chamber.

The reaction of the gathered senators and spectators to Lance's startling entrance was instantaneous disbelief and a gasp that rippled around the chamber like a sonic boom. He strode around the speaker's podium, causing some seated there to actually move away in shock, no doubt, he thought vaguely, from the smell of dried blood encrusting him.

Cairns faced away from him, directing his prattle to the audience at large. But the stunned ripple through the room gave him pause, and he must have noticed the direction of every eye because, still speaking, he turned slowly. And then he recoiled in open-mouthed astonishment. Whatever he'd planned to say next was lost in the stunned look on his face, and he exclaimed loudly, "Lance!"

Lance released Chris's hand and stepped up to the man. He wanted to be close enough for Cairns to see every cut, every bruise, every speck of blood, to smell everyone who'd died because of him. He could feel his wounds slowly and inexorably killing him. He knew he'd lost an extreme amount of blood and that Excalibur was merely putting off the inevitable. But he would not look weak for this man, and he determined to live long enough to see his Dad once more. And to kiss Ricky goodbye.

"Didn't expect to see me again, did you, Senator?"

Cairns' eyes flicked from Lance to Chris, and then to Ryan and the officers standing just behind them.

"I don't know what you're talking about, Lance," the man said feebly, his strong voice of a moment before now reduced to that of a frightened child.

"Your wealthy donor, the one who bankrolled your campaign, he tried to kill me," Lance explained, making sure his voice carried throughout the chamber. He heard loud gasps of shock from the lawmakers. "He tried to kill Chris, and he did kill some of my family."

Cairns genuinely looked perplexed, and Lance couldn't help but shake his head in disgust.

"A useful idiot indeed. That's what Edwin called you."

The senator's face collapsed in shock. "Edwin? My intern?"

Lance nodded. "And the real man behind the alter ego who backed you," he explained, forcing his eyes right into the man's own and pinning him in place. "Son of my enemy became my enemy. And you helped him." He turned to Ryan. "*Nino*, the senator is finished with his filibuster. Arrest him, please."

Ryan nodded to the senate police officers and they immediately flanked Cairns, who still looked stunned with disbelief.

"You're under arrest, senator," one of the officers said. "Will you come willingly or do we need to cuff you?"

The man looked to Lance like he'd aged twenty years in the last twenty seconds. He turned his pale, bloodless face toward the cop and said, "I'll go with you."

They began leading him down the long aisle, past all of his silent, speechless colleagues, when Cairns turned to look back at Lance. "Lance, I swear I didn't know."

"Because you didn't want to, senator. All you cared about was getting elected."

Cairns cast him one more abject look of defeat before being led from the chamber in silence.

Lance turned to face the Senate Majority Leader and the other officers seated up on the dais before him. They stared at him in shock, as though disbelieving this moment was even occurring.

"Mr. Senate Majority Leader, I apologize for my appearance. No disrespect intended, but there wasn't time for me to clean up."

He heard gasps of surprise from behind him, as though the other lawmakers couldn't believe he would even think to apologize after what he'd obviously been through.

"I have to go now," Lance went on, sighing heavily. "To see if my father and my... and the boy I love are still alive. Now that the senator has stopped his filibuster, I respectfully ask that you proceed with a vote on the Children's Bill of Rights."

Then he offered a respectful bow, reached out to take Chris's hand in his, and strode purposefully from the chamber the same way he'd entered.

Ryan glanced up a moment at the stunned expression on the majority leader's face before hurrying after his godson.

†††

Walter Reed couldn't loom before the windshield fast enough for Lance. In their haste to depart the Capitol, both he and Ryan had forgotten to grab a cell phone from someone to call Jenny. As Ryan sped through the streets of Washington, siren blaring and blue light flashing atop the driver's side window, he offered to stop and use his federal ID to commandeer someone's phone, but Lance nixed the idea.

"We'll know soon enough," was all he said, his voice tired and resigned. Knowing he would collapse the moment he allowed Excalibur to slip from his grasp, Lance continued to grip the sword firmly, while his other arm remained just as firmly wrapped around Chris. His little brother hadn't spoken since leaving the compound and Lance knew the boy's mind was focused on the same question as his – would they see their dad and Ricky alive again?

They left D.C. behind and barreled through the rural beauty of Maryland's woodlands and Lance watched tree after tree whip past his view as he stared listlessly out the window. What was happening in the Congress, he wondered? Was the senate voting up or down on the CBOR? To think all this death and destruction and anguish could be for nothing if the politicians acted as politicians usually did – in their own self-interest.

He suddenly sat bolt upright as the mammoth hospital came into view. He exchanged a quick look with Chris and gave the boy a loving squeeze as Ryan flashed his badge at the guard gate and they were waved on through.

"I'm taking you straight to emergency, Lance," Ryan said in his best no-nonsense voice as he spun the car through the parking lot toward the emergency entrance.

Lance just grunted and nodded his head, knowing that no such thing was going to happen. Dad and Ricky first. No argument.

And so when Ryan finally stopped the car, Lance flung open the door with his left hand and, waving Excalibur about like a madman, he bolted toward the sliding glass doors marked "Emergency Entrance Only." He heard Ryan shouting, "Lance, wait!" but he kept right on running.

Nurses and orderlies and security personnel all gaped at him in astonished surprise, obviously recognizing him, and stunned by his bloody, wild-eyed appearance. Intensive Care was on the first floor and Lance pelted headlong down the corridors, ignoring every call for him to "Stop" or "Slow down" or "Watch that sword, kid!"

And then he saw the two Secret Service Agents standing outside the door. They looked over as he bolted down the hallway toward them. Like the hospital personnel, they weren't sure what to do, knowing he was under the direct protection of the president, so they hesitantly stepped to each side of the door and Lance burst through into the room.

The first thing he saw was Arthur, sitting up in bed and gazing silently out the window.

"Dad!" he shouted in ecstatic joy.

Arthur turned, and the worried, fearful look on his face breached into the biggest smile of relief Lance thought he'd ever seen.

"Lance, thank God!" the king exclaimed.

But then Lance turned his head to Ricky's bed, and gasped. It was empty. And the bed was made, as though waiting for the next person to occupy it.

A guttural wail of pain rose from within him. "No," he wailed. "No, no, no."

And then, legs feeling like rubber, his heart frozen in his chest, Lance turned to stagger out of the room into the corridor. He heard Arthur shout, "Lance, wait!" but he ignored it.

Ricky was dead! Oh God, no, the most amazing boy in the world, the boy who made his heart and soul complete, was dead.

"Nnnnoooooo!" he shrieked, drawing every eye from the nurses' station to those by the elevator. Lance staggered a few more steps, and then vomited what little he had in his stomach. He retched up mostly blood and the water he'd drunk on the drive over.

He staggered, the life force gone from his body, from his soul. Ricky was gone. There was nothing to live for. He let Excalibur go, and the sword clattered to the linoleum floor with a thudding echo.

Suddenly all the pain, all the weakness, all the light-headedness from loss of blood swamped Lance and took him to his knees. Then he crumpled back against the wall, his vision swimming.

Then he heard it.

Faint.

Uncertain.

His name.

"Lance?"

Lance lifted his head and gazed through confused, blurred vision toward the end of the corridor. He was sure the lady standing by the wheelchair was his mom. And the boy in the chair was—

"Ricky!" he blurted with desperate abandon. It wasn't a name. Or a word. It was every emotion he had left.

Drawing on wells of strength that shouldn't have existed, Lance pushed and struggled to his feet, forcing one leg in front of the other, staggering drunkenly toward the boy who made his life worth living. He vaguely heard people shouting, calling for help, but none of that mattered. He stumbled to the wheelchair where a terrified Jenny grabbed him and pulled him into a hug of joy.

"My God, Lance, what happened to you?"

But Lance could barely hug her. He didn't have any strength left. Just enough to touch the boy he loved one last time.

Ricky's beautiful face had pulled itself into a mask of horror and fear. "Lance, what happened?"

Lance shook his head. He didn't have much time. "Ricky, I thought…." He gulped, his throat tasting of blood and bile. "Your bed… it… was… empty. I thought…."

Ricky reached out to take his hand, ignoring the blood, gently caressing the fingers the way Lance always loved. "I left you?"

Lance thought he nodded, but everything was swimming. He leaned forward, free hand on the arm of the wheelchair, knowing if he let go he would topple. He heard Jenny shouting for help and more running footsteps. But he had eyes only for Ricky, embedding forever in his heart and soul that most perfect of faces.

Ricky lifted his other hand and gently touched it to Lance's bruised cheek, tears brimming, a look of tortured pain on his face. "What part of 'for now and always' didn't you get, fool?"

Lance tried for a smile, but had no idea if he succeeded. Ricky was safe. Ricky lived. Nothing else mattered. He could sleep now.

His hand slipped off the arm of the chair and he collapsed in a heap at Ricky's feet.

"Lance!" Ricky cried out in horror. "Mom, help him!"

And then Jenny was there, cradling his head, telling him to hang on and screaming for a doctor to help her son.

Lance barely understood what was happening. It was all so ethereal and vague, like wisps of fog on a summer morning, gone almost the moment they appeared.

All he could see in his limited field of vision was Ricky hovering above him, crying, leaning forward in the chair and begging him to hang on.

It was all good, Lance thought as the darkness began to take him. The boy who'd made him whole was safe and sound. It was perfect.

"Ricky…" he heard himself say, though he couldn't tell if it was a whisper or a shout. "I… love… you…."

And then Ricky disappeared, and there was nothing more.

†††

Chapter Ten

I Should've Told You Before You Died

Ricky sat in stony silence in the surgery waiting room holding Chris's hand and staring off into space. Because of the wheelchair and the back injuries he'd sustained, Ricky couldn't cradle Chris on his lap and hold him the way he wanted. But Chris understood and dozed in a chair beside him, never letting go of his brother's hand and resting his head lightly up against Ricky's arm.

The hospital had allowed Chris to shower and clean up, which he hadn't wanted to do after Lance was rushed into the operating room, but Jenny had insisted and Ricky urged him to "Keep Mom busy." Chris's long, blond hair had finally dried after so many hours of waiting, and he'd been unable to keep his eyes open any longer. Ricky, however, couldn't have slept if they'd injected him with every drug in the book.

Shortly after the chaos in the corridor, after the nurses and doctors had gotten the unconscious Lance up and onto a stretcher, as Ryan and Chris arrived on the scene, the boy Ricky loved was wheeled off into surgery, with not a word for nearly five hours. During that time, Reyna, Justin, and Kai had all been admitted and operated on. Justin's feet would require many skin grafts and plastic surgeries, but eventually he'd walk again.

Dakota's bullet wound was in no way life threatening, due to the vest he'd been wearing and the side angle in which it had entered, and his surgery had been relatively brief.

The bullet that had entered Reyna broke her collarbone and deflected into her left shoulder. The injuries were not extensive, but she'd lost a lot of blood, and currently lay in the post-op recovery room. Esteban had apologized to Ricky and Arthur for not waiting with them, but he'd said he needed to be with Reyna when she awoke, and they agreed.

"She's your life, Este," Ricky told him, his mind's eye seeing only Lance as he'd crumpled to the floor at his feet. "That's where you belong."

Esteban looked long and hard at Ricky. "Lance was as badass as I've ever seen him, Ricky. We'd all be dead if it weren't for him. He's like, the most epic hero I ever saw. And he doesn't quit. You know that. He'll pull through." Then he placed one brotherly hand to the boy's shoulder and tried for a smile of encouragement. "He's got you waiting for him, right?"

Ricky's eyes went wide at Esteban's summation of Lance, and he nodded his thanks. Then the anxious man hurried off to the recovery area to wait.

The arrowhead had been removed from Kai's upper torso and the area cleaned and dressed. But the Indian had lost a lot of blood, and the beginnings of an infection had set in. He lay in the recovery room being pumped full of antibiotics. Dakota, patched up and groggy from the anesthesia, lay on a gurney by his side, gently holding his hand.

So that left Ricky waiting with Chris, Arthur, Jenny, Merlin, and Ryan for word on whether or not Lance would live or die. There'd been no time for a doctor to even speak with them. Lance's condition was so desperate he'd been prepped and readied without delay.

Five hours ago.

Five hours!

Ricky eyed Excalibur leaning up against one wall near where Arthur sat in his wheelchair cradling Jenny's head against him. The blood had been cleaned off and the sword gleamed regally beneath the overhead fluorescents. Merlin sat by himself gazing without expression out the window, while Ryan paced back and forth anxiously.

The aged detective had already been to check on Justin and found his partner's son woozy, but in no pain, his feet bandaged up past the ankles. He must not have spent much time there, Ricky had noted, because he was back with them quickly.

Yeah, Lance had that effect on people.

Ricky felt weighed down by guilt and intense pain. He'd left Lance, and now Lance might die. He'd made a promise that he'd broken, and it may cost him the most precious boy in the world. Both parents had reminded him that he'd been shot and near death himself, and he knew what they were saying was true, but he couldn't help that sense of failure, that he *hadn't* been there when Lance needed him most.

Jenny had told him how Lance never left his side while he was unconscious, and only did so because he had to save Chris. Ricky felt a warmth fill him, and somewhere deep within he recalled Lance's voice speaking to him as though from another universe. He even remembered some of Lance's words, remembered how desperately he'd wanted to respond, how urgently he'd wanted to tell this boy of boys he loved him and would never leave him.

Except I did leave him.

And now he's dying.

Ricky had refused food and all attempts at commiseration. He'd allowed Jenny to hold him awhile, but that was all.

Night had fallen long ago, and the only sounds were rattling carts and calls over the intercom system for this doctor or that one to call this station or that. When he'd awoken suddenly yesterday, having been in the middle of a frightening dream in which Lance was imperiled, Ricky found himself in an unfamiliar bed, with Arthur in the next bed over quietly conversing with Jenny.

Both parents had been ecstatic at his awakening, and the doctors had all rushed in to check his vitals, making sure he could feel his legs and move his toes. Having no clear idea about anything that had happened since he'd been shot, Ricky insisted that he felt okay. "Except for the pain in my back."

Jenny explained everything that had happened since the attack, and Ricky had been shocked to hear about those who'd died. He told her he knew Lance was gone because Lance had told him why, and she allowed Arthur to recount the episode of the assassin Jenny had taken down with the bedpan.

His mother's violent defense of him had surprised Ricky, especially given her distaste for physical conflict of any kind, but his mind and heart continued to be with Lance and how the boy he'd vowed to protect was out there without his protection. He'd brooded even when the doctors insisted he get into a wheelchair and stroll the halls with Jenny. And that happened to be where he was when the other half of his heart stumbled down the corridor toward him.

Ricky forced the image of the collapsing Lance from his mind and thought back on all their time together. He'd felt an instant attraction to the boy the first time he saw him on YouTube. He'd already been growing his hair out, but seeing the long and luxurious hair Lance wore made him want to let his own grow longer as a tribute to his idol. His father had mocked him and upbraided him and hit him all the more because of the hair, but that had made him even more determined to let it grow.

Meeting Lance on the streets had been the only shining light in his sorry life up till that point. Seeing him die had ripped his heart out, and watching him return filled up his soul with immeasurable joy.

It had been a long journey they'd taken together, but it was only supposed to be the beginning. They were supposed to have their whole lives ahead of them. Wasn't that what adults always said? Yeah, one of many stupid things adults said to kids. Didn't grown-ups realize that kids didn't always have their whole lives ahead of them? Jack hadn't. Neither had John or Lavern or Darnell or Techie. Even Michael, who Ricky had hated because Michael was in love with Lance. Even Michael's life had been cut short.

And now Lance might join them.

The clock on the wall pressed forward inexorably, the second hand sweeping endlessly around in circles, minute-by-minute, until another two hours passed. Chris continued to sleep with his head resting on Ricky's arm, while Jenny slept with her head against Arthur's shoulder. Ricky looked at his father again for the hundredth time and saw the same pain he'd seen every time they'd passed each other in the night at New Camelot, back when Lance was incarcerated. Except this pain was worse. This time Lance might not get out of jail, because death was a sentence that lasted forever.

Finally, an exhausted-looking, middle-aged man wearing green surgical scrubs, with a face mask pulled down below his chin, entered the waiting area. Ricky's heart instantly flew into his throat and he nearly stopped breathing.

The man looked so somber....

Arthur turned his head and Jenny immediately snapped awake, as though she knew this was the moment.

Ricky shook Chris awake gently as the doctor approached and sighed heavily, eyeing the adults and the kids with equal gravity.

"Is Lance all right?" Jenny asked anxiously, her voice dry and tight with sleep.

Arthur squeezed her hand, but glanced over at Ricky and Chris with more fear in his eyes than Ricky had ever thought possible.

"For the moment," the doctor answered, the fatigue in his voice as obvious as the slumping of his shoulders. Then he shook his head in amazement. "How that boy is still alive is beyond me, Lady Jenny. He must have a will of steel."

Ricky's heart thundered in his chest. That was his Lance, all right, a will of steel. And he lived!

"The bullet lodged in his appendix, which we removed," the doctor went on, rubbing one hand through his slightly thinning hair. "The knife did the most damage. It nicked the right kidney, punctured the liver and the gallbladder, damaged a number of arteries. He lost a prodigious amount of blood."

Arthur cleared his throat as Jenny's hand had flown to her mouth. "Will he live?"

Ricky heard in his father's voice the strain of having to say the three most painful words ever spoken by a parent.

The doctor looked at both adults without hope in his brown eyes. "I can't make any promises. He's in critical condition. For any other patient, I'd say the chances were slim. But with Lance...."

He shrugged and glanced over at Ricky, and Ricky's breathing stopped.

"When can we see him?" Jenny asked breathlessly.

"He'll be out of recovery in a couple of hours and in Intensive Care. He can't have too many visitors, so you'll have to go in one at a time. The next forty-eight hours are crucial."

He turned to leave, and Ricky said quietly, "Do you have bigger beds than the one I was in?"

The doctor looked momentarily caught off guard. "Yes, I think we have some for our... larger patients. Why?"

Ricky pinned the man with his gaze, ignoring his parents. "Can you put Lance in one of those beds when he comes out of recovery?"

Ricky saw Jenny's uncertain look, but he could tell Arthur already understood.

"I suppose so," the doctor answered, obviously confused.

"Good," Ricky affirmed quietly, but firmly. "Cuz I'm gonna sleep in the same bed with him."

The doctor frowned and looked at the adults.

"Honey," Jenny began gently, "I don't think that's—"

Ricky surged with emotion as he fixed his mother with an intense look. "Mom, I'm not leaving him again. Ever."

The doctor looked concerned and turned to Arthur. "He might dislodge an IV or some vital piece of equipment, King Arthur. I don't recommend it, at least not for a few days."

Arthur turned to Ricky and studied the face of his son.

Chris suddenly found his voice, almost startling Ricky because he'd been quiet for so many hours. "It's okay, Dad. Lance needs Ricky more than he needs those machines."

Ricky turned to his brother, saw the magnified blue of his eyes blurred with tears, and pulled him in close, both gazing at their parents with a beseeching expression. He knew Chris was right. Lance needed him now more than ever.

Arthur exchanged a look with Jenny, and Ricky could see they both understood. "It's all right, doctor. I give my permission."

The doctor nodded silently and left the room. Arthur and Jenny turned to look at their sons, and the boys at them. Then Chris ran from Ricky to engulf both adults in a desperate and fearful hug. Ricky rolled his chair over and joined in the hug as far as his limited reach would allow.

†††

And so the vigil began, not just for Ricky and the family, but for the whole world. Over the next two days it seemed nothing else happened on the entire planet except updates on Lance's condition. Headlines ran the gamut from "Will America's Royal Family Lose its Crown Prince?" to "Has the Boy Who Came Back Run Out of Lives?"

Everyone tweeting, everyone Facebooking, everyone on every social networking site was talking of nothing but Lance, his life, his accomplishments, his impending death. Every news outlet gave hourly updates on the boy's condition, coupled with almost 24/7 coverage on Edwin's dual personalities and bloodthirsty quest for vengeance.

Kai told Dakota and Arthur that he'd been dozing on and off when he heard Sylvia approaching in the dark. When she first appeared, he'd felt a moment of hope. But her clothes were different than when she'd been kidnapped, and her hair, too. An artist always noted details like that, he told them, so he was ready when she got close and revealed the knife, whipping the gun up and firing wildly. He'd been so weak most of his shots missed, but he'd been sure he heard her cry out before she bolted into the woods.

Ryan told them the entire area had been combed for the body, but nothing was found. Her trail of blood led into the trees, and then disappeared. She was presumed alive and a massive manhunt had begun, to find her and whoever might be harboring her.

Sir Phillip reported to Arthur that the New Camelot website and Facebook pages were inundated with cards and messages and prayers, everyone hoping and praying for Lance's recovery.

The media took up permanent residence outside the entrance to Walter Reed. Every few hours, Arthur and the surgeon gave brief updates on Lance's condition. No pictures of the wounded boy had been released to the public and all staff were forbidden from bringing their phones into his room.

Ricky knew all of this, but none of it mattered. True to his word, he slept by Lance's side from the moment his beloved came out of recovery. The only time he left him was to use the bathroom. Despite admonitions from Jenny and his own surgeon that he needed to strengthen his back and legs by using a walker, Ricky refused.

"Never again," was all he'd say each time one of them suggested it.

When Ricky first saw Lance in Intensive Care, the tubes and heart-rate monitors, the oxygen mask and IVs snaking into and out of his battered body, the tears forced their way from his eyes to spill onto the floor. And he cursed himself for being weak. He was a man now. It was after midnight. He and Lance were eighteen years old, and men weren't supposed to cry.

Except Ricky did cry. He held most of the tears at bay while Arthur and Jenny and Chris each had their brief time with Lance. Jenny had helped him out of his wheelchair and, with the aid of a nurse, eased him into bed beside the boy he loved. He still wore the requisite hospital gown with the back tied, but open, and felt momentarily embarrassed. But once he lay beside Lance, everything was as it should be.

Just as on those long-ago nights when some traumatic need had brought them together, lying now beside Lance was exactly where he belonged. He ached to lift the oxygen mask and kiss those lips that had become so much a part of him these past two years, but knew he couldn't.

So he settled for gently entwining his fingers within those of his beloved, and allowed his lips to gently brush Lance's pale, bruised cheek.

"Lance, you can't leave me, man." More tears welled and spilled onto the pillow, some entangling with his splayed hair. "For now and always, remember? I love you, fool. You're the only reason I have to live. Come back to me. *Please!*"

The tears continued, the sounds of his quiet weeping mingling with the *beep beep beep* of the heart monitor and the whooshing sound of the oxygen tank. Nurses came in every hour to check on them, probably, Ricky thought later, to make sure he hadn't accidentally unplugged anything. But Ricky was beyond careful. He merely lay beside Lance, holding his hand, listening to the even breathing, and cried until he had no more tears left to shed. Then he finally drifted off to sleep.

Ryan told him the following day that the president had come by during the night and had sat with them for a brief time, but Ricky didn't remember that. Throughout the day there was a steady stream of visitors, mostly doctors and nurses, but also the surviving members of the Round Table.

Kai came in wearing jeans and an open shirt, his entire chest wrapped tightly with a bandage. Despite his obvious pain, his focus was on Lance and he'd prayed some Navajo prayers his grandmother had taught him before wishing Ricky a happy birthday and leaving.

Dakota came next, his upper chest bandaged beneath his loose-fitting shirt, his face looking more solemn than Ricky had ever seen him. He knew Dakota worshipped Lance as an amazing leader and mentor, and he watched the Indian take Lance's hand in his and speak to him, first in Lakota and then in English. He told Ricky he would gladly give up his life if it would save Lance, but he knew Lance was out of his reach now.

"He needs you more than anything else," the Indian intoned with more passion than Ricky expected from him.

Reyna showed up with her arm in a sling. Her beautiful face bore no makeup and her long, curly brown hair tumbled carelessly around her shoulders. But her normally potent eyes looked weak and afraid. She stared down at the boy lying in the bed as though she couldn't believe what she was seeing. Ricky understood. It didn't even look like Lance in the bed with him, lying still with tubes running in and out and equipment attached everywhere, his astonishing green eyes closed, his face pale, his whole demeanor fragile. This wasn't Lance. Lance was all energy and strength, buoyant love and passion, steadfastness and indomitability. Yes, Ricky understood her look, because he felt the same way every time he looked at that pale face and closed eyelids.

Reyna leaned down to kiss Lance on one cheek, and then did the same to Ricky. Standing up, she gazed at both of them, her eyes beginning to well.

"Happy birthday, baby boy," she whispered to Lance, causing Ricky to gasp slightly, recalling her saying those exact same words the day after the California election two years before. Then Reyna turned to him, "And happy birthday to you, baby boy number two."

With that, the tears came and she fled the room.

Justin rolled in and sat in his wheelchair at the foot of the bed, head bowed silently. He told Ricky how he wouldn't even be there but for Lance, and Ricky had to fight back the tears once more.

Esteban came in last, and Ricky nearly gasped. This massive man, who'd always seemed to Ricky like a solid mountain of rock, looked frail and small and lost as he gazed upon the silent, bruised, pale face of the younger boy he idolized. His wrists were bruised and the skin shorn off, and it looked painful. But the only pain Esteban displayed was directed at the unmoving Lance.

"You know Ricky," he said sadly, "I never thought I could love another guy. I was all macho as shit out there, but I love Lance, you know? He's my *carnal*, but he's more than that. He's like the best part of me besides Reyna. Just being around him makes me better."

Ricky nodded, more tears forcing their way out despite his best efforts not to let them. But he needn't have worried about looking weak in Este's eyes, for his, too, were welling and the older man made no excuses for that.

"You should've seen him, Ricky, all powerful and strong and almost godlike," Esteban went on, his voice slightly trembling. "When Edwin stabbed him in the back... I felt like it was me he stabbed." He raised his eyes from Lance's silent face and fixed them onto Ricky's expectant one. "He's the toughest, baddest, greatest kid I ever knew, Ricky, and he doesn't know when to quit."

Then he did something that shocked Ricky – he bent down and kissed Lance on one cheek before hurriedly leaving before his emotions overwhelmed him completely.

Most of the time Arthur and Jenny took turns sitting beside the bed, but the others drifted in and out throughout that day and into the next. Ricky was told that the pope had sent out messages to all the faithful worldwide to pray for "The health and recovery of Sir Lance." The president also issued several statements to the American people to hope and pray for the boy's recovery. As on the night Lance "died" the first time, when the world seemed to grind to a halt in shock, it happened all over again. Everyone, it seemed, wished him well, even those who'd been opposed to him and his bill of rights.

Once the entire story was revealed about Edwin being R.'s son and his carefully plotted plan to destroy the Round Table, the American people rallied around Lance and Arthur. For the moment, anyway. Ricky knew it wouldn't last. He'd seen enough of the fecklessness of people to know that if Lance recovered, his naysayers wouldn't wait long before going on the offensive again.

If he recovered.

No, Ricky forced himself to say over and over again, *when* he recovered.

Throughout that second day, many members of Congress dropped in for a visit, and the president showed up again, this time with the House Speaker and the Senate Majority Leader. Ricky was glad they were not in any way gloating, nor did he ask about the CBOR. At this point, all he cared about was the boy beside him. Everything else could wait.

It was late on that second day, while Ricky lay alone with Lance, talking to him about whatever came to mind, that the heart-rate monitor suddenly went flat-line, and Ricky sat up screaming desperately for help.

†††

Lance dreamed.

He was on that hillside again. The same one he'd visited before. Only this time there was no one there. The magnificent wall of light lay just along the top ridge as it had before, spreading outward as far as his eye could see.

It called to him.

And he went.

He realized he was wearing a hospital gown and no shoes. The grass felt so soft and soothing against his bare feet that he moved up the hill slowly, relishing the feel of the grass, the touch of a warm breeze wafting through his dangling hair, the light ahead seeming to call him by name. He wasn't bruised anymore, or even in any pain. In fact, he'd never felt better.

Up close the light looked more like a barrier separating his side from the other. He tried to peer into it, but the opacity made it impossible to get a clear picture. And then suddenly Jack was there, on the other side, as though he'd just appeared out of nothingness. Lance gasped, momentarily startled, but Jack smiled, looking both happy and sad to see him. Lance felt his breath almost stop – did that happen in dreams, he wondered? But Jack looked so strong and handsome and toweringly beautiful, all light and ethereal, that Lance couldn't help but gape.

"Jack," was all he could say. The name itself said it all.

The image of Jack was slightly blurred and distorted, as the barrier seemed to undulate with various shades of light and shadow.

"You look amazing, Lance," he said, his voice sounding like Jack's, but different, too. "The most beautiful man I ever saw. Like I knew you would be."

Lance reached for Jack, and his hand passed through the barrier of light. It felt warm and misty and not at all unpleasant. Jack took his hand and gently squeezed.

And then just as suddenly Mark stood beside Jack, blond and white with those eyes of translucent blue that made Lance's heart lurch.

"Mark...."

Mark looked so radiant in the light, and so happy. Both he and Jack wore their billowy tunics, but they were spotlessly white and so were their brushed leather pants.

Mark looked out at Lance, those pools of blue almost sucking him through the barrier. "See, Lance, I told you everything would work out the way it was supposed to."

"What?" Lance asked, confused. "All those people who died? Or me here with you?"

Mark shrugged and grinned, and Lance felt momentarily overcome with the old guilt.

"I love you, Mark," he said quietly. "I should've told you before you died."

Mark's smile grew even larger. "It doesn't matter, Lance. I already knew."

Jack hadn't taken his eyes off of Lance since arriving, but Mark didn't seem to mind.

"I knew he'd fall for you," Mark said, tossing off that shy little smile Lance had loved. "How could he not? But I guess him and me were meant to be together."

Lance looked from Mark's shy smile to Jack's wide eyes and loving expression.

"Can I come in now?" Lance asked. He wanted to go. He wanted to be on the other side. He wanted to be with Jack and Mark again. But there was something he was forgetting, wasn't there?

Jack looked suddenly sad, and shook his head. "Not yet, Lance. You have to go back."

"He's right, Lance," Lance suddenly heard from his left and turned in shock to find Michael standing there, blond and handsome, on the same side of the light as him.

"Michael!" he exclaimed, pulling his hand back through the barrier in shock.

Michael tossed off that smirk that Lance had by turns hated and loved, and then turned to Jack. "I'll take it from here, brother. You guys're gonna get in trouble again."

"I know," Jack said quietly. "But we had to see him one last time."

Lance felt nothing but confusion as he looked from one brother to the other. Mark hung by Jack's side and gently took his hand. Jack sighed, and smiled at Lance with such love that he felt his heart fill, and tears began to form at the backs of his eyes.

"Michael will explain everything, Lance," Jack said. "We have to go. We're not really allowed to hang around down here. But don't worry. Lavern sends his love. So does John. And Techie. Oh, and Lady Helen and Sergeant Gibson are here, too. It's been pretty crazy down there, hasn't it?"

Lance nodded sadly.

Jack and Mark smiled again, making Lance feel warm and afraid all at once. "We're all okay, Lance," Jack added. "And we'll see you again someday."

They began to fade away into the light.

"Wait!" Lance called out, trying to reach through the barrier for them, but this time the light forced him back.

"I *am* proud of you, Lance," were Jack's final words, and then he and Mark were gone.

Tears dropped from his eyes as Lance turned to face Michael. The taller boy, clad in his black tunic, jeans, and Nikes, had lost the smirk and looked genuinely compassionate.

"Walk with me, Lance," he said, extending one hand. Lance eyed the large hand a moment before taking it, and they started down the hill away from the light.

"Why aren't you in there with Jack and the others, Michael?"

Michael tossed him one of those looks of his and said, "I did some pretty bad stuff down there, Lance."

Lance frowned, enjoying the feel of Michael's fingers entwined with his. He'd wanted that for so long, but now it somehow didn't feel right. What was he forgetting?

"But you were good in the end, Michael," Lance protested.

Michael nodded. "Oh, I'll get in eventually. Just have to wait, you know, to atone, I guess."

"For how long?"

Michael shrugged. "Don't know. Time works differently here. Oh, and Darnell's wandering around somewhere. I guess he pulled some bad stuff on the streets, too."

Lance nodded. Somehow it seemed to make sense.

They stopped on a soft, grassy knoll and sat side by side. As far as Lance could see in all directions were endless green fields and hills.

"Why can't I go in, Michael?" he asked, suddenly fearful. "Cuz of bad stuff I did?"

Michael snorted. "You never did bad stuff, Lance, not bad *enough* anyway."

"Then why?" Lance wanted to go.

"Because it's not your time," Michael answered, turning those soft brown eyes onto his face. Lance marveled at how gentle they looked now, so different from the violent, vengeful Michael of the past. "You have too much left to do down there. Too many people are counting on you, Lance. You have to go back."

Suddenly Lance felt afraid and small and vulnerable. "But I'm tired, Michael," he said softly, his shoulders slumping. "I'm tired of fighting all the time. I'm tired of carrying the whole world by myself."

Michael smiled, a smile that lit up an extraordinarily handsome face. "You're not carrying it by yourself, Lance," he said more gently than he'd ever said anything when he'd been alive. "You're forgetting your promise."

Lance felt confused. "Promise?"

Michael nodded. "For now and always. Remember?"

And suddenly Lance did. How could he have forgotten? Even in a dream, how could he have forgotten?

"Go back to him, Lance," Michael said quietly, his eyes filled with regret and loss. "He'll help you carry the world." Then he laughed, a genuine laugh of delight. "And God help the world."

Feeling overwhelming gratitude and a renewed sense of purpose, Lance gushed, "I'm *so* happy I met you, Michael."

Michael looked startled, and then grinned. "Nobody ever said *that* to me before." Then he laughed again, a childlike laugh that Lance loved. "See ya when I see ya, Jesus, Harry Potter, and the Ivory Tower all rolled into one." He paused, those brown eyes wide and sincere. "I love you."

Lance smiled, felt the tears coming, and then with a powerful shock, like lightning striking his chest, he was violently flung backward, ripped away from Michael, from the field of grass, from the light.

†††

Suddenly his eyes flew open and he nearly cried out in surprise.

Ricky's face hovered above him, wide-eyed and tearful and terrified. He saw his mother and father, she in his arms sobbing. And there was a man in a mask, wearing ugly green clothes and holding paddles of some kind in his hands, gazing at him with relief.

But it was Ricky's lost and stricken look that Lance focused on as he tried to clear his thoughts after that weird dream.

"What?" he blurted, feeling annoyed to find people staring at him like that.

"You were dead, Lance!" Ricky blurted breathlessly, and Lance saw Arthur nod, cradling Jenny in his arms. She looked so happy she couldn't even speak.

"Again?" Lance said, still trying to focus.

Ricky nodded, hands gripping the walker for stability, tears dropping from his face onto the bed.

"For a little over a minute," said the man behind the mask.

Lance took a moment to digest that. He'd been dead. It hadn't been a dream. He *had* seen Jack and Mark. Jack *was* proud of him. And Michael was there, too. Then he smiled to himself.

"Thank you, Michael," he whispered softly.

Ricky sucked in a breath. "Michael?"

Lance smiled weakly. "He reminded me of my promise."

Ricky's eyebrows shot up questioningly.

Lance tried to laugh, but it hurt his abdominal muscles, so he smirked. "What part of 'for now and always' didn't *you* get?"

And then Ricky grinned so broadly Lance thought the dimples would sink right into his face, and his lips were on Lance's a second later, pressed together with his as gently, but firmly, as Ricky dared. And Lance kissed him right back, suddenly feeling a surge of energy flow through his body even greater than that first time they'd kissed.

"Whoa, whoa, Ricky," Lance heard Jenny say anxiously, her voice trembling with a mix of joy and fear. "Shot and stabbed, remember?"

And then Ricky's lips left his all too abruptly and he felt empty.

"Sorry," Ricky said sheepishly, his breathing suddenly ragged. "I couldn't help myself." But his eyes were only for Lance.

Lance no longer looked pale, but flushed, and he glowered up at Jenny. "C'mon, Mom, that's what I need more than anything."

That got a relieved and joyful laugh from the adults. Jenny leaned in to gently kiss Lance on the cheek, and then a visibly relaxed Arthur did the same. By that point, more doctors had arrived and told everyone to step outside so they could examine Lance.

"We have to make certain everything is working all right," said Lance's surgeon.

That caused Lance and Ricky to exchange a look. Lance turned even redder, and Ricky obviously knew why because his face reddened, too. Then both of them cracked up before the room was cleared and the newly revived Lance was given an examination. The doctors checked everything possible without a full battery of tests, but the cursory assessment they gave him he passed, according to his surgeon, "With flying colors."

Yeah, Lance thought, as the doctors proclaimed him miraculously out of danger, *all the flying colors of love.*

Because it was love that brought him back.

Thank you, Michael. You saved me again.

†††

Of course, the moment the doctors left and declared Lance fit for visitors, his room became home to more traffic than the 405 freeway back in L.A. Chris bolted into the room with a huge grin on his face and practically smothered Lance with hugs. Jenny had to forcibly restrain him to keep the boy from hurting Lance or dislodging some equipment.

Everyone crowded in, despite the disapproval of the nurses, and Lance lay in his bed surrounded by the surviving members of the Round Table. Reyna shed tears of joy, and Esteban had a visibly hard time restraining his own. Kai and Dakota stood grinning at him. And naturally Jenny stood beside Arthur in his wheelchair. Everyone seemed to be talking at once, but all Lance could think about were those he'd lost along the way. And Ricky. He asked Este to help Ricky climb back into bed with him, relishing the touch of Ricky's bare arm against his and the bare skin of their legs brushing against each other beneath the covers. But he also felt a funk threatening to take him down again.

Techie was dead. And Darnell. And Sergeant Gibson, and Helen. And so many more. Because of him. Because a whacked out man who'd chosen to be a monster wanted revenge for something Lance hadn't even done!

Arthur told him he would need to make a statement to the press as soon as he was stronger, and Lance agreed. For now, Reyna took several pictures of the family with her phone. Ricky and Lance lying side by side on the bed with Chris trying to grab both of them while standing alongside. Jenny stood on one side of the bed and Arthur on the other. Though still weak, the king stood for the picture. Everyone smiled happily and Reyna uploaded the pictures to Sir Phillip at New Camelot. He released them to the press, tweeted them, and posted them up on the Facebook page with the status update: "Lance Lives!"

What Lance wanted more than anything was time alone with Arthur to talk about the rescue operation. He desperately hoped he hadn't disappointed his father in his first command situation, mostly because he'd lost some of the knights he'd been entrusted to lead.

He even more desperately wanted time with Ricky because there was something he so badly needed to talk about. But even at night for those next few days there was a steady stream of nurses and doctors checking on him and giving him sleeping meds so the pain wouldn't be too extreme.

Lance determined to get back on his feet as quickly as possible, but could clearly feel the piercing agony in his lower back every time the pain meds started to wear off, and he knew it might be a pretty long recovery process.

Over those next few days as Lance got stronger, he was released from Intensive Care and placed into a regular room, with Ricky recuperating in the bed right beside him.

On the fourth day after Lance's "Return from the dead – again!" as the media had dubbed his brief brush with death, the president, flanked by the requisite Secret Service agents, appeared in the boys' room. The president found Ricky sitting beside Lance's bed, the two of them talking.

"Well, Sirs Lance and Ricky, you're both looking a hundred percent better today," the man said in his deep, resonant voice. Then he grinned, and Lance could tell it was genuine.

"Thanks, Mr. President, we're feeling a lot better," he said.

"I have something I want you to see, Lance," the president went on, "and I purposely ordered a news blackout of this hospital until I could be here to see it with you. Do you have a remote for the television?"

Lance and Ricky exchanged a quizzical look before Lance fumbled around under the covers and found the remote.

The president stepped to one side of the bed so his head would not block the TV screen mounted to the wall. He took the remote under Lance's watchful eye and turned the TV to CNN.

Lance sucked in a surprised breath, and he heard Ricky do the same. But his eyes were glued to the television screen as the words "Children's Bill of Rights passes both houses of Congress – now being ratified by the states." The anchor explained that the states had already indicated how each would vote and the ratification process was a mere formality.

"History has been made today as the Constitution of the United States has ten new amendments," the anchor informed the viewers in that usual monotone voice they always used.

All but Helen, Lance thought, a wave of sadness intermingling with his joy.

"The Children's Bill of Rights is now the law of the land," the anchor continued, "all because of the determined efforts of one boy and his followers. May Sir Lance have a speedy recovery from the recent attempt on his life."

The anchor continued, but the president muted the sound and looked at Lance very solemnly.

Lance eyed the man in shock, and then exchanged a look with Ricky. He hadn't given the CBOR much thought the past few days since Congress had taken a brief recess so many of the lawmakers could visit him. At least that's what they told him when they continuously streamed in and out of his room.

"We won, Ricky," Lance whispered, finally finding his voice. "We won."

Ricky grinned. "Dumbass. *You* won. *You* did this, Lance. Not me, not even Dad. Just you."

Lance grinned right back, his heart hammering with joy and a myriad of other emotions be couldn't begin to describe. Then he turned his head to observe the chief executive studying him with an uncertain expression. "You mad at me, Mr. President?" he asked, suddenly feeling small and insignificant despite having just made history.

The president chuckled. "Not at all. This whole business has gotten me closer to my own children, Lance." He looked pensive for a moment. "I've listened to them more in the past year than I ever did before. The law of unintended consequences, I suppose. But I have you to thank for that."

Lance grinned. Michael and his law of unintended consequences, he thought. It just kept coming back. "You're welcome, sir."

That got a laugh from both the president and Ricky. The president gazed at Lance with a look of extreme admiration.

"I underestimated you, Lance," he said with a shake of the head. "We all did. You were just a kid, and kids weren't to be taken seriously." He paused and looked thoughtful a moment. "That attitude will have to change now, because of you." Then he chuckled. "If you ever decide to run for president, I pity your opponent."

Lance laughed at that, and pain shot through his abdomen and lower back. Meds were wearing off again. "Don't worry, Mr. President, I don't want your job."

The president smiled wryly. "You don't need it anyway, Lance. You're already a bigger player on the world stage than me."

Lance studied the man's face. When he'd first met the president he'd sensed that the man was jealous of him and his influence around the world, and now he'd just admitted that Lance did, in fact, have such influence. Except his soul whispering skills told him the president didn't mind anymore, that maybe being the most powerful man in the world wasn't all it was cracked up to be and that maybe, just maybe, he was cool with Lance getting more attention.

Lance extended a hand and the president shook it. "Thank you, Mr. President, for all you did."

The president's eyebrows shot up.

Lance laughed. "I heard you twisted a few arms in congress to vote my way."

The president winked. "Being president has to have some advantages, right?"

At that moment the door opened and Jenny strolled in with Arthur. The king still wore the required hospital robe, which made him look goofy, Lance and Ricky had both told him, but he was using a walker with much more strength in his steps, and the sight warmed Lance's heart.

Chris trailed in after them, followed by Reyna, Esteban, Merlin, Ryan, Justin in his wheelchair, Dakota, and Kai. They all gushed over the passage of the CBOR, having just seen it on the news. The mood within the crowded room became festive and joyous as everyone congratulated Lance and, as Ricky had done, attributed the passage solely to him and his determined efforts, and said he should be proud of what he had achieved.

As they all chatted with the president and each other, Lance took a moment to reflect on that idea. He *had* accomplished something almost unheard of, hadn't he? Sure, he'd been stubborn and intractable, and he'd had a lot of help and support along the way, but was what Ricky said true? Would this moment never have come to pass if not for him? His passion for self-doubt and second-guessing his choices attempted to grab hold of his psyche, but he forced it back.

I changed history, he said to himself. *Me, the boy nobody loved till he was fourteen years old!* It felt like a fairy tale of some kind.

And then he knew this was the moment. He'd never get another like it. He called out loudly for everyone's attention, and gradually the room settled into a pregnant silence as all eyes turned to him with anticipation. Even Ricky sat further forward in his wheelchair so he could look more directly into Lance's eyes.

Lance shivered slightly. Suddenly he was scared, even more scared than he'd been on their rescue mission. He looked out at all those eyes, all those expectant faces awaiting his announcement, and he momentarily froze. His heart began to pound. He drew in and expelled a deep breath.

"I just wanna say how much I love all of you and thank you for standing with me, even when I did stupid-ass stuff that embarrassed you."

That drew a laugh from everyone, and Ricky grinned broadly.

Lance's face grew solemn and thoughtful. "I know it's an old expression that God works in mysterious ways, but it sure looks that way in my life. It all seems so random looking back, how I met my Dad, how I got here to this place in time. Maybe that *is* how God works, you know, making the random pieces all come together to make everything work out the way it's supposed to."

Ricky held up a hand and twirled his finger, smiling and rolling his eyes. Lance reached out and shoved him lightly. "Okay. Dumbass says I need to speed it up."

His family laughed at that, and Lance saw even the president looking attentive and amused.

"I don't know if all of this was supposed to be my destiny," Lance went on, "but what I do know *was* destined was Ricky and me." He eyed Ricky almost shyly, like they had when they'd first gotten to know each other. "I knew it the moment I met him that night on the street with Jack. I was just too scared to admit it. Like John said, we're two parts of the same toy and neither can work right without the other." He sighed heavily. "I've almost lost him too many times already. I don't wanna risk that again. We promised each other we'd be together for now and always."

He paused again, finding it so difficult to go on with Ricky's soft brown eyes fixed on him with such love and expectation.

"We're eighteen now," Lance went on, "legal adults. And I want to… that is, I want him to…." He sighed again before planting his gaze squarely on the most beautiful face in the world. "Ricky, I want you and me to be together, like we always planned. Will you… Oh, crap, why is this so hard?"

Ricky smirked. "Yes, Lance."

Lance looked momentarily taken aback. "Yes, what?"

The smirk got bigger. "Yes, I'll allow your dumb ass to marry me."

Lance heard a gasp from his mother and saw her hand fly to her mouth. Reyna nearly squealed, but Esteban hushed her as everyone waited with intense expectation.

"That's what you're trying to ask, right?" Ricky added with a laugh.

Lance pulled himself up a little straighter in the bed. "Well, yeah, but you didn't let me finish."

Ricky squinted at him. "And why do you get to ask, huh, fool? I'm a man, too."

Lance suddenly felt flustered and tongue-tied. "Well, cuz, I… I'm older."

Ricky tilted his head in a dismissive gesture. "You are not."

"Okay, I have longer hair," Lance blurted, which drew a laugh from Merlin and the Indian boys.

Ricky gazed at him. "Nice try. But I'm a man, too, and I have just as much right to propose as you."

"Uh, Lance," Jenny started to say, but Arthur's arm on hers silenced her thought.

Lance barely glanced their way. "Hold on, Mom," he said quickly, looking Ricky straight in the eye. "We're gonna handle this like grown men. Okay?"

Ricky nodded.

Lance bit his lip, considering his options, and then looked at Ricky sheepishly. "Rock, paper, scissors?"

Ricky rolled his eyes and just shook his head. "For a guy who changed the country, Lance, you sure suck at this whole proposing thing."

"That's cuz you screwed it up," Lance protested. "If you'd just let me—"

"Ahem!"

That was Reyna's voice, and past experience made both Lance and Ricky whip their heads around. Under no circumstances did either of them want to piss off Reyna.

She stood, right hand to her hip, a mock glower on her lovely face. "On three."

The boys looked at each other, and Reyna began to count. "One... two... three."

Simultaneously, both boys blurted out, "Will you marry me?" And then immediately answered, "Yes" at the exact same time.

They looked at each other a moment before cracking up.

"See, that wasn't so hard," Reyna said with a laugh, and nudged Esteban in the ribs. He began clapping.

Then everyone else burst into applause, Ryan and the president louder than the rest. Jenny looked dazed, but Arthur merely grinned and kissed her. Ryan appeared happy, which Lance hadn't seen at all since Gibson's death. He grinned at his godfather, and Ryan grinned right back.

Then Reyna squealed and started jumping up and down as much as her sling allowed. "Oh, this is so awesome! My baby boys are getting married. Jenny, we have to have the wedding at New Camelot the same day as me and Este. Oh, it'll be so amazing!"

Lance and Ricky both looked at Jenny, and she seemed overwhelmed with emotion, tears already forming in her eyes.

Lance smiled and flicked his eyes toward Kai and Dakota. "Let's make it a three-fer, eh, Reyna?"

Reyna stopped gushing and looked over at the Indian boys in surprise. "You guys too?"

Dakota turned red, which made Kai laugh. "Yup," he said, wrapping his arm around Dakota, careful not to squeeze where his chest was bandaged.

Reyna grabbed Jenny's hand with her uninjured one. "Oh, Jenny, three weddings at one time! Oh, we have so much to plan. You know guys can't plan anything for a wedding so it's up to us. Oh, it'll be so cool!"

Jenny laughed now, caught up in the excitement pouring forth from Reyna. Then Chris leapt forward and said, "And I get to carry *all* the rings."

That got another laugh as Chris grabbed Ricky in a tight hug and then clambered up onto the bed to hug Lance.

The president stepped up to the bed with a big smile on his face. "Well, that was quite an announcement. Am I invited to the wedding?"

Lance grinned. "Of course. Bring the wife and kids."

The president tossed back his head and laughed. "It's a deal."

"Oh, but don't tell anyone just yet," Lance said in all seriousness. "I want all the states to ratify before we announce this. That way the haters will have something new to bag on me for."

"Well at least they can't say we're living in sin," Ricky added with a grin, and Lance leaned over to punch him in the shoulder.

"Fool!"

The president laughed again and made his exit, followed by his bodyguards.

Now the boys were swamped with handshakes from the men and kisses from Reyna and Jenny. Kai and Dakota likewise were given hearty handshakes, and kisses from the ladies. Lance laughed at Dakota's obvious discomfort, and Kai kept playfully flipping the man's long hair every time he didn't smile.

Lance felt happier at this moment than he'd been in a long while. Despite everyone they'd lost along the way, the future glowed with promise.

After a while, the nurses shooed everyone out of the room except Arthur and Jenny, who were allowed to stay. "For just a little longer," the nurse said firmly. "These boys need their rest."

Arthur gazed down at his sons with a look filled with equal parts love and astonishment, as though he couldn't believe they were even grown up, let alone to be married. His brown eyes were misty and wistful, but his face bespoke nothing but happiness.

Jenny, however, seemed concerned. She retracted the side panel of the bed and sat beside Lance, gazing long and deeply at her two boys.

Lance knew exactly what she wanted to say and saved her the discomfort. "I know, mom, we're young and we have our whole lives ahead of us and marriage is such a big step. That's what you were gonna say, right?"

Jenny's eyebrows shot up so high even Arthur laughed. Then she blushed. "Well, yeah, something like that. I mean, you are—"

"Really young?" Lance finished for her, taking Ricky's hand in his and squeezing it gently.

She nodded.

"So was Techie," Lance answered somberly, the Asian boy's big grinning face appearing before his mind's eye. "And he never even got the chance to tell Ariel he loved her." He glanced at Ricky and knew his soul mate understood. Then he returned his gaze to Jenny. "None of us know how much time we have down here, Mom. I know that better than anyone. And I want to spend every minute I have with this fool I love."

She opened her mouth to say something more, but Lance placed his free hand atop hers lovingly and flashed that winning smile. "Don't worry, Mom," he assured her in all seriousness. "I promise not to get him pregnant right away."

Arthur guffawed as Jenny's face collapsed in shock. But her look was nothing compared to Ricky's. The boy's mouth hung open in astonishment, and then he shoved Lance harder than he probably should have. It hurt, but Lance laughed anyway.

"I am *so* gonna kick your ass for that, Lance," Ricky said with a shake of his head. "As soon as we're better."

Lance chuckled. "Bring it on, little man."

"I'll 'little man' you," Ricky retorted and they looked prepared to grab each other when Jenny stood and put her hands between them.

"Okay, enough before you hurt yourselves," she said, exchanging a look with Arthur.

Arthur grinned and that grin made Lance extraordinarily happy to see. "Have I mentioned today that I love you both?" the king said.

The boys grinned. "You just did," they said simultaneously.

Then it was time for the parents to leave, and the two young men gazed at one another a moment in silence. Lance looked into Ricky's eyes and felt his whole body tremble.

"I told you when I married your fool ass we'd invite the whole world, didn't I?"

Ricky grinned. "And you know Reyna will. Live TV coverage and everything."

Lance suddenly felt his mouth go dry, and his heart almost skipped a beat. "I love you so much, Ricky."

Ricky's grin broadened and the dimples went crazy. "I love you more."

And then Ricky leaned forward, and Lance leaned downward and their lips pressed against each other. They reached for one another, but their awkward positions made closeness next to impossible. It didn't matter. The kiss sealed the deal all by itself.

†††

The following day Lance finally had some time alone with Arthur. Jenny had taken Ricky down to physical therapy and Chris had gone with them. Ryan was preparing to fly back to California with the bodies of the dead to return them to their families and help make arrangements for the memorial service. Reyna, Esteban, Justin, and Merlin would accompany Ryan and the fallen. Reyna wanted to begin planning the triple wedding so it could happen the moment the boys were well enough and she got her arm out of its sling. Dakota and Kai chose to remain behind with Lance and Ricky and would return home with the family.

Arthur still needed a walker to get around, and when he wasn't using the walker he sat in a wheelchair, just like Lance and Ricky were required to do unless engaged in PT with the therapist.

Arthur sat that morning in his chair and Lance pulled himself high up in the bed after Jenny wheeled Ricky from the room. Father and son gazed at one another a long moment in silent contemplation. Lance couldn't even recall the last time they'd spent time together, just the two of them.

Arthur cleared his throat uncomfortably and gazed at his son. Lance feared the worst. "Lance, at the risk of bringing up painful memories, I wish to discuss the rescue operation you led while I was unconscious."

Lance blanched and lowered his eyes to the bed, humiliation washing over him. "I'm sorry, Dad. I screwed it all up."

Arthur's eyebrows shot up in surprise. "How did you screw it up, son?"

Lance looked up, suddenly overwhelmed with sadness and guilt. "I lost Darnell, Dad." He choked back a sob. "And Techie."

Arthur nodded solemnly. "And you saved the others, including your brother." He sighed deeply, a sigh filled with painful reminiscences. "Alas, Lance, I lost many a good man in battle. Such is the nature of warfare. That is why war should always be the last resort." His eyes met those of his son and shimmered with a mix of compassion and pride. "You did what you had to do, Lance, and you saved far more lives than you lost. You're a hero, son."

Lance's eyes became so wide they looked like green beacons shining in the night. "You're not disappointed in me?"

Arthur sighed, his own eyes moistening with impending tears. "I could not be more proud of you if I lived a hundred lifetimes, Lance."

Lance blew out a heady breath. "Thanks, Dad. I'm still trying to be like you."

Arthur smiled warmly and lovingly. "You have far surpassed me, son. It is I who needs to be more like you."

Lance nearly gasped in shock at his father's words. Here was the greatest man he'd ever known saying *he* was better?

Then he frowned as another thought entered his mind. "What about Sylvia, Dad?" He felt chills every time he remembered her face, and that knife in her hand.

Arthur sighed sadly. "Alas, James and the FBI feel she was spirited away by the cartel Edwin took over from his father. Likely she is in another country by now."

Lance nodded. "Do you think she'll change, or become more like Edwin?"

Arthur smiled. "As you proved to the world, Lance, hope endures."

Then he turned the chair and rolled it to the closet. Lance watched uncertainly as Arthur pulled out Excalibur. The sword was sheathed, but its jeweled hilt still shimmered beneath the fluorescent lights from above.

Arthur placed the sword across his lap and wheeled back to Lance. He held the sword out to his son.

Lance instantly recoiled, pushing back into his pillow as though his dad held a King Cobra in his grasp. "No, Dad, it's yours. I only had it while you were hurt."

Arthur merely laid the sword down onto the bed beside Lance and offered an amused smiled. "What is that expression I've heard, humor the old man?"

Lance's mouth dropped open in surprise and Arthur smiled cryptically. "Keep Excalibur by your side, Lance. Take hold of its hilt often each day. You will recover with greater rapidity."

Those words filled Lance with the same dread he'd felt in Vegas, and then again within Edwin's compound when he'd felt the power of Excalibur flow into him. But he didn't want to disobey his father so he said, "Okay. But you get it back soon as I'm better."

Arthur nodded, reminding Lance once again of Merlin and those knowing looks he often flashed.

And then the two men simply sat and chatted about the wedding and the future of New Camelot and what the new bill of rights might mean for Chris, and about a whole host of other issues until Jenny returned with Ricky an hour later. For Lance it was a magical hour, reminding him of the days he'd spent with Arthur way back in the beginning when the crusade was in its infancy, when it was just the two of them sharing the kind of one-to-one intimacy only a loving father and son could share.

Later, Lance would think back on this one-on-one time with his dad and cherish the memory.

††††

Chapter Eleven

And The Children Shall Lead

Three days later it was agreed Lance would make a statement to the throngs of press camping outside Walter Reed. Now that the Children's Bill of Rights was officially part of the Constitution, everyone clamored even more for the boy who'd made it happen. It wasn't out of false pride, Lance told Arthur and Jenny, but more out of the need to look and feel his strongest in front of the crowd that made Lance veto the use of a wheelchair or a walker.

He remembered his mother teaching him about President Franklin Roosevelt and how the president seldom appeared in his wheelchair when speaking in front of people because he felt world leaders might think him weak.

"I'll hold Excalibur," Lance assured Jenny when she'd tried to force the issue. "It'll keep me strong. Ask Dad."

Jenny looked very dubious, but Arthur assured her Lance spoke the truth. So at noon, dressed in his finest knightly tunic, pants and boots, his hair brushed and held back by a gold circlet, most of the facial bruises having faded with the daily aid of Excalibur, Lance clutched the unsheathed sword in his right hand and allowed himself to be wheeled from his room to the lobby. Ricky, still weak in the back from his bullet wounds, was forced by his doctor to use a walker, but had also dressed himself up in his princely attire, his flowing hair restrained by a silver circlet.

Feeling renewed as he always did when clutching Excalibur, Lance stood easily from the chair and grinned at his parents. The nurses and others in the lobby burst into applause and Ricky flashed Lance a thumbs up.

And so The Boy Who Amended the Constitution strode purposefully forward, Ricky at his left and Chris at his right, with Arthur, Jenny, Merlin, Kai and Dakota trailing behind. Ryan had already departed with the others in an Air Force cargo plane bearing the bodies of their dead.

When Lance stepped through the double glass doors he nearly gasped. There must've been a thousand people gathered, and almost as many video and still cameras. Many, he knew, were members of the press, but the general public would not be kept away and there were hundreds of average citizens amongst the multitude, jostling each other and craning their necks, hoping for a glimpse of him. More than ever, he felt humbled and small.

The cameras were already rolling as he stood a moment at the top of the steps. The massive crowd burst into deafening applause while reporters simultaneously shouted out questions.

Lance stepped up to the podium with ease, though he knew it was the nascent power within Excalibur propping him up. If he let go the hilt, he'd topple, so he used it as a sort of cane, keeping the point down at his side and pretending to lean on it for the cameras.

Ricky moved to Lance's left side and Chris to his right, like bookends in case he needed the support. The applause died down and he leaned into the microphone sheepishly.

"Thank you for that reception. I'm happy I'm alive too."

That brought a new round of applause from the members of the press and public. When it subsided he said, "I guess I'm making a habit out of dying, but that's gonna stop," he offered with a sheepish look at Ricky beside him. "Ricky told me if I die again, he'll kill me."

That brought on some laughs and helped relieve the tension. It was as though a dam had burst and Lance felt the difference. Many, if not all of these people, would've been sad, if not devastated, had he died. He still couldn't get over that.

Ricky punched Lance lightly on the shoulder. "Fool."

Lance smiled, but then turned serious as his eyes scanned the faces below. His body shook with an intense sadness at not seeing Helen's lovely, eager face looking up at him, and Charlie by her side giving him a thumbs up sign when he was doing well.

"My doctors say I can only stand here about fifteen minutes or they're gonna haul me back in by force, so I'll be quick. We lost some amazing people in the past couple of weeks, people I loved, people who died for me." He paused to catch his breath as his chest tightened with grief. "When you grow up without a family, everyone who comes into your life and cares about you *becomes* your family, and that's how I feel about all of them. I won't be able to attend the memorial service in person, but I will speak to their families on a live feed from here and tell them what their loved ones meant to me."

He scanned the crowd again, and saw lots of children out there he hadn't noticed the first time around.

"The Children's Bill of Rights is now the law of the land," he went on soberly. "The Constitution of the United States has ten new amendments, and I want to thank the president and all those lawmakers, both state and federal, who supported us in this cause. But mostly I wanna thank you, the children out there, the young people of this country. You did this. You showed the adults that you matter, that you have power, that you deserve equal protection under the law."

He smiled sadly. "I would be saying 'we' did it, except I'm not one of you any more. I turned eighteen last week, so yeah, I'm still a teenager, but legally I'm an adult now and the original Bill of Rights applies to me. But unlike so many adults in this country, I don't plan to take those rights for granted. And I don't want you kids out there to do that with yours, either. You now have more rights than most kids in the whole world, so don't abuse them, please. Keep doing what you've been doing, what I tried doing when I was one of you – show the adults how to make things better, not worse, how to *not* be so self-absorbed. This country has been reborn today, and the children shall lead the way to making it greater than it's ever been. You kids rock!"

He raised Excalibur over his head and threw his left arm up as well, fist clenched. Chris did the same, and Ricky threw up one fist in solidarity, his other hand clutching the walker for support.

The crowd cheered, and Lance could now hear the voices of children shouting louder than the rest.

When it died down, Lance said, "I have a few more minutes for questions."

Every hand amongst the press corps flew up, and Lance almost laughed. Again feeling awash in sadness that he could not first call upon Helen, he spotted another blonde reporter from CNN waving her hand, and pointed to her.

"Sir Lance," she said almost breathlessly. "Have you been following the investigation into the man who tried to assassinate you?"

Lance was momentarily taken aback by the word 'assassinate.' Hadn't he learned from Jenny that the word was only used for important people like presidents or kings? Had the president been right? Was he that big a player on the world stage?

He glanced at Ricky, who reached out and placed a calming hand on his arm for just a moment before retracting it. Lance smiled his thanks and then answered the question. "Edwin was his father's son, just like I'm my father's son. My father is a great, decent, and honorable man. Edwin's father was a monster, and he raised his son to be a monster. But Edwin didn't have to stay that way. I saw my friend Michael go from monster to hero by choice. Edwin chose to stay a monster and he deserved to die for that."

The blonde wasn't finished yet. "What about the sister who escaped, and Senator Cairns?"

Lance's breath caught in his throat a moment. Sylvia's betrayal still haunted him. It turned out her supposed mother in L.A. didn't even exist – just a phony address and another dead end. "She's still young enough to change," he said, trying hard for a positive tone. "Hopefully, once she's found, that change will happen. As for Senator Cairns…." He paused and shook his head in dismay. "I guess like so many politicians he didn't care where his money came from as long as he got elected. If you're asking do I think he knew Edwin wanted to kill me, no, I don't think so. But that doesn't make him any less guilty and he should go to prison for a long time."

Lance felt a hand touch his shoulder and he turned to find Jenny gesturing behind her. His doctor was flashing him the "wrap it up" sign. Lance nodded and turned back to the crowd. "My doctor is telling me to wrap this up so I'll take one more question."

He scanned the crowd and gasped slightly. Yellow Hair was in the media pool. The tabloid journalist, and at one time his biggest heckler, grinned as he waved a hand. Throwing caution to the wind, Lance pointed to him.

"Is it true, Sir Lance," the man called up with a smirk on his face, "that when you return to Los Angeles you and Sir Ricky are getting married?"

If a bomb had gone off within the crowd there couldn't have been more tumult. Everyone erupted with surprise, and Lance felt his breath leave his body. He looked aghast at Ricky. How in the hell…?

He put up a hand and quieted the crowd, gazing down at the smirking Yellow Hair in amazement. "Where did you hear that?"

The man chuckled. "With someone as famous as you, Sir Lance, there are always little birds everywhere waiting to chirp."

Lance exchanged another look with Ricky, who shrugged and held out his hand. Grinning, Lance took it and faced the crowd. He exhaled and then flashed his world-renowned smile. "The answer to that question is… yes."

Now the cameras went wild again and more hands flew into the air, but Lance quelled the ruckus by raising Excalibur majestically with his right hand and Ricky's arm with his left.

As the uproar gradually quelled, Lance beamed with joy and lowered his arms. "This fool right here is my soul mate," he called out loudly to the expectant crowd. Ricky laughed and mock-shoved against their clasped hands. "Everybody says we're too young to get married." He shrugged. "We almost lost each other many times over the last few years, so we know how fragile life can be. We love each other and plan to stay together forever. So yes, we're getting married, some time around Christmas. And not only us, but our own Lady Reyna and Sir Esteban will marry and so will my Native brothers Kai and Dakota. All on the same day."

He turned and waved the Indian boys forward, and a laughing Kai practically had to drag the petrified Dakota to stand beside Ricky. Kai grabbed the hand of his beloved and grinned out at the crowd.

"This'll be the most epic wedding ever," Lance shouted excitedly, "and you're all invited!"

The multitude burst into applause as Lance grinned joyfully for the cameras. Ricky stood flushed and beaming beside him.

By this time, Lance knew he needed to go in and lie down. Excalibur could only carry his ravaged body along so far. Despite the sword speeding his recovery, as his father said it would, he couldn't risk a relapse. He'd made a promise, after all. He found himself smiling at the thought, causing Ricky to lean in. "What?"

Lance smiled more broadly. "Just you," he said quietly, feeling lightheaded.

Ricky chuckled and shook his head. "Dumbass."

Then the family re-entered the hospital, leaving the excited crowd to disperse.

For the next week, Lance, Ricky, and Arthur went through daily physical therapy regimens for at least an hour. Most of it involved walking while holding on to parallel bars, and later with a walker for extended periods of time. Lance seemed to heal at an astonishing rate, at least according to his dumbfounded doctors, even faster than the other two despite having been more badly injured. Lance knew his recovery had everything to do with Excalibur, and usually held Ricky's hand while also clutching the hilt so perhaps some of the magic would seep into him, too. There might have been a small effect, but nothing like what the sword did for him.

On more than one occasion, he insisted on Arthur keeping the sword with him, to help heal him faster. But the man always tossed off that cryptic Merlin-esque smile and assured Lance he was mending just fine and that the sword should remain with him. Lance never liked the tone of those words, but he didn't press the matter and kept Excalibur in his bed.

Fallout from the Children's Bill of Rights continued to dominate the news, and kids all across the country reacted with glee at their new status, gladly returning to school and promising to do their best on the retake of those standardized tests they'd purposely failed. However, the kids vowed to use their new standing as real citizens to reshape the school system into something that would meet the needs of all students as individuals and replace the "one size fits all" mantra of the past.

Only time would dictate, Lance knew, the real effects of everything they'd done, and it would likely fall to him and Ricky and everyone at New Camelot to gauge the progress being made, and to help offset Michael's law of unintended consequences, which Lance already knew would inevitably rise from the ashes like a phoenix and throw some kind of monkey wrench into the whole deal. Oh well, he mused as he easily navigated the hallway with his walker, Ricky grinning by his side, as long as he had this man beside him he could deal with anything, even a zombie apocalypse.

About a week and a half after Lance's first public press conference since "coming back" the second time, the memorial service took place for those who'd been murdered in Maryland. The families of the dead had held their own private funerals, but now all but the families of the slain Secret Service agents gathered in Pastor Tom's church to memorialize their loved ones. Pastor Tom and Father Mike were the facilitators, and Lance felt a slight jolt of comfort seeing those two good men together again.

A camera had been brought in by CNN to broadcast Lance's eulogy live to those in the church via a large screen, as well as to everyone watching it on television. And everyone, it seemed, had ceased all activities to watch. The entire service was broadcast or streamed on nearly every news outlet and Internet site, including the New Camelot website.

Lance and Ricky sat side by side along with Arthur, Jenny, Chris, Kai, and Dakota in a cordoned-off waiting room, camera and cameraman ready to begin the live feed of Arthur and Lance's remarks. While they awaited their turn, Lance watched the church fill to capacity with knights from all over the city, as well as family members of the fallen, most of whom he didn't even recognize. How could he, he suddenly realized, since most of them had never visited their loved ones at New Camelot? Not once, not even to see what they were doing with their time. Carelessness. There was no getting away from it, he knew, and the CBOR wouldn't change that. New Camelot would always be needed as a safe haven for the neglected, abused, and abandoned children of America.

Lance held Ricky's hand, squeezing more and more tightly as the service unfolded on the flat screen mounted above them. Family member after family member stepped to the podium to memorialize his or her loved one.

Helen's older sister, Rachel, also blonde and leggy and attractive, very much a sibling, almost set Lance to sobbing with her heartfelt words. He gripped Ricky's hand all the tighter and allowed the tears to seep from his eyes.

Rachel spoke of Helen's dream, even at a young age, to be a journalist. By the time she'd hit high school several of her stories had actually gotten into the local paper. Theirs was a small-town in Indiana, but Helen's ambitions were big – New York or Los Angeles. She'd finally opted for L.A. because of the weather.

That had gotten a slight chuckle from the mourners. But then Rachel talked about him, and that's when Lance had to be gently cradled by Ricky.

"Helen never wanted kids," Rachel went on solemnly. "She wanted the career and perks that went with it. No husband, no kids. Until she met Lance. She loved that boy from the first moment she interviewed him. I don't know how many times she told me that if she could have a son like Lance she'd happily give up her career."

Lance nearly choked when she said that. He felt like his whole body was made of stone and sinking into the floor beneath his chair. He'd known Helen loved him, but not that much.

Rachel looked directly into the camera now, and Lance felt the weight of her eyes on him even through the glass of the television screen. "I know you're watching, Lance, and I wanted you to know that. Meeting you and your dad and following your story these past four years was the best thing to ever happen to her. And I know she'd do it again in a heartbeat, even if she knew how it would end. So don't you feel guilty, Lance. She was doing her job and knew the danger. She loved you and so do we for making her so happy."

Her own tears had begun trickling down her face as she concluded, and then she hurried back to her pew.

Lance had his head bowed, his chest tight, fighting for control. But it *was* his fault, he knew. None of them would be dead if not for him, if *he'd* never come back. Was that how God worked, or was it just that cosmic chaos thing Merlin spoke about? He didn't know, but it didn't matter. Nothing anyone said would ever remove the stain of guilt from his soul.

Arthur's hand on his shoulder and Ricky's cheek nuzzling his slightly calmed him, but Lance knew the worst was yet to come because Justin was now speaking in halting tones about his murdered father. Again, culpability swept over Lance, but he forced his eyes up to the screen to watch and listen.

Justin looked handsome and very much a man, Lance noted as he wiped the blur from his eyes with his left hand. His right hand remained firmly within Ricky's, the rock that kept him from falling. Justin had cut his 'fro, the hair now close-cropped and very much resembling the style his father had sported. He was dressed in a dark suit and tie, with Gibson's sergeant's badge pinned proudly to his left chest. It sparkled under the church lighting as though Justin had polished it for hours. Justin stood awkwardly with crutches, his shoes big puffy things, obviously to help support his damaged feet.

"My father was a great man," he began, his deep voice easily carrying out over the heads of the mourners. "But I didn't always think so. Growing up, I thought my dad hated me. He never spent any time with me. He was always working, always telling me how he wanted to keep kids my age from going to jail. I guess he thought that would make me happy, but it just made me madder. So I joined a gang and sold drugs to get back at him."

He hung his head. "I'm ashamed of that now." He looked back up. "Arthur and Lance, they showed me how a father and son were supposed to be, and they showed my Dad, too, cuz he changed. These past three years my Dad and me were tight, and I loved that feeling. I loved being able to talk to him, you know, man-to-man, about stuff and have him listen."

He broke a moment and had to pause, fighting to control his shaking, fighting back the tears. After a moment, he looked up at the people and the camera.

"My father showed me how to be a good man and I'm gonna be that man," Justin went on, his voice quavering, yet strong. "I'm gonna be a detective like him and walk proud through the hood like him and let kids like me know that they can be whatever they wanna be. I have my brothers in the Round Table to help me, and my dad's partner. 'Tween him and Arthur, I got two good men to lean on."

He looked straight into the camera now. "Lance, like Lady Rachel said, don't you go blamin' yourself for my Dad's murder. That's *pura paja* and you know it. Someone who fooled us all killed him, and he died protecting you and that's something he would never regret. You're my brother, Lance, and I love you." He lowered his gaze to the mourners. "I loved my Dad, and I'm gonna honor his memory by being the best man I can be. Thanks, Dad, for being my hero."

Lance choked back more tears as he felt both Arthur's and Jenny's hands on his shoulders. He glanced at Ricky and saw tears in his eyes too. They rested their heads against each other as the service continued.

Finally, it was Arthur's turn. He sat in a chair before the camera, and the operator pointed at the king to begin.

As always, Arthur spoke eloquently about the strength and courage of those who'd been killed, of their loyalty to him and his family, and his undying appreciation for those freely given gifts. He likened Gibson to himself, a man who believed that the hope of the world lay in its children. "He was a man who saw the future of his country in the youth he served, and he gave his life so those youth would have a better one."

He especially praised Darnell and Techie for their service, their dedication to protecting Lance, and their ultimate sacrifice in saving Chris.

Lance heard Chris softly crying behind him, but knew if he turned to his brother he'd start bawling too. So he kept his eyes on his father, steeling himself to follow.

Arthur finished with a prayer for the souls of those lost and his fervent hope and belief that God would cherish them for eternity.

Then the king sadly returned to sit beside Jenny, and cradled the crying Chris in his strong arms.

Lance looked up at the flat screen and saw it was split. Half showed the mourners in California, and the other half showed him and Ricky. It was his turn to speak, and his throat suddenly went dry with dread. Ricky lightly squeezed their intertwined fingers.

He gazed sadly at the camera, struggling his hardest not to cry. At least not yet. The tears would come. As had been the case so often these past four years, there was no way to stop them.

"I wish I could be there with you all because everyone who died was family to me." He sighed. "Even the Secret Service agents. Especially Brooks, who Ricky and me called The Rock. He was awesome. He sparred with us and messed with us and protected us. Even the ones who didn't act like they cared, they cared. Ricky and me would be doing something dumbass like always and I'd see them sneaking little smiles with each other."

He glanced at Ricky, who flashed him "the look," and that renewed Lance's flagging resolve. He looked back at the camera with its creepy red light and mad dogging eye and expelled a deep breath. "Darnell was my brother, a kid who started out an enemy and ended up dying for me. That's family for you. But he died way too soon. He so desperately wanted someone to love who would love him back, but he never found her, and now he's gone. But he loved his mom, and those were his last words."

Almost as if on cue, the cameraman at the church zoomed in for a close up of Darnell's weeping mother, clad in a large black dress, her thick hair in dangling curls, her round face filled with sorrow.

Lance's heart lurched at the sight, and he squeezed Ricky's hand more tightly. "I never met you, Mrs. Brown, but I promised Darnell I'd tell you and the world that your son was a hero, a great man who died to save my ten-year-old brother. Thank you for sharing him with us."

He took another deep breath before speaking about Techie. He'd never even met the boy's mother and Techie had never spoken of her, only to say once that she didn't take much interest in his New Camelot activities because they interfered with her drinking. Lance wondered if she was even present.

"And then there was Techie, Sir Thuy," he began, his voice tight and his breathing unsteady. "He was an amazing friend that I never appreciated until it was too late." He heard Ricky's slight intake of breath, but kept his eyes on the camera. The tears began, small at first, just little blurs before his vision. "He did everything I ever asked him to do, even if he didn't like it."

He paused as the first large teardrop slid slowly down his cheek. "When I went through my bad boy stage, he protected me from the worst hate coming at me on the Internet. When Ricky and me were slammed for being in love, he slammed them right back even though I know he didn't understand why we were the way we were. I know I thanked him, but I don't think I ever treasured him." More tears fell and he bit his lip to keep his emotions under control. He sighed again. "He volunteered to go with us to save Chris, even though he was never a fighter. He gave his life for me and my brother. He did those things because he loved us."

Now tears began to stream and Lance made no move to even swipe at them. What was the point? "Ariel, he loved you more than anyone in the world and he wished more than anything that he had told you that. He so wanted you to know."

The camera had now zoomed to a close shot of Ariel, cradled in Bridget's arms, sobbing.

"He said to tell you to have a happy life."

Seeing her sorrow so close to him, larger than life on that screen, broke Lance and he couldn't continue. He lowered his head, his own body wracked with wrenching sobs as Ricky pulled him in and whispered words of love and support into his ear.

The mourners sat in a stony, saddened state, apparently viewing on their own large screen both young people crying.

After a few moments, Lance raised his head and pulled away from Ricky, but still clasped tightly to Ricky's hand. "I loved Techie and I told him that before…." He paused a moment. "He was the best friend a guy could ever have and I'm blessed that he was mine."

He sighed again as he spotted Justin and Sandra clutching each other as the church camera returned to a wide shot. "I didn't know Sergeant Gibson at first, not until after I… well, died the first time. I've been more blessed than most boys cuz I had three amazing men as role models, and he was one of them. He always told me that I'm the one who brought him and Justin together, but it was my Dad and his unconditional love that did that. Sergeant Gibson, like my godfather, loved me and swore on his life to keep me safe. I wish he hadn't done that or he'd be alive right now. But it was his choice. I understand that part better now that I'm grown. I also learned from him, just like I've learned from my *nino* and my Dad, what being a real man means, and I'll never forget what he taught me."

He lowered his blurred eyes again for a moment before looking back up at the camera. "Justin, I know you said it wasn't my fault, but I still feel guilty. You lost your Dad, and Lady Sandra you lost your husband, because of me. And you shouldn't have."

He paused again, squeezing Ricky's hand as new tears forced their way from the back of his eyes to the front. He trembled and felt coldness wash over him. He pulled Ricky in closer, and Ricky willingly obliged.

"I saved Lady Helen for last because she was the first person out of all those who died that I got to know first." He searched the screen behind the cameraman for Helen's sister, and as though reading his mind, the church camera zoomed in on her.

"Lady Helen was like a mom to me," Lance continued, trying not to choke on his words. "So what you said, Lady Rachel, hit me right to the heart. From the first time I met her she helped me relax and feel comfortable in front of the camera. She taught me how to deal with paparazzi and guys who wanted to use me in commercials. She taught me how to talk to the press and crowds of people."

He paused as tears tumbled down his cheeks. "She always made time for me in those early days even when my Dad didn't. She was an astonishingly good person and I loved her. But I never told her that."

He broke again and kept shaking his head slowly from side to side to regain control. He couldn't last much longer. He knew that. He would break down and that would be that. So using every ounce of willpower he had left, he looked back up at the camera, his face riddled with recrimination.

"I planned on telling her," he went on haltingly, "but the time never seemed right, you know? I guess I thought there'd always be time, like Techie thought about Ariel. But there isn't always time. I forgot again what Jack taught me back in the beginning, that it's the things we don't say to each other that make the biggest difference. So I say it now, Lady Helen, and I know you can hear me. I love you. You were like another mom to me and I'll never forget you."

He choked back another sob as he saw Rachel break down in her husband's arms. He had one more thing to say and struggled to keep his voice steady. "To all of you watching out there, don't be like me. Don't think you have all the time in the world. If you care for someone, if you love someone, don't *not* say it. Tell them how you feel. Tell them while you still can."

And then he was done. He released Ricky's hand and threw both arms around this astounding young man who was his everything, and Ricky's strong arms enveloped him.

"I love you, Lance," he heard Ricky say with intense passion.

Lance pulled his head back and through blurred eyes focused on that face of pure love that made his life worth living. "Oh God, Ricky, I love you so much!"

They hugged again, a fierce clench that pressed them together so tightly Lance could feel Ricky's heart thumping against his chest. Then he saw over Ricky's shoulder that the split screen was still up and everyone at the church and around the world could still see them. He raised one hand and did the slashing motion across his throat, and the camera operator turned off the feed.

With the rest of the service unfolding without him, Lance felt the need to rest his head against Ricky's solid chest and just cry. Ricky's own tears dripped down from above and mixed with his as they silently watched the final goodbyes for their friends. Chris sat on Lance's lap, his round face streaked with tears, and the family huddled together in love.

†††

It was Thanksgiving week before the boys were declared fit enough by their doctors to fly back to Los Angeles. Arthur had already been up and around without the aid of a walker for more than a week and both parents felt ecstatic to finally be taking their children home.

This time the president offered Air Force One as transport to L.A. and promised to meet them at Andrews Air Force Base for the departure. At first Lance objected, worrying over the cost of the flight to the American people. The president had laughed and said he was thinking "Like a true politician." But, he assured the boy, "You're as important to the American people as I am, maybe more." He added the last part with a chuckle, but Lance could hear an almost wistful disappointment in the man's voice.

And so the family was driven to Andrews in a limo sent by the president, and the man himself met them by the enormous hulk that was Air Force One. It practically dwarfed Air Force Two, Lance noted as they exited the stretch limo and stepped out onto the tarmac. Painted blue and white, it boasted a small American flag on the tail and in huge lettering "UNITED STATES OF AMERICA" across each side.

The president stood beside his own limo, wearing the usual dark pants and tie, but no jacket this time. He wore a light blue long-sleeved shirt with the sleeves rolled up. He grinned broadly as Lance and the others approached, gripping the boy's hand heartily and then shaking everyone else's.

"You look great, Lance," the man gushed, clearly surprised. "Like nothing happened to you."

Lance exchanged a quick look with Arthur before saying, "A little magic goes a long way, Mr. President."

The president pulled a confused face, but Lance's brilliant smile turned it into a grin. "Okay, keep your secrets. Arthur, I've authorized my people to give you full access to the plane."

"That's most gracious of you, Mr. President," Arthur replied with a nod of thanks.

The president grinned and winked down at Chris. "Just don't let this one fly it."

That drew a laugh from the boy.

Lance looked up at this man, the most important man on earth, with a respectful smile. "You're still coming to the wedding, right?

The president's grin grew even larger. "Wouldn't miss it for the world."

For some reason that made Lance feel especially good inside. He thanked the president, and then they boarded the most secure plane on the planet. Lance and the others marveled at the lush interior and all the various levels. Of course he sat with Ricky and Chris, while Kai sat beside Dakota, and Arthur beside Jenny.

After takeoff, true to his word, the president's personal assistant took them on a grand tour – everything from the presidential suite with its elegant furnishings to the other bedrooms and offices, the kitchen, and even the cockpit where Chris gaped at the controls with bulging eyes. The copilot allowed the boy to put on his headset and listen in on the air traffic chatter coming over the airwaves. Lance thought Chris had died and gone to heaven.

For most of the flight Lance and Ricky talked about the wedding and their future together. Lance noted Kai and Dakota huddled together and suspected they were doing the same. Arthur and Jenny chatted while Chris played *Madden Football* on his iPad and creamed the computer in game after game.

All too soon the flight was over and the plane taxied to a stop at LAX where the family found Ryan and a large limo awaiting them. Lance felt an intense rush of emotion upon seeing his godfather and, adult or no, he hurried forward to hug his "second" father lovingly. Where once upon a time Ryan would've balked at such a hug, now he welcomed it.

Then they were in the limo and navigating their way through the excited throng that had gathered to welcome them home. The November day was crisp and bright and sunny and Lance felt happier than he had in months.

†††

That first night at New Camelot was the day before Thanksgiving and, as had become customary, everyone would arrive the following day for the traditional dinner. Thus this night belonged solely to the family, which now included Kai and Dakota. And Merlin, of course, who, as usual, said little and merely observed the interactions with a studied gaze.

Reyna had set the weddings for the Saturday before Christmas to allow herself and the others more time to heal, and everyone's excitement level began to rise even that first night back. Because there had been no opportunity, and due to the loss of their loved ones, there had been no celebration of Lance and Ricky's birthday, so it was agreed that the communal dinner the following night would be a combination Thanksgiving/birthday celebration, albeit a quiet one. Neither boy wanted to make a big deal of his birthday given all that had recently happened, and the wedding day would be the big party anyway. So it was agreed to be low-key on the birthdays this year, despite Lance and Ricky turning the seminal eighteen.

When Chris left the table for more ice cream after everyone had finished eating, Lance observed Arthur and Jenny exchange a quick look before eyeing him and Ricky uncertainly.

"Lance," Jenny began haltingly, "While Chris is gone we wanted to let you know that, well, since you and Ricky are adults now and almost married, well, it's all right with us if you want to sleep in the same room."

Arthur took her hand and Lance almost laughed at her obvious discomfort. Arthur nodded his affirmation, causing the boys to exchange a look. Lance also glanced over at Kai and Dakota across the table, and they were watching the exchange with intense interest.

Lance sighed, reached for Ricky and placed their linked hands atop the table. "Thanks, guys, for the support. But Ricky and me talked on the plane and we're gonna stay in our own rooms until the wedding."

Arthur's eyebrows went up. "Indeed?"

Lance tossed off that shy smile he'd adopted from Mark. "Remember, Dad, how you and Mom had your own rooms before you got married?"

Both adults nodded.

"I mean, we don't know if you guys, well, you know, did anything when we weren't looking," Lance went on, smiling mischievously at Jenny's mortified look and Arthur's stoic face. "But you wanted to set a good example for us and Chris and we're gonna do the same." Then his face clouded with uncertainty. "I'm still not even sure where I am with, you know, all that, anyway."

"Me, either," Ricky confirmed, looking equally embarrassed.

"But we do want to set a good example for Chris, you know?" Lance went on with conviction. "That way, if he's sixteen and wants to have his girlfriend over for the night, we can say no and he can't ever say we're hypocrites."

Arthur grinned and Jenny laughed with delight.

"I love you both so much," Jenny gushed with another grin, drawing a laugh from the boys, as well.

Then Arthur fixed his sons with an intense, but loving gaze. "Wise beyond your years, the both of you."

"We had good teachers," Lance said, then he and Ricky high-fived.

"Uh," they heard from across the table, and everyone turned to Dakota and Kai. "Cloudy and me'll do the same, Lance," Kai affirmed while Dakota nodded shyly. "You're right about setting a good example. That's what the whole crusade was about, right, helping kids and showing them how to be better?"

"Here, here," Merlin said, startling everyone with his calm, but firm voice. He had his glass raised, and then everyone joined in. They were clinking glasses when Chris reappeared with a heaping bowl of chocolate ice cream. He stopped a moment and gazed at the adults clinking their glasses as he set down the bowl.

"What are you toasting?" he asked as he resumed his seat.

Lance grinned and held out his glass to his brother. "You."

Chris's face broke into an enormous smile. "Damn straight!" he gushed and then up flew his glass of milk. Everyone laughed as he clinked Lance's glass and then made the rounds of everyone else's. It was another family moment none of them would forget.

†††

Thanksgiving proved to be a joyous reunion. Despite the recent tragedies, or maybe because of them, everyone felt intensely grateful to be together. Reyna and Esteban were there, along with her parents and his mother and sister. Jaime, Sonia and the now three-year-old Arturo also arrived to a great amount of gushing over the rapidly growing little boy.

Justin and Sandra and Phillip came with Ryan and while they all wore the loss of Gibson and Techie plainly on their faces, they were happy to join with everyone for a festive day of peace and gratitude. Sam wore his Scottish sash and regaled everyone with tales of the old country. Other knights dropped in throughout the day, and even Mayor Soto and his wife joined them for dinner. The roly poly man who loved Lance and whom Lance deeply respected, gushed over the weddings and their triumph with the Bill of Rights, and filled everyone in on the progress he and the knights of New Camelot had made in Los Angeles during their absence.

The biggest development, which had just become finalized, was the non-profit New Camelot Foundation buying out the Church of Kabbalogy, making the old Manor Hotel the permanent home to the Round Table and no one else. Sam and the mayor had been working on the sale for months, and it had finally gone through. That was the deal Soto had hinted at over the summer. Arthur and Lance were thrilled, for now New Camelot could openly house any homeless or abused or rejected child who arrived on their doorstep.

John's mother, Karen, also arrived bearing gifts of wine and flowers and crushing hugs for Lance and Ricky. The boys hadn't seen her in months and she looked radiant upon setting eyes on her "adopted" sons. The boys vowed to have her over more often because they missed her pleasant face and engaging smile, and her resemblance to the young boy who'd died way before his time.

Of course, the massive wedding looming in less than a month was the primary topic of conversation, with the mayor filling in the family on the logistics of pulling off the event of the century. Every news outlet wanted to be on hand, and with the president attending, security would be at the highest possible level.

Lance and Ricky rolled their eyes. Here we go again, their expression seemed to say. Then Lance leaned in and laughingly whispered, "Told you we should've eloped."

Ricky grinned and shoved him like always.

As per custom, everyone offered their thanks for something, and with such a large group the process took some time. Lance grinned when Dakota volunteered to go first.

"This family and everything I've learned from them has made Thanksgiving something us natives *can* celebrate. Thank you!"

He nodded at Arthur and Jenny, and then grinned over his glass at Lance and Ricky.

Lance chuckled. "No more shooting Indians on Thanksgiving."

Both Dakota and Kai laughed and the process continued. One after another, people expressed gratitude for their loved ones and the opportunity to be able to tell those loved ones how important they were.

Lance smiled to himself. It seemed what he'd said at the funeral had an impact. *Thank you, Jack.*

Arthur expressed thanks for the health and safety of his family, and especially to Lance for risking death to save Chris. That sentiment earned an embarrassed Lance a hearty toast from all.

Chris held up his glass of milk. "I wanna thank my big brother Lance for being my hero."

Lance reddened even more as everyone raised a glass and said, "Here, here."

Ricky expressed gratitude for the love of his life sitting beside him and the extended family who'd swept him in and loved him unconditionally.

Lance went last, as had also become the custom. He was grateful for Ricky in his life because Ricky was everything. But then he added, "But I'm also grateful for everyone here, and to those we've lost along the way. Every one of you has helped make me the man I am today and I just can't imagine what I'd be like if I hadn't met you. So I thank all of you. You're amazing."

He offered Mark's shy smile and raised his glass in salute. Everyone solemnly did the same, no doubt considering how Lance's words could apply to each of them. What would they be like if their lives hadn't collided in the ways that they had? That was a question for the ages.

Once dinner ended, a large birthday cake was brought to the table and the two boys happily blew out the eighteen candles. Of course Reyna, left arm still restrained by the sling she frequently called "Annoying as hell," supervised the cake cutting and distribution of presents, most of which she'd bought, since Arthur and Jenny had been in Maryland.

Reyna waxed with giddy joy as she handed each of them her most special gift, something she insisted, "You have to wear at the wedding!"

Lance and Ricky exchanged an uncertain look as they clutched the flat gold boxes on their laps, like they expected snakes to leap out at them. When the boxes were opened, however, both stared at the contents with wide-eyed wonder.

Each box contained an identical golden, crown-like circlet, easily an inch tall with thick gold strands woven into intricate Celtic patterns that glittered beneath the chandelier lighting of the dining room.

Excitedly, Reyna snatched them up and placed one on each boy's head, fussing and arranging their hair so the circlet wrapped across each forehead and around the back.

"They're like extra large wedding rings, " Reyna gushed excitedly, and Esteban rolled his eyes at the boys. But Lance was deeply touched and he knew Ricky felt the same. Both hugged Reyna and gushingly thanked her, vowing to wear them always.

"You'd better," the girl said with mock sternness and everyone laughed.

Later that night, after everyone had gone home, Lance stood with Ricky in their adjoining doorway, each wearing his new circlet. They kissed long and lovingly, and once more gave thanks for each other, their amazing family, and their new life together, a life symbolized by the circlets they would for now and always wear.

†††

For the next two weeks there was nothing but wedding preparations, which included decorating New Camelot to look even more like a castle than ever before. Tapestries were hung, Arthur's suit of armor, which he hadn't worn in full since the first night he'd met Lance in that alley, was put on display in the lobby. Lance and Ricky, in addition to preparing for the wedding, insisted on adding to the display honoring their fallen dead. As Knights of the Table, both Techie and Darnell's swords were placed in the display cabinet and Lance wrote short dedications for each. While not officially knights, Helen and Gibson had been honored members of the New Camelot family and the boys put up displays honoring them too. Chris eagerly assisted his brothers, seemingly wanting to spend every minute with them, as though feeling that somehow once they were married he would no longer have such opportunities.

Lance easily surmised the boy's fear and constantly assured him that he would never be forgotten and would forever be their brother. It occurred to Lance while they were working that both he and Ricky needed a best man for the wedding, and with less than a week and a half to go would have to choose somebody fast. They spoke about it in private and both agreed on the perfect choice.

"Say, Chris," Lance said one morning while they were finishing up the tribute to Techie. Chris looked up from the sword he was polishing, wide blue eyes filled with expectation.

Lance looked down at the boy who'd once been so tiny and now suddenly seemed huge by comparison. "We know you were kind 'a hoping to be the ring bearer, but that seems like a job for a little kid, don't you think?"

Chris squinted up at both brothers with a suddenly quizzical, but understanding expression. Lance could tell the boy liked what he'd heard.

"Here's the deal, Chris," Ricky went on conspiratorially. "This fool and me both need a best man for the wedding, see, and we both want you."

"So," Lance jumped in as though interrupting, "to keep me from kicking this fool's ass, we were hoping you'd be best man for both of us. What'chu say, bro?"

Chris's eyes bulged so wide Lance thought they'd burst right out of his head, and the boy grinned from ear to ear like there was no tomorrow.

"Damn straight I'll be your best man!" he exclaimed, leaping up and throwing his arms around them both and pulling them in together, pushing their grinning faces right up against each other and necessitating the need for a quick kiss. Then Lance grabbed his little brother and tackled him to the lobby floor, where the two rolled and laughed and tickled and pinned each other with gleeful abandon while Ricky, whose back still wasn't up to such antics, clapped and cheered.

Esteban, Lance knew, had asked Arthur to be his best man and the king had gladly accepted. But there was something troubling Arthur throughout that week. Merlin too. Lance could sense it. On several occasions Lance would come upon the two old friends huddled in the library or one of the lounges deep in a serious-toned conversation. Upon seeing him, they would instantly stop talking and inquire if all was proceeding as planned for the wedding, but he knew they were hiding something. His dad had that same expression on his bearded face that Lance had seen several times over the past year. But, because he feared the unknown, Lance ignored the anxiety that slowly crept up his spine and kept nipping at his heart.

He didn't mention these surreptitious conversations to Ricky because he didn't want to dampen his intended's mood before the ceremony. The two of them had decided not to wear traditional tuxedoes, but rather put on their finest Round Table regalia. Arthur would also loan them some of his kingly cloaks, the full-length one for Lance, who was next in line for the throne, and a shorter half-cloak for Ricky. Both would sport their matching, glittery gold circlets Reyna had given them and Lance would also wear the crown Arthur had presented him on his sixteenth birthday.

They worked closely with Kai and Dakota in planning their vows and discussing attire. The two Native men, both healing rapidly from their own wounds, planned an elaborate combination of Round Table and Native American apparel, complete with some of their fancier powwow regalia. To show solidarity with their Native brothers, Lance and Ricky accepted the offer of fancy feathers for their hair, courtesy of Kai, and hand-made neck chokers from Dakota.

Of course, Reyna had overseen all the wedding preparations, including the ordering of wedding bands for the men. She'd measured their ring fingers prior to leaving Maryland and had ordered the rings as soon as she returned. Even Lance hadn't seen them, but he knew Reyna's style and they would no doubt be exquisite. He and Ricky didn't worry about those details. Neither did Kai and Dakota. They simply basked in the presence of the ones they loved and felt relieved that someone else was handling the details.

The four of them sat one night atop Lance's bed and looked at each other in blissful silence. They'd been battered and bruised, all of them, but they'd survived. No, triumphed. Lance had fully recovered thanks to Excalibur; Ricky could walk and even lightly jog on the treadmills within the hotel health center; Dakota sported what Lance thought was a wicked looking scar on his right chest; and Kai could almost use his arm and shoulder with full range of motion. Yes, they'd triumphed over their enemy, they'd given the children of America a new birth of freedom, but their greatest triumph lay mere days in the future – the day each would commit himself to the one who completed him.

"You guys look happy," Lance said, grinning and elbowing Ricky, who elbowed him right back.

"Thanks to you, Lance," Kai shot back with a thankful smile.

"Yeah, right," Ricky said, shoving Lance and almost knocking him over. "This fool?"

"He's right," Dakota said, flicking his long hair back off his face and gazing at Lance with deep respect. "What you told me on the rez, Lance, about all I needed?"

Lance nodded. He remembered, involuntarily reaching for Ricky and feeling the soft hand back where it belonged.

"I haven't wanted a drink since," Dakota finished with a shy smile, giving his own version of a shove at Kai, who laughed and pushed right back. "Laughing Boy is all I need."

Lance felt a wave of happiness rise up and fill his being with joy. Yes, he knew, these two would be happy forever, just like him and Ricky. Soul mates from the get go, and yet the road to that realization had been long and hard to navigate, just as his own had been. He sighed heavily.

"What?" Ricky asked, tilting his head and shifting the hair to one side.

Lance smiled. "I was just thinking how all of us almost missed the chance to be with the one we love because we listened to the wrong people. Life is crazy like that, huh?"

The other three nodded silently and there was a moment of unspoken truth filling the air with its palpable weight. Then, with a mischievous grin, Ricky snatched up a pillow and whacked Kai across the face. The Indian took only a second to be startled before he grabbed for it and threw the pillow right back. Then all of them had pillows and the battle commenced. By the time the four laughing, giggling young men had breathlessly finished their mini-war, the air in the room looked like a blizzard for all the tiny feathers they'd sent flying as the pillows ripped and split apart.

Hair wildly askew, feathers stuck to their faces and arms with sweat, the four Native Knights collapsed in a group heap atop the bed and laughed and talked and joked around, enjoying the last remnants of boyhood. But they were happy, and looked ahead to their adult lives with excited anticipation, and that was what mattered most.

The day before the weddings was frantic. One Direction would be flying in later that day to stay the weekend. Harry had called Lance and asked if he and the boys could sing for the wedding, and naturally Lance said yes. Ever the troublemaker, Harry laughingly promised to dance a slow dance with him and get the tongues wagging anew. Lance had laughed and signed off, but he liked the self-confidence of this young man. Nothing seemed to ruffle his feathers and he almost thrived on the foolishness perpetrated on him by the media. Lance wished he could be that way, but knew he was a little too emo.

The president would arrive with his family just prior to the start of the ceremony. Mayor Soto would perform the weddings for the men, while Father Mike would marry Reyna and Esteban. The latter was at Reyna's parents' insistence since they were at least nominally Catholic and wanted their daughter married by a priest. That was all good with Lance, who couldn't wait to see the man again. He wished Father Mike could perform his and Ricky's wedding, too, but that wasn't possible yet and Mayor Soto was so excited and flattered that it would all work out as it was supposed to. Just like Mark said. Thinking of his first friend with those big, sad pools of blue pulled a wistful smile to Lance's lips as he continued to lay out his wedding clothes.

Reyna and Esteban and their families would spend the night at New Camelot to avoid the gridlock the following morning would bring. Camera stations had already been set up all around the lobby and the exterior gardens, and the outdoor stage had been adorned with the same style arch that had been used for Arthur and Jenny's nuptials, except this time the flowers adorning it displayed every color of the rainbow.

Because of the president's attendance, security would be extraordinarily tight. Thus the ceremonies were not slated to begin until two o'clock so all the attendees would have enough time to be screened by Secret Service when they entered. As Lance had predicted, the weddings would be carried live on every network and cable news outlet, and streamed on many an Internet site, including the New Camelot one. The media had gone berserk with the buildup ever since Lance confirmed that indeed he and Ricky would marry. Billed as the Wedding to End All Weddings, the event had been hyped so ceaselessly that Lance himself was tired of the coverage and figured the American people must be too.

But no. According to the polls, ninety-four percent of Americans planned to watch some, or all, of the event, and the number worldwide was even higher.

Sir Phillip kept him apprised of the Internet chatter regarding his nuptials, even though Lance didn't care what the world thought. Not any more. He had long ago stopped trying to be what everyone wanted him to be. But surprisingly, the majority of people weighing in about the wedding – on websites, Facebook, Twitter, etc. –

didn't even mention the fact that Lance and Ricky were both male. The two had become so big that most people no longer cared.

While Lance and the others had agreed to make the ceremony mostly about Reyna, the only bride, he understood that, to the world, *he* was the main attraction, mostly because people honestly loved him. That was a tough concept to grasp for the boy who'd grown up unloved and unwanted, and the worthiness issue kept creeping into his subconscious when he'd least expect it to.

Ricky had repeatedly told him he was beloved by the world, and even the president had said the same. And while Lance knew he'd never understand why, he had to accept the reality of it. He *was* beloved by the masses, and their beloved boy had become a man before their very eyes, and now he was getting married.

Sir Phillip, who Lance was growing to like more and more each day, grinned with glee as he displayed these stats, and the two fist-bumped like old friends.

Lance vowed to spend more time getting to know Phillip, rather than just depending on him for technical advice or Internet services. As a start, he'd asked Phillip to be one of the groomsmen for the wedding, and the bespectacled boy's pale, pinched face lit up with pride and happiness. And the fact that Lance's skin was brown and Phillip's white made no difference. Lance could clearly see that. Despite his parents' attempts to brainwash him into a racist lifestyle, Phillip had rejected it, and that rejection showed in those wide, worshipful eyes as he excitedly accepted Lance's offer.

Other groomsmen chosen by the celebrants included Justin, Jaime, and Charley. Reyna had chosen Jenny as her matron of honor, to Jenny's great surprise and joy. Bridget and Sonia would be Reyna's bridesmaids, but Ariel chose not to accept one of those slots. She was still too devastated by Techie's death to handle a wedding, but she wished Reyna, and especially Ricky, all the best over a Skype call. Ricky nearly choked up and could barely respond with his thanks, but Ariel seemed to understand and offered a small smile before signing off.

Arthur had insisted on Lance keeping Excalibur in his room with him, despite the fact that he was well and healed and no longer needed the magic so deeply embedded within the sword. Lance had tried to argue, but Arthur would hear none of it. However, the day before the wedding, Arthur came for the sword, explaining that he had a need for it. Lance was only too happy to give it back to his Dad, still fearful over the sword's almost symbiotic relationship with him.

The guest list ran into the hundreds, and that didn't even include members of the media who'd be wandering the reception interviewing people at random. Everyone had been required to RSVP two weeks ahead of time because the Secret Service needed to vet each name and do a background check prior to the event.

Lance had been surprised that last day to find Dakota pouring over the list, Kai leaning over his shoulder as he did. Dakota's hair hung about his bowed head as he flipped through several pages and then silently handed the list off to Kai before striding across the lobby and up the stairs. Kai made eye contact with Lance and shook his head. Lance sighed sadly, patted Kai on the shoulder and then made his way to the computer lab.

†††

Dinner that night was a festive energized affair, doubling as the rehearsal dinner since the only topic of conversation was the following day's events. But there had been no formal rehearsal – just a basic walk-through choreographed by Reyna so everyone would know where he or she was supposed to stand.

Reyna dominated the dinner with her incessant chattering. Her sling was gone and she had most of her mobility back, at least enough to gesticulate wildly as she prattled on about this or that aspect of the event. Her parents were there, as was Esteban's mom. Reyna would gush over her awesome wedding dress or the gorgeous flowers and Esteban would roll his eyes and elbow his mother beside him. She'd flash him a frown and elbow him right back, always causing Reyna to flash that "What?" look she'd perfected over the years.

Esteban laughed and the other young men joined in. Having planned it out beforehand, all of them in unison chanted, "Reyna, you're such a girl." This time she laughed heartily and threw a napkin at Esteban in mock annoyance while everyone chuckled.

Chris looked puffed up with pride at having the grown up job of best man, and he brought the table conversation to a standstill by announcing that he should have had a bachelor party for Lance and Ricky and somebody should've told him. Lance nearly spit out his water and looked over at Chris, a mortified look in his eyes.

"How do you know about bachelor parties?" He glanced at Ricky fearfully.

Chris just flashed that knowing look he had, and shrugged. "I Googled 'best man' to see what my job was and it talked about the bachelor party."

Arthur and Jenny exchanged a nervous look as Lance felt the blood drain from his face. He hoped Chris had only looked at Wikipedia and not something more risqué.

"And what did it tell you about the bachelor party, Chris?" Jenny asked cautiously.

Chris took another mouthful of mashed potatoes and shrugged again in that nonchalant way young children seemed to have perfected. "Oh, naked ladies jumping out of cakes and stuff like that."

Esteban stifled a laugh while Reyna glared at him. Lance and Ricky groaned inwardly and turned red.

"Anyway, I figured Lance and Ricky wouldn't wanna see any naked ladies so I decided to skip it," Chris replied with complete sincerity and innocence.

Both Kai and Dakota had to cover their laughter with their hands and Esteban piped up with, "I'll take the naked ladies," to which his mother responded with a hard elbow to the ribs and Reyna flashed a stormy scowl.

Lance was mortified and wanted to sink down into the floor and vanish. He looked at Ricky and saw the same feeling in the other's eyes.

"Uh, thanks, Chris," Lance finally said hoarsely. "You know, for the thought and all."

Chris beamed. "What are brothers for?"

Reyna reached out and tousled the boy's unruly mop of blond hair and chuckled. "Too smart for your own good, that's what you are."

Chris smiled even more brightly. "Thanks, Reyna. When I get a girlfriend someday I hope she's just like you."

Reyna's eyebrows shot up and she nodded approvingly, tossing a smirk across at Esteban. "Now there's a boy who knows a lady when he sees one."

Esteban laughed and raised his glass to his bride-to-be and she happily clinked it with her own.

Lance glanced around at a table full of happy, chattering people. Even Reyna's parents, once so proud and haughty, laughed and joked with Este's mom and Arthur and Jenny like they'd grown up together. In a sense, Lance considered, maybe they had. They'd all grown up these past four years, and they'd all grown better.

Then his eye returned to Kai and Dakota and saw Dakota with his head bowed, Kai whispering into his ear. Dakota hadn't looked so morose since he'd left the rez in South Dakota months before.

"What's up?" Lance asked quietly since the other two were directly across from him.

Kai looked up, his usual smiling face drooping with pain. "Cloudy's mom isn't on the RSVP list."

Lance felt momentarily numb, and guilty. He'd been so caught up in his own joy that he hadn't even thought to say anything, suddenly recalling Dakota's reaction to the guest list yesterday. "I'm sorry, Dakota," he said, feeling an unusual inability to know what to say. His soul whispering skills clanged like alarm bells and he felt the Indian's intense feelings of rejection.

Dakota looked up at him and Lance's heart lurched at the sadness etched across his handsome, aquiline features. "I just wish she didn't hate me."

"Hey, my *má* loves you," Kai chirped, trying to sound upbeat.

Dakota looked at him sadly.

"And so do I," Jenny said from behind him, causing Dakota to spin around in surprise.

Lance hadn't even noticed her get up and move. She was just suddenly there, looking into Dakota's face with love and acceptance. And Dakota smiled, grabbing her around the waist in a tight hug. She cradled his head against her and stroked his hair a moment while the table fell into a respectful silence. Most didn't understand what was happening, but it didn't matter.

Jenny returned to her seat and Lance observed Dakota swiping at his eyes a moment before exchanging a look with Kai. Kai offered his own alluring smile, and that drew one from Dakota.

Lance visibly relaxed and looked at Ricky so intently that Ricky blinked. "What?"

"We have the coolest mom in the world, don't we?"

Ricky grinned. "Damn straight."

That got a universal laugh and a toast from Arthur to his amazing wife and mother to his sons. Jenny blushed as everyone raised a glass in tribute.

Dakota's "Here, here" was loudest of all.

†††

Chapter Twelve

Once Upon A Time...

The wedding day dawned bright and clear with not a cloud in sight. While the temperature would only hit seventy for the high that day, this was a typical Southern California December day and perfect for an outdoor event.

When Lance awoke that morning alone in his bed it suddenly hit him like a rockslide – *I'm getting married today. This is the last time I sleep in this bed alone.* He also felt an intense wave of panic slap him like a hand to the face. Would Ricky expect him to do, like, *everything* right away? They'd talked about the sex part of their relationship in very vague terms because both still hadn't decided just what they'd be comfortable with and how soon.

"We'll go slow, Lance," Ricky kept assuring him. "I need that as much as you."

Then he relaxed and luxuriated a moment within the comfortable sheets. Ricky wouldn't push anything, and neither would he. They knew each other too well, could literally read each other's mind and mood, and everything would work out just fine.

Lance slipped on a pair of workout shorts and quietly opened Ricky's door. The love of his life still slept, his hair splayed out all around the pillows as Lance snuck over silently to gaze down at him. He knew most guys would think he was crazy, but more than any sex between them, Lance longed to wake up every morning with this man beside him because he loved watching Ricky sleep. The peaceful expression on that beautiful face always sent Lance's heart into overdrive and would make waking up each day a gift unto itself.

Like he always did when Lance watched him sleep, Ricky sensed the presence of his beloved. The lids popped open, and those soft brown eyes fixed upon Lance and melted him right into the carpet beneath his bare feet. Ricky smiled.

"Happy wedding day, dumbass," he said, pulling his arms out from beneath the sheets and reaching for Lance.

Lance could scarcely breathe, very often his response to seeing Ricky awaken. "Happy wedding day to you, dumber ass," he whispered, his voice breathy and weak. And then he was in Ricky's arms, lying atop the other man and kissing him gently and lovingly, running his hands through Ricky's hair while Ricky's arms encircled his back.

After a deep and satisfying kiss, Lance rolled off him so they could lie side by side, both breathing heavily and luxuriating in this quiet, peaceful moment.

Their hair lay intertwined and spread out behind them as Lance turned his head and gazed lovingly at Ricky.

Ricky grinned with giddy delight, and that drew out the most beautiful smile he thought he'd ever seen from this most beautiful man in the world.

They lay like that a few minutes, fingers intertwined, a blanket of love covering their hearts and souls. Then they reluctantly separated and rose to get ready.

†††

The One Direction boys had arrived the night before and bounded down the stairs that morning rife with energy, dressed in the same tunics and pants they'd worn for Arthur and Jenny's wedding. It was Chris who met them this time, assuring them that his brothers would be down soon.

"They're doing each other's hair," he said with a satisfied smirk, which drew laughter from the band members. Harry reached out and tousled Chris's hair with a chuckle.

"Your own hair's getting' pretty long there, mate," Harry said with a laugh. "And you look quite spiffy today."

"I'm Lance and Ricky's best man so I got to look good," Chris answered with all seriousness, generating more good-natured laughter from the Brits.

Jenny had dressed Chris in a royal blue tunic, his standard brushed leather pants and boots. Ricky had presented Chris with the golden circlet Lance had given him for his sixteenth birthday, the one still memorialized on the downtown mural. Mayor Soto had made the mural a permanent fixture as a reminder of what Lance and Arthur had done for the city.

The circlet wound around Chris's blond hair and the ghostly white locks tumbled about his shoulders and partway down his back. More than ever did he resemble Arthur, though the king's hair was light brown rather than blond. Feeling large and important in his role as best man, Chris happily escorted the One Direction boys to the dining room for breakfast.

†††

Arthur soon joined Chris in the lobby to begin welcoming their guests, while Jenny and the bridesmaids prepared Reyna in one of the upstairs rooms. Reyna's dad had apparently been convinced by his wife to look in on Esteban, in case the young groom needed any help, and he'd reluctantly agreed. Arthur watched the tightly wound man ascend the stairs and would have loved the opportunity to observe their interaction. Just the thought of them alone together amused him. He knew Justin and the other groomsmen would be nearby, so nothing untoward should occur.

The hotel swarmed with Secret Service, and the streets outside with LAPD officers to control the already enormous crowd, many of whom had camped out over night to get a glimpse of the invited guests and have a clear view of the big flat screen TV that had been mounted just above the main front gates.

Ryan arrived early, with Justin, Sandra, and Phillip by his side. Arthur noted that his friend looked especially well-groomed and decided Sandra must have had a hand in that. Despite having just lost her husband and Justin his dad, both seemed happy and excited to be present. Justin and Phillip excused themselves to get ready for their groomsman duties, Phillip helping Justin navigate the stairs because of the big, cumbersome support shoes he was required to wear.

Sandra decided to wander out to the gardens, but Ryan hung back. He and Arthur looked long and hard at one another, a look equal parts friendship and astonishment.

Ryan shook his head. "Can you believe Lance is getting married, Arthur?"

The king grinned through his beard, which he'd trimmed and clipped just that morning so it would look perfect for the ceremony. "No, James, I cannot," he confessed. "It seems only yesterday he was just a boy."

Ryan smiled and Arthur realized for the first time that it was an engaging smile. "He was never just a boy, Arthur. You know that better than anyone."

"True enough, James. He has always been a miracle."

"Am I a miracle, too, Dad?" Chris asked, looking up at his father expectantly.

Arthur grinned. "For now and always, son." Arthur reached for the boy's hand, but Chris pulled it away quickly, looking around in embarrassment.

"Not now, Dad, I'm best man, remember?" The boy looked horrified that Arthur could have forgotten something so important.

Arthur laughed and Ryan joined in. Then the detective excused himself to be with Sandra. "I think she needs some company right now."

After that, the guests began entering in waves. A metal detector had been set up on the front porch and everyone had to pass through it, even Mayor Soto. Arthur had merely shrugged and said, "Oh well…" as he shook the hand of his friend and colleague. The mayor looked especially dapper in a light blue suit with a burgundy red tie and his thinning hair looked more stylish than usual.

His wife, Darlene, an attractive forty-something woman with short, curly hair, long legs, and a good two inches on her husband, gushed over the décor and how cute Chris looked, which caused the boy to frown.

"Ma'am," Chris said in all seriousness, "I'm the best man. I *can't* be cute."

Everyone laughed at that, especially Arthur who patted the boy on the back and congratulated him on taking his job so seriously. The compliment drew a fierce look of pride from Chris and he beamed.

All morning the guests streamed through the open double doors. They marveled at the suit of armor, stopped reverently at the shrine to the fallen, and wandered about with excited chatter. Arthur warmly welcomed Karen, who arrived wearing a bright green dress because it had been John's favorite color. Arthur embraced her, and the small Filipino lady stooped to hug Chris, praising him on how big he'd grown.

"And you're John's age now," she said with a wistful shake of her head. "My, how time flies."

Karla and several teacher friends of Jenny arrived, decked out with wild hair and dangling jewelry, looking ready to party.

Even Mr. Mills and his wife appeared. Arthur hadn't seen them since visiting Mills in the hospital following the train crash. The older man grinned happily and embraced the king, and then high-fived a grinning Chris. Arthur thanked him for coming, and the man winked.

"Wouldn't 'a missed it," he said with a laugh and then excused himself to show his wife around.

And, of course, Arthur's knights streamed into the hotel from all over the city, dressed in their finest tunics and pants and miffed at having to be "wanded" before entering a place they considered home. Arthur merely shrugged as if to say, "That's life in this era, I'm afraid," and greeted each with great joy.

Helen's sister, Rachel, her husband and their two children, showed up and she expressed a great desire to hug the boy who had taken her sister by surprise and turned her world upside down. Arthur assured her there would be plenty of time to chat with Lance after the ceremony, and they wandered off.

Several knights had volunteered to give tours to anyone who wished them, and others had been assigned seating duties for the outside gardens.

Kai's mother, Dezba, arrived with another lady from the reservation whom she introduced as Kai's aunt. Dezba wore a formal dress, adorned with traditional Native earrings and jewelry, and once more displayed the same wide smile and infectious laugh as her son.

"So where is my handsome son and soon-to-be second son?" she asked excitedly.

"He's upstairs getting ready," Chris answered. "Want me to go get him?"

She laughed. "No, that's all right. I'll see them soon enough." Then to Arthur she added, "This is quite a place you have here, Arthur."

"Thank you," the king replied with his usual graciousness.

Chris looked up at the two women with curiosity. "How come Dakota's mom isn't here?"

Dezba exchanged a look with the other lady before saying, "It's complicated."

The boy's eyes turned to angry slits. "It's not complicated. She's just mean like my first mother. I saw the way she looked at him. Just like my mother looked at me." He proudly gazed up at Arthur. "Now I have a Mom and Dad who love me."

Arthur smiled at the boy, and then addressed the two women. "He's at that age where he speaks his mind."

Dezba smiled knowingly. "And his mind speaks true." She nodded at Chris before leading her sister through the lobby toward the back gardens, following the flow of the crowd.

The president and his family arrived around one-fifteen and he strode into the lobby with a big grin on his face. The usual phalanx of agents milled around him scanning every face and every corner for threat assessment. The First Lady looked radiant in a designer gown, and both of the children were smartly attired, and eager to see Lance again.

"I am, too, Arthur," the president said with a grin. "Where is America's son?"

As though on cue, Lance appeared at the top of the stairs, Ricky at his side. Kai and Dakota stood just behind them.

All conversation in the lobby ceased as the men of the hour, most especially, as the president had put it, "America's son," began descending the stairs.

Arthur couldn't keep himself from gaping. He'd always known both of his sons to be handsome youths, but today they looked almost supernaturally resplendent in their tunics adorned with his cloaks. The long and luxurious hair on both spilled over their shoulders and down their backs like shimmering damask, adorned with large feathers to celebrate their Native heritage. Lance wore the choker Dakota had given him and it complemented the rest of the outfit, while Ricky sported a small, dangling beaded necklace given to him by Kai. Reyna's matching circlets glimmered beneath the lobby lighting and the crown atop Lance's head nearly stopped Arthur's breath in his throat. His son had never looked so much like a king as at this moment, and Ricky a prince. And Arthur had never felt so much love and pride. Pride could easily be a sin, he knew, if abused. But through his interventions, these two extraordinary young men were about to embark on a lifelong journey, taking on the woes of the world as a team, and Arthur was speechless.

Trailing behind them, Kai and Dakota looked equally splendid in their traditional colorful headbands, fringed moccasins, draping chest plates and dangling feathers intermingled with their knightly tunics and pants. Kai's hair had been turned into a single long braid, and Dakota's hair fell about his face and chest unfettered and free, restrained only by the regalia around his head.

Uncertainly, Lance stopped before his dad, Ricky at his side. They smiled cautiously. "Well?"

Arthur's frozen moment broke and he grinned broadly. "You look like a king, Lance. And you, Ricky, every inch a prince."

The boys broke into big grins at the compliment and the president stuck out his hand to them. "I couldn't agree more."

They shook his hand and Lance tossed off a laugh. "Thanks, Mr. President."

The president stared at them a moment as though verifying what he was seeing, and then grinned anew. "You two are remarkable." The First Lady stepped forward. "You remember the wife and kids." He winked and Lance laughed, shaking the hand of the First Lady and then the two kids. The First Lady proclaimed them "Gorgeous" and hugged them warmly.

The First Children gushed over the Children's Bill of Rights and the older one thanked Lance for giving them something to use when "Dad gets too uppity in his 'dad' role." It was clearly a joke, but the president momentarily frowned before getting it. Then he laughed, patted Lance fondly on one shoulder, and then led his family off to "Work the room." Lance watched a moment in amusement. Politicians!

Suddenly he and Ricky were swamped with well-wishers. So were Kai and Dakota. The Indians had earned the respect of all Arthur's knights for their heroics and strong character, and felt at home amongst these disparate young people united under a common cause.

Chris proclaimed the four boys "Toweringly beautiful," which made Lance feel wistful and happy all at once, and Arthur stood gazing in wonder at his two sons, and the two who had unofficially joined the family.

He grinned broadly. "To quote my son, you all look amazing."

They laughed at that and Ricky gave Lance a little shove.

"You all, including you, Chris, have been the greatest gift a man could ask for. Each and every one of you is a man to be reckoned with, a man of honor, a man unafraid to do what's right, rather than what's easy. I remain forever proud of you."

As always, Lance choked up under Arthur's praise, but not as strongly as he had in the past. All five gazed at the taller man with an almost reverent expression, and then Lance broke the moment open by throwing his arms around his father. After, Ricky did the same. Though they hesitated, Arthur motioned the Indians forward and hugged each in turn.

Then Arthur stepped back and placed one hand on the shoulder of Lance and one on Ricky's. "Well, my sons, I think the time is now. Are you both ready?"

The boys exchanged a grin. "Damn straight," they said together, and Arthur laughed.

Then the king watched his five sons cross the vast lobby and head back toward the gardens. He observed them with a wistful sadness, both for them growing up and away from him, and for what that growing up might soon mean for the entire family.

He spotted Merlin loitering by the stairs and waved the wizard over. With something clearly unspoken passing between them, the two older men followed the younger ones out to the garden.

Kai spotted his mother straight off and Lance watched him drag Dakota by the hand over to where she stood with his aunt. Because Jenny would enter with Reyna, Lance and Ricky would walk up the aisle side by side without her. Esteban would walk his and Reyna's mothers down the aisle and seat them, and then Kai and Dakota would escort Dezba to her place of honor. Lance overheard Kai's aunt begging off and saying she would sit somewhere on her own.

"He's *your* son," she told Dezba with a grin at her smiling nephew. "They both are." Then she kissed both men on the cheek and drifted off to find a good seat.

The crowd was much larger than that which attended Arthur and Jenny's wedding, Lance observed, as he and the other grooms stood with Chris and Dezba awaiting the arrival of Esteban and Jenny. Esteban's mom found them and they introduced her to Kai's mother. Dakota looked happy, Lance could see, but inwardly sad. He was doing a good job of hiding it, but Lance could read him too well. So could Kai, who kept their hands clasped together, his eyes firmly fixed on those of the man he loved, and showing nothing but unwavering support.

Esteban finally stepped out of the hotel with the groomsmen, all of whom wore their knightly attire, despite Esteban sporting a traditional tuxedo as a concession to Reyna's parents. Lance whistled seductively upon laying eyes on Esteban, who looked by turns handsome and uncomfortable.

"Looking pretty hot there, *carnal*," he jested as Esteban loosened the tie and pulled down on his black vest. Elbowing Ricky, Lance said to the older man, "Maybe I should throw over this fool and marry you, eh?"

Ricky busted up at Esteban's shocked look, and then the big man punched Lance in the chest with a chuckle.

Arthur and Merlin joined them, and the bridesmaids a few moments after that.

Lance and Ricky held hands and gazed around them at the magnificent gardens with most of the trees stripped of leaves, but adorned with white garlands of fresh flowers. They marveled at the sea of chairs spread out before and around the outdoor stage, and at the numerous circular tables dotting the gardens beyond the stage.

It's my wedding day, Lance thought with rising excitement, squeezing Ricky's hand lovingly.

Ricky looked over and must've sensed something because he said, "What?"

Lance expelled that breathy little laugh. "I promised you the whole world, didn't I?"

Ricky grinned, the dimples going into hyperdrive. "Damn straight you did."

Lance so wanted to lean in for a kiss and felt his body temperature start to soar.

No. Gotta wait for the ceremony.

Jenny arrived at just that moment to distract them with the news that Reyna was ready and the ceremony could begin.

Lance gaped a moment at this woman who had started out as his favorite teacher and gradually evolved into the only real mother he'd ever known. If possible she looked younger and more radiant than ever as she hurried over to sweep his hair back over his shoulders and adjust the crown on his head. Then she did the same for Ricky, standing and just staring at them a moment.

"I'm so happy for you both, and I love you so much," she gushed breathlessly, leaning in and pulling both into a hug.

"I love you, too," they said at the same moment, causing her to laugh and shake her head. Then she hugged Kai and Dakota and Dezba, frowning slightly. Kai's mother met her eyes and shook her head. Jenny understood and stepped back with Arthur and their sons to await the start of the ceremony.

Lance squatted down before Chris and adjusted his hair and circlet, placing both hands atop the boy's broadening shoulders. "Ready to do your job, best man?"

Chris grinned. "Damn straight. I go up and tell everyone to sit cuz we're gonna start. Then I wait for you guys. Piece of cake."

The boy's earnest, confident expression caused Lance to laugh, and he kissed Chris on the cheek before sending the boy up the red carpet toward the stage.

Some of the milling, chatting guests took note of Chris's entrance and turned to observe the boy as he strode forward. Father Mike and Mayor Soto appeared from behind Sir Khom and his D.J. setup, and stood just to one side of the arch awaiting Chris's arrival.

Lance watched as his younger brother confidently ascended the steps leading up to the stage and walked over to Sir Khom for a microphone. The grinning knight handed it over and Chris stepped forward to face the throng of people, some of whom were sitting, others standing and talking. He tapped the microphone several times, sending a rasping, scraping sound out and over the crowd and drawing them quickly down to silence.

Chris beamed out at them, his blond hair almost glowing beneath the afternoon sun. He raised the mic to his lips and said, "Hello everybody."

A chorus of "Hellos" flew back at him, rising like an erupting volcano and making the boy laugh.

"I'm Sir Christopher Pendragon and I'm the best man for my brothers," he announced with the kind of formality he'd learned from Round Table gatherings.

"Hi, Sir Christopher!" many in the crowd shouted out, much to the boy's delight.

"It's my job to get this show on the road so my brothers and sister can get married," he went on, eliciting a laugh from the attendees. "So if everyone could take a seat, we'll get started."

Lance almost laughed at Chris's serious and formal delivery, squeezing Ricky's hand all the more.

As everyone in the gardens scrambled for their seats, Chris walked back to Sir Khom and handed him the mic. Then he moved to his assigned position to the right of the gigantic arch.

At this point, Lance observed Arthur give Jenny a quick kiss and then she re-entered the hotel to emerge later with Reyna. The D.J. struck up music Lance and Ricky had downloaded from a movie about King Arthur, a rousing, heraldic fanfare of horns and brass that seemed the perfect procession music for the men.

He glanced at Arthur, who grinned like a boy, suddenly looking to Lance ten years younger than he had during their darker hours these past few years. Then the king, decked out in his finest tunic and pants, but sans the crown and cloak, strode forward up the red carpet and onto the stage. He winked at Chris before assuming his proper place in the center of the archway.

Then Justin linked arms with a shimmery Bridget and they proceeded up the carpet. Lance had nearly gasped when he'd seen Bridget step into the garden mere moments before. She looked more radiant than ever. The pale purple bridesmaid dress and glittery tiara, courtesy of Reyna, made her look like a princess. She'd stepped over to Lance and kissed him on the cheek. Then she'd kissed Ricky and told him to take good care of the most beautiful boy in the world.

Ricky had laughed and swore he would, and Bridget smiled lovingly at Lance before joining Justin for the procession. They ascended the steps to the stage, Bridget assisting Justin because of his injuries, and stood at their assigned locations. The other groomsmen and bridesmaids strode forward to do the same.

Then it was Esteban's turn. He had one arm linked within his mother's, the other within the arm of Reyna's radiant mom as he led them up the aisle and seated both in the front row. He joined Arthur up on the stage where the two men shook hands before Esteban proudly stood beside the king.

Next came Kai and Dakota, each with an arm linked through one of Dezba's, who walked happily between them. When they arrived at the front row, she kissed both men and then took her seat. The Indians stepped up onto the stage and took their positions to the left of the arch.

Lance and Ricky strode forward on their own, heads held high, huge grins on their faces as they acknowledged those sitting on the aisle seats with smiles and head nods. The music reached a crescendo of brass and drums and horns as they stepped up onto the stage, turned to the right, and moved to stand beside Chris, who grinned mightily.

Now Jenny finally entered and moved slowly up the red carpet, and Lance once more noted how beautiful she appeared, especially in her own pale purple dress and golden tiara that made Bridget's look like something out of a Cracker Jack box. A queen she was and a queen she looked, Lance thought, as she grinned at them with delight just before Arthur stepped over to help her up the steps to his side.

The fanfare music climaxed with a clash of cymbals and everything went silent for a moment. Then the strains of "Here Comes the Bride" burst forth from the speakers.

Lance fixed his gaze on the double doors leading into New Camelot, and could see everyone else rubbernecking to do the same. Reyna stepped through those doors, and Lance heard Ricky gasp beside him. His own breath had stopped and he knew his mouth had to be hanging open like a fish.

She had never looked so luminous as she did at that moment, he realized. So accustomed was he to seeing his sister in pants that the sight of her in this long tiered and flowing, sleeveless side-draping white gown, accented with lavender appliques around the waist and up along her bustline, reminded Lance just how stunningly gorgeous she was. Her hair flowed down her back, accented by a sheer white veil that looked as delicate as fairy wings. Her upper back and shoulders were visible beneath an even more sheer covering adorned with tiny lavender flowers.

Her makeup was subtle, yet brought out the soft brown of her eyes and highlighted her wide, ingratiating smile. Her father, dressed in a standard black tux, had his arm linked in hers and for once, Lance noted as they moved slowly up the red carpet, he didn't look like he'd swallowed a rotten egg. He actually looked happy.

Lance found himself grinning foolishly, glancing over at Ricky and seeing the same goofy grin on his face, too. This was their big sister who could kick the ass of any guy out there, and she looked like something out of Cinderella. He watched as Mr. Hernandez walked his daughter up the steps and then held her hand out to Esteban.

The younger man smiled with pure joy at the older one, and took Reyna's hand warmly in his. Then Mr. Hernandez kissed his daughter lightly on the cheek, descended the steps, and joined his wife in the front row.

Father Mike and Mayor Soto strode forward now to stand before the crowd. Both men welcomed the attendees and explained that the ceremony for Kai and Dakota would be first, performed by the mayor.

Father Mike took a step back beside Reyna and Esteban as Mayor Soto waved the two Indians forward. That was Lance and Ricky's cue to break away from Chris and join them. Lance nervously patted his pocket, suddenly not sure if he had brought Dakota's ring or not. With an exhalation of relief, he felt the satisfying press of metal against his fingers as Ricky shook his head with amusement beside him.

The chief executive of Los Angeles looked out over the enormous crowd and said, "As mayor of Los Angeles, it gives me great pride to have the honor of uniting these two fine young men in marriage. While they were new to our city a scant two years ago, they have proven themselves heroic and brave and invaluable. They have prepared their own vows and will share those with each other now."

He stepped back to give the young men space, and the quiet filling the gardens held an almost otherworldly quality. Lance and Ricky watched, grinning and feeling like foolish little boys, as Kai and Dakota turned to face one another. Lance saw the nervousness on Dakota's face, but the formerly hard, squinty eyes now fixed softly upon the face of his beloved, shutting out the world.

"I never told you this, Laughs A Lot," he began, his voice soft and almost breathless. "But when I was six and first met you, I kept telling my mother, I wanna kiss that boy over there, and she just kept slapping me every time and saying boys didn't kiss other boys."

He smiled then, the memory one he obviously cherished. Kai's own smile grew so wide it filled his whole face.

"I never got the chance to do that till we were eighteen," Dakota went on, his voice filled with passion and love. "And I thought I'd die right there on the spot. Thank you for loving me. Thank you for wanting to spend your life with me. I don't deserve you, but I'm gonna keep you."

That drew a laugh from Kai, and from the spectators.

Now it was Kai's turn. He took Dakota's hand and held it. "I never told you this, either, Cloudy Boy, but after I met you at that first powwow when we were six, I molded you out of clay and kept you in my room like a totem." He laughed – a light, airy laugh of delight. "I wasn't so talented then and you looked like a diseased snowman, but I kissed you every night before I went to sleep. Crazy, huh?" He laughed again happily. "I am so happy that you love me and want to spend your life with me because I can't imagine life without you."

He finished, and Lance watched the two gaze at each other with pure joy. Then, hands still clasped, they turned to Soto, who maintained that beaming smile on his round face. He went through the standard civil ritual and each man firmly declared, "I do," before Lance and Ricky handed them their rings. As each slipped the ornate gold rings onto the other's finger, the mayor pronounced them married and bade them kiss.

Lance's heart jumped for joy as his two friends pressed their lips eagerly together and then separated to a healthy dose of applause, especially from the assembled young knights. Then Kai and Dakota turned to the crowd, beaming broadly, and Lance heard Dakota gasp.

His searching gaze flew out over the crowd, following Dakota's fixed look, and sucked in his own shocked breath. Dakota's mother stood in back of the rows of chairs, staring solemnly and intently up at her newly married son. Lance glanced over at Dakota and saw a look of surprise on his handsome features. Then the moment passed as the couple stepped back, and Lance and Ricky returned to Chris.

Now it was Father Mike's turn to step up. The impish grin was in full force, Lance noted, as the priest flashed it toward him before motioning Reyna and Esteban forward to the center of the arch.

Lance nudged Ricky and nodded toward Esteban. The once hyper-confident, badass gangster looked like he might faint he was so nervous. Yet he looked happier than Lance had ever seen him.

"We are gathered here today," Father Mike, dressed in his finest vestments, began with that slight Irish brogue, "to unite this man and this woman in the bonds of holy matrimony, in the sight of God and each other."

He went through the first part of the standard ceremony just like he'd done with Arthur and Jenny, and then deferred to the young couple before him to exchange their own personal vows.

Esteban went first. He took Reyna's hand in his, paused, exhaled a nervous breath and said, "Reyna, you had me that first night in Griffith Park when you threatened me with an arrow."

Reyna laughed and the crowd joined in.

"I was too tough and hard to admit it," he went on, his deep voice easily carrying out over the crowd. "I never told you this, but almost three years ago when my *carnal* Lance was messing up, I told him I was gonna marry you one day, if you'd have me."

Her eyes went wide and she turned her head to toss a mock glower at Lance for not telling her. Lance grinned and shrugged. Reyna turned back to Esteban, smiling broadly.

"The only girl I couldn't have my way with is the only one I fell in love with, and I'm so happy you agreed to have me. We're too much alike in all the wrong ways, but we're perfect together, and I can't wait till we have kids." He grinned at her shocked expression.

Reyna flashed that pretend glower. "Don't push your luck, mister," she said, to much laughter from the people. "Este, you were easily the most arrogant, egotistical knucklehead I ever met, and also the most drop-dead gorgeous." Again, the attendees chuckled with delight. "Just so you know, you had me the moment you got your ass handed to you by Lance and still agreed to follow him."

Lance laughed even as Esteban turned red. He was still grinning, though. That playfulness, Lance knew, was another reason these two were so perfect together.

Reyna grinned. "I am so happy you *finally* got around to asking me to marry you, and I can't wait to spend my life with you."

Esteban smiled, all nervousness gone, and Reyna returned it. Father Mike resumed the ceremony. Once Arthur had presented each with the ring and both had been slipped onto the appropriate finger, Father Mike said, "I now pronounce you husband and wife." Then to Esteban, who looked frozen with amazement, he added, "You may kiss the bride."

And Esteban did. He grabbed Reyna and pressed his lips so hard against hers, and she did the same right back, that Lance almost turned red from embarrassment, glancing shyly at the grinning Ricky beside him.

Everyone burst into applause as the newly married couple gazed out at the crowd and Reyna blew them a kiss. Then they stepped back along with Father Mike and Mayor Soto once more took center stage beneath the arch. Because of Lance's status as heir to the throne, it had been unanimously decided that his and Ricky's ceremony would be last.

The mayor grinned over at them to join him. Lance looked at Ricky, and Ricky at Lance. They stood frozen in place a moment, locked within each other's eyes.

Then an amused Chris gave them both a shove forward and they laughingly complied, the little one trailing behind.

They stopped before Soto, and acknowledged him with a smile before facing each other.

"Ladies and gentlemen of the world," the man said, his lapel mic easily transmitting his voice throughout the gardens and, via the cameras, across the planet. "It is my distinct honor and privilege to unite these two outstanding young people in marriage. There is nothing that I can say about either of them you don't already know, except that I consider myself proud to be their friend and colleague, and I look forward to many more years working side by side with this amazing couple to improve the lives of children everywhere."

Lance and Ricky's eyes never left each other's, and Lance's heart pounded with excitement, his blood rushing to his head at the realization that finally, for now and always, Ricky would be his.

The mayor invited them to exchange their vows. Both hesitated, and Lance realized they forget to decide who would start.

Ricky laughed and said, "Okay, fool, I'll go first."

Lance grinned and the people laughed.

Ricky took a deep breath and looked so beautiful to Lance that he could scarcely breathe.

"Lance, the second I saw you on YouTube giving that first interview I was in crush city," Ricky said, his voice soft and filled with emotion. "I never imagined I'd ever meet you, let alone be standing here with you today. Yeah, I know I'm stronger and better looking—" Lance chuckled and laughter wafted up from below. "—but you are and always will be the most beautiful boy I ever saw, and from the first time I met you on the streets you *were* the *guardién de mi corazón*. Because I'm a dumbass and you're a dumber ass it took us forever to figure that out." Ricky grinned and waited for the laugher to subside. "But you have my heart, Lance, for now and always."

He smiled and Lance felt weak in the knees. *God this boy was so perfect!* And to think he'd almost let Ricky slip away from him. Shivering at the possibility, Lance took Ricky's hand in his and pressed it up against his wildly beating heart.

"I knew the first time I met you that we were meant to be together," he began breathlessly. "I wasn't sure how back then, but I just knew we were connected. Yes, you are a dumbass and I'm a dumber ass and we almost screwed everything up between us. That's what listening to the wrong people gets you."

A few in the crowd chuckled, and Mayor Soto nodded in agreement.

Lance's eyes grew wide with love as he pressed Ricky's hand more firmly against him. "I don't care what you or anybody says about me, *you* were the most beautiful boy and *are* the most beautiful man I will ever see, and I can't imagine living my life without you. It is true you never could kick my ass in any of our sparring matches—" He grinned as people laughed. "—Until that first time you kissed me in front of the whole world. Then I was down for the count, and still am every time you do. I love you, Ricky, for now and always."

He blew out his famous breathy laugh, and Ricky did the same. Lowering their hands, they kept them clasped together as the mayor stepped up and performed the ceremony. "Do you, Ricky Pendragon, take Lance as your lawful wedded husband, to have and to hold, in sickness and in health, till death do you part?"

"I do," Ricky said without hesitation.

The mayor turned to Lance, who realized he should try to look more dignified for the cameras, but couldn't help the foolishly stupid grin he knew was plastered to his face.

"Do you, Lance Pendragon, take Ricky as your lawful wedded husband, to have and to hold, in sickness and in health, till death do you part?"

"Damn straight I do," Lance said, breaking into a grin that had the desired effect on Ricky because the other man grinned right back.

That line got yet another laugh, even from the mayor.

Then Chris stepped proudly forward with the rings. Ricky eagerly slipped his on Lance's finger and Lance reciprocated with a huge smile and a quick wink Chris's way.

The mayor then officially pronounced them married and said, "You may kiss each other."

And kiss they did. Lance put his hands on each side of Ricky's face and pulled the other man in for a kiss he wished could never end. Ricky's lips felt more perfect than ever, and the blood rushed to every part of him that mattered, filling him with passion and desire and not the slightest sign of a freak-out. Ricky's arms flew around his neck and they pressed together so tightly they might have been one and the same person.

Chris cleared his throat in annoyance. "No making out in front of the little brother, remember?"

That got a huge laugh from everyone and caused Lance and Ricky to bust up with glee, pulling them apart in their laughter. They grinned down at Chris's stern expression and shrugged sheepishly at the little boy's look of mock annoyance.

"Ladies and gentlemen," the mayor intoned in a very serious voice. "Per instructions of the groom, I present to you Mr. and Mr. Dumbass."

Lance whipped his head around to face Ricky at the exact moment Ricky did the same, and both blurted, "You didn't!"

Then they realized they had both given the grinning mayor the same instruction and cracked up again, high-fiving, and taking each other's hand happily.

The three couples stepped forward, each hand in hand, and stood in front of the arch as pictures were snapped, cameras rolled, and the entire crowd rose to its collective feet, applauding and cheering with abandon.

Lance snuck a look at Kai and Dakota and Este and Reyna, and relished the sight of their happiness, even as he squeezed Ricky's hand more intensely and exchanged a look of pure love with the one person he was always meant to be with.

✝✝✝

Official wedding photos were taken in the same spot as those for Arthur and Jenny, and seemed even more endless than before. Chris, in particular, looked ready to scream if the photographer asked him one more time to pose this way or that. Lance and Ricky just stood by and laughed, recalling the same antsyness when their parents had married two years before.

Ricky leaned in to Lance's ear and whispered, "Still wish we'd eloped?"

Lance looked over at him in wonder. "And miss sharing you with the world? Hell no!"

The food serving was under way by the time the newly married couples entered the dining area to great and thunderous applause. With so many tables and so many attendees, and with news cameras following them everywhere for the live broadcast, the couples split up to work various parts of the venue.

Lance and Ricky chose the section with the president and his family. The president stood when the two young men approached. He grinned as the First Lady congratulated them with a huge smile and the kids eyed them with their usual awe.

"Congratulations, Lance," the president said, extending a hand. Lance shook it. "Ricky," the man added, offering his hand to Ricky, who shook it with a big smile. "Your vows were, well, unique."

The boys laughed. "Thanks, Mr. President," Lance said honestly. He knew being present for the wedding of The Boy Who Amended the Constitution would likely boost the president's public image with all but the most die-hard haters, but Lance genuinely felt that he'd touched something in this man, had softened him a little, smoothed out the hard politician's edge he'd noted the first time they'd spoken. He and Ricky chatted a few more moments with the First Family and then excused themselves to make their rounds.

Lance was especially surprised to see Mr. Ryerson seated at a table with several probation staff from Sylmar. Mr. Mansfield warmly embraced Lance and shook Ricky's hand with abandon. Ryerson stood at awkward attention, as always, like he was so detached from his emotions that getting in touch with them was a major challenge. Lance knew that's how Ryerson kept from caring about the clients he represented in court, but he was happy to see he'd touched something human in this man, too. The normally aloof attorney smiled as he shook their hands and congratulated them. As they moved away from the table Lance caught Father Mike's impish grin and realized the chaplain must've been the one to invite that group. He returned the grin and they moved on.

Mr. Mills gave him a huge hug and shook Ricky's hand, introducing his wife. Lance was happy and touched to see this man, a virtual stranger who'd entered his life in a moment of need and stayed around as part of his extended family. He felt blessed, and thanked them for attending.

After nearly an hour of chatting and thanking people, Lance and Ricky finally joined Esteban and Reyna, Kai and Dakota, Arthur and Jenny, Chris and Merlin at the largest table reserved for them. Not a moment too soon, Lance realized, because he was starved. He'd been too nervous to eat breakfast and it was already late afternoon.

Just before sitting, he stepped over to Reyna and gave her a kiss. She looked radiant with joy and beamed at him.

"My baby boy is married," she said with a lyrical laugh. "I can't believe it."

Lance laughed right back. "My badass big sister is married. I can't believe it."

They gazed at one another a moment with a sense of deep love and respect passing between them.

Then Reyna grinned. "You know we're naming our first son 'Lance', right?"

Lance flashed her a look. "You better."

They cracked up and held each other, basking in the love they shared and the bond they'd forged over the years.

A couple of throats cleared loudly behind them, and they separated in surprise. Esteban had a glower pasted to his face. "Trying to steal my wife, *carnal*?"

"Trying to steal my husband, Reyna?" Ricky said right beside him, affecting a mock tone of anger. Then all of them busted up and took their seats for the meal.

Before the food was served, however, Lance and Ricky stood to toast Dakota and Kai. Ricky picked up the wireless mic that had been left on the table for their use and grinned at his Native brothers seated beside him.

"I congratulate Kai for noticing right after he joined the Round Table that I'm much hotter than Lance," he said in a serious tone of voice, drawing a laugh from the crowd and a shove from Lance, "and for making dumber ass jealous because you should see this fool's face when he's jealous."

He pointed to Lance, who playfully shoved him again, and both Indians laughed along with the crowd.

"But seriously, I salute Kai," Ricky continued happily, "on the beginning of his new life with the soul mate who completes him."

He raised his goblet of cider and drank, while everyone in the gardens did the same. Then he handed off the mic to Lance with a grin and sat down.

Lance eyed the Indians with tightness in his chest. These two had come out of the night like shadows into his life, and then lodged themselves in his heart forever. He offered a radiant smile as he put the mic to his lips. "Unlike this fool I married, I'm not going to say something stupid, even though Kai was right and Ricky *is* hotter than me."

He paused as people around them laughed and Ricky nodded vigorously.

"What I do want to say to my brother Dakota is, thank you for being you. You're a great man, a hero." Then he chuckled. "Oh, and thanks for showing Ricky there are guys more emo than me."

That brought on another laugh and Dakota reddened with amused embarrassment.

Lance grinned and raised his goblet. "I'm proud that you're my *carnal*." He took a swig, and everyone else followed suit.

Dakota nodded in gratitude as he and Kai took sips from each other's goblets and grinned like little boys.

Then Lance handed the microphone to Arthur and reseated himself.

Arthur stood and raised his goblet of wine, looking down at Esteban with pride.

"I have been more blessed in this lifetime than in my previous one," he began, his voice strong, yet filled with emotion. "My family is the greatest gift I have ever received, and I count this man and this woman as part of that family. Sir Este has always been a young man of deep passion and commitment, and never a man to be trifled with. But he has learned that the essence of manhood is not fighting or warfare or conquests of any kind, but rather the acceptance of honor and a commitment to principle. Today he has committed himself to Reyna in front of the world, and I know he will never take that commitment for granted." Then he grinned. "If he does, Reyna will kill him."

That got a huge laugh from everyone, Esteban most of all, with Reyna mouthing, "That's true."

Arthur raised his glass. "I salute Sir Este and his lovely bride, Lady Reyna. Long may they thrive."

Everyone throughout the dining area raised a glass in toast and drank.

Now Arthur reached across the table and handed the microphone to Chris before reseating himself beside a beaming Jenny. He took her hand and both awaited their youngest son's tribute to their two older.

Lance watched Chris looking strong and confident and so grown up as he climbed up onto his chair and put the mic to his lips. "Lance and Ricky are the two most amazing big brothers a kid could ever have," he began in his still boyish voice that sailed sweetly out over the crowded gardens like hundreds of butterfly wings flapping in the breeze. "Even when they make out in front of me," he added, drawing laughter and sheepish looks from his brothers.

He looked out at the sea of faces, seemingly studying them for their reactions. "They read to me every night, and we been through lots of books together," Chris went on excitedly. "My favorite is *Peter Pan* cuz I used to imagine myself flying around Neverland and never getting old and never growing up. I think maybe Lance and Ricky didn't wanna grow up either, cuz they were afraid to be in love with each other. I think love scared 'em like it did Peter. And I remember Peter saying 'to die would be an awfully big adventure' cuz he was a kid so long he probably got bored, like I sometimes do in school when my mom talks too much."

That got another big laugh and Jenny looked sheepish this time.

"But Lance did die, twice," Chris went on solemnly. "'Cept it wasn't such a big adventure cuz Ricky wasn't with him. I don't understand it, but they *are* part of the same toy, like my brother John said, and they gotta be together no matter what. And that means they had to grow up to do that. So I wanna grow up, too, and be just like them."

Now he shrugged and grinned. "Sorry, I'm talking too much like Lance always does."

That generated more laughter and Lance tossed his napkin at Chris, who laughed and dodged it. Then Chris turned and looked straight at his two brothers with pure earnestness. "I just wanna tell you guys I love you and to please, please remember the other thing Peter said, but was too scared to do. 'To live would be an awfully big adventure'. So live the adventure and be together for always."

Then he raised his glass of sparkling cider and called out, "Lance and Ricky forever!"

Every glass was raised on high and a loud chorus of "Lance and Ricky forever!" arose and filled the gardens like a roaring tornado.

Chris grinned and leapt down from his chair and faced his newly married brothers. "Did I do good?"

"You did amazing," Lance whispered, his voice tight with emotion, as he grabbed the boy and pulled him into a group hug with Ricky. "Thank you *so* much for being our brother," he added into Chris's ear, to the little one's obvious delight.

By the time everyone had eaten, it was nearly five o'clock and the sun was setting. Glowing lights had come on throughout the gardens and the strings of pearly white Christmas lights added by Reyna gave the entire area a magical, ethereal feeling, almost like being within the enchanted forests of Neverland, Chris commented as he went off to find Harry Styles and his group. It was now time for the traditional first dance.

All three couples had agreed it would be most appropriate for their first dance that One Direction perform "Little Things" as they had for Arthur and Jenny. Somehow the uniformity of it all appealed to the young newlyweds.

As everyone chatted and laughed and enjoyed each other's company, Chris finally appeared up on the stage and tapped the microphone again. Lance glanced over and saw that the arch had been removed and the area around the front of the stage cleared for dancing. Chris called the three couples forward.

Esteban winked at Lance, stood, held out his hand to Reyna and escorted her forward. Lance glanced at Ricky, and then at his Native brothers across the table, and shrugged. He held out a hand to Ricky and Ricky held out one to him and together they pulled each other to their feet, laughing the whole time. Kai and Dakota did the same.

They moved out onto the softly lit dance floor under Chris's watchful eye. When all were in place, Lance looked up at Chris.

"And now, ladies and gentlemen," Chris began, sounding like a circus barker. "All the way from England for your entertainment, we have One Direction performing the first song for these people down here to do, you know, that first dancing thing like my Mom and Dad did." He started to turn away, and then remembered. "Oh, and they're gonna dance to 'Little Things.' Don't know why, but hey, it's their wedding."

Lance's mouth dropped open and Chris grinned mischievously as he handed the mic back to Sir Khom and exited the stage.

Harry and the boys stepped out onto the stage, but this time they each carried little stools and sat on one. Harry made eye contact with Lance and winked. Then the music started, and they began to sing.

Lance and Ricky, Kai and Dakota stood a moment to allow Esteban and Reyna to go first. Esteban placed one hand on Reyna's waist and took her hand in his other and with a grin of pure joy began sweeping her around to the almost mournful strains of the heartfelt ballad.

Kai looked at Dakota and Lance at Ricky. Lance saw from the corner of his eye the two Indians place hands on each other's waist and begin dancing. But his focus was Ricky alone. He placed his hands gently at Ricky's waist, and Ricky wrapped his arms around Lance's neck, and they began to move, the lyrics filling them with the meaning of this day and all the days to come.

Lance rested his forehead against Ricky's and the world fell away. They swayed and moved. Their lips came together and they kissed. And nothing else mattered. No one else was even there. Just him and Ricky and this moment of perfect synchronicity.

It seemed like the song went on forever, but in truth it lasted only a few minutes. He suddenly became aware that no music was playing, and forced his eyes away from Ricky's. The other dancers stood watching them with huge smiles on their faces, Esteban's grin the largest of all. Lance blew out his breathy laugh, and Ricky did the same.

Then it was time for the parents to join in as Harry and his boys began another of their slow songs. Esteban's mom moved forward to dance with him and Reyna's dad took her in his arms. With great agility, the man moved his daughter lightly around the floor, while Esteban lovingly held onto his mother and they swayed gently to the music. Reyna's mom stood to the side awaiting her turn with her new son-in-law.

Lance nudged Ricky as Kai's mother approached, Dakota's mother in tow. Dezba smiled like she usually did, but Dakota's mother looked like she might bite someone's head off, like *she* usually did. Dakota nervously looked at his mother, forcing himself to make eye contact. She nodded before Dezba went straight to Dakota, and directed Dakota's mom to Kai, and then they began to dance.

By this time, Jenny was there, looking magnificent and gleefully happy as she gazed at her two grown sons in amazement. "So which of my sons do I dance with first?"

Lance waved a hand toward Ricky. "You may have my husband, fair lady."

Jenny laughed and reached for Ricky. He grinned at Lance as she swept him out onto the floor while Lance stood to one side with Chris. Before he knew what was happening, Harry was there, dragging him out to the dance floor and spinning him around. Lance laughed and gave him a quizzical look as they moved to the music, Harry's hands on his hips.

"You don't expect me not to dance with the most famous groom in the world, do you?"

Lance laughed again. "You're crazy, Harry."

"Course I am, mate," he said with a wink.

After a few minutes, Jenny tapped Harry on the shoulder and the Brit turned and handed off Lance to his mother, simultaneously grabbing Ricky's hand and spinning him into a tight embrace, causing both of them to crack up.

As Lance danced with Jenny he looked into her eyes and saw dampness there. "You okay, Mom?"

She smiled. "Yeah. I just can't believe you boys are grown up and married."

Lance smiled back. "Don't worry, Mom. We're not going anywhere."

That drew from her an even brighter smile, and their dance continued. Something caught Lance's eye and he nudged his mother to look. They turned sideways in time to see Dezba pull her own son into the dance and pass Dakota off to his mother. At first mother and son stood frozen, gazing at one another uncertainly.

"Thanks for coming," Dakota whispered cautiously.

Dakota's mother did something Lance thought was impossible. She smiled. A small smile anyway, and then she reached for her son. He took her in his arms and without another word they began to dance.

Jenny smiled. "That's progress."

Lance grinned. "Yup. One step at a time."

After the song ended, the bridesmaids and groomsmen joined them for the next dance, and the floor opened up to any of the attendees who wished to join the wedding party. The president and the First Lady joined in for several dances, as did Mayor Soto and his wife.

True to his goofy nature, Harry grabbed Chris and spun him around the dance floor before handing him off to Reyna who wanted to dance with "My favorite little man in the world."

Lance and Ricky were vaguely aware of these developments, but would only notice them while watching the playback of the ceremony in the days that followed. That's because they could seldom see past each other. Most of the songs were slow songs, at Lance's insistence, because he wanted to dance every single one with the keeper of his heart.

Of course Reyna insisted on everyone doing "The Cha Cha Slide," and Lance cracked up at the sight of the president and his family goofing it up to the crazy antics of the song. Harry and the boys joined in, and Lance also spotted Father Mike, Merlin, and even Ryan yucking it up to the dance and laughing all the way.

If only life could always be this way, he thought as he flapped his arms and waved his hands and did all the other nutty things the song commanded. At times like this nobody was left or right or hateful or evil or greedy or selfish or black or white or brown or gay or straight. *At times like this*, he mused, *with everyone just having fun, we're all exactly what God had in mind when he made us - human.*

Finally, Chris got back on the microphone and announced that it was time for cake. The dance floor cleared as three enormous multitiered wedding cakes were rolled out to "Oohs" and "Aahs" from the crowd. Reyna and Esteban's had been decorated with the traditional bride and groom at the top, but the groom held a sword and the bride wore a bow and quiver of arrows over one shoulder. The cake for Kai and Dakota was decorated with native colors that matched their traditional regalia, and was adorned with horses, bows, and arrows.

But it was the third cake, the one for Lance and Ricky that caused the biggest stir. Unbeknownst to either man, Chris had arranged this cake himself. It was three layers, all connected and taller than the other two and shaped like a gigantic stone, only the frosting was rainbow colored and decorated with swords and shields made out of chocolate. Excalibur protruded from the top of the cake, its hilt sticking up with eight inches of its blade visible. Chris had asked Arthur to get a plastic sheath made that would fit inside the cake and house the sword.

It was Chris who gleefully made the announcement that inadvertently signaled the beginning of the end.

"Cuz Lance and Ricky are a team now," Chris said, looking at his two brothers who stood gaping at the sword in the cake, "they have to pull Excalibur from the stone at the same time. That was my idea."

He grinned broadly and everyone clapped and some called out "Speech! Speech!"

Waiters had placed two chairs in front of the cake for Lance and Ricky to stand on. Grinning at each other, they clambered up onto the chairs and stood gazing down at Excalibur glimmering in the mood lighting overhead. Lance felt a chill ripple through him at the sight, but he didn't know why.

Chris began clapping and echoing those in the crowd, "Speech, speech!" and handed the mic up to Ricky.

That shook off Lance's mood and he smiled shyly at Ricky. Standing atop these chairs making them so visible, he suddenly felt more vulnerable than when they'd been on the ground. He nudged Ricky. "Go ahead, fool."

Ricky nudged him right back and looked out over the crowd. Then he sighed and cast a sidelong look at Lance. "I'm just glad Chris didn't use that other famous line from Peter Pan."

That threw Lance off guard. "What line?"

Ricky smirked something fierce. "I do believe in fairies, I do, I do."

Lance's mouth dropped open and he stared aghast at Ricky, appalled and amused at the same time. Ricky smirked all the more.

The crowd roared with laughter.

"I can't believe you just said that, fool!" Lance said with mock annoyance. Then he pulled the mic toward him and said to the crowd, "Does anyone know if it's against the rules to kick a guy's ass on his wedding day?"

"No, it's not!" many women shouted, and there was another wave of laugher.

Ricky pulled his hand back with a laugh. Then he turned to the crowd. "This *is* a fairy tale, though, for real. I mean, isn't it always when soul mates find each other? And this fool is for now and always my soul mate, and I don't even mind getting old like Merlin so long as I have Lance with me. Oh, and so long as I never like country music." The crowd laughed and Lance saw Arthur nudge Merlin in the ribs. But Merlin seemed lost in thought, and Lance wasn't sure he'd even heard the joke. Then Ricky thrust the mic into his hands, and he had to pause a moment to collect his thoughts.

"I know this sounds crazy," Lance finally said as the words came to him, "but once upon a time I thought the best moment of my life was right before I died." Then he quickly added, "The first time," which engendered laugher, and a grin from Ricky.

"The reason was cuz Jack and my Dad both told me they loved me, and nobody ever did that before." He paused a moment to take another breath. "Then I thought the best moment of my life was the first time Ricky kissed me. I thought I'd melt away I was so happy. But now I think *this* is the best moment of my life, today, when Ricky said he'd be mine forever."

He hesitated, trying to gather his thoughts and say them the best way he could. "I guess what I'm trying to say is what Chris was saying before. To live is an awfully big adventure and there are always 'best' moments. Those moments I mentioned were the best of my life when they happened, at least until the *next* best moment. And now that I'm grown up and have this fool beside me, I know the best is yet to be."

He handed Chris the microphone to the accompaniment of cheers and applause. Then it was time to pull Excalibur from the cake.

While everyone watched expectantly, the young men each lifted a hand and wrapped it around the fabled hilt. Lance hesitated a split second, but no tingly vibrations or warmth shot up his arm this time. With big grins for the cameras and the wedding photographer, and with great dramatic flair, they slid Excalibur from its plastic sheath and raised the shimmering blade high above their heads in gleeful triumph.

That was when the sword began to glow, and Lance along with it.

The crowd gasped and the sudden warmth startled Ricky, forcing him to pull his hand away like he'd been shocked.

Lance felt the now familiar heat and tingling and gazed upward in fear at the blade glowing a bluish green, and his arm glowing along with it. Terror clamping on to his heart, Lance whipped his head around and found his father below in the crowd. Their eyes met, and Arthur's looked wide and filled with so much sadness Lance began to tremble.

Arthur broke eye contact and turned quickly to Merlin, who looked upward at the glowing sword and the young man wielding it with glazed resignation in his gray eyes. He turned to Arthur and, in a voice devoid of inflection, yet somehow sad all the same, said, "It is time, Arthur."

Jenny gasped as she looked from her husband to her son holding the glowing sword aloft.

Ricky looked in bewilderment from Lance to Arthur to Merlin and back to Lance as the nascent young king slowly lowered the sword and the glow began to fade, absorbing itself into him this time, rather than vanishing into the metal as it had done before. Ricky saw tears welling in Lance's eyes and instantly reached for him.

"Lance, what's wrong?"

Lance fixed his blurry green eyes on the man he loved and whispered the words he'd prayed he'd never have to say, "Dad's leaving."

Ricky's mouth dropped open in shock, his own eyes burning with impending tears as he whipped his head around to look down at his father.

Jenny clutched at Arthur's arm, fearful he might vanish from her sight if she didn't. But Arthur's gaze met those of his sons, and Ricky saw the truth of Lance's words painted clearly across the stricken features of the man.

Suddenly Lance thrust Excalibur into Ricky's hands and leapt from the chair, pelting frantically through the crowd toward the hotel entrance.

"Lance!" called Ricky, his heart pounding with dread.

He jumped to the ground and made to follow, but Arthur held out an arm to stop him.

The crowd was milling and murmuring in confusion. Only those closest to the cake had heard Lance's words, but everyone saw the young man run away and knew something was wrong. Ryan was at Arthur's side within moments as the king held Jenny close and looked into Ricky's eyes. Chris ran forward, his soft blue eyes swimming pools of tearful sadness.

"Is it true, Dad?" Ricky asked, terrified of the answer.

The pain in his voice pierced Arthur to the heart, and he sighed heavily, unable to speak.

"What's going on, Arthur?" Ryan asked anxiously. "What's wrong with Lance?"

Arthur met Ryan's eyes a moment and patted the man on one shoulder. Then he ushered Merlin over as Reyna and Esteban, Kai and Dakota surrounded Ricky and Chris and looked fearfully at the king.

The wizard, dressed in his formal tunic, stepped to Arthur's side.

"When, Merlin?" the king asked.

Merlin looked solemn. "Midnight."

Jenny gasped again and tears forced their way out.

Ricky put a frantic hand on Arthur's arm. "Dad, what's going on? Tell me!"

Arthur moved his gaze from Ricky to Chris and then to Jenny. "Jenny, I must speak with Lance alone. Please explain to Ricky and Chris and then bring them to me in the throne room. Give us twenty minutes."

She nodded, but seemed so devastated Arthur could scarcely look into her tearful blue eyes. He turned to Merlin. "Merlin, explain to the people here, and I shall return shortly to address them."

The wizard's expression of anguish was clearly readable to Ricky, who stood before the two men with terror gripping his soul.

"Dad, is what Lance said true?" he asked breathlessly, clutching Chris's hand in his. "Are you leaving?"

Arthur met his son's fearful eyes for a moment before looking away. "Your mother will explain."

He reached for Excalibur, and Ricky silently handed the sword over, his hand shaking as he did so. Then without another word, Arthur turned and hurried through the murmuring, confused, and uncertain crowd into the hotel.

Ricky's eyes welled up with tears and he pulled Chris into him like he never wanted to let go. He looked into his mother's eyes and saw the answer to his question. Then, despite being a man who wasn't supposed to cry anymore, Ricky did just that.

†††

Lance huddled in Arthur's throne struggling not to cry, and losing the battle. He sat with his legs pulled up and his arms tightly wrapped around him, head buried in his lap – the same closed-in posture he used to assume as a boy when life came crashing down on him with all its invisible, but ponderous weight.

He'd failed after all. He'd failed Arthur and that's why the king was leaving. He'd failed.

He heard the door to the Throne Room open, but didn't look up even as heavy footfalls approached. He couldn't face his father now. Not when he was such a failure that Arthur had to leave….

"Lance."

Arthur's voice was soft in his ears, not harsh or angry. But then, Arthur never got angry, just disappointed. Lance didn't look up. He couldn't.

"Lance, look at me," he heard Arthur say firmly, but still with that gentleness that always spurred people to action.

Lance pulled his head from under his arms and gazed tearfully up at this man who had been everything to him. All his old fears, all his old childhood insecurities instantly rose up and smothered him. His face collapsed into utter despair. "What did I do wrong, Dad?" he blurted desperately. "Tell me and I'll fix it. I promise! You don't have to go. I'll make it right!"

Arthur's face dissolved into a look of stunned horror. "You have done nothing wrong, Lance. You've done everything right. It's...."

Lance saw him trail off helplessly, struggling for the right words, and his greatest fear reared its head again. "Is it because...?" He almost couldn't say it. "Because I'm not *really* your son after all?" He held his breath.

Arthur looked appalled, and his face filled with love. "You *are* my son, Lance, for now and always." He paused a moment, and Lance could clearly see how hard this was for him. "It may not please your mother or your brothers to hear this, Lance, but there is no one, has never been anyone, and never will be anyone I shall love as much as I love you."

The dreaded burning sensation instantly filled the backs of his eyes, and Lance fought desperately to keep more tears at bay. He saw a tear work its way from Arthur's eye and realized that men did cry after all. "Then why?"

The tear made its slow journey down Arthur's cheek to lodge in his beard. "Alas, Lance, my destiny has never been mine to choose, in either of my lifetimes. Some of us are called upon to serve the greater good, and some of us volunteer to serve it, like you. Avalon is a place beyond time and space, and even Merlin knows not its origin. I am at its beck and call to serve mankind as needed, but when Avalon bids me return that means I have succeeded in my mission. It also means I have no choice."

Lance felt frantic, desperately searching his mind for any argument to keep his father with them. He leapt from the throne and pointed at Excalibur. "But Dad, you're still the king. We need you here."

Arthur shook his head, sadness and pride fighting for control of his expression. "You are king now, Lance." He held the sword out, but Lance backed away, shaking his head. "Take it, son."

Lance found his eyes fixed on Excalibur. "No, Dad, that was just when you were in a coma, just for rescuing Chris."

Arthur shook his head. "You've been king from the moment you pulled Excalibur from that stone in Las Vegas."

Lance remained silent, green eyes locked fiercely on the brown of his father's.

"But you already knew that, didn't you, son?" Arthur said quietly.

Lance didn't break eye contact, but he also didn't respond. He *had* known, known it from the moment he'd touched the hilt and felt that powerful tingle run up his arm and straight into his heart.

He nodded, suddenly realizing something else. "You knew it, too, didn't you, when we were attacked in that field?" he said almost without breath. "When you sent me back for Excalibur. You *knew* it wouldn't protect you."

"But I knew it would protect *you*."

And Lance knew for certain the truth of his father's declaration. He *had* felt bullets kick up all around him that day, but none had struck him. Just like in Edwin's compound. He *was* the king.

"But I don't need to be king, Dad," he blurted suddenly, breathlessly, hopefully.

Arthur gazed at him with admiration. "The king doesn't choose Excalibur, Lance. Excalibur chooses the king. And she has chosen you."

Once again feeling the weight of immense responsibility settle upon his shoulders, Lance reached forth with trembling arms and took the sword in his hands, gazing at his father through blurred vision.

"But Dad, what will I do without you? Everything I am, everything I've done is because of you."

Arthur placed both hands lovingly on his son's shoulders, and smiled with more pride in his eyes than Lance had ever seen. "Everything you are, Lance, you were from the moment I met you. I merely helped you realize that."

Lance's breath stopped, the tears trickling down his face unheeded.

At that moment, the Throne Room doors burst open and in pelted Ricky and Chris, who bounded to Arthur's side, their devastated expressions only increasing Lance's pain.

Jenny entered behind them and closed the double doors before silently joining them. The spring in her step had vanished. The joy of seeing her boys married and about to begin a new life together was gone, replaced by the pain of losing the man she loved.

Chris threw himself at Arthur and enveloped the man's waist in a sobbing embrace.

Ricky reached for Lance's free hand and Lance gladly offered it, pulling his beloved in and wrapping an arm around him as the family gazed in agonizing silence at the man who had given them everything. For once, Arthur looked like he didn't know what to say. He looked broken and defeated, exactly how Lance felt.

Heart hammering, Lance asked the question he most feared the answer to, "Will I ever see you again?"

Arthur and Jenny exchanged a look, and then the king turned back to his son. "Should a great need arise, Lance, should you be threatened or face mortal danger that could topple New Camelot, Excalibur will awaken me, and Merlin and I shall return."

The king must've seen the hope dancing in those pools of green because he cautioned, "As much as I would give anything to be with you again, and your brothers and your mother, I do not wish for such a calamity to befall you, for it could prove fatal."

Lance nodded sadly, glancing at Ricky. Ricky's eyes reflected the same sting of losing the father both of them had shared all too briefly.

Arthur looked around at each of them now, taking in their faces, searing them into his memory for eternity. "I love you all so much there are no words to express it. And I am forever proud of you. This world is a far better place because you made it so. Especially you, Lance. Even should I never have occasion to return, I know I have left the world in good hands."

His words didn't comfort Lance, who felt as bereft and lost as he'd ever been as a child on the streets. He released Ricky's hand and both young men joined Chris and Jenny in hugging their father, and Arthur gripped them all like a man on a precipice, holding on for dear life. The family remained thus for a time before silently and sadly returning to the gardens so Arthur could address his knights, and the world, for the last time.

✝✝✝

Arthur held Jenny's hand as they emerged from the hotel into the gardens. A phalanx of reporters and commentators instantly began throwing out questions about his departure. Lance followed just behind, his eyes lowered to the pathway, one hand holding Ricky's and the other gripping Excalibur, while Ricky held Chris's hand. It was obvious from the questions that Merlin had announced the king's imminent parting.

The crowd fell silent, the previous jovial wedding mood having turned funereal. And to Lance this *was* a funeral, the worst ever.

Esteban, Reyna, Kai, Dakota, Merlin, and Ryan were already up on the outdoor stage where they had been obviously speaking to the people, maybe even answering questions. Lance couldn't tell from their shell-shocked expressions. He still felt like he'd been punched in the gut and all the air had been pushed from his lungs, so he suspected the others felt the same way.

Arthur had made all of this happen. How could they go on without him?

The reporters ceased calling out questions because Arthur ignored them. He stepped up onto the stage and the family followed. Reyna released Esteban's hand and rushed at Lance. He saw she'd been crying and her makeup had smeared. As she engulfed him in a hug, he flashed back to that night he'd saved his Dad's life and he'd seen Reyna cry for the first time. Now she just held him in a loving embrace.

Esteban approached Ricky and Chris, his own face damp with tears he obviously hadn't been able to fight. He grabbed Chris and lifted the boy up, holding him against him with one arm while gripping Ricky's shoulder with the other.

Kai and Dakota stood in a stunned silence, watching the grieving family and feeling lost. They'd never been a real part of anything, and Arthur had treated them like they were his own, and now he was leaving, maybe never to return. The joy of their wedding faded into such bittersweet sadness that neither man could do anything but hold each other close.

Arthur met Ryan's gaze and saw the same grief he'd seen the night Lance had seemingly died. He tried to offer a hopeful smile, but knew it probably looked like a frown. Hope though he might, Arthur knew his chances of ever seeing his family and friends again were slight.

Merlin stood with the microphone in hand and looked at Arthur with genuine loss in those steely gray eyes. Arthur understood. Despite his natural reticence and reluctance to allow closeness to others, Merlin loved these kids and this era and was loath to leave.

Arthur took the proffered microphone, and realized his hand was trembling. He exchanged a look with Jenny before turning to the vast crowd spreading outward beneath the peaceful lighting of the gardens. He saw Justin crying, being held by Bridget in a comforting embrace. He eyed the devastated Mayor Soto and realized he needed to speak with the man before his departure. He hoped the mayor would continue as an advisor and friend to Lance and New Camelot, feeling certain he would.

He spotted Sam McMullen in the throng, also looking shocked and grief-stricken. Even the president and his family appeared genuinely sad. But it was his knights he sought out, both young and now grown. These were his children, his Round Table. These were the ones who had taken his lead and run with it, who were still in the long-term process of transforming this society into something better. He needed them to continue. He needed them to follow Lance as they had followed him. He needed to inspire them more at this moment than ever before, because he'd not get another opportunity.

He gazed out over the vast sea of stunned, yet expectant faces. "I address these final words to the people of the world. My all-too-brief sojourn in your era has been, as my son would say, amazing. Humanity has become equally inventive and wasteful, and I pray you all will continue the work we have begun here in America. Children are our most precious resource, not something to be squandered, or worse yet, mistreated. And that means all children, no matter their color or their upbringing or status in life or whether they fall in love with girls or boys."

He paused a moment, his voice fighting for the strength he knew people expected from him. But this was difficult, more difficult than any other moment in either of his lifetimes. "Cherish the children. All of the children. For they are the hope."

He paused again, once more scanning the crowd and making eye contact with his hundreds of knights. Most of them wore a look of devastation on their shadowy faces, as though the end of the world was at hand.

"My noble and blessed knights," he said, projecting in his voice all the love and pride he could muster. "You are beyond pearls of great price. You are exceptional human beings, and I have never been so honored to lead anyone as I have been to lead you. Most of you came from nothing, thought you *were* nothing, yet you have accomplished more in four years than most do in a lifetime. I'm humbled by your greatness."

Normally such a compliment would have engendered a rousing cheer, but this time there was just scattered applause wafting up through the darkness.

"Life is about change," Arthur went on wistfully. "Alas, as much as we would wish things to remain as they are forever, such is never possible. But change is good, for it keeps us fresh. As my son Chris said earlier, to live would be an awfully big adventure. And live you all must. Continue to serve New Camelot and your communities. Continue to grow as leaders. Teach the precepts of chivalry to your siblings and your own children not yet born. New Camelot will thrive and grow so long as *you* keep it alive."

This time a cheer arose from the youth, a cheer tinged with sorrow. Arthur turned to Lance, who stood beside Ricky staring at him with wide-eyed abandon, and ushered him forward.

Still clad in the crown and cloak, Excalibur clutched in one hand, the young man stepped to his father's side. They made eye contact, and Arthur smiled. Lance did not.

Arthur turned back to the crowd. "You are not losing a king," he said with deep fervor, "but gaining one. Lance has been king from the moment Excalibur chose him back in Las Vegas."

That started a spate of excited murmuring and low chattering amongst the adults and the young people.

"With all due respect to my other sons and to all of you, Lance was the most extraordinary boy I ever encountered, and he has become the most extraordinary man I will ever know," Arthur said firmly, one hand resting on Lance's shoulder. "He is your king now. Follow him as you have me. And remember that wherever I am, you all will never be far from my thoughts and dreams. I shall hold you in my heart forever. I give you your king."

He stepped back before Lance could say or do anything as the crowd burst into loud and increasingly thunderous applause. Behind them, Reyna and the others began to clap vigorously and with great passion. Lance gingerly took the microphone from his father and gazed out at the clapping people, some young, some old, some child and some adult. He scanned the faces of the knights within his field of vision and saw something the surprised him – support. They believed in him. Even with his dad leaving, they believed in him, that he could lead the way forward. The realization stuck in his throat and nearly rendered him speechless.

Finally, the clapping died down. "I honestly don't know how I'm going to go on without this man who took me in, who taught me everything, who loved me when no one else ever had before." He began, fighting the emotions welling up and threatening to overcome him. "I was a screwed up kid, but he believed in me before I ever believed in myself. I know I can't be my father for you because he's irreplaceable. But I can be the man he raised me to be." Then he blew out his nervous, breathy laugh. "But I'm new at being a man, and I'm gonna need help. I have Ricky and my family, but I need all of you, too. Let me know if I do something stupid, which will probably be, like, every day."

A few laughs floated up out of the shadowy darkness.

"I need all of you to help me be a good man because we still have a lot of work to do. Sure, we got the bill of rights passed, but do you really think that means people will stop abusing kids? You know it won't. So New Camelot isn't going anywhere. It will always be a safe haven for you and any kids who need it. We're gonna keep fighting to make sure things get better, not worse."

He paused a moment to force back the tears. "My father has been everything to me. He started this crusade, but I'm gonna finish it. He may be leaving, but Ricky and me and Chris and Reyna and Este and Kai and Dakota and all of you, we're not going anywhere." He recalled Mark's soft, gentle features and piercing blue eyes, and the memory brought a wistful smile to his lips. "We're like the Avengers, a team, and we've only just begun. Like Mark once said, it's gonna be epic!"

He thrust Excalibur high into the air in triumph, and the knights in the crowd erupted with excited, youthful fervor, clapping and cheering and chanting. "Long live Lance! Long live the king! Long live Lance! Long live the king!"

Despite his best efforts, the emotions of the day and the tumultuous support he was receiving yanked yet another tear from Lance's eye and he allowed it to roll unheeded down his cheek. He may be a man and he may be king, but first and foremost he was human. And humans cried.

He glanced over at Arthur, clutching Jenny and Chris to him and smiling with pride. Then he caught Ricky's eye. The most amazing man in the world gazed at him with pure love, and Lance's heart melted anew. Excalibur still held aloft in his right hand, he extended his left and felt complete the second Ricky's hand took it. He pulled the man in, smiled sadly, and then thrust their clasped hands on high to join Excalibur in reaching for the heavens.

The crowd went even wilder at the sight, and the chanting continued. Ricky's hand in his made the pain bearable, and his soul surged with the prospect of a bright future, despite the darkness currently descending. He didn't know if he could be half the leader his father was, but he knew with Ricky beside him he could do anything.

✝✝✝

Despite the pall that had initially settled over the proceedings, Arthur insisted that the wedding celebration continue with the cake cutting. Lance's heart wasn't in it and he could see the other couples merely going through the motions, as well, but as the cakes were cut and distributed, Arthur and Jenny stood beside the double doors into New Camelot. He had announced his intent to shake the hand of every guest, and, most especially, every knight in attendance, as the festivities began to break up and people took their leave.

True to his word, as always, the former king did precisely that. He thanked those who thanked him and praised each and every knight whose hand he shook, while Lance did the same where the cake was being distributed. He felt heartened by words of support from Mayor Soto, who vowed to continue his assistance to New Camelot, from the president and his family before Secret Service escorted them from the premises, even from Harry Styles and his mates, who promised to keep in touch and visit any time they were in town.

Lance would later think back on this part of the evening as "the long good-bye" because it took hours for everyone to pay his or her respects to him and to Arthur before heading home. Prior to his departure, Father Mike hugged Lance and vowed to continue working alongside him for social justice, which made Lance happy. He'd need the man's spiritual strength now more than ever.

Reyna's parents, Esteban, Kai, and Dakota's mothers were the last to leave. Lance overheard Kai's mother inviting the newly married couple to live on the reservation, but they declined. Lance felt good hearing them affirm their love and dedication to him and New Camelot and their desire to remain. Reyna and Esteban also planned to live at New Camelot and continue the work Arthur had begun. Now that the Church of Kabbalogy was gone, the entire facility could become the safe haven for kids Lance had always envisioned it to be.

So by ten o'clock, only the family, the newlyweds and Ryan remained. They quietly began assembling within the Throne Room after changing out of their formal attire. It was nearly ten thirty by the time everyone but Lance and Ricky had gathered, and a solemn pall settled over the room as the clock ticked inexorably toward its midnight deadline. Merlin explained that Avalon would appear wherever he and Arthur were assembled, in this case, likely beyond the double doors normally leading into the main hallway.

Lance and Ricky changed in their own rooms because their clothes hadn't yet been moved to the penthouse suite on the seventh floor that would become their new home. Lance laid Excalibur gently atop his bed. There had been no more glowing, no more tingling. Somehow, he knew, that last pulling of the sword from the cake, with Ricky's hand on his, signified the sword's final endorsement of him as king.

With a heavy heart, he removed the crown that had once belonged to Arthur and was now his, recalling Merlin's words that day in the chapel, "Uneasy lies the head that wears the crown." Appropriate words, he thought with a heavy sigh, as he placed the crown atop his dresser, for he felt uneasy in his new role. Then his eye caught sight of the picture stuck into the corner of the mirror, that favorite one of him and Ricky yucking it up on the roof. He looked so young and boyish, and Ricky looked so magnificently beautiful that Lance grew warm with love just looking at it.

Such a long way he'd come on the road to manhood.

Will it be this hard for Chris, he wondered? *Not if I can help it.*

He knew the teenage years were going to be harder for Chris with Arthur gone, and he determined to fill that void as best he could. He and Ricky both. Chris would always be loved and nurtured, and Lance would never put his wants or even his needs above those of Chris. Never. Otherwise, everything they fought for and championed would be for naught, and he'd become something he detested – a hypocrite.

A cleared throat drew his eye to the connecting door and a rush of blood pounded through him. Ricky stood there wearing workout shorts, skate shoes, and holding his Team Lance shirt in one hand. Lance's eye took in the sight of Ricky's perfect torso, the curves and ridges of his defined muscles, and his heart rate quickened. Ricky smiled, and Lance nearly dropped the photo and collapsed. But it was a sad smile, and it pulled him back into the moment, to what was about to happen, and his own sadness returned in force.

"C'mon, Lance," Ricky said, his voice edged with urgency as he slipped into his shirt. "We don't have much time left with Dad."

That jolted Lance out of his musings and he quickly began shedding his clothes under the watchful eye of the man he'd married.

Five minutes later, with Lance wearing his Team Ricky shirt and matching workout shorts and skate shoes, they joined the family in the Throne Room for their final moments with the man they cherished.

They found everyone seated on the floor, and quickly joined them. Arthur sat with Jenny to one side, but had left an empty space for Lance and Ricky. Lance scooted in beside his father and brought his legs up and crossed them, while Ricky did the same. Just being this close to Arthur, touching the man arm to arm made Lance feel strong and safe, like it had when he was a boy.

Arthur informed him that Ryan would be moving into New Camelot to take up permanent residence and help run the operation.

"I gotta keep an eye on my godson, right?" Ryan said with a nod toward Lance.

Lance knew his godfather was trying for a cheerful tone, but the downcast look only deepened his depression. "Thanks, *nino*. That'll be great." And it would be, too, under regular circumstances. But with his dad gone, would anything be great around there ever again?

There was some attempt at small talk, mainly by Arthur, but the mood was somber, and everyone looked like they'd just come from a funeral, rather than a wedding.

Then a thought occurred to Lance. "What will happen to Llamrei, Dad?"

"She will remain, as will all of the weapons and clothing Merlin brought here for the crusade," Arthur answered. Then his gaze travelled to Kai and Dakota, sitting side-by-side holding hands. "I had hoped perhaps Sir Dakota might keep Llamrei as his own."

Dakota looked up from beneath his sheltering hair and flicked it back to gaze wide-eyed at the man. "I could have her?"

Arthur nodded. "She seems to have taken quite a liking to you. While I know Lance cares for her, I have seen that you love her."

Dakota sat up straighter and glanced over at Kai, who nodded vigorously. "It will be my honor, Arthur," he answered. "She'll be well cared for."

Arthur smiled. "Of that I've no doubt."

Everyone fell silent again. Jenny clutched Arthur's hand firmly and Chris sat huddled up against Ricky with his head bowed in despondency.

Reyna sat with her head resting against Esteban's chest, his arm encircling her and pulling her in close. Both looked morose. Ricky lay up against Lance, while Lance had his head resting against Arthur's shoulder.

Arthur eyed Merlin, but the wizard merely shrugged, obviously unable to provide any assistance. Arthur finally cleared his throat and said, "Reyna, why not tell Dakota and Kai about the first gathering you attended within the storm drains?"

She lifted her head from Esteban's shoulder, and when Arthur smiled warmly and gestured to the Indians she sat up and proceeded to tell the story. Some of it they knew because of their little show in Vegas, but not all the details. Despite their melancholia, they smiled, and even Lance grinned slightly at the recollection.

Then Lance said to her, "Remember how you blew me that kiss right before I fought Este and how pissed off he got?"

She grinned and nudged her husband.

"I did not," Esteban protested, but her look coupled with the one Lance shot his way caught him up short. "Okay, I was jealous as hell."

That drew a laugh from Ricky. "Of Lance?"

Esteban nodded. "Hell, yeah. Pretty boy like him, I thought she was into him and not me."

Now Lance laughed. "Yeah, right. Reyna scared the crap outta me."

Now Reyna looked surprised. "I did?"

Lance nodded. "Hell, yeah."

That got a chuckle from the entire group.

Then Chris lifted his head. "I think my favorite was when Lance and Dad were running from the cops on Llamrei," he said with rising excitement. "I saw it on YouTube and it was so cool."

Lance glanced over shyly at his dad. "Yeah, and Dad wanted to jump the L.A. river."

Now Jenny turned to Arthur, aghast. "You didn't?"

Arthur grinned sheepishly. "Alas, I did not know how great a span it was."

"So he jumped her over cop cars instead," Lance added, elbowing Arthur and laughing.

And then they were all laughing, recounting story after story of their adventures over the years, including those on their travels across the country. The mirth even infected Merlin who recalled aloud how appalled Lance and Ricky had been by his country music. "They said to me, Arthur, 'that is so wrong.'"

Arthur busted up and Ricky called out, "It was!" And that sent Lance pitching over on the floor, holding his stomach from laughing so hard.

Then a giggling Reyna said to Lance as he righted himself, "Did you ever tell your parents what I said to make you relax before your big speech to congress?"

Lance blanched. "No, and don't you dare!"

"Reyna!" Ricky said pleadingly.

"Tell us, Reyna," Jenny said with a big smile.

"They were kissing, *as usual*, in the senate parking garage!" the girl began in mock disapproval. "So I told them to break it up because I promised you guys neither of them would get pregnant on that trip."

Lance and Ricky turned beet red as Kai and Dakota busted up at the memory and Jenny's mouth dropped open. "You didn't?"

Reyna nodded, and Arthur laughed, nudging Lance with his elbow.

Esteban smirked at Lance. "Well, it worked, right, *carnal*? No bun in the oven for either one."

Humiliated, Lance slipped off his shoe and tossed it at the laughing Esteban, who tossed it right back.

Story after story flew back and forth, each of them trying to one up the other by recalling something humorous. Even Ryan got into the act, recounting the chewing out he'd gotten from Chief Murphy for letting Arthur and Lance slip through his fingers at Round Table Pizza.

The despondency had lifted as the extended family recalled their precious and humorous moments together, those moments that had united them and provided memories that would endure forever.

But then, all too soon, it was eleven forty and Arthur reluctantly stood to say his final goodbyes. Merlin rose stiffly and stood just behind the former king. The mood shifted on a dime and the reality of impending doom closed over everyone as they rose to their feet and shuffled uncertainly.

They all lined up before the man who had led them to such heights of success and achievement, the man who had loved and believed in them when no one else had, the man none of them could ever forget.

Lance mournfully watched the father he adored move first to Kai and Dakota, who stood at the end of the line. Arthur took each young man by the shoulders, smiled warmly, and embraced him as a father would his son.

"Sir Kai and Sir Dakota, thank you for your loyalty," Arthur said, his voice sounding weaker than Lance had ever heard it. "It may not be according to your customs, but in my heart you will always be my sons."

Lance saw Kai choke back tears as Dakota's arm flew up and enveloped his shoulder.

Arthur stepped next to Ryan, who Lance felt for certain was about to cry. But the aged detective managed to keep the tears at bay as he faced the man who had become his closest friend.

"Thank you, James," Arthur said, gripping his hand firmly. "You love Lance as I do and I know he will be in good hands."

"They all will, Arthur," Ryan croaked, his voice more gravelly than ever. "I promise."

Arthur smiled his gratitude and released the wrinkled hand before moving onto a tearful Reyna.

"Oh, Arthur," she began, forgetting how tough she liked to appear, and simply allowed her sorrow dominance. She threw her arms around him and held on tight.

"You have perhaps made the greatest journey of all, Reyna," he said lovingly into her ear. "You learned what is of true value in life, and that's the greatest gift you can pass on to your children."

She pulled back and wiped at her tears, struggling to smile. "I will, Arthur."

Arthur smiled sadly and stepped up to Esteban. The younger man looked bereft, more lost than Lance had ever seen him. The pain in those usually hard brown eyes exacerbated Lance's own, and he gripped Ricky's hand fiercely.

"Sir Este," Arthur said with a knowing look. "My other son. You are a man who will accomplish much in your lifetime, but your greatest role will be father to your own sons and daughters. I leave the next generation in the best hands possible."

Esteban looked ready to crack. "Arthur, I…." He trailed off, collecting his thoughts. Then he said, "You've done more for me than anyone because you believed in me when I thought I was shit. I can never repay you for that."

Arthur placed a hand on the man's brawny shoulder. "Yes, you can. Do the same for your children, and teach them to do the same for theirs. That is a true legacy."

Esteban nodded, and then grabbed the man in a tight hug, holding on a moment before yanking himself back and grabbing Reyna as though he might collapse.

And now Arthur stood facing the woman who had captured his heart the first night they'd met. Jenny had placed herself in line before the boys because she knew they needed the final goodbyes, especially Lance. So she stood looking at Arthur and he at her. And then they kissed, long and lovingly, a kiss Lance wished would never end. Because if it didn't end that meant Arthur wouldn't have to leave. But it did end.

Arthur had his hands on Jenny's shoulders and smiled at her lovely face, etching it into his memory forever. "I love you, Lady Jenny," he said in a voice filled with passion and tenderness, his eyes looking lost at the thought of never seeing her again.

"And I love you, Arthur Pendragon, and always will," she said, her voice almost without breath. "These past two years as your wife have been better than two lifetimes without you."

"I shall dream of you without end," Arthur replied before dropping his hands to hers and squeezing them gently.

Chris was already sobbing when Arthur scooped the boy into his arms, cradling him against his shoulder, and soothingly rubbed the boy's back. "I love you, Chris, and I wish more than anything to stay with you. But you have your mother and your amazing brothers."

"But I want you, Dad," the boy sobbed into his shoulder.

Arthur's eyes welled with tears. "Alas, my son, we cannot always have everything we want. Just know that you have been a gift to me and will always be so."

He made eye contact with Jenny as the clock on the wall ticked over to eleven fifty-five. She reached out and took their son, barely able to hold him any more. Chris grabbed her fiercely around the neck and continued crying.

Arthur stepped in front of Ricky and Lance and looked at them with such intensity and love that Lance's eyes burned once more with tears.

"Ricky, you came to us like a miracle," Arthur said as he placed a hand on his son's shoulder and squeezed. "I believe God sent you because Lance needed you. But you captured my heart almost at once with your sincerity and strength of character. I am and ever shall be blessed to call you my son, and I love you."

Ricky's tears spilled forth, and he grabbed Arthur in a desperate hug. "I love you, too, Dad, *so* much!"

Arthur held on a moment before letting him go. The clock read eleven fifty-seven. Arthur looked at Lance's destitute expression and wet cheeks. "Walk with me, Lance."

Arthur turned and waved Merlin toward the large double doors at the far side of the room. Stiffly, Lance fell in step beside his father as they approached those doors Lance wished would never open. He wished it with all his heart. But he knew they would. And they'd take his father from him forever.

Arthur turned to Lance as they stopped in front of the closed doors. Merlin stepped forward and pulled them open. Lance gasped, and heard similar reactions from his family behind him. Where normally there was a hallway leading to the lobby, now there was a glowing, translucent chamber with what looked like slabs of stone standing in the center. The image shimmered and wobbled like it existed outside of this world.

Merlin turned to Lance and smiled. "You are an outstanding king, Your Majesty. I have been honored to serve you." He glanced back at the others and gave a slight bow. "All of you." Then he turned and passed through the translucency, becoming a shimmering part of the chamber beyond. He turned and awaited Arthur.

Father and son stood facing each other, sad and lost and desperately wishing this moment had never come to pass.

"I love you, Lance," Arthur said with quiet passion, his voice tremulous with emotion. "You have been the greatest gift I ever received, and you will live on in my heart for eternity."

Now Arthur began to cry, softly and despairingly, and Lance broke into tears.

"Oh, Dad, I love you so much!" he said as he grabbed the man in a final desperate hug.

Arthur patted him lovingly on the back, pressing the young man's face against him, never wanting to let go. But let go he did, for the clock in the Throne Room struck midnight.

Father and son separated and locked eyes, bereft green with sorrowful brown. "Take care of your mother."

Lance nodded, his heart shattering into a million pieces. "I will."

Arthur offered a sad smile filled with love. "We began as a team, son, you and I. But now you have Ricky and he is all you'll ever need. Love and cherish him. As your mother so astutely said, with you and Ricky against the world, I pity the world."

That drew a tiny smile to Lance's lips as Arthur stepped back and eyed the shimmering threshold before him. He turned one last time, drinking in the sight of Lance and Jenny and Ricky and all of them, all of those who'd entered his life and made it beyond worth living.

"I treasure all of you," he said quietly before turning to cross over the threshold, the doors slowly closing and cutting him off from their sight.

"Dad!" Lance called out and rushed to the double doors. He flung them open and stared, heartbroken and solemn.

The hallway had returned.

And Arthur was gone.

Lance shook his head in despair, every emotion possible churning through him. He clenched his fists in fury and then bolted from the room to disappear down the hall.

Ricky instantly made to follow, but Jenny's hand to his arm stopped him. "Give him a little time, honey, and then go to him. Hold him and love him."

He looked into her tearful eyes through his own, and nodded.

Feeling dazed, but knowing she had to be strong for the younger people, especially Chris, Jenny clung tightly to him and said, "I'm going to take Chris upstairs." She looked over at Reyna, Esteban, Kai, and Dakota, all of whom looked lost and forlorn.

"Why don't you newlyweds go on up to bed," she suggested. "This is your wedding night, after all."

She tried for a smile, but fell short.

Reyna eyed her from within Esteban's arms and frowned. "The worst wedding night ever."

Jenny tried to sound positive. "There's no such thing, Reyna. Go on up to bed. Hold each other close, feel the heart of the one you love beating against you. That's the best medicine for sorrow."

Reyna exchanged a look with Esteban, and he nodded. Slowly, leaning on each other, the couple ambled out of the Throne Room.

Jenny eyed Kai and Dakota, who stood uncertainly watching Ricky, and no doubt worrying about Lance. Jenny seemed to sense this and said, "You boys do the same. Ricky will take care of Lance."

The young men looked over at Ricky.

Swiping at his damp eyes, Ricky nodded his agreement and his Native brothers strolled dejectedly from the room.

Jenny turned to Ricky, still cradling Chris in her arms.

"You want me to help you with Chris, Mom?"

She smiled lovingly. "No, sweetie. You have someone who needs you more."

She leaned in and kissed his cheek before carrying the softly crying Chris from the room.

Ricky stood and looked around. His eyes fell on the throne. He recalled the moment Arthur had knighted him, the day Arthur asked if he wanted to be adopted, and the day the adoption became final. He even recalled his total dejection when he'd thought he'd lost Lance forever. So many amazing things to cherish, and now so much pain to endure. That was life, he supposed. You couldn't have the one without the other.

He needed to find Lance.

And he knew just where to look.

As Ricky exited the Throne Room and entered the lobby, there came a knock at the front door. Hesitantly, and not without a twinge of rising fear, he stepped up to the door and peered through the beveled glass at a boy standing outside, a young boy if the distorted image was any indication.

He opened the door and looked out uncertainly. The boy appeared dirty and homeless, clad in a wife-beater, tight jeans, and wearing a light windbreaker that likely came from a thrift store. Ricky's heart instantly beat with compassion.

"You're Ricky, right?" the boy asked, his voice trembling from the cold.

God, he must be freezing out there, Ricky thought. "Yeah. Come on in, kid."

The boy grinned with gratitude and eagerly stepped into the lobby, eyes going wide with wonder at the suit of armor and the other decorations. Then he shyly looked at Ricky.

Ricky noted how small the boy was, and how frightened. "What's your name?"

"Billy," the boy answered, his voice barely at that puberty stage. "I'm, uh, I'm twelve."

Ricky nodded sadly. "How long you been on the streets, Billy?"

"About a week," the boy answered, still shivering. "I was living with my aunt and uncle, but they kicked me out."

"Why?"

The boy looked humiliated. "Cuz I told 'em I liked another boy at school."

Ricky groaned inwardly. *Here we go again....*

"I knew you and Lance, well, you wouldn't care about that," Billy went on, hope in his voice. "You think maybe I could stay, be part of the crusade?"

Ricky fought his own painful memories that threatened to engulf him. He suddenly saw his whole childhood in this young boy's eager face.

"Damn straight you can, Billy," he said, placing one hand on the boy's timorous shoulder, and grinning. "New Camelot, the next generation."

Billy beamed so brightly that Ricky's breath caught in his throat a moment. "C'mon, man, let's get you some food and a room."

He placed his arm gently around the relieved boy's shoulders and led him down the hall toward the kitchen.

†††

Lance sat on his usual spot upon the parapet of New Camelot, bare legs dangling over the side, a cool December breeze wafting his untamed hair about his face. He shivered in the light t-shirt he wore and absently reflected that he should be wearing his hoodie.

But it didn't matter. Nothing mattered now. His father was gone. The man who had come out of the distant past and given him a life, given him love, helped him love himself, was gone, and Lance knew he'd likely never see him again.

His teary eyes looked out at the glittering city lights surrounding him, but didn't see them. Nor did the constant, almost soothing hum of freeway traffic eight stories below register in his conscious mind. All he saw were images and memories of these past four years.

His life before Arthur seemed like something out of a book he'd read, some kind of horror tale where the main character was terrorized and tortured the entire time. It felt to him like someone else's story. He'd slammed the door on Richard long ago. He still had minor flashbacks, but knew they would all vanish under Ricky's gentle ministrations. He knew he could make Ricky happy in every way because Ricky was everything, and there wasn't anything he wouldn't do for him. But he also knew Ricky would be happy however their relationship progressed, because Ricky loved him more than he loved himself.

Even the old tacked-on surname, Sepulveda, seemed like it had once belonged to someone else, someone who didn't exist anymore. Maybe it had, he mused wistfully. He wasn't that boy any longer. He was a young man who, thanks to the most amazing father a boy could ask for, had become someone of value, someone to be reckoned with in this crazy world.

"Everything you are, Lance, you were the night I met you." His father's words filled his mind and heart and nearly stopped his breathing. As hard as it was for him to admit, him who'd been told he was worthless his entire life, he knew those words to be true. Arthur had never forced him to do anything he hadn't wanted to do. True, he'd done them to please the man, to earn his respect and pride. But he *had* done them, and now the entire country was profoundly changed. Hopefully, for the better. Only time would tell. What would Michael's law of unintended consequences bring next? That, he supposed, was what made life worth living – the things yet to be.

He thought about Michael, how Michael had forced him to confront himself and be true to who he was and what he could do. Just like Jack. And Mark. And

†   316   †

John. Just like all those who'd touched his life along the way. He'd learned something from each of them, something about being human, about being a positive force in the world. And they'd all loved him, just like Arthur had from the start. He hadn't forced them to love him; they simply had, and their love gradually made him realize that maybe he wasn't worthless after all. Maybe he *was* worth loving.

"If someone loves you, Lance, that means you're worthy," Jack had written in his farewell letter.

Lance sighed and shivered as Ricky's beautiful features filled his mind's eye.

I guess I'm worthy, he thought, as the image of the most amazing boy in the world drew a smile to his sad face.

As though knowing Lance was thinking of him, Ricky suddenly appeared, slipping into his usual perch and holding out a paper plate with some wedding cake on it. A tiny chocolate sword jutted up and out at an angle from the slice. Lance hadn't even heard him approach.

"Hey," Ricky said.

"Hey," Lance replied.

Ricky offered his own sad smile and held out the plate. "You never tried your wedding cake."

Lance eyed the cake forlornly. Wedding. The happiest day of his life had turned into the saddest. He reached up and brushed Ricky's own wafting hair from his desolate eyes.

"Neither did you."

Ricky shrugged. There were two plastic forks sticking out of the cake. Lance gingerly took one while Ricky reached for the other. Silently, hearts heavy with equal parts love and grief, the two young men picked at the cake until only the sword remained.

Ricky indicated the sword with his fork. "That's for you, Lance. You're king now."

Lance eyed him in the shadowy darkness a moment before picking up the sword with two fingers. He held it up so the roof lighting could reveal its reality to them both. His eyes met those of his beloved.

"We're a team, remember?"

Then he slipped the hilt end into his mouth and leaned into Ricky. With a tiny smile, Ricky closed his lips over the blade and they dissolved the chocolate in their mouths, gradually moving together until their lips touched in a gentle kiss.

Pulling apart, they sat silently gazing out over the city. Their hands slipped into each other's as their thoughts ran side by side. Neither needed to read the other's mind to know what each was thinking. Not this time.

"Some wedding night, huh?" Lance finally said with a heavy sigh.

"Yeah," Ricky said in reply, exhaling his own weighty breath.

Lance felt that burning behind his eyes again. "Oh, Ricky, what are we gonna do without him?"

Ricky squeezed his hand, his voice tight and constricted. "We're gonna do everything he taught us, just like you said. We're gonna follow his example and pass it on to Chris and the kids we adopt someday. He's gonna live on, Lance, in us."

Through blurred vision, Lance eyed Ricky's sad, but resolute face. "How'd you get so smart all of a sudden?"

Ricky offered a slight smile. "I had a good role model."

Lance smiled back. "Me, too. The best."

They sat a moment in silence, holding hands, just letting everything be, the cool breeze brushing their hair up against each other's shoulders. Finally, Lance turned his head and said quietly, "I am so lucky you found me, Ricky."

Ricky eyed him knowingly. "Luck had nothing to do with it, Lance. We were always meant to be together."

Lance considered that a moment. "You're right. I've been thinking that, well, maybe everything that's happened to us, the good and the bad, is all part of that big adventure that scared Peter Pan so much. He is *so* missing out."

"You still scared?"

Lance squeezed the hand gently and offered his famous smile. "No. Not so long as I have you."

Ricky returned the smile and they looked out over the city once more.

After a few moments, Ricky yawned and said, "You wanna go downstairs and go to bed?"

Lance turned his head quickly, and he must've looked startled because Ricky instantly lowered his eyes in embarrassment. "I, uh, you know, didn't mean it like that," he stammered. "I just meant we could lie there and hold each other close. Mom says that's the best cure for sadness." He raised his eyes and found Lance's poignant green ones peeking shyly out at him from beneath those long, wavy lashes.

Lance offered his version of Mark's shy smile. "We could do more, if you want."

Ricky's eyes widened, and his heart rate quickened. "Yeah?"

Lance maintained eye contact. "Yeah," he said in a wisp of breath. "I wanna make you happy, Ricky."

Ricky smiled lovingly, and Lance's heart melted all over again. "You do make me happy, Lance." Then he patted his left chest, right over the heart. "I got you."

Lance patted his own chest. "And I got you."

Ricky's eyebrows lifted. "For now and always?"

Lance smiled broadly, his heart fluttering like angel wings. "For now and always."

They looked into each other's eyes, saw the mix of love and desire, and shared a gentle little laugh.

Just as they made to stand, the door burst open and Chris pelted across the gravel roof toward them. He wore his favorite football-themed pajamas and slippers and looked terrified.

"Chris, what's wrong?" Lance asked, suddenly afraid as he slid the boy in between him and Ricky and they cradled his shivering form.

"I had a bad dream about Dad," Chris said urgently, his voice trembling as much as his body. "I'm too big to ask Mom, so can I sleep with you guys tonight? Please?"

His soft pale face looked so distraught, so small and afraid, that Lance's heart melted.

The young men looked at each other over the top of Chris's blond head. Lance saw on Ricky the same expression he knew he wore – incredulity and amusement mixed together.

"Irony, Lance?" Ricky said with a wry grin.

Lance grinned right back. "Irony, Ricky."

Chris tilted his head upward at his brothers. "Does that mean yes?"

Lance blew out his breathy laugh, and tousled Chris's unkempt hair. "That means yes, little man, for as many nights as you need."

Chris's tight face instantly relaxed and Lance already felt the trembling of his body subsiding. "Thanks. You guys are the best."

Lance and Ricky exchanged another look, and then shrugged at how things worked out.

"You're our little brother, Chris," Lance said softly, stroking the boy's hair gently. "You always come first."

"Always," Ricky affirmed, pulling the boy in more closely between them so the three could feel each other's body heat.

They were a family, after all. And the children had to come first.

"Do you think we'll ever see Dad again?" came Chris's sleepy voice to break the silence.

Ricky looked over at Lance and smirked. "Yeah, Chris, I do. You heard him. Soon as Lance gets in big trouble, he'll be back."

Lance's eyebrows shot up in surprise. "*If* I get in big trouble," he replied solemnly, like the possibility was unlikely.

Ricky grinned. "Fool, when *don't* you get in big trouble?" He chuckled at Lance's comical expression and then inclined his head toward Chris. "Right, little man?"

But Chris was already slumbering peacefully, sound asleep in his brothers' arms.

With a tiny laugh, Ricky looked up at Lance and shook his head in wonder. "How does he do that?"

Lance shrugged. Ricky was right, as usual. The way his life had gone so far, they'd likely have Arthur back sooner, rather than later. Not that he was planning on getting into big trouble, but trouble always seemed to find him no matter what he did.

It's all good, he thought as he locked eyes on those of his soul mate. Ricky's were filled with such love that Lance could scarcely breathe. They leaned in over Chris's head and rested their foreheads one against the other, gazing deeply into each other's eyes. They were happy. Sure, they'd have to put off their wedding night to take care of a child in need, but that was as it should be, all part of that big adventure called life.

It's not like we won't have plenty of time for each other, Lance thought happily, finally content and at peace, with himself and the world.

After all, for now and always had only just begun.

Once upon a time in the City of Angels,

a boy grew up…

and a country grew with him.

†††

THE KNIGHT CYCLE

Book I:
Children of the Knight

Book II:
Running Through A Dark Place

Book III:
There Is No Fear

Book IV:
And The Children Shall Lead

Book V:
Once Upon A Time In America

†††

Michael J. Bowler is an award-winning author of seven novels—*A Boy and His Dragon, A Matter of Time* (Silver Medalist from Reader's Favorite), and The Knight Cycle, comprised of five books: *Children of the Knight* (Gold Award Winner in the Wishing Shelf Book Awards), *Running Through A Dark Place, There Is No Fear, And The Children Shall Lead,* and *Once Upon A Time In America.*

His horror screenplay, "Healer," was a Semi-Finalist, and his urban fantasy script, "Like A Hero," was a Finalist in the Shriekfest Film Festival and Screenplay Competition.

He grew up in San Rafael, California, and majored in English and Theatre at Santa Clara University. He went on to earn a master's in film production from Loyola Marymount University, a teaching credential in English from LMU, and another master's in Special Education from Cal State University Dominguez Hills.

He partnered with two friends as producer, writer, and/or director on several ultra-low-budget horror films, including "Fatal Images," "Club Dead," and "Things II," the reviews of which are much more fun than the actual movies.

He taught high school in Hawthorne, California for twenty-five years, both in general education and to students with learning disabilities, in subjects ranging from English and Strength Training to Algebra, Biology, and Yearbook.

He has also been a volunteer Big Brother to eight different boys with the Catholic Big Brothers Big Sisters program and a thirty-year volunteer within the juvenile justice system in Los Angeles.

He has been honored as Probation Volunteer of the Year, YMCA Volunteer of the Year, California Big Brother of the Year, and 2000 National Big Brother of the Year. The "National" honor allowed he and three of his Little Brothers to visit the White House and meet the president in the Oval Office.

He is currently at work on a horror/suspense novel based on his screenplay, "Healer."

You can find him at:
www.michaeljbowler.com
FB: michaeljbowlerauthor
Twitter: BradleyWallaceM
Blog: www.sirlancesays.wordpress.com
tumblr: http://michaeljbowler.tumblr.com/
Pinterest: http://www.pinterest.com/michaelbowler/pins/
Instagram: StuntShark

Made in the USA
San Bernardino, CA
02 February 2015